THE ASHRAM

By The Same Author

Felicitavia
When the Time Comes
Devi
Anandamurti: The Jamalpur Years

THE ASHRAM

DEVASHISH

InnerWorld Publications
San Germán, Puerto Rico
www.innerworldpublications.com

This is a work of fiction. Names, characters, places, and incidents either are the product of the author's imagination or are used fictitiously. Any resemblance to events or persons, living or dead, is entirely coincidental.

2nd edition
Copyright © 2010 by Devashish Donald Acosta

All rights reserved under International and Pan-American Copyright Conventions. Published in the United States by InnerWorld Publications, PO Box 1613, San Germán, Puerto Rico, 00683.

Library of Congress Control Number: 2010907422

Cover Design © Lourdes Sánchez (Mukti)

No part of this book may be reproduced or transmitted in any form or by any means, electronic or mechanical, including photocopying, recording, or by any information storage or retrieval system, without permission in writing from the publisher, except for the inclusion of brief quotations in a review.

ISBN: 9781881717027

The fact that the fortune of every individual, not only of this earth, but of the entire cosmos, has been wreathed together will have to be admitted one day by humanity.
— Shrii Shrii Anandamurti

Prologue

It had been quite a game, and the boy was feeling rather proud of himself. He had reached base four times in six tries and had narrowly missed a home run in his last at-bat when his sharply hit line drive caromed off a tree and back to the outfielder. The tying run had scored from first on the play as he slid under the tag with a triple, and moments later he was crossing home plate with the winning run on a grounder up the middle.

As he turned the corner of Wisteria and Vine and headed down the final block to his house, he replayed that long line drive in his head, but this time the abandoned lot was replaced by a professional stadium, the fans cheering wildly as his rocket caromed off the third tier for a grand slam in the bottom of the ninth with two out and the home team down three runs. It wasn't the first game-winning home run he had hit while walking home after the evening pickup game with his buddies, but it might have been the most dramatic.

It was nearly nine and already dark when he entered the house through the back door and deposited his glove and bat in the corner. He peeked cautiously into the empty kitchen. Then, gathering his courage, he headed for the stairs as quietly as he could, hoping that his parents were already upstairs in their room with the door closed, watching TV or reading. His luck, however, did not hold. As he passed the living room, he noticed his father reclining in his favorite armchair, reading his business magazines.

"Isn't it kind of late to be getting home, buddy?" his father said, without looking up from his magazine. "Correct me if I'm wrong, but I thought we'd agreed that you're to be back evenings at eight?"

"The game went extra innings, Dad," the boy replied, trying to keep the dismay from his voice. "It wouldn't have been fair to the guys if I had skipped out with the game on the line. I had the big hit, a triple in the last inning."

The boy's father closed his magazine and laid it down deliberately on the coffee table beside his chair. "And that's supposed to make it all right to get home so late, that you won the game with a triple?"

The boy did his best to appear crestfallen. "No. I'm sorry. I should have paid more attention to the time. It won't happen again, I promise."

His father nodded. "See that it doesn't. Otherwise we're going to have to reconsider letting you go out after dinner to play ball. Isn't that right, Irene?"

The boy turned to find his mother standing at the top of the stairs.

"Absolutely. He's got to learn that life has consequences. You screw up; you have to pay the piper. It's as simple as that. Now get ready for bed, young man. You have school tomorrow, in case you've forgotten."

The boy scurried upstairs to brush his teeth and change for bed. A few minutes later his mother came into his room to say goodnight.

"So, you won the game with a triple, did you?"

The boy grinned. "Yeah. Well, I drove in the tying run with a triple and then scored the winning run."

She laughed and gave him a pat on the head. "Good work, slugger. Just try to get the game over with a little earlier next time so your father doesn't get bent out of shape. You know how he is."

"Don't worry, mom. I will."

"And don't stay up too late reading. You know how groggy you are in the morning if you don't get enough sleep."

She leaned down and kissed him on the cheek, and then left the room, shutting the door behind her.

Once the door was closed, the boy reached down to the bottom of his night table where he kept the book on the San Diego Padres that his father had given him for his last birthday. He had read the book cover to cover many times and could almost recite parts of it by heart, but that didn't lessen the thrill he felt when he read the familiar text and looked once again at the historic photos. As usual, he turned to the second-to-last chapter. Steve Garvey, the boy's all-time favorite player, was about to lead the home team to the 1984 National League pennant. As he looked at the pictures, he could hear the cheering of the crowd, almost as if he were in the stands with the rest of the fans—as he had been one year earlier with his dad for game four. Finally, he turned off the light and laid back on the pillow, still watching Garvey in his mind: striding to the plate in the ninth inning with the score tied five-five and the fans going crazy, the dramatic windmill swing, the collective stopped breath as the ball soared toward the stands, the explosion that erupted when it landed. The roar of the crowd was the last thing he heard as he drifted off into sleep, a deafening swell that seemed as if it were never going to end.

The boy's slumber was full of the usual dreams—family, friends, school—until early in the morning when he stepped into a landscape he had never seen before: a yellowed field of course grass on a night when the fog was so thick it threatened to swallow the earth whole. As he looked around, trying to peer through the milky envelope, a strong wind began to blow. It blew stronger and stronger until he felt it lift him up and carry him through the air, as if a tornado had swept down and plucked him up by the shoulders. He was scared, as any young boy would have been, but as he gave himself up to the sensation of flight, an unseen voice seemed to accompany him, assuring him that he was safe, as though a part of him were aware that it was only a dream. Sure enough, the wind began to die down. He felt himself being lowered down gently until his feet touched the ground. The mist began to thin and was soon blown away by a last preemptory gust.

When it cleared, he saw that the insistent wind had deposited him on the bank of a small slip of a river that wound like a ribbon through a dry, desolate landscape broken here and there by a few wind-scarred trees. It was a dark, moonless night, but there was starlight enough to see by. He glanced up and down the river, wondering where he was, until he noticed a dark figure sitting cross-legged on a boulder by the river's edge. As he drew near, he saw that the man was naked except for a loincloth and a necklace of thick, corrugated beads. His eyes were closed, he had long, matted locks that hung down to his shoulders, and his entire body was smeared with ash. When he got within a meter or two, the man opened his eyes and motioned for him to climb up on the boulder and sit beside him. The boy scrambled up and sat down facing the man, who was sitting on what appeared to be a tiger skin.

"Who are you?" the boy asked.

"I have many names," the man replied, his lips curving into a smile, "but you can call me Ashutosh."

"What is this place?"

"Don't you recognize it?"

"No."

The man laughed. "How quickly you humans forget! Look around you. This is not the first time you have been here."

The boy looked around. For some reason, the landscape started to seem familiar, though he couldn't figure out why that should be, since he had never been there before.

"I see that you are starting to remember. Good. I chose this place to meet you for a reason, so that it might remind you of your purpose. But those memories can wait."

"To meet *me*?"

"Yes, I have been waiting for you. "

"For me? But how could that be? I don't know you."

"Indeed. And that is the crux of the matter. How can you hope to know who you are if you do not know who I am? But we can talk of that later. Now it is time. You have been asleep long enough."

"Time for what?"

"Time for you to learn what I have called you here to learn. Contrary to what you have been taught in the world in which you now live, it is magic that rules the creation. Everything that you see around you has been created by magic, and what I am about to teach you will give you the key to that magic. But before I can teach you, you must agree to two conditions."

"What are they?" the boy asked, his mind suddenly astir with the possibility that this strange figure could teach him how to harness the unseen magic that ruled the world.

"First, you must promise that you will never harm any living being, either by thought, word, or deed. Second, you must promise me that as long as you are in this world you will utilize all your actions for the welfare of others. Are you ready to promise?"

"Yes," the boy replied, his excitement mounting.

"Good. Then repeat after me."

The boy put his hand over his heart, as he did each morning during the pledge of allegiance, and repeated the oaths as the sage instructed him.

"Now, sit as I am sitting, with your legs crossed. Fold your hands in your lap, like this, and keep your spine straight."

When the sage was satisfied with the boy's posture, he closed his eyes, raised up his right hand, palm outward, leaving his left hand, palm upward, on his left knee, and began a slow and solemn chant that lasted for several minutes. His voice had a haunted quality that mesmerized the boy. Every drop of his attention remained riveted to the sonorous but unintelligible syllables that poured forth in a precisely modulated stream from the sage's throat. When the sage finished his chant, he opened his eyes and pulled a soft clump of vermilion paste from a small pouch. He smeared a bit on his thumb and then pressed his thumb between the boy's eyebrows and twisted it back and forth.

"Now, close your eyes and visualize a point of light at the base of your spine. Surrounding this point is a golden square and around that square, four rose-colored petals…" For the next twenty minutes the sage taught the boy an intricate process of visualization, ending up at the spot between the eyebrows. Then he taught him a secret word—a mantra, he called it—that he was to repeat over and over again while visualizing himself as a point of light merging into an infinite ocean of light. He had the boy practice the technique until he was sure he had it right. Then he told him he could open his eyes.

"Now, listen carefully. I'm going to explain to you the real secret of life, the secret that is not a secret, no matter how well it remains hidden. Just as you can create a whole world inside your mind by thinking, the Creator of this universe does the same. He thinks of a tree and a tree appears. The difference between you and him is that you think the tree is real, while he knows that it is just a thought."

The sage tapped the boulder with his fingers. "This rock we are sitting on, you, me, the sky above us—all of these are just thought waves in the mind of the Creator, everything, from an elephant to a tiny blade of grass. We are all drops in an infinite ocean of consciousness. Do you follow?"

The boy nodded his head. He had never thought about the world in this way, but it seemed to make sense.

"The curious thing," the sage continued, "is that everyone thinks that this is all real, but they only do so because they can't see the person standing behind the curtain who is making it all appear and disappear. Have you ever watched a magic show?"

The boy told him about the shows he had seen on television and the book on magic and magicians that he had checked out of the library. He had even tried a few simple tricks.

"Very good. Then you know that the whole art of the magician is to make the audience believe in the illusion. As long as the audience doesn't know what is really happening, they believe whatever the magician wants them to believe. This world is exactly the same. We think that everything is solid and everything is separate, but that's the illusion. That's what the magician wants us to think. The truth is that there is only one Consciousness; this is all just a magic show in his mind. But if you can go behind the curtain and meet the magician and learn his secrets, then the illusion no longer remains an illusion. And that is the whole purpose of the game. It is a game of hide-and-seek where the object is to find the Cosmic Magician. And the way to find him, the only way, is by meditating on him. The more you meditate, the closer you get, until one day you and he come face to face. When you do, you will realize that you and he were never separate. You are, and have always been, the one who is creating this magical universe. When you realize this, you will have the key to the magic of creation. Whatever you wish for will be yours. And when that day comes, I will come back and ask you the same question you asked me: Who are you?"

The sage laughed. At that moment the wind started picking up again, ruffling his matted locks. He picked up the trident that was lying beside him, held it upright, and stared intently at the boy with an amused expression on his face, his eyes glowing like two coals in the night. The mist returned and began to swirl around them, thicker and thicker, until the boy felt the wind lift him up and carry him away, the sage's laughter following him as he flew.

Then the boy woke up. For a few moments, he felt disoriented. He rubbed his eyes and blinked as he looked around at his surroundings, startled to see the four walls of his room illuminated by the dim glow of the night-light, his books on the night table, his clothes thrown in a heap on the floor beside his bed. At first, he had the feeling that the scene he was seeing was completely unreal—that this was the dream and that he had somehow fallen asleep. Then he remembered who he was, remembered his parents asleep in the next room and the baseball game that had ended a few hours before. He realized that he had been dreaming, and the moment he realized this he could feel the dream start to slip away from him, the strange image of the half-naked sage and the silver glint of the river growing more and more indistinct with every passing moment. But then he remembered that he had learned something, and all at once it came back to him: the odd ceremony, the oaths the sage had made him take, his enigmatic words about going behind the curtain to meet the Cosmic Magician. He remembered the process with its secret mantra, as clearly as if he had been practicing it for many years. Immediately, almost instinctually, he got up and went to the bathroom to wash; then he came back to his bed, sat down with his legs crossed, and began meditating. The clock on the night table showed four thirty. It was not yet five thirty when he finished, but for some reason he didn't feel sleepy. Rather, he felt alert and full of energy. He got up and went to his desk and opened his books, and he remained there until it was time to get ready for school.

In the days that followed, the boy went to bed each night wondering if he would dream again of the mysterious sage; and early each morning he was met again by the same great wind that carried him to the edge of the river, where the sage was waiting for him with the same burning eyes, more instructions, and a laugh that followed him into his room. On the seventh day the dreams stopped. Though he kept hoping each night that he would return to that desolate but magical landscape, his hope grew fainter with every passing day, until eventually he accepted that the dreams were part of his past. But what he had learned from the sage was part of his present, and he practiced what he had been taught whenever he had the chance: mornings when he woke up, at night before bed, even sometimes before dinner. He took care to hide this from his parents, suspecting that they might not understand—especially since he did not really understand himself. Gradually, his practice became as familiar a part of his daily routine as eating and sleeping. As he started to get good at what was to him a private game, he began to feel a mild intoxication whenever he experienced good concentration in his meditation. Soon he was looking forward to his practice as much as he looked forward to playing ball with his friends. He still wished he could meet the sage again and learn more about how to unlock the magic of the universe, but for the time being he was happy enough just closing his eyes and exploring the new world the sage had shown him.

One night, seeing the light off and thinking her son to be asleep, the boy's mother cracked open the door to his room to peek in on her little angel. She was startled to see him sitting up on the bed, his legs bound in the full-lotus posture, his eyes closed and his hands folded in his lap. She could see that he was meditating, but she couldn't, for the life of her, fathom why, or where he might have learned it. After watching him for a minute or two, she began to feel uneasy, as if she were spying on him, so she closed the door and went back to the living room to tell her husband. Her husband looked up from his magazine and arched his eyebrows. "Meditating? Are you sure? What is a nine-year-old boy doing meditating?"

"I haven't the foggiest idea, Ralph. I'm just as surprised as you are. But he's definitely meditating. There's no doubt about it."

Her husband frowned. "Okay, let's talk to him about it in the morning. Tomorrow's Saturday. I have to go into the office for a little while—this business with HP is really driving me up the wall—but it won't hurt if I go in a little late. We'll talk it over at breakfast. One of his teachers probably showed them in class—although what they're doing teaching something like that in a public school, I have no idea. Maybe it has something to do with developing concentration so they can study better, who knows, but you can rest assured I'm going to talk to someone about it."

Irene felt calmer now. Ralph was right. Why worry about it until they had a chance to talk to the boy.

When the boy told his parents about his dreams, it did nothing to allay his mother's concerns. Both she and her husband had dabbled briefly with Zen while they were in college. It had been the sixties, and nearly everyone who considered themselves liberal minded had tried meditation at least once, in the same way that just about everyone had tried pot at least once. They still retained something of their liberal outlook, and because of this she felt hesitant to say anything negative to the boy. After all, she thought, it could be a lot worse. God knows, considering the things kids were getting into these days, even kids his age, they should be grateful he was taking this deep end to jump off of. But this matter of the dream, especially the way he referred to the figure in the dream as his teacher, gave her pause for concern about his contact with reality. Even then she hesitated to say anything to him, and Ralph was just as quiet. He had a line from Shakespeare on his desk at the office that he was fond of quoting—"There are more things in heaven and earth, Horatio, than are dreamt of in your philosophy"—and it was she who had framed it and given it to him as a birthday present.

Instead, she decided to consult with her elder sister, who was a professor of comparative religions at USC and a specialist in the esoteric disciplines of the East. Her husband wasn't crazy about the idea. He had always considered her sister a few face cards short of a full deck, but he didn't have any better ideas and didn't put up much of a fight. Her sister, to her credit, was considered something of an authority in her field. Her most recent book, *Surfing with the California Masters*, had come as close to best-seller status as one could reasonably expect from an academic study of esoteric movements in the California hinterland, and she had been a guest on regional talk shows on more than one occasion.

One evening Irene invited her sister over for dinner, having forewarned her about her nephew's dreams but without supplying any details. Her sister had sounded intrigued when they talked on the phone, but that was nothing compared to the obvious surprise that showed on her face when the boy described the sage and the initiation process and then steadfastly refused to share any details about the meditation technique he had learned. After dinner the boy went out to play ball, and the three adults retired to the living room with an after-dinner liqueur.

"So, Carmen, is my son going crazy, or is there a rational explanation for all this?" Ralph was smiling but there was concern in his voice. His wife gave him a cautionary look, but she was just as anxious to hear what her sister would say.

The boy's aunt looked up from the goblet she was holding cupped in her hands, gently rolling the liqueur around in the glass to bring out its aroma. "Michael is most assuredly not crazy, Ralph. In fact, I suspect he may be saner than any of us in this room. What can I say? I'm stunned. Literally. This dream of his was an authentic spiritual experience—and a very powerful one, very powerful. There's no doubt about it. No doubt, whatsoever."

Ralph appeared startled by her answer. "How can you be so sure?"

"This is my field, Ralph. This is what I've spent my life studying. His description of the yogi he met, the ritual involved in the initiation, the invocatory mantra, the yogi's teachings—it tallies far too closely to be anything but an authentic experience. Carmen placed her glass deliberately on the coffee table. "First of all, the place is India and the man he described is a Shaivite monk."

"A what?" Ralph said.

"A Shaivite monk. There are many different orders of ascetics in India, and each has certain distinguishing characteristics. The Shaivites are followers of Shiva. The matted locks, the smeared ashes, the trident, the tiger skin—these are all symbols of Shiva, part of the Shaivite tradition. Shaivites practice Tantrism, and the ritual involved in Michael's dream was his initiation into Tantric practice. Every detail corroborates this, right down to his reluctance to talk about the meditation process he learned."

"Okay," Irene interjected, "so it fits the description of a Shaivite monk. We'll take your word for it. I don't really see how that matters so much. After all, he could have seen a picture of a Shaivite monk in a book. What makes you think that it's not just an ordinary dream that Michael is somehow confusing with reality? It wouldn't be the first time that a nine-year-old boy overindulged in his fantasy world, you know."

Her sister shook her head emphatically. "I'm quite sure that if you go through every book he's ever been exposed to, you won't come across such a picture. And even if you did, it's neither here nor there, because there is no way he could have known about that initiation process. I would have known it was a Shaivite monk simply from the initiation ritual itself—leave aside the description. That's what really surprises me. Even nowadays that kind of initiation is still very rare and very, very secret.

You won't find anything written about it anywhere in any kind of detail. Believe me, I know what I'm talking about. I've gone to a lot of trouble for a lot of years investigating these things, and I tell you, as sure as I'm sitting here, there is absolutely no way Michael could have learned what he learned except from a Shaivite adept. Allowing foreigners or even Indian non-practitioners access to this kind of knowledge has been taboo for centuries—millennia, in fact."

Ralph squirmed in his seat, looking decidedly uncomfortable. He glanced questioningly at his wife. Carmen didn't seem to notice. She took another sip from her liqueur and continued to stare into the glass, even after she resumed speaking. Her voice became softer, as if she were musing to herself rather than addressing her sister and brother-in-law. "Oh yes, it's an authentic experience alright. Quite extraordinary, really. I would scarcely have believed it if I hadn't heard it from Michael with my own ears. For a boy who's not ten yet to be initiated into Tantric meditation by a Shaivite monk in a dream? My word! And in Southern California of all places, nine thousand miles from the nearest practicing Shaivite. It's extraordinary, absolutely extraordinary, and not just a bit ironic also. I've been chasing down these kinds of things from Big Sur to Tibet, and here it happens in my own family."

"But what does it mean?" Ralph insisted. "If it is an authentic experience, as you seem so convinced it is, then why Michael? Why my boy? There has to be a reason. This is not India, you know. It's not Tibet. It's La Jolla, for chrissake!"

Irene fidgeted beside him and put her hand on his shoulder, sharing his discomfort.

Carmen looked up from her glass and stared at her brother-in-law for a moment, glancing only briefly at her sister. "Yes, Ralph, you're absolutely correct. There most certainly is a reason, though I'm not quite sure that I'm the right person to answer that question. My guess—and it's only a guess, mind you—is that the sage in Michael's dream is his teacher from his past life—his guru, I should say—and that it's time for him to begin his spiritual journey again in this lifetime. In other words—now don't freak out on me here—in his last life Michael was almost certainly a Shaivite, living in India, meditating in burial grounds and forests, the whole nine yards. And for him to be initiated in a dream, at such a young age—well, the only possible explanation is that he must have been a very advanced soul when he died. Otherwise this simply could not have happened."

"You expect us to believe—"

"Ralph, please," his wife said, a pleading tone in her voice.

"Yes, Ralph, please," Carmen continued. "Don't be so quick to dismiss what you are not qualified to evaluate. You're far too intelligent for that."

She tapped her glass with her fingernail and set it down again on the coffee table. "And one thing more. I'm convinced that Michael has a very special destiny ahead of him." An edge crept into her voice now as she pointed a finger at her brother-in-law. "As I believe I remember you saying one time, everything happens for a reason. Let him seek his own destiny. He is going to find it, one way or another, but it will be much better, for all of you, if you help him to get there. Or at the very least, if you don't put any unnecessary obstacles in his way."

Ralph kept stone quiet, visibly offended. A few awkward moments passed before Irene broke the silence.

"So what do you think we should do then?"

"I don't think you need to do anything, really. This is between him and his teacher, or between him and his karma, if you prefer. If I were in your shoes, I would just accept it. Try to act as if it were something completely normal, like playing ball after school. However concerned I might be, I would do my absolute best not to let it show; otherwise, it will just make things worse, I guarantee it. And really, you don't need to worry. He's a bright boy with a unique destiny. He'll be just fine. But..." Carmen began to rub her chin. "You might want to get a second opinion, so to speak. I can give you the number of an Indian guru who has an ashram in Topanga Canyon. He's considered to be an enlightened being by people who know about these things. He'll probably be able to tell more about what's going on with Michael just by looking at him than I could after a year of research. If anybody in America can give you proper advice, it's him."

Two weeks later, Irene and her husband were waiting apprehensively by the living-room window when a black Mercedes-Benz 500 SEL pulled up in front of the house shortly after ten in the morning. Two men dressed in white opened the front doors and stepped out. One of them opened the back door and out stepped an attractive blond in a long white dress, followed by a dark-skinned man with a long graying beard, a receding hairline, and a full-length orange tunic.

"That's a pretty fancy ride," Ralph commented. "The guru business must be doing pretty well these days."

"Please, Ralph, don't start. Okay? This is not the time."

"Okay, okay. I was just pointing out the obvious, that's all."

"Of course you were."

Irene opened the door and showed their guests into the living room, where she had set out a pitcher of grape juice and a tray of crackers and cheese slices. She felt awkward at first. Neither she nor her husband had any idea what to expect from this exotic-looking Indian monk and his gleaming disciples, but she was soon put at ease by his effortless charm. Their visitor radiated such warmth and such a profound sense of repose that she quickly felt as if they were having a long-overdue chat with a favorite uncle. He asked about her husband's business concerns and her classes and listened to their answers with such attention and interest that she nearly forgot about the reason for his visit, until the guru himself brought the subject up. He listened quietly to everything they had to say and then asked if he might have a few minutes alone with the boy.

"Of course, certainly," Ralph volunteered. "There's a deck out back with a nice view of the gorge." Ralph went upstairs and returned a minute later at the heels of a slightly built but strikingly handsome young boy with wavy black hair. The boy glanced curiously at the guru and his entourage while his father introduced them, and then led the guru out to the deck where they sat down on a pair of adjacent lawn chairs that looked out on the gorge.

"So your dad tells me you're quite a ballplayer," the guru asked, once they were seated.

The boy shrugged his shoulders.

"What position do you like to play?"

"Centerfield."

The guru raised his eyebrows. "I see. Important position. A lot depends on the centerfielder. Who's your favorite centerfielder?"

"Kevin McReynolds."

"The hometown favorite and a good pick, but if it were my team and I had my choice, I would pick Ricky Henderson. He has better range in the field, which is why he can play so shallow. And he has better concentration at the plate. That's what makes him such a good clutch hitter. McReynolds has very good range, and he's a better than average ballplayer. Plus he's young; he can only get better. But Ricky will come through for you when the game is on the line. Concentration is the key, Michael, not just in baseball but in anything you do. The better your concentration, the better you will be at anything. That's part of why we meditate, but of course it's only the beginning."

The guru now had the boy's full attention. By the time they began talking about his dreams, Michael was eager to hear what he would say. He even disclosed things he had kept from his parents and his aunt. There had been questions bubbling up inside him ever since that magical week and no one whom he could ask—until now—and he took full advantage of the opportunity.

As they were getting up to go in, the guru reached out and patted Michael on the head. For a moment the world seemed to grow hazy; his eyes clouded and his mind went blank. Then, just as suddenly, the world cleared. He reached for the chair to steady himself and found the guru smiling and patting him on the shoulder. The experience had been far more than he'd expected, it seemed, though he hadn't really known what to expect. As they walked back into the house, the boy still felt strangely disoriented, but even so, he decided he would ask his parents if he could visit the guru from time to time. He just wasn't sure how to broach the subject.

As it turned out, there was no need to ask.

"I realize how strange this must seem to both of you," the guru told his parents when they went back in. "Such occurrences are simply not part of the Western cultural experience. But I assure you, such things do happen and they are perfectly normal, rare though they may be. Michael is an unusual boy, but I mean that in the best of senses."

Ralph winced as he exchanged looks with his wife. "Then you agree with what my wife's sister thinks?"

"Your sister-in-law is a remarkable person and a wonderful scholar. She's done a lot to make esoteric matters intelligible to the academically trained Western mind. However, in this case, I don't agree with everything she said. It is not Michael's teacher from a previous life that he saw, but what he saw was heavily influenced by past-life memories. It was a dream, and in dreams the impressions stored in the mind can be woven together in the most fantastic of ways. But the source of whatever one sees is the mind itself and its stored-up memories. Nothing can appear in a dream that is not already present in the mind, no matter how hidden it might be. In this case, it was material from his past lives that surfaced, which is not as unusual as it may sound. Past-life memories often express themselves in the dream state, but they are almost always so well disguised that we never recognize them for what they are. What is unusual is the clarity and the nature of his memories. I can tell you for certain that the meditation technique he learned in his dream was the same technique he was practicing in his previous life. It is very unusual for such memories to awaken, but it does occasionally happen with advanced yogis, and in virtually all cases it happens before they reach the age of twelve. Once the child reaches puberty, those memories become inaccessible—unless and until he attains a high state of spiritual elevation through his meditation practice."

"I can't honestly say that I believe in reincarnation," Ralph said.

The guru nodded his head. "I don't expect you to, but neither do I expect you to disbelieve it. It is not something that can either be proved or disproved by modern science. I will say, however, that it is the most logical explanation, not only of your son's experience but of the workings of the world in general, and I'll leave it at that." Then he grinned. "Except to add that the reason I talk about reincarnation in such emphatic terms is that I remember my past lives, as does every yogi who reaches a certain level in their spiritual development."

Ralph and Irene looked at each other for a moment and then broke into sheepish-looking smiles. They talked for a few more minutes about the differences between the Western and the Eastern worldviews, and then the guru invited them to bring Michael around to his ashram whenever they liked.

"There are always certain pitfalls associated with doing spiritual practices without a proper guide," he told them. "The great sages of the past have always been quite firm on this point. You wouldn't think of studying classical piano without a proper teacher; meditation is no different. I can promise you that I will look after Michael personally whenever you bring him by."

Ralph and Irene discussed it among themselves for a few minutes, and Michael was thrilled when his parents accepted the guru's offer. Ralph's job required him to spend one or two Saturdays a month in LA, and from his very next trip he started dropping his son off at the ashram in the morning and picking him up in the evening, a routine that would continue until Michael was old enough to drive.

Part One

Topanga Canyon

1

Mukunda opened the front door of the Bungalow and stepped out to savor the freshness of the early morning air. He breathed deeply, drinking in the sweet, heady scent of jasmine and frangipani, the most potent of the flowering shrubs that made the courtyard of Gurudeva's compound an olfactory delight in the spring, when the perfumed atmosphere that enveloped the sprawling Spanish-revival-style ranch house seemed to announce its proximity to heaven. The sky was cloudless, typical for a spring morning in Topanga Canyon, an azure lake that flowed serene and stately over the receding hills until it merged into the distant haze that hung like an eternal backdrop to the City of Angels. Outside the compound walls, the musicians had assembled beneath the shade of the old tamarind tree, as they did every morning at this hour, seated in a semi-circle on the grass with their backs to the gnarled trunk, chanting their way into the heart of the universe while the arriving disciples gathered round, swaying to the hypnotic pulse of the tablas and mridanga. He could hear their low voices singing one of the ashram's favorite *bhajan*s, the mystic syllables of the ancient Sanskrit chant rising and falling to the modulations of a harmonium, the familiar sounds muffled by the compound's thick adobe walls but still loud enough to tug at his heart with their rhythmic charm. He glanced instinctively at his watch—still a few minutes to go before he needed to see to Gurudeva's breakfast; time enough to enjoy a bhajan or two before his duty called him back inside.

He ambled up the walkway to the gate and exchanged smiles with the gatekeeper as he waited for him to nudge open the trellised doors. He passed under the stucco archway, crowned with bougainvillea, and paused to contemplate the sweeping expanse of the hundred-year-old tamarind on the other side of the gravel drive, stretching out like a bridge between heaven and earth. Its vaulted crown towered more than sixty feet into the air, casting a gentle, unbroken shadow across the drive and up the compound walls. Bright yellow flowers streaked with red mingled among its intricately leafed branches, glowing softly in the morning light. This had been the first tree he had ever truly looked at as one living being looks at another—curious, respectful, open to the myriad questions and countless mysteries that such an encounter supposes. He had been nine then, awed by the sheer size of it, conscious of its foreignness in this sparse land of oak and sycamore. He was twenty-seven now and if anything even more awed by this majestic being who lived life to a rhythm so different from his own, a rhythm with stillness as its heartbeat. He had meditated in its shade more mornings than he could remember, looking for that heartbeat, searching for the same stillness inside himself, yet always thwarted in his efforts by the quicksilver in his veins and the dreams that ran him from one day to the next. His heart felt a twinge of sadness, as it verged on the murky shallows that had troubled him in recent months, but then the music slipped past the curtain of his attention and called him from his thoughts. The summons started with the syncopated glide of fingernails on nylon strings; it was followed by a voice—a vigorous, clear soprano that soared above the chords. The voice stirred the cauldron within and the quicksilver leapt from its bubbling froth.

He scanned the crowd until he saw Gita kneeling beside the tablas, strumming her guitar with her eyes closed, her ash blond hair flowing over her loose-fitting cotton blouse like molten gold down a white sand beach. Her voice called the disciples to a chorus of *Hari om, Hari om, Hari Hari om.* Mukunda sang softly along, tapping his thighs with his fingers as if he were playing the tablas, but his eyes remained fixed on the singer's form. He would never admit it to her, but she was his favorite singer. Not Deva Premal, not Krishna Das, not Jai Uttal. Ever since that evening, six months ago, when she had risen from the ashes of his past and materialized in front of the dais at Sunday *darshan*, singing with the ashram band. The sleeveless leather jacket and Rasta braids were missing, but there had been no mistaking her crystal blue eyes and feline grace, the impossible-to-counterfeit remnants of a girl he had once thought of as the anti-yogi, the epitome when he was growing up of everything unspiritual. For a fleeting moment, he remembered their fifth-grade talent show when she had belted out "They Built This City" in an ear-wrenching Grace Slick imitation. He had found it painful to listen to, though he could not deny the talent (his classmates and teachers had risen to their feet in a thunderous, chair-rattling outburst of applause), but seventeen years later, and about as far as one could get from the smoke-filled bars and all-night raves that had been her usual habitat, her voice was as true as a precision-crafted platinum flute and far richer. She sang as if her soul were joined to the music, soaring heavenward with each succeeding, tear-inducing note. If ever there was a butterfly, he thought, poster child for the possibilities of transformation—

"Mukunda."

He turned to see Rashmi—short and trim in an organdy sari and as always a tad too earnest for his taste—escorting a young, well-dressed couple up the drive. The woman wore a stylish black gown; the man, tailored slacks and a dress shirt—both noticeably out of place amid a sea of jeans, t-shirts, yogi pants, and tie-dyes.

"Mukunda, this is Jessica and Saul, from Santa Barbara. It's their first visit to the ashram. Do you think you could give them a quick orientation before Gurudeva comes out?"

Mukunda stiffened, but he did his best not to let it show. For some reason, Rashmi still insisted on treating him like a pliant younger brother, even though he had been Gurudeva's personal assistant for more than a year now, a position that should have exempted him from such requests. He mustered a dutiful smile and escorted the couple a few meters down the drive so they could talk without disturbing the singers. One look at their faces, however, made him forget his annoyance. Though they were dressed more for a dinner party than for an ashram, they showed the same slightly overwhelmed, self-conscious eagerness that he had seen so often in new disciples. He knew the symptoms and he knew the cause. The thought of seeing an enlightened being for the first time was enough to unsteady the ground on which you stood. There was nothing you could do to prepare yourself for it, no matter how many books you read or how many trails you wandered in the Himalayas with your backpack and your Sherpa. It was the ones who took it all in stride that made him wary. Time had taught him that they were either spiritual tourists, collecting darshans the way some people collected jade carvings and African masks, or else dull as a board.

Heedful of their uncertain smiles, he animated his voice as he explained to them about Gurudeva's daily practice of going for a walk each morning with a small group of disciples in some scenic spot. These were intimate, informal sessions, he told them, during which the master would chat with his disciples about whatever was on his mind. He would ask them how their spiritual practices were going, give advice and instruction, tell stories and crack jokes. Going on morning walk was one of the high points in a disciple's life, a chance to pass a couple of uninterrupted hours by the master's side—and waiting outside the Bungalow to see him off or welcome him back was the next best thing. Gurudeva would usually spend a few minutes chatting with the crowd and bestowing his blessings—sometimes as long as twenty minutes, especially if the bhajans were particularly strong that day.

Mukunda explained the importance of guru darshan, how the mere sight of a realized being brought unimaginable blessings to whoever was fortunate enough to have that opportunity. He quoted the same lines from Kabir he always quoted: "If God and guru are standing in front of you, whom should you salute first? You should salute the guru, because it is the guru who shows you God." He could see the anticipation in their eyes as they listened, likely for the first time, to words that had inspired disciples for centuries, as potent as the day they first fell from the poet-yogi's lips. Taking that as his cue, he excused himself and went back into the Bungalow to check on Gurudeva's breakfast. He would have preferred to stay and listen to the bhajans a while longer, but as usual his duties left him little time for personal preferences.

As he entered the Bungalow, he saw Bhishma still sprawled out on the sofa at the foot of the stairs—his sentry box, as he liked to call it—deep into his surf magazines. Bhishma glanced up momentarily and then buried himself again in his maritime meditations. Mukunda was sure that Gurudeva was the first and only spiritual master in history to have a tank-topped Brazilian beach rat for a bodyguard, but then, as all good yogis knew, appearances were invariably deceiving. Anyone who had seen Bhishma go through his daily martial-arts routine made sure he stepped softly whenever he was within hailing distance.

Mukunda passed the foot of the stairs, where he could hear the TV going up in Gurudeva's quarters, and continued on into the immaculate, ultra-modern kitchen. Everything looked ready. On the counter was a heavily laden silver serving tray with buttered whole-wheat toast, a platter of freshly cut fruit, a glass of fresh-squeezed orange juice, a bowl of homemade yogurt, and several smaller bowls with Gurudeva's breakfast favorites: blueberry-almond granola, roasted cashews, and mixed dried fruits. Ganesh, Gurudeva's short, round, and ever-jovial cook, was humming along to a *kirtan* CD while he lifted the last of the banana-blueberry pancakes off the griddle with a spatula. He glanced over his shoulder at

Mukunda and smiled. "Just the way Gurudeva likes them. Golden brown with almond sauce and maple syrup on the side."

"Smells great. I hope there's some left over for us."

Ganesh covered the plate of pancakes with a silver top. "There's more batter in the fridge, enough for a battalion of hungry yogis."

"My man. How about the maple yogurt and blueberries from yesterday, any left?"

Ganesh cocked a finger toward the fridge and turned off the gas flame. "Shall we?" he asked. Mukunda grabbed the serving tray and headed for the stairs while Ganesh followed with the pancakes.

They found Gurudeva in his usual morning mudra: leaning back in his plush recliner with his arms draped over the armrests, the remote firmly anchored in his right hand. He was staring into a state-of-the-art entertainment system with a sixty-inch wide-screen TV and five pro-logic surround-sound speakers. Onscreen the familiar face of CNN's Peter Arnett was paying homage to one of the leading figures in American politics.

"Take a look at this." Gurudeva motioned toward the screen with the remote while Ganesh and Mukunda deposited their trays on the teak coffee table and arranged the silverware. His gold Rolex and emerald and sapphire rings—gifts from his more affluent disciples—flashed as he moved his hand, reflecting the light streaming in through the sliding-glass balcony doors. To Mukunda he seemed the perfect image of an ancient Indian sage, with his flowing white locks and magnificent ochre robe. Had it not been for the house, they could have easily been back in the time of the Upanishads, two disciples harking to the words of an immortal *rishi*.

"Look at those fools," Gurudeva exclaimed, "running after these politicians like they were gods. And what for? For spreading ignorance wherever they go and doing all sorts of nasty deeds when they think no one is looking. If they had any sense, they would avoid them like poison gas. Meanwhile, the Buddhas of the world pass by completely unnoticed. Tell me, Mukunda, when was the last time CNN reported what the Buddhas were up to? Eh? What do you say?"

Mukunda smiled but kept silent. He loved the sound of his guru's voice, that melodious basso drawl with its lilting North Indian intonation. He loved to watch his movements, every gesture so graceful, so harmonious, so relaxed. The master's prize piece of jewelry hung from a silver chain around his neck, a gem-encrusted medallion engraved with Sanskrit mantras that had belonged to Krishna, who had worn it around his neck thirty-five centuries earlier alongside the much more famous Koh-i-Noor diamond, now on display in the Tower of London. Gurudeva had never told him how it had come to be in his possession, but it created an aura about him, a misty presence of centuries past.

The master muted the volume with the remote. He rolled up his sleeves, pulled up his feet into a cross-legged posture, and leaned over the coffee table to sample the different dishes laid out in front of him, attending to his breakfast with a connoisseur's single-mindedness. Mukunda stood on one side while he ate and Ganesh on the other, both ready to anticipate their master's slightest need. As usual, Gurudeva kept up a running commentary while he ate. He told a few jokes, compared Eastern and Western cuisine, and inquired about some of his disciples and the goings-on in the ashram. He ate leisurely, sometimes pausing for several minutes to better tell a joke or finish an anecdote, especially when he needed both hands to talk, which was not infrequent. When he finished eating, he wiped his chin and mouth with the cloth napkin that he had tucked into the neck of his robe, picked up the glass of orange juice, and drained it in one go. He motioned for his two disciples to sit down on the carpet, wiped his mouth again, and dropped the napkin onto the tray. Then he flushed a toothpick from a hidden pocket and began telling a Mullah Nasruddin story while he cleaned his teeth.

Mukunda could not resist a grin. He loved these Mullah Nasruddin stories. They never failed to amuse him, though there was always a message behind the chuckles and the tears. Gurudeva loved to make his disciples laugh and he was brilliant at it. As far as Mukunda was concerned, he was the world's greatest actor, a master of voice inflection and mannerisms, one whose panache and flair for the dramatic extended to each and every encounter with his disciples.

"Once the mullah went to Tabriz to pay a visit to some of his disciples. He arrived in the morning and decided to go straight to the market to break his fast, but when he got there all of the shops were closed, including his favorite sweet shop. Everyone he saw was hurrying in the direction of the Blue Mosque as fast as their feet could carry them. Nasruddin managed to stop one of them long enough to ask where everybody was going. Half out of breath, the man told him that the Sultan of Mashhad, reputed to be the world's richest man, was at that very moment in the square in front of the Blue Mosque; naturally all the shopkeepers had closed their shops and gone to catch a glimpse of the great man.

"This is bad, very bad, the mullah thought. All the shops are closed and it has been hours since I have eaten. Let me see what can be done."

As Gurudeva recounted the mullah's dismay, he added some righteous indignation to his voice and shook his head resentfully. Mukunda exchanged an amused glance with Ganesh, thoroughly enjoying the masterly dramatic touches.

"The mullah decided to go to the mosque himself. When he got there, he saw a huge crowd assembled around the sultan's caravan. Knowing the great affection that his people held him in, and the awe that his august presence generated, the sultan had deigned to step out of his canopied wagon and give his blessings to the crowd. People were praising his beneficence: 'Ah what a great soul he is. How lucky we are to have him among us!' When the mullah heard this, he started laughing in his booming baritone voice. Those within earshot became angry and tried to shout him down. 'Can't you keep quiet, you disrespectful old fool? Can't you see that the sultan is giving us his blessings?'

" 'I can't help it,' he replied. 'This is one of the world's great farces. It gets better every time I see it.' "

As Gurudeva dramatized the shouts from the crowd and the mullah's replies, he changed voices, from rank annoyance couched in a vaguely Persian lilt to something close to a British upper-class accent that reminded Mukunda of John Cleese. Gurudeva's mannerisms were so perfectly suited to what he was dramatizing, and his shifting voices so compelling, that Mukunda had to sit on his hands to keep from clapping. Suddenly Gurudeva lowered his voice and changed tone again, shifting back to the conspiratorial narrator, using his hands for emphasis with every modulation of phrase.

"Two city scribes happened to be standing nearby, and they were deeply offended. They recognized the mullah, whom they knew to be a great fool, and decided then and there that he needed to be taught a lesson. That evening a few of the mullah's disciples gathered together at the house of a local baker to hear some words of wisdom from their teacher. The two scribes also attended. They had prepared a few questions especially designed to show the mullah up in front of his disciples. They waited patiently until the mullah finished his talk and then they pounced. One by one they asked their questions, and one by one the mullah foiled their designs with his clever answers. But they had saved their best for last. 'Have you ever seen God?' they asked, thinking that if he said yes, they would accuse him of blasphemy, and if he answered no, then he would lose face in front of his disciples.

" 'Now it's funny you should ask that,' " Gurudeva had shifted back to his venerable-yogi version of John Cleese, drawing appreciative chuckles from his two disciples. " 'Just yesterday God and I were having a long talk; he told me that two scribes from the city would be paying me a visit and that both of them were guilty of embezzling funds from the government exchequer.' The faces of the two scribes turned beet red. They had in fact been embezzling funds from the government exchequer; and, as everyone knew, the offense carried a penalty of death.

"The mullah paused while he looked first at one scribe and then the other. Then he said, 'God told me that he was sending them to me because he was busy with some other more important cases; he was leaving it up to me to determine their punishment. The only problem is that I am also very busy. A knotty problem, indeed. I am considering letting them decide their own fate. What do you two think?' "

Gurudeva extended his hands, palms upward, as if Ganesh and Mukunda were the two scribes and he were the mullah asking them to decide their fate. They kept silent, waiting for Gurudeva to finish the story.

"The two men gulped in unison and let out a couple of strangulated sounds that no one could understand. The mullah smiled indulgently. When no words were forthcoming he turned his attention back to his disciples. The next day public notices appeared on the city walls extolling the virtues and spiritual wisdom of Mullah Nasruddin; a small footnote was all that the sultan's visit merited. Soon afterward, certain funds that had disappeared unnoticed from the government exchequer mysteriously found their way back into the government coffers."

Gurudeva broke into an impish grin and signaled for Ganesh to remove the leftovers. As was often the case, Mukunda didn't really understand the point of the story, but he didn't care. The entertainment was an end in itself. The master could be so charming when he wished to be that Mukunda sometimes had to consciously restrain his smile to keep from getting a facial cramp. As usual, a few minutes with the master had been enough to banish his unruly emotions.

Ganesh scuttled away with the remnants of breakfast while Mukunda stayed to discuss the arrangements for morning walk. It was his job to choose the place and select which disciples would accompany the master. When he first became Gurudeva's personal assistant—or PA, as everyone called it—he had spent a lot of time trying to find new and interesting places for the master to walk, but he soon found out that Gurudeva was happiest when he rotated between his dozen or so favorite spots, with no more than an occasional novelty thrown in. Mukunda had scheduled this morning's walk for the hiking trails behind the Griffith Park observatory. It was a good ride from the Topanga Canyon ashram, but it had one of the best views of the city and Gurudeva never tired of going there. That was the easy part. Choosing who would go with him was a different story, a constant headache as far as Mukunda was concerned. A small coterie of Gurudeva's oldest and most trusted disciples had the rare privilege of being able to go on walk whenever they wished; this normally left only four or five additional spots in the two-car convoy. The competition for these remaining spots could be downright fierce. He remembered how he had resented it when Madalasa or Markandeya wouldn't let him go back in the days when they had handled the PA duties. Now he felt the same kind of subtle or not-so-subtle pressure, but being as young as he was, his fellow disciples were far more likely to voice their discontent. To shield himself from their criticisms, he had drawn up a set of fixed criteria—how long since their last walk, how active they were in ashram activities, and so on—and had it affixed to the office bulletin board along with a formal application system. It hadn't stopped him from hearing complaints, but at least no one accused him of playing favorites.

After the brief discussion, Mukunda went downstairs and informed Bhishma that Gurudeva would be down in a few minutes. From the window he could see the master's recently purchased silver Mercedes S320 parked just outside the gate, the latest in his growing collection. He continued outside to double check that everything was ready. As he approached the gate, he could see Sarathi, Gurudeva's personal driver, standing outside the passenger door of the Benz, assiduously wiping the side-view mirror with a cotton cloth. Quick-witted and easygoing, Sarathi doted on the cars he drove like an over-protective parent. They arrived in front of the master's gate freshly washed every morning, glistening with a sleek wax sheen that he seemed to be constantly polishing. As Mukunda passed under the archway, Sarathi gave him the thumbs-up. Both cars were in position and ready to go. The devotees had formed a tight ring around the two cars and down a good portion of the drive that led from the house to the main entrance. The musicians had left their seats beneath the tamarind tree and were now standing by the side of the master's car, stoking the devotional fervor with their pulsating rhythms. Some of the disciples were dancing with their arms raised to the sky, stepping from side to side and tapping the big toe behind the heel in the traditional kirtan step. Others were dancing free form, many of them with their eyes closed, carried away by the moment.

Markandeya and Madalasa, Gurudeva's senior-most disciples, were standing just outside the gate. Mukunda signaled to them, and they entered the courtyard and took up their positions outside the Bungalow door to escort the master to his car. Leela was already waiting in the courtyard, her eyes focused on the doorway as if the world for her would not exist until the master stepped through it. The three of them would go in Gurudeva's car along with Bhishma, as they usually did. The others who had been selected for this morning's walk were waiting near the BMW, ready to jump in once the master was inside the Benz.

His mental checklist complete, Mukunda relaxed and surveyed the scene. His gaze came to rest, as it often did these days, on Gita. She was singing in inspired abandon, her eyes closed, guitar strapped over her shoulder, leading the chant that would welcome Gurudeva to his car. He still found it difficult to get over the transformation. La Jolla's foremost teenage rebel, the queen of grunge rock and illicit drugs, thumbing her nose at the system every chance she got—and now here she was, about to go on morning walk with an enlightened master. How many times had he heard his folks discuss the grief she was causing her poor suffering parents? If anyone had told him then that one day she would be bringing tears to the eyes of the devotees with her devotional singing, he would have questioned their sanity. But karma was a strange animal. It made paupers of kings and turned sinners into saints. He thought back to that darshan six months ago when he had seen her sitting with the band and wondered if his mind were playing tricks on him. After he had escorted Gurudeva back to the Bungalow, he had gone out to see if he could catch her before she left. He found her waiting for him outside the Bungalow gate. His astonishment must have been graven on his face, because as soon as she saw him she said, "Well, you look like you've seen a ghost. Am I that scary?" It wasn't fright, of course; it was shock. They took a seat under the tamarind tree, on a crisp fall night studded with stars, and she started telling him the story of how she had turned up in his Topanga sanctuary after years of running in the opposite direction, while he looked at her as if the road she'd traveled had twice circled the earth after winding up the stone steps from Hades. By the time she finished her story, the moon was beginning its slow rise above the canyon, adding a golden shimmer to Gabriela's already golden tresses. Like everything about her, there was nothing ordinary about what she'd gone through to get here. She had survived things he had only read about or seen in movies, and somewhere along the way her lifelong passion for social justice had transformed itself into a hunger for something she couldn't put a name to, but which led her slowly but surely into the world of spiritual ambition that raised its banners on the Coast of Dreams. As she began her fledging pilgrimage from one spiritual group to another, wary of charlatans and disdainful of the plumes of escapism that seemed to sully the New Age sky, she had wondered if she would see him in one of those events, if he were still sequestered in his ashram in the hills. Then one day she got a call from Kamal asking her if she'd be interested in singing backup on what turned out to be an ashram CD. When Kamal told her about the ashram one afternoon at the studio, her intuition went off like the warning light in the control room. She told him about her old friend and was not surprised to learn that he was living there. A few days later she accepted Kamal's invitation to sing with the band at Sunday darshan, knowing that the look on Mukunda's face when he saw her would go down with the best of her memories.

Smiling at his own memories, Mukunda looked again at Gita and was surprised by a flash of crystal blue. She had her eyes open now and was looking directly at him, as if she had caught him at his thoughts. He hoped his embarrassment didn't show. Fortunately, he was rescued a few moments later by a shout that went up from the crowd: *Gurudeva ki jai, Gurudeva ki jai*, victory to Gurudeva. He turned and hurried back to the Bungalow, where the master was standing in the open doorway in his elegant one-piece ochre robe, orange ski cap, and mirrored sunglasses. His hands were folded to his chest as Leela knelt down and devotedly slipped on his sandals. Markandeya put a conch shell to his lips and blew a long sustained blast that momentarily silenced the chanting. Setting down the conch, he opened an umbrella to protect the master from the still-weak sun, and Gurudeva began his stately march up the walkway to his car, where the thronging disciples had taken up a new chant, the one they traditionally sang from the time the conch shell blew until the moment the master's car disappeared out the gate: *gurudeva sharanam, sharanam gurudeva*, we take refuge in the guru, the dispeller of ignorance. Markandeya and Madalasa walked on either side of the master, with Bhishma and Leela flanking them and Ganesh pulling up the rear, carrying two thermoses with chilled juice and water, a couple of clean towels, and some light refreshments packed in a thermal shoulder bag. As Gurudeva passed under the archway, the chant softened to a whisper. Sarathi opened the rear door of the Mercedes and stood stiffly with one hand on the handle, hidden behind the same model sunglasses as the master. Gurudeva paused by the open door and started conversing with the crowd, looking around from face to face with his charismatic smile, calling on several disciples by name and recounting a short anecdote about the Buddha's first sermon at Sarnath. Mukunda smiled as he noticed the couple from Santa Barbara struggling to shoulder their way toward the front, straining to hear what the master was saying, their earlier decorum entirely absent now that the master was in full view. It was a promising sign.

Finally, Gurudeva gave the crowd his blessing and climbed into the Benz. Markandeya and Bhishma got in on either side of him. Madalasa and Leela squeezed into the front seat next to Sarathi, who eased the car down the drive toward the main gate with the BMW and its allotted passengers following close behind. Many of the devotees ran after the car, jockeying to catch a final glimpse of the master, until the car exited the main gate and turned right onto Topanga Canyon Boulevard.

Once Gurudeva was gone, the crowd quickly dispersed. Most of the disciples wandered off in twos and threes and fours toward the Buddha Café or the ashram cafeteria. For Mukunda, however, it was going to be a working breakfast. He caught up with Rashmi and Ganesh, and the three of them went back to the Bungalow for their meeting. Mukunda and Rashmi laid the kitchen table while Ganesh heated up a skillet and prepared some fresh pancakes. Once the pancakes were on their plates, they settled into a light conversation, content to enjoy their meal before they took up the pedestrian details that awaited them.

"The kundalini's going to be jumping at this retreat," Ganesh remarked buoyantly as he dove into his breakfast with the steadfast gusto of a hungry man. Mukunda knew he was probably right; he also knew that it didn't matter much to Ganesh whether or not he felt that tickle in his spine. He was content to cook for his guru, to enjoy his food, and to tend to the hundreds of potted plants that spiced the veranda with their pleasing scents and made Mukunda feel as if he were in a jungle every time he looked out his bedroom window. Ganesh spent his days doing exactly what he loved to do, and he did it, moreover, while living at the center to which all paths led: the inner sanctum where the echoes of an enlightened master traveled down the banister at night and crept into the kitchen where he worked. But then, Ganesh also rolled on the ground in ecstatic trance during big kirtans when the energy swirled like an incipient hurricane. Mukunda would have given anything to feel his kundalini jump like that, but he had grown used to seeing other disciples fall to the ground or dance in wild abandon while he attended to his charismatic master and felt nothing, just a windless sea and empty sails. Even prim, oval-eyed Rashmi, whom he rarely caught smiling, had her moments when the heavens opened: she was describing one of those moments now as she reached for the maple syrup. On and on she went as the last of the pancakes disappeared into her maundering mouth: how she had seen Gurudeva turn into Lord Shiva at the end of Sunday darshan a few weeks earlier; how light had poured out of the master's third eye and straight into her heart. The fervor in her voice and the tremulous excitement that radiated from her face made Mukunda long for the privacy of his room and the solace of a good book. Unfortunately, this was not an option. He forced himself to smile and nod appreciatively, and consoled himself with the thought that their meeting would soon come to his rescue. Not that he was jealous. He was glad, in fact, that someone was enjoying the spiritual waves that had left him stranded on the beach. But it was tiresome to be reminded all the time that what he most longed for in life—spiritual experience—was being handed out free of charge to everyone it seemed but him. It hadn't always been this way, and that only made it worse. There had been a time, not so long ago, when he'd been sure that he was one of the privileged few who would reach the shores of illumination in a single lifetime. For years he had found meditation easy, and whenever he had his doubts, Gurudeva would assure him that his future was already ordained: he had been born a yogi, and a yogi he would be. But somehow in the last couple of years the well had begun to dry up. His practice had grown mechanical, the respect he enjoyed among his fellow disciples had become a disquieting burden, and even the healthful balm of Gurudeva's smile could only sustain his spirits for short periods of time. When he remembered the times when his mantra had led him to the edge of an interior ocean where the silence was more beautiful than music, where clouds of understanding decorated the sky, he could see that the certainty that had once filled his life was gone. Those experiences were merely memories now, faltering images fading into a growing mist that made him question whether they had truly been as profound as he had once taken them to be, or whether the industrious hands of self-indulgence had built them up from molehills into mountains. His present (and his present now stretched well into his past) was a low tide in a marshland, obscuring the horizon with its murky vapors.

He was relieved when Ganesh reached for a folder that was lying on the counter and pulled from it a couple of typewritten sheets with his suggestions for the retreat menu. Mukunda helped Rashmi ferry the empty plates and bowls to the sink and shied her away when she volunteered to help with the washing. From there the conversation slipped into a pool of mundane details: lists of what to purchase and where, how to divide up the *seva* volunteers for food prep, how much extra staff they would need, a long discussion on desserts, the ubiquitous questions of how to avoid going over budget. Mukunda felt himself on firmer ground now, glad for the chance to escape his thoughts. When he was done with the washing, he lent his attention to the few administrative details that required his input and trusted the rest to Ganesh's expert hand. Ostensibly, Rashmi was in charge of the ashram cafeteria, and she did fine when it came to the day-to-day affairs of running the collective kitchen, but all creative matters were still handled by Ganesh, who had trained her and still watched over her like a doting uncle, though he was a good ten years her junior. Outside the window, Mukunda could hear the sharp twittering of sparrows darting among the ordered battalions of hanging plants. He leaned back in his chair and sought the marbled streaks of blue that appeared in the spaces beyond the twisting stems and dangling, many-shaded leaves. While Rashmi and Ganesh bent their heads over the array of papers in front of them and pointed at figures and nodded, his mind drifted out the window and into the future. He pictured himself in the meditation hall, seated on the platform to the left of his guru, as insubstantial as a glint of cloud on a far horizon. In front of the stage he could see bright currents of energy coursing through the disciples, their bodies twisting like live wires flashing blue and white sparks as they jumped. He wondered if this might be his time to feel heaven's lightening in his spine, if he were finally ready, or if he would just continue to sit there: transparent, weightless, to the point where he could walk through himself and never feel his step.

2

They ought to ban strong perfume in public places, Gita thought, as she stepped out of the BMW into the observatory parking lot and took a long-overdue draft of fresh air, feeling as if she had just been released from captivity. It ought to be regulated, like cigarettes and car exhaust. Make them pay a fine, especially these leggy brunettes who insist on being called actresses when they've never even been in a cat-food commercial. She was aware that she still used perfume herself and that she had spent her adult life in and out of smoke-filled bars, half the time with a lit cigarette wedged between the strings of her guitar, but this morsel of self-awareness was not enough to elicit her sympathy, especially when the girl hadn't stopped talking the entire forty-minute drive from the ashram, an artsy monologue straight from the pages of *Variety*. Her Sanskrit name was Pushpa Devi, the flower goddess; Gita suspected that Gurudeva had been enjoying a private joke when he gave her that name.

She fetched her guitar from the trunk and joined the small group of disciples gathered around the master, careful to station herself on the opposite side from her perfumed nemesis. She could feel the relaxed excitement spreading like a contagion as the group began making their way up from the parking lot to the observatory. Even tall, debonair Markandeya, Gurudeva's oldest and most respected disciple, was not immune. Despite his graying sideburns and immaculately tailored Armani casuals, the wealthy fifty-something wizard of the financial markets turned into a starry-eyed youngster whenever he was around his guru. Gurudeva had this effect on practically everyone, herself included, though she wasn't entirely sure why. It was something she was still trying to figure out.

The group reached the observatory grounds and started strolling down the walkway, attracting curious glances from the light smattering of tourists wandering the grounds with their cameras slung around their necks and their guidebooks in their hands. Their attention was something Gita had gotten used to on previous walks. Gurudeva looked as if he had stepped out of a guidebook to spiritual India, with his flowing white locks and ochre robes, surrounded by a gently moving spiral of billowing white cotton dresses, tie-dyes, and yogi pants. She would have been gawking herself had she come across this group a year ago, before the spiritual bug had gotten into her and begun making a mockery of her so-called sanity.

As Gita took in the scene, she could hear the intonations of different languages mingling in the atmosphere like birdsong. It was what she liked most about the tourists, the chance to hear different languages, disconnected syllables careening through unfamiliar cadences, far more interesting to her ear than the often-tedious music of English. The locals tended to be quieter, as if they were trying to store up whatever peace they could find before they traveled back down the hill and into the restless grip of runaway civilization. She knew the feeling. She had thought San Diego over the top, but that was before she had actually lived in LA, instead of just driving up every once in a while for a night of neon vapor trails and West Coast jazz. She had been living in the city six months when she finally discovered what Griffith Park was all about: the precious opportunity to pretend for a few hours that you didn't live in a city where the concrete swallowed up your dreams and left you somnambulant in the smog.

As they passed through the thin shadow of the Astronomers Monument, Markandeya mentioned to Gurudeva that when Galileo was young he had wanted to be a monk and lead a life of contemplation. Gurudeva smiled and paused in front of the monument. The disciples gathered in a semi-circle around him, Leela and Madalasa flanking him on either side like zealous bodyguards.

"Galileo had a modern spiritual sensibility," Gurudeva commented, "very unusual for his time. He refused to let himself be bound by the dogmas that weighed down even the best minds of his era, but he was also pragmatic enough to recant when the church left him no choice. Some people nowadays think less of him for this, but it is very difficult for people of the twenty-first century to understand what a stranglehold the church had on cultural and political life in Europe in the sixteenth century."

"Kepler was also supposed to have been very religious," Markandeya said.

"It went with the territory. Both Kepler and Galileo were essentially cosmologists. We think of them as astronomers nowadays, but if you strip away the trappings of science you will find that the astronomers of today are nothing but cosmologists in modern garb. In Galileo's time, the scientists who studied the heavens were aware that it was the heavens they were studying, not simply outer space. They were trying to comprehend God's creation and the divine laws that govern it. Unfortunately, our modern material culture has divested our scientists of that awareness. Their discoveries may be more factual than those of Galileo and his contemporaries, but they are also less significant—precisely because that awareness is missing. They are like blind men examining an elephant. One person feels the leg and thinks it's a kind of pillar; another grabs the tail and compares it to a rope; a third feels the tusk and says that it's like a solid pipe. None of them can gain any true conception of the elephant because they lack the gift of sight. Until you realize the role of consciousness in the creation, the universe is nothing more than a meaningless sea of cosmic dust; and the person looking through the lens of his telescope is no better than a blind man.

"Recently, however, some modern physicists have begun to realize that they are indeed cosmologists. The deeper they go in their investigations, the closer they get to the Divine Intelligence that lies at the heart of the cosmos. This is beginning to force them out of their materialism. Einstein, for example, realized this early on in his career. As physics evolves, it has no choice but to capitulate to metaphysics. It is a process no scientist can stop, no matter how deeply he buries his head in the sand."

Gurudeva looked up at the sculptures, saluted them with folded hands, and started moving leisurely toward the opposite end of the grounds, where the hiking trails began, while the disciples swirled in formation around him. Gita loved the solemnity in this simple gesture. She found it quaint yet moving. To all outward appearances, he was paying his respects to a lifeless monument, but she could feel his regard pass from the symbols to the men, oblivious of the limitations of time and space, honoring their contribution to human history and their continued presence in the daily lives of generations past, present, and future. There was something very Indian about it that became universal the moment she touched the spirit behind it. She smiled as she remembered the song from the Indigo Girls that she used to sing when she was young and nobody was listening: "I call on the resting soul of Galileo, king of night vision, king of insight." It had been a kind of silent anthem for her at one point in her life, though it had been years since she had listened to the song. She looked over at Gurudeva; as she did, he glanced at her with a knowing smile. She felt a twinge of embarrassment, as if her thoughts were on display in front of the master. It was not the first time she had felt this around him, and each time it happened she became more and more convinced that the occult powers the older disciples attributed to him might well be more than a devotee's fanciful tale.

The entourage left the grounds and started winding their way up one of the narrow hiking trails. They fell into groups of twos with Leela and Madalasa walking just behind Gurudeva. It was a clear, bright morning. The sun was in their faces, suspended between the sky's zenith and the hills in front of them, reflecting off the scraggly brush that crept up the mountainside. Gita had been on morning walk with Gurudeva in these hills once before; now, as then, the master maintained silence until they reached the top of the trail. As they walked, she turned her attention to the sounds of their footsteps on the dirt path, gliding polyrhythms scrunching into the compacted soil. In the background she could hear a faint hum rising from the sprawling megalopolis that covered the valley floor. Occasional voices from the observatory punctuated the soundscape: high-pitched, almost bell-like phrases, too distant to separate into words. They reminded her of a wind section in an avant-garde symphony, catching her ear for a tremulous moment before they disappeared into the void. Her thoughts continued to drift as she listened to the chorus of the world around her, melding into dreams of the music she longed to give birth to. The sounds of melodies, both foreign and familiar, called her inward, toward the part of her being that lived to express itself in music, calling her to a world unique and complete in itself. This was her own night vision, a solitary look into a secret space in which she could see gestating the music she was destined to create—faint, meandering, colored wisps of sound tinged with unrecognizable emotions. It was something she hesitated to describe, even to herself, something far more than mere notes and rhythms spread in orderly arrangements across the fabric of her mental sky. It was a presence that lived inside her, using her as a host while it grew and nurtured itself on her aspirations. Gurudeva had called her a *gandharva* when she first sang for him. She had no idea what it meant, but the word struck an instant chord in her mind. The next day she looked it up in a Sanskrit dictionary and discovered that a *gandharva* was a mythological being that had left behind a body of flesh and blood for one of celestial music. Perhaps it had been this ethereal, musical life form slowly taking shape inside her that he had been referring to, this incipient music that left her soul restless for what could be. She had been writing songs ever since she'd first picked up a guitar in grade school, but something had changed since she'd begun meditating. Her earlier songs had been written from the outside in, self-conscious productions that had never truly satisfied her—this new music was writing her from the inside out. It was something she had no control over, but which she would gladly give her life to see born. She had read of saints who talked of a divine music that blew through them without any conscious design on their part, a sacred wind that chose them as a reed. She wondered if she dare hope for the same divine visitation, though for now she could only watch and listen, and pray that her destiny would make it so.

The walkers crested a ridge and paused for a few minutes to catch their breath. The sun was closer now and hotter. Gita removed the long-sleeve blouse she was wearing over her t-shirt and tied it around her waist. She edged a little closer to the master, who began conversing with the disciples about the city that lay spread out beneath them. As always, he enchanted them with his unique blend of philosophical insight and understated humor, while he dissected the follies of his adopted homeland, both spiritual and material. He was a guru who loved to talk and could do so about seemingly any topic under the sun. As he pointed to the various landmarks, hazy in the distant smog, he regaled the disciples with colorful historical anecdotes that cast each of those landmarks in a novel light. Gita had once overheard Madalasa remark that in the early days Gurudeva used to read as many as ten books a day. She had found it difficult to believe, but the more time she spent around him, the more it seemed within the realm of possibility.

The conversation continued during the return journey down the winding trail. Gurudeva passed from one subject to another with the ease of an accomplished skier bending through a turn. Everyone got a chance to ask a question or two, led by the perfume lady who continued to talk as if she were an animated advertisement for *Variety*. She even had the temerity to tell Gurudeva about a script she was working on—a spiritual romantic fairy tale, no less. From the rear of the troupe, Gita caught Leela's eye and made a desperate "gag her" sign, eliciting a wicked gleam and a silent laugh from the older woman. How does she get away with it? Gita wondered. Does she lull everyone with her perfume, stun them with her legs, and then attack with the saccharine and the sugar? She hoped someone would be blunt enough to tell her to be quiet, but she knew it was too much to ask. It was all very New Age-y in the ashram, all peace and love, at least on the surface. This had taken her a good deal of getting used to, especially once she realized that there was just as much going on behind closed doors and closed eyelids as anyplace else she had ever been. She had come to the conclusion that human beings were still human beings, no matter how much they meditated. There were plenty of times when she would have loved to set loose the sharp tongue she had spent years honing, but it didn't go over well in the ashram, as she had quickly discovered. It had galled her at first—at times there seemed to be a willful disregard among the disciples of the darker side of human motivation—but she was honest enough to admit that she had something to learn in this regard. There was something to be said for maintaining one's serenity under trying circumstances, even if it were only on the surface. If Gurudeva could listen so patiently to mystical Barbie without losing the beatific smile he was so famous for, then she could certainly make an effort to learn from him.

By the time they made it back to the observatory grounds, they had been walking for more than an hour. At Gurudeva's suggestion they went to the back terrace to sit and meditate. They found it deserted, except for a young couple at the telescope. Markandeya placed Gurudeva's blanket and cushion in one corner of the terrace, in the broken shade cast by the James Dean statue. Abhay and Paritosh unfolded a pair of blankets for the disciples to sit on. Once everyone was settled, Gurudeva called for a bhajan. Gita pulled her guitar from its gig bag, checked to see that it was still in tune, and selected a popular bhajan from the ashram songbook: "Ragupati Raghava Raja Ram." Bhishma and Madalasa produced hand cymbals and started marking time, while the rest of the devotees clapped in rhythmic accents. Gita closed her eyes as she sang, still conscious of the young couple behind her, surveying the city through the telescope. How strange this invasion from an alternate reality must seem to them. She suspected they wouldn't be there for long. It was what usually happened when Gurudeva and the disciples sang and meditated in public.

By the time Gita completed the second stanza, she had forgotten about the couple, startled once again into rapt attention by the now-familiar transport of a music unlike any she had known in her twenty-seven years. There was something about these spiritual songs—the bhajans and the kirtans—that acted on her in a way no other music could. It was as if she were dough being kneaded into unimagined shapes by these simple notes and the syllables that accompanied them. Part of it, she had come to understand, was her own attention to the devotional sentiments they evoked, her willingness to surrender to emotions that had been put to sleep by a society almost entirely impervious to the promptings of the soul. She had often heard Indian devotional songs during her year and a half at Ali Akbar College of Music, where she had gone to study Indian vocal and instrumental music, inspired by John Coltrane's microtonal explorations of the world's most sophisticated melodies, but somehow it had never penetrated her interiors until she began singing the kirtans and bhajans herself in her first studio sessions with Kamal at The Record Plant. Rafael, a friend of hers from AACM who was on his way to becoming California's finest non-Indian tabla player, had recommended her for the gig when Kamal invited him one day to play tablas on an ashram CD. Kamal was looking for backup singers with a background in both jazz and Indian Classical—not an easy combination to come by—and Rafael had recommended her in the same breath. The sessions lasted a week: five kirtans and a half dozen traditional bhajans in three different languages: Sanskrit, Pali, and Hindi. The musicians and the backing singers were mostly Western—in keeping with the eclectic Indian-jazz fusion Kamal was looking for—but the feeling was pure esoteric India, the mystical atmosphere of a Himalayan peak. Kamal spent much of the first day coaching them on how to feel their way into the spirit of the music. It took Gita a little while to loosen up, to trust the notes and the rhythms to her musical instincts and throw herself into the emotions that the simple phrasings conveyed—in some respects her musical training only served to get in the way—but when Kamal talked to them about music as meditation, something clicked. A world behind the notes opened up, and it was as deep and as unexplored as the world inside her own heart. She staggered out of the recording studio at the close of the second day, intoxicated by a music that went to her head like the finest Lafite-Rothschild, a nectarean sampling from a land rimmed round by magic. When Kamal caught up with her in the lobby, she wondered aloud why she had never been able to feel the magic in these songs before. "It was only a matter of time," he told her. "You've been chosen. And once you've been chosen, you know, you can never go back." He wore the smile of an imp on his dusky face, but his eyes gleamed with a benevolent earnestness that was beyond reproach. Later, after she had accepted his invitation to attend Gurudeva's Sunday discourse and subsequently taken initiation, he insisted that it was the music that had brought her to the yogic path, acting on her like leavening until she was ready to be molded. She was convinced that it had more to do with seeing Mukunda again after all those years—though she knew he would be there, her heart had still skipped several beats when she had seen him walking by Gurudeva's side. He was more handsome than ever and even more mysterious, possessed of a powerful calm that instantly awakened her dormant hunger to experience that same unaccountable self-possession. But maybe there was something to Kamal's claim. This music had a strange power that went far beyond the interior attention she brought to it, a power that was impossible to explain.

Gurudeva called for a second bhajan and then a short kirtan: *om namah shivaya*. By the time they closed their eyes for meditation, the music had returned her to a place she wished she never had to leave, carried by the wings of mantra to the land of quiet that lay beyond the tempests of her mind. The vistas that opened up inside her felt like a tidal motion carrying her toward the unseen font of her existence, silent sweeps of a landscape so immense the planet underneath her was reduced to a spinning particle of dust. For a moment she felt as if her heart might burst open, so glorious was the feeling, but it didn't last long—it never did—a short stretch of seconds that had the impact of centuries. Then her breath, which had been swallowed by her momentary rapture, came rushing back—and with it, the incessant too and fro of thoughts that was her customary inner climate. She continued to chase her mantra, as if it were a boat battered by winds, pitching and plunging on the waves as she sought in vain the elusive thread of a joy that had disappeared into the distance, veiled by a darkening horizon; but as usual whenever her concentration wavered, she felt the tug of other attractions, more earthbound and immediate. A sweet, almost overpowering fragrance invaded her senses, a field of poppies like the fabled Valley of Flowers. In her case, the opium-laden air was flecked with images of Mukunda (a name it had taken her a long time to get used to). Only a couple of hours ago she had caught him looking at her from across the drive, separated by a crowd of devotees and the sobering implications of their residual karma. Though her eyes had been closed, she had felt him watching her, narrowing the chasm that at times felt unbridgeable. But when she had opened her eyes and returned his gaze, he had looked away, seemingly unconcerned, no evidence of any interest apart from that which he might give to a leaf in the tamarind tree or the perch of a sparrow. She had been left wondering for the umpteenth time if her mind wasn't just doing a brilliant job—yet again—of inventing something that simply didn't exist.

In this respect, not much had changed since their childhood. She had always liked him, as far back as she could remember, but he had never given any sign that the interest was mutual, at least not once they'd reached the age that she'd begun to think in such terms. They had grown up together, had splashed around in the same inflatable pool as toddlers, had played together in their respective backyards while their mothers talked for hours on end in the La Jollan sun. They had sat together in her father's SUV at the South Bay Drive-in on many a Saturday night, two only children circling in the shadows of parents who had been best friends since college. But in grade school they had begun drifting apart, each into their own circles at that awkward age when the girls huddled together at lunch and talked incessantly about the boys they liked without ever having the courage to start up a conversation with one of them. They had still stopped to talk in the halls and at recess, had still been thrown together when their parents met up for dinner, but the easy companionship of their childhood years soon disappeared into what eventually seemed to her like a bottomless chasm. By middle school they had become as different as two twelve-year-olds could be. By then she was already well on her way to her deserved and long-nourished reputation as the quintessential bad influence, a natural-born agitator, someone all well-bred girls were warned to stay away from; he had somehow blossomed into a precocious New Ager, hanging around yoga centers and ashrams with people two or three times his age, talking about reincarnation and enlightened beings with the same single-minded enthusiasm that most kids reserved for pop stars and hanging out at the beach—like it was the only thing in life that mattered. While she was getting high on drugs—along with every other kid in school who wanted to be cool—he claimed to be getting high on consciousness, a claim that seemed as strange to her at the time as it did to everyone else.

By the time they reached high school, her rebellious streak had erupted into full-bore volcanic activity. Anything that served to shake up the status quo she considered a virtuous deed, from sneaking into the high school auditorium at night and spray painting "down with capitalism" and "say no to economic terrorism" over the business exhibits for the annual career fair—how she had loved that escapade; everyone had known who the culprit was but nothing could be proved—to pinning a real marijuana leaf to the "legalize cannabis" t-shirt she wore to the junior prom (she had been "asked" to leave after fifteen minutes, five minutes longer than she'd predicted). Above all, her music provided her with a means to get under people's skin and call attention to the causes that kept her constantly on fire. She started her own punk band in her freshman year and within months had built up a fanatic following composed mostly of school delinquents.

She accumulated a collection of leather-ware and outrageous t-shirts that provoked a revision in what had been until then a nearly non-existent school dress code. Her band changed musical styles almost as fast as the seasons but her following loyally rode the changes, and even the kids who criticized her music—and there were plenty of those—still listened to it, for how else could they keep up with what was going on at school? Most of the new bands that became the rage for a time were bands she turned them on to, and the causes that caught everyone's attention were more often than not the ones she brought to their attention. There were other kids in school who considered themselves activists of one sort or another, but no one who could raise hell like she could and shout it into everyone's ear. But for all that she prided herself on marching to the beat of a different and better drummer, Mukunda's rhythm section was straight from another planet. There was no one else like him and everyone knew it, no matter how eccentric they found him. His was another kind of cool. When everyone in school seemed bent on calling attention to themselves—no one more so than she—he seemed bent on deflecting it. Half the time he talked, no one had any idea what he was talking about, even their teachers, but he was so calm about it, so self-possessed and unflappable, that no one ever minded. She was the most well-known and most talked-about student in high school, for better or for worse, but he was the one that everyone secretly envied, though they could never quite figure out why. She remembered how strange she had felt when she watched him graduate, ten minutes after she had accepted her diploma (unnaturally docile for her parents' sake), knowing that he was leaving the next week for LA, to his ashram in the hills, wondering if she would ever see him again, remembering how close they had been as kids and how far apart they were now, recognizing how much she still liked him and wishing for one fleeting moment that she could be going with him. And now here she was in the shadow of the Griffith Observatory with the LA haze stretched out below her, frosting the tops of the distant palms and acacias, unable to meditate properly because this ghost from her past was threatening to take over her present and fully capable of doing so. And only because it was the one invasion she wanted, and perhaps had always wanted.

But was it at all what he wanted? She couldn't tell. Did he like her? Of course he liked her. He liked everyone. But he was so damn spiritual about it that she couldn't tell whether he felt any different about her than he did about his mother or Gurudeva's cat. That was what was so exasperating about it. He'd smile at her when he saw her walking up the drive like heaven had lit up his heart, and then he'd flash Ganesh the very same smile. At first she had wondered if he might be gay. It was a thought that had crossed her mind a time or two during high school, especially when she was piqued at his insistence on being the one person who never paid any real attention to her. But she was old enough and schooled enough now to tell the difference. She knew now that he had been raised on the yogi's version of universal love, and as far as she could see, that kind of thing could be very confusing. Not only for her. There were all kinds of romantic entanglements tripping up the ashram residents. She had been hip to that straight away, which was no great feat since no one was making any great effort to hide it. Romantic entanglements were served along with breakfast at the ashram. They were impossible to avoid with everyone frantically trying to open their hearts and singing spiritual love songs all day long. But when everybody was supposedly trying to see God in everybody else, it could be almost impossible at times to know if someone was attracted to you or just really good in his spiritual practices.

And then there was this whole celibacy thing that she had yet to wrap her head around. Gurudeva had made it clear that he supported both paths equally: asceticism or the Tantric partnership—after all, this was California not India; celibacy wasn't exactly common fare in these parts. But although it might have few practitioners, there was a mystical aura in the spiritual community that surrounded the celibate path, and as far as she could find out from her sisters-in-arms, Mukunda was about as ascetic as they came. Either that or he hid his tracks better than anyone could imagine. In the real world she would have just gone up to him and asked him if he were interested, ready to deal with it if he wasn't. But things didn't work like that in the ashram. It would have been considered too brazen, too crude—downright unspiritual, in fact. "It's all up to your karma," she had been told when she'd brought up the subject with a sister devotee. "If it's meant to be, it will be"—as if only worldly people took karma into their own hands. It was a bit too hypocritical for her taste, this sanctified, leave-it-to-God attitude, but when in Rome, it was best to learn Italian, unless you wanted to remain a tourist all your life. Sisters openly on the make were heavily frowned upon in the ashram—unfettered libido was considered bad for the soul—so whatever signals she sent out had to be subtle enough that no one would call her on it; and either Mukunda had his antennas down or he wasn't buying.

Gita sighed as she made another half-hearted effort to concentrate on her mantra. Anyhow we are friends, she thought, and we do have history together. She grimaced as she caught the strident, grating rumble of tedious cliché. But as much as it made her cringe, some clichés could not be avoided. Pitiful as it sounded in her ear, it did give her a leg up on the competition, far from negligible in a closed community that universally acknowledged Mukunda to be its most eligible bachelor, however ignorant he might be of the fact. She needed whatever advantage she could get. She had always been a determined wench, used to getting whatever she set her sights on, but this was a whole new playing field. She didn't have the same cachet here that she had in the outside world. Her former exploits and her musical talents were good for some colorful stories and a bouquet of compliments, but here it was how "spiritual" you were that mattered most—especially with somebody like Mukunda who had grown up on the ashram Kool-Aid—and as indefinable as that word might be, she knew she was well behind the competition.

At that moment Gita heard the low tones of Sanskrit mantras intruding on her reverie—the sound of Gurudeva's voice signaling the end of the meditation. She furrowed her brow, as if to shake the cobwebs from her thoughts, and joined the chant. When it ended she opened her eyes and glanced at her watch. Forty-five minutes. At best, twenty of those minutes spent meditating; the rest wasted in fruitless daydream, the same recurring fantasies that had been plaguing her for the past few months. She would have to work on this. If she were going to daydream about Mukunda, she might as well do it when she wasn't meditating. Of course, that was easier said than done. There was something about meditation that seemed to draw all this stuff to the surface, including things she never thought about at any other time. She had read in one of Gurudeva's books that it was a normal part of the process—"spiritual spring cleaning" he called it. "The act of meditation draws the detritus up from the depths of the subconscious, like a receding tide that reveals the ocean's hidden floor." The trick was to not cling to any of those thoughts or emotions. "Observe," Gurudeva was always saying. "Observe your thoughts and let them pass like birds in the sky. You are the consciousness that witnesses the material of the mind. Be one with that consciousness. Appreciate the play of the ego, its infinite wiles, but don't allow yourself to get caught up in it." Oh yes, she understood the theory. The practice, however, was a different matter. Sometimes those thoughts were just too pleasant to let go of. And even when they weren't, even when they were downright unpleasant, there was always some part of her that was unwilling to let go. She was making progress, but oh, did she ever have a long way to go.

Now that her eyes were open, her preoccupation with her recalcitrant mind was quickly forgotten. Gurudeva signaled with his hand to Madalasa and Leela, who fetched the two baskets of snacks from the thermal packs and placed them in front of the master. He held his hands over them and recited some Sanskrit mantras. Then he took a small sweet from one basket and a savory from the other and began nibbling on them, officially turning the rest of the snacks into *prasad*, holy offerings to the guru. Madalasa and Leela picked up the baskets and began handing out the snacks, dropping them into reverently outstretched palms. Gurudeva was in a lighthearted, jovial mood, as he usually was after meditation. He began telling a story about a simple-minded devotee and his guru and soon had the disciples pealing with laughter. The sun had climbed overhead by now. The shade had all but disappeared and it was growing uncomfortably warm. Gurudeva told a couple of more stories and then asked Gita to sing a bhajan before they left, "an English one this time." Gita felt her pulse quicken. She had been hoping for just this opportunity, without ever really believing it would come. Three weeks ago she had finished her newest composition, a traditional-style English bhajan that she had been guarding zealously, hoping to have a chance to sing it in front of Gurudeva before anyone else heard it. As she grabbed her guitar and fingered the opening chord, a sense of gratitude welled up inside her. She sent her silent thanks to the master and began singing.

Gurudeva listened with his eyes closed, while the disciples sang along with the refrain. When Gita finished singing, the master clapped his hands softly and said, in his drawn-out, North Indian drawl, "Beautiful. Very devotional. I haven't heard that one before. Is it one of yours, Gita?"

Gita felt tears wetting her eyes as she nodded. The master had known her desire and he had answered it! As they were getting up to go, Leela squeezed her arm and whispered that it was one of the most beautiful bhajans she had ever heard. Gita was too flushed to reply. Leela's words seemed to be a pure extension of the master's.

Halfway down the path to the parking lot, Markandeya dropped back beside her and told her how much he liked the bhajan. "Are you planning on recording it anytime soon?" he asked.

"I hadn't thought about it. Kamal did mention the possibility of my doing a record on the ashram label at some point. Nothing concrete though."

Markandeya nodded thoughtfully. "I think you should go ahead and make a record. You seem to have Gurudeva's blessing, judging by what just happened. What do you say I tell Kamal that I've okayed the project and that he should give you whatever help you need—getting the musicians together, arranging the studio time, and all that? What do you think?"

"That...that would be amazing," Gita stammered, not quite willing to trust her ears.

Markandeya laid a brotherly hand on her shoulder. "Consider it done, then. I have a feeling this is going to be a special album. Why don't you keep me posted on how it's going, okay?"

By the time they reached the cars, it had hit her like a sudden fall into cold water: she had just been given approval to record her first album. As they rode back to the ashram, even the frilly chatter of the perfume lady couldn't put a damper on her spirits. Her first album! It was something she had dreamed about ever since she had first picked up a guitar. She had recorded a couple of funky EPs in her garage with her high school band and afterward had made some reasonably polished demos of her songs in a San Diego studio, but that was a far cry from recording an actual album. This was the real deal. The ashram label could be found in the New Age section of every record store in California and in most record stores across the country. It had more than thirty titles, ranging from traditional Indian bhajans and kirtans to New Age instrumental albums, and it generated a sizable income for the ashram. Having the backing of the ashram label meant that people in the New Age community all over the US and even overseas would be listening to her music, not just ashram devotees. The thought was enough to send a thrill through her. It even helped her to look more kindly on Pushpa Devi, despite the oppressive perfume cloud that persisted in the backseat of the BMW like the fallout from Hiroshima. When Pushpa Devi started telling her how much she loved the song, her words no longer sounded so saccharine or so out of place. She sounded like a fan, and that was something Gita had no problem with, no problem whatsoever.

3

As the Benz merged into the light morning traffic on Pacific Coast Highway and sped westward toward Malibu, the aureoled sun glinting off its sleek silver contours, Mukunda gazed out his window toward the nearby ocean, acutely conscious of Gurudeva's potent presence next to him in the backseat but drawn irresistibly nonetheless toward the azure swells and surging whitecaps that bridled, restive and untamed, under a hazy sky. The master had just asked Leela to sing a bhajan, one of his favorites, a sixteenth-century celebration of the love between Krishna and Radha by the poet-saint Mirabai. As Leela's throaty contralto filled the cool air-conditioned interior with the rich, exotic sounds of the Braj language, Mukunda's gaze fell on the distant black shapes that were bobbing on the waves like indolent pelicans. He glanced momentarily at Bhishma in the front seat, wedged in between Sarathi and Leela, and saw him gazing wistfully out the window at his former haunts. The bhajan's melody had a mournful edge, the tear-driven longing of the devotee as she wonders when Krishna will come back to her, ready to wait eons if necessary for her divine lover to sweep her up, once again, into the blinding, blissful whirl of the *rasalila*, the eternal dance between the lover and her beloved. Mukunda thought he detected the presence of those same plaintive emotions in Bhishma's gaze, but in his case he knew it was not entirely brought on by Leela's song. Bhishma's eyes clouded over with longing every time he got within sight of the sea without a board in his hand, separated from the object of his desire by the choice he had made to chase the waves of a inward ocean, a choice that had left him landlocked in the Topanga hills, thankful to be walking in the shadow of his guru but always aware that just over those hills lay the inchoate rumblings of the sea.

Ironically enough, it was the sea that had brought Bhishma to

Gurudeva—more specifically a wave, a thirty-foot half-mile-long curling lip that had lifted him within sight of heaven before it pancaked him into the benthic underworld and kept his foot on his neck until he was ready to renounce his worldly desires and cleave to the spiritual path. Mukunda had heard the story at least half a dozen times over the past ten years, and each time it turned his insides watery with the raw, unforgiving ferocity of nature, once all but unheeded by non-surfing Californians until the gaping lesson of the Loma Prieta quake, followed soon afterward by a series of devastating fires and the calamitous return of El Niño. Bhishma had virtually grown up on the California beaches after moving to LA from Rio in his early teens, already a master of the fiberglass shortboard. He had fooled around with meditation, but he had never taken anything seriously that wasn't shaped of water and composed of metric tons of sheer propulsive energy until he heard of the storm that was making its way across the Pacific, prompting small-craft advisories and high-surf warnings for the whole of the Northern California coast. Within minutes he had thrown his sharply tapered, ten-foot longboard—a board he had kept in waiting for precisely this purpose—into his battered old Toyota pickup and headed for the 101 North onramp, his entire body electric with the adrenalin-laced certainty that the fabled break at Mavericks was about to be conjured into existence by the hand of God and his own pent-up longing to be a big-wave rider. He was not mistaken. When he reached Pillar Point, eighteen miles south of the San Francisco city limits, just after four the next morning, the dirt parking lot near the old shipyards was already overflowing with cars. As he doused his lights, he could see stark silhouettes standing by their rides, gazing silently at huge black shadows barely visible a half mile offshore, punctuated by explosions so loud they seemed like the predawn bombing of a Japanese beachhead. No one seemed to be aware of his neighbor. Each and every soul was transfixed by a spectacle so awe-inspiring it had dumbed them into silence. He walked out toward the point and stared in near disbelief at blackened ramparts larger than anything he had ever seen, while below him in the tidal shallows the churning salt spray boomed its apocalyptic warning. Soon the ocean lightened, black edging toward purple and then to blue. He walked back to his pickup where a quiet minority was solemnly pulling on wetsuits. He pulled his own from behind the seat, feeling as if he had arrived at the summit of his life, finally ready to brave the hand of God and stake his claim to the heights of the human experience, something that no one would ever be able to take away from him—should he successfully scale that peak and live to tell the tale.

The sun was still hidden behind the eastern horizon when he followed the other winter warriors into the sea, some of them as young as he or younger, paddling toward what he knew to be his destiny, a monolithic surge of primal energy that he felt he had been paddling toward all his life, lifted by succeeding waves, each one greater than the previous, until they had pronounced him ready to face life's ultimate challenge. There were a dozen of them as dawn broke that made it to the edge of the break, mere blips on the horizon to the growing crowd on shore that had now been joined by several journalists and a local TV station. A helicopter appeared over the promontory and began flying lazy circles above the rising walls of water that now took on the aspect of translucent mountain ranges in the gathering light. A young Asian boy, no older than himself, was the first to rise to his feet and turn a defiant face to nature. They had been lying near each other on their boards, staring intently into the approaching walls of water but occasionally glancing into each other's eyes for signs of the courage that each knew he would need to brave what was approaching. And then a wave appeared, a huge, lifting wall of water easily twenty-five feet from trough to lip. The boy started paddling toward it. Suddenly he sprang to his feet and an instant later he was dropping down its face like a falcon exploding from the falconer's fist, chasing perfection with a harrier's impassioned eye. And then it was Bhishma's turn. It was 7:18, he was told afterward, the sun just beginning to throw emblazoned shafts across the water, when he caught sight of a set of three huge whitecaps bearing down on him. He set his sights on the outside wave, letting the first two pass underneath him, unable to believe its size as he turned and began to paddle, more than twice the size of any wave he had ever bested, as tall as a three-story building and a hundred times the mass. But this was a moving building, a glacial mountain careening at twenty-five knots across the face of a watery plain, a force of nature as irresistible and as pitiless as the thunderclap of Zeus. As he readied himself, it crossed his mind that he was a mere mortal trying to best the gods in sport, a puny speck of biological insignificance getting set to wrestle with the universe. And then the lip was carrying him to his feet and there was no more time for thought.

As the lip soared upward, suspending him in motion between earth and sky, he was struck by a moment of clarity so timeless, so utterly perfect, that he would forever associate it in his mind with the rush of insight that struck the Buddha under the Bo tree. For one fleeting, perfect moment, the meaning of his existence coalesced into a tapestry of beauty that extended beyond the azure sea above and the foaming sea below, and out into the circumambient universe that cradled him like a June bug in a child's palm, an infinitely loving gaze fixed upon him from beyond the stars. It lasted only a moment, but it was a moment that would still hold him in thrall years later. And then he began to drop, rushing down and across the face of the wave at a dizzying, electrifying speed. As he flew, the wave began to break. A sheet of water curled over his head and engulfed him, thrusting him into a translucent liquid tunnel as vast and as surreal as Carlsbad Caverns, his ears deafened by the roar. For a moment he caught a flash of daylight at the other end of the tunnel, and then he was flipped into space, wiping out inside a collapsing wall of green. The water drove him thirty feet straight down into the reef and held him under in its cold, black grip. He knew then that he had ridden a death wave. And yet he felt neither panic nor remorse, just a lingering sense of the beauty and perfection that was hidden in the world and a sense of gratitude for having had a chance to witness it. But then he felt the grip on his neck relax, as if Yemanjá had decided on a whim that she was satisfied with his devotion. He swam for the surface, almost as a reflex action, and breached like a dolphin singing for air. Moments later his board surfaced nearby, snapped in two. He grabbed the bigger half like he was embracing a trusted friend and let it carry him shoreward, offering himself up gladly to the surging energy of the sea and the dominion of the sky that now welcomed a rising sun, shining directly in his eyes. Two months later he was living in Gurudeva's ashram, searching for the perfect big wave inside himself, knowing now that it existed, thanks to the death wave at Mavericks, which he would forever look upon as a kind of counselor, a spiritual advisor who was ready at any given moment to show him the humbling face of reality, should he begin to lose his way. He still surfed the outer waves—on Gurudeva's instructions, in fact, ordered out at dawn to Malibu twice a month by the master, who never failed to choose the onset of a respectable break to give his faithful bodyguard the day off. From time to time he even brought Mukunda with him, schooling him firsthand in the beauty and the power of nature, but he no longer entertained any hubris with regards to the sea goddess Yemanjá. He brought her flowers and perfume along with his board and humbly asked her to return him safely to his guru before he stepped into her wordless, watery domain and replenished his Brazilian soul with the energy from her waves.

When Leela finished her song, Gurudeva reached out and patted Bhishma on the shoulder. "So, Bhishma, how do you feel? Hmm?"

"A little like Mira, I imagine," Bhishma answered, turning to face the master, his hands folded at his heart chakra. "By your grace."

"Yes," Gurudeva continued, drawing out the *s* until it resembled the dying whisper of a flute. "And by the power of the bhajan. You have caught the wave, Mira's wave. It is not the music of the sea. That is a wilder music, very difficult to catch. This is the music of the human heart. Now do you understand why they say that music soothes the savage beast?"

Bhishma nodded.

"Of course, the savage beast is inside us, not in the jungle or the forest or the sea. Do you agree?"

The four disciples voiced their agreement in unison.

"Of course, forest animals also enjoy music. They even sing, as dolphins and whales do. All creatures are attracted to music, to a lesser or greater extent, and even undeveloped creatures can feel its subtle power, but only human beings are able to harness that power for self-transformation. The right music has the power to lift us out of our savagery and into our divine self; thus the sages have always paid the highest respect to music. In fact, they have declared that music is itself a form of *sadhana*, of spiritual practice. Of course, they weren't talking about the commercial self-indulgence that passes for music nowadays in large parts of the world. In ancient India, all music was devotional in character, even instrumental music. People had so much respect for music, in fact, that they didn't dare use it for any other purpose. They would have considered it blasphemy, like practicing meditation for material prosperity instead of as a path to God. Not merely blasphemy, but a fruitless waste of time."

Gurudeva shook his head. "Of course, nowadays even in India much of the music is nothing but self-indulgent crap. Our ancient tradition still exists, but it is gradually being swallowed up by the mud of commercialism."

"Most of the popular music I hear these days just disturbs my peace of mind," Leela said, "or else it makes me depressed."

Gurudeva nodded. "It is one of the innate characteristics of music that it alters your mood, for better or for worse. Traditionally, spiritual music has always focused on creating a devotional mood, partly by imparting a calming effect to the mind. When someone sings a devotional song, your flow of thoughts calms down and as a result your mind elevates easily, almost effortlessly. Then, when you sit for meditation or begin your work or start your spiritual conversation, it will bear better fruit. The idea is to sanctify the atmosphere before you start your practice or your activity. That is what we have done here. We are taking a trip, so I asked you to sing in order to sanctify the atmosphere. Not only are we taking a trip, we are traveling into the eye of the storm, directly into the stronghold of the material world. It becomes doubly important in such situations to prepare oneself to withstand the shocks that one is bound to face. You have heard of soldiers singing in order to gather courage before going into battle? This is the same, only the stakes are higher. There you have only your body to lose. Here it is your very existence, your spiritual self. So you must always prepare yourself when you leave the ashram and go out for an encounter with the world."

At that moment they were cruising past Malibu Colony, arguably the most famous and costly beachfront in Southern California, an area that had once belonged to a Massachusetts millionaire who had made the shores of the sundown sea his private kingdom before he began selling it off to the Hollywood nouveau-riche. Here, with their spacious glass windows facing the ocean, sat the privileged dwellings of movie stars and entertainment industry magnates, rock musicians and the CEOs of the California corporate culture, the rich rubbing shoulders with the famous and each basking in the other's reflected glory.

On a gesture from the master, Mukunda opened the small refrigerator tucked into the back of the front seat and removed a cherry-lime spritzer, Gurudeva's favorite backseat drink. He poured it into a glass and handed it to him along with a cloth napkin, then turned his eyes again to the magnificent and so widely publicized scenery that was slipping by their windows, one he knew the master had never tired of, not in all the years that Mukunda had known him.

"Whenever I have to leave the ashram for some work," Leela said, "I always sing a bhajan or two before I go, or some kirtan. It makes the whole day go better."

"A wise strategy, indeed," Gurudeva said, after a sip of his sparkling juice. "Of course, if you sincerely want to realize God—instead of merely wanting to want God, as is the case with so many spiritual seekers—then the best course of action is not to leave the ashram at all, unless absolutely necessary. Of course, this is hard medicine for most people, but a terminal disease demands a radical cure. In the meantime, if you do need to leave, then take the ashram with you when you go. Don't worry about what other people might think or say. If you want to sing or dance or shout because the spirit moves you, then go ahead. Don't hesitate, even if you're on a bus or waiting in line at the grocery store. Sing your devotional songs wherever and whenever you please. One of the great achievements in spiritual life is having the confidence and the conviction to express your spirituality no matter what the situation. People may call you crazy—in fact, they *will* call you crazy—but it is also a fact that the real history of the world is the history of the crazy-wisdom teachers who have shaken the people from their sleep. The Christs, the Buddhas, the Rumis, the Meher Babas—wherever they went the so-called sane people condemned them, but now who remembers those sane people? No one. They've vanished without a trace, while the ones they called crazy still march on, with millions and millions of followers right behind them. So I say, if you can't be in the ashram, then take the ashram with you."

Bhishma now followed with a question. "Gurudeva, is the same true once you reach enlightenment? Can an enlightened person also be harmed by too much contact with the material world?"

Gurudeva shook his head. "No. Enlightenment means that you are a free man. You are free from all rules, all constraints. Nothing can bind you, nothing whatsoever. You may act in a certain way to set an example for others, but that is entirely up to you. When a tiny banyan tree is young, you have to surround it with a fence so the cows and the goats don't trample it or eat it, but when it grows into a huge tree then it gives shade to those same cows and goats. For an enlightened soul the whole universe is an ashram. Wherever he goes he brings the spiritual environment with him.

"Once there was a great saint in Bihar who used to live in a garbage dump on the edge of town. His main company were the pigs who would come every day to root for food. Everybody thought he was just a crazy man, a great fool who wasn't even aware of the filthy conditions in which he lived, but actually he was a realized saint. For him there was no difference between the filth of the dump and the luxury of the greatest palace. In his eyes, everything was an equal manifestation of the Supreme. The reason he lived in the dump was because he didn't want to be bothered by worldly people, and a dump is a great place for that. Nobody will bother you in a dump. The only people who visited him were a few spiritualists who were able to recognize him for who he was. And the people used to call them crazy also.

"An enlightened soul can do whatever he wants; no one is fit to pass judgment on him. But until you reach that point, you must do your best to keep clear of the filth of the world. If you don't have the necessary strength, then you will get corrupted; your spiritual life will suffer. If a baby elephant wanders away from the protection of the herd, he may be eaten by a lion or a tiger or a pack of hyenas. But once the elephant grows into an adult, those same lions and tigers and hyenas steer him a wide berth."

Mukunda knew exactly what Gurudeva was talking about. He had moved into the ashram a week after his graduation from high school, feeling like a convict who had just been paroled. As soon as he had stepped out of his car in the ashram parking lot, a resident at long last rather than a visitor, he had lifted his folded hands to the heavens in recognition of his great fortune, though his long-awaited sanctuary was still, for the time being, a part-time proposition. For the next four years he spent most of his days and some of his nights on the UCLA campus in West LA, majoring in comparative religions and Oriental philosophy. The campus, and especially his esoterically inclined department, was a protected enclave in a grim, complex, and often overwhelming city that was still largely foreign to him—his frequent childhood visits to the crossroads of the north had been mostly confined to the interiors of the ashram—but even so, it presented more than its share of challenges for a young spiritualist trying to navigate the tightrope between a yogi's discipline and student life on a freewheeling LA campus. The UCLA facilities were spectacular, as were the opportunities for stimulating intercourse with a rich amalgam of fascinating minds from all cultural and socioeconomic backgrounds, but so were the distractions, everything from hip and beautiful women eager to educate him in the pursuit of worldly pleasure to charismatic professors who did their utmost to fill his head with well-intended notions about the illustrious destiny that awaited him should he follow in their eminent footsteps. Nor was he immune to succumbing to those temptations. But he had a refuge to return to in the evening and a hideout for his weekends, a chance to regroup before he dove back into turbulent waters—and that made all the difference. The ashram had its own distractions and temptations, to be sure, but they didn't prevent him from recognizing how blessed he was to be living in such a charmed space. The bubbling cauldron of unrest that spilled over the rest of Southern California might as well have been simmering on another planet for all that it seemed to affect life within the ashram's secluded borders. Once he graduated, he slipped behind those protected walls and disappeared from the city's sight—forever, as far as he was concerned. Had he been born in India, he would have sought refuge in the Himalayas, but the Topanga Canyon Hills were just as potent in his eyes, specifically the ashram's five hundred well-tended acres, seeing that they came provided with the daily company of an enlightened master and the effortless seclusion guaranteed by the rights of private property in an industrialized society.

The Benz was now approaching downtown Malibu. Sarathi maneuvered the car into the right lane and took the next exit. A few blocks later they arrived at the clinic, a large, gleaming single-story edifice with a façade of polished black marble and mirrored glass. Sarathi pulled the car up in front of the entrance and jumped out to open the door for Gurudeva. Mukunda jumped out the other door and led the way into the clinic while Sarathi stayed behind to park the car.

As they walked up to the reception desk, the patients waiting in the lobby snapped to attention, bringing a smile to Mukunda's face. Over the years he had come to enjoy the vicarious celebrity status that was conferred on those who moved with Gurudeva in public. He was Southern California's most successful resident guru, and in a town where many celebrities made a point of being "spiritual," he was, in a way, a star among stars. Mukunda had seen his own face on television more than once, standing next to or behind the master; he had even generated some sound bites of his own when reporters had asked him questions about Gurudeva or the ashram and then aired his answers. Even in a place like the clinic lobby, where few people would recognize who Gurudeva was, the master's flamboyant tunics and the magnetism he exuded were enough for most Los Angelenos, with their finely tuned celebrity consciousness, to assume that he was "somebody." Certainly, the tunic Gurudeva had chosen to wear today was especially eye-catching. It was one of Leela's recent designs, a white outer gown with billowing sailor's sleeves and winged shoulders, open in the middle where it framed a floor-length jet-black inner gown. The matching white fur hat with its black stripe and the tinted two-toned sunglasses combined with the long white beard to create the image of a sage who had just stepped out of a future where fashion had replaced tradition in the wardrobe of the saintly.

Mukunda completed the formalities at the reception desk; minutes later Gurudeva was ushered into the examination room by his regular doctor, a trim, cherubic forty-something who occasionally attended hatha yoga classes at the ashram and clearly considered it a feather in his cap to be the regular doctor to a famous Indian sage. Mukunda and Leela found three vacant seats in the waiting area while Bhishma wandered over to the soft drink and candy dispensers and started carefully sizing up his options. Moments later Sarathi walked in; he went straight to a pile of magazines on a table, chose a couple of entertainment rags, and found a free chair in the corner.

Mukunda leaned back and lowered his voice to a conspiratorial whisper.

"So, what's this I hear about you and Bhishma becoming a hot item? I haven't seen any evidence of it at the Bungalow, but where there's rumor there's usually fire."

Leela opened her eyes wide in a gesture of mock surprise and then broke into a broad grin. "What can I say? I like younger men."

They had an easy-going relationship that stretched back to Mukunda's childhood. She had been his hatha yoga teacher at the beginning, an angular Irish woman with the flexibility of a gymnast who still retained her brogue despite her twenty-plus years in California. Once he moved into the ashram, she began training him to become one of its regular instructors. Mukunda loved her joyful irreverence, the uncanny knack she had of taking the serious edge out of practically any situation. He could joke with her in a way he couldn't with any of the other senior disciples, without ever worrying that she might get offended or take things the wrong way. And he had always appreciated the way she had looked after him from the moment he first appeared in their community, instantly adopting him as the child she would never have, one she was never shy of chiding with her saucy humor.

"Doesn't that qualify as cradle-robbing?" he asked.

"Oh absolutely, my dear boy, absolutely. If we were back in County Cork the gossipmongers would be wringing their hands and wagging their lips. Oh, it would be fun. But alas, this is Los Angeles County; it doesn't even merit a raised eyebrow here. Or do I detect one waiting in the wings? Have you now become such a fuddy-duddy?"

"Nah, I'm just playing with you. Bhishma could use a matronly touch in his life."

"Oh, now that's hitting below the belt, lad." Leela wagged her finger at Mukunda as Bhishma came up and sat down next to them with a 7-Up in one hand and a chocolate bar in the other.

"Well, while we're on the subject, Mukunda, how are things progressing between you and Gita?"

Mukunda flushed. "What do you mean?" he murmured, uncomfortably aware of Bhishma's look of surprised curiosity. "There's nothing between me and Gita."

Leela nodded sagaciously. "You mean to say you haven't made your move yet? Or are you waiting for her to take the initiative?"

Mukunda started to squirm. "C'mon, what are you talking about? It's nothing like that."

"You could do worse, ol' buddy," Bhishma offered, between bites of his chocolate bar. "She's kind of foxy, and man, what a voice! She is a bit trippy, though."

Leela patted Bhishma on the leg. "Bhishma, why don't you be a dear and go read one of those gaudy magazines so Mukunda and I can have a chat."

"Okay, okay. I can take a hint. I've got my iPod anyhow. I'll just tune in a little Djavan and tune you guys out." Bhishma gave Mukunda a look of commiseration and went over and sat near Sarathi.

"I'll level with you, Mukunda. I have a feeling about this one." Leela had softened her tone, and Mukunda knew she wasn't teasing him any longer.

"I've been watching the two of you these past few months. You have some very strong karma together. Just exactly where it will lead you, I can't say, of course, but the mere fact that you inhabit bodies of the opposite sex, same age, both physically attractive, and so obviously attracted to each other… well, the Cosmic Mind usually takes the simple route when it comes to the karmic webs it weaves."

"Honestly, Leela, I like Gita, I don't deny it, but not in that way."

Leela cocked her head and looked at him in obvious disbelief.

"The thing is, it's complicated," he said, shying away from her gaze, which he often found uncomfortably perceptive. "I've known Gita basically since we were born. We grew up two houses away from each other. Our parents have been best friends since college. There's a whole a lot of history there, and to tell you the truth we never really got along when we were kids, at least not once we got to high school. And since then we've taken very different roads to get here. To be honest, just the fact that she's here at all still feels rather strange to me, even after all these months. I really don't want to have to deal with all that old stuff on top of everything else. And anyhow, I'm not looking for a relationship. You know that."

"Well, my dear, relationships have a funny way of looking for you. Especially when you try to avoid them. And I think you're going to have a tough time avoiding this one." Leela crossed her arms. "Now, come on. Don't look at me like that. It's not a death sentence."

"You know, you're scaring me a little now."

"I know. I just haven't figured out why."

Leela continued to peer at him, probing him with her eyes while she fingered the wheel of her thoughts and sent it spinning. Mukunda hoped that topic of conversation was over, but his karma said otherwise. After a full minute of silence, Leela raised her finger as if she had just found what she'd been looking for.

"I should get Madalasa to do your composite chart and run your progressions, see how they compare." Leela was nodding confidently now. "Yes... That may be just what we need to unravel this karmic knot."

Mukunda felt like he was sliding deeper and deeper into quicksand. He knew he should keep still if he were going to have a chance of escaping, but his natural defense mechanisms were too strong to keep under control.

"The last thing I want is for you to repeat this conversation with Mada. I can just imagine what she'd say if you did."

"First of all, young man, you have two spiritual mothers in this ashram, Mada and myself. It's our divinely ordained duty to take care of you, no matter how grown up you've deceived yourself into thinking you are. And how do you expect us to take care of you if we don't know what's going on in your life? This is a very important phase you're moving into, a critical phase in fact, and you're going to need our guidance."

Mukunda could hear the unspoken "whether you like it or not." It may have had something to do with neither of them having children, but whatever the reason, Madalasa and Leela had adopted him the moment he first set foot in the ashram, an eager but bewildered nine-year-old boy. He had enjoyed the attention, the confidences they shared, and the steady counsel that had helped him steer a course through the many shoals and rapids he had faced while growing up as a yogi in Southern California. But he was twenty-seven now, Gurudeva's PA, and if there was anything a son didn't like discussing with his mothers, spiritual or otherwise, it was his love life—or lack thereof. Unfortunately, neither Leela nor Madalasa had ever stopped to consider that his private life might include areas that were off-limits to them. The composite chart was as good as done. Leela would bring the idea to Madalasa. She would hit a few keys on her computer where she kept the ashram database and the birth charts of practically everyone she knew—whether they were aware that she had done their charts or not—and before the ink was dry they would be sitting together debating Mukunda's romantic destiny and devising how best to guide him. And there was nothing he could do to stop them. He would just have to remember who was at the wheel and be prepared for the curves up ahead.

A few days later, Mukunda was relaxing in his room after lunch with a copy of the *Yoga Journal* when he heard a knock at the Bungalow door. As he got to his feet, he wondered who it might be. Those few disciples who had free access to the master's house never knocked. The reporter from KTTV was due at three, but that was still an hour away, and anyhow Markandeya had left instructions at the main gate to call him as soon as they arrived so he could meet them there and escort them to the Bungalow. When Mukunda opened the door, he was surprised to see Gita standing behind the screen with her guitar slung over her shoulder, looking every bit the typical devotee in a thin white cotton blouse and a long, tawny stonewash skirt tied in the center with a tasseled chord, clothes that suited her far more than the leathers, the studs, and the torn jeans that used to be her trademark dress.

"*Namaskar*, Mukunda. Leela asked me to be here for the interview in case Gurudeva asked for a bhajan. She told me to be here early, just in case, though I didn't expect to get here so quickly. For some reason the 101 was virtually deserted today."

"That's a surprise. The 101 at lunchtime is usually a disaster. Here, come on in."

"I know," she said, as he opened the screen door and let her in. "That's why I gave myself so much time."

As Mukunda led her to the couch, his senses suddenly on alert, he glanced momentarily over his shoulder, half expecting to see Leela or Madalasa peering in through the window, waving their composite chart and watching gleefully to see if he would fall into their trap. There was no one there, of course, but even so, he had the uncanny feeling that he had gotten caught inside the gear shaft of a runaway vehicle: wheels within wheels, one irreversible revolution after another, spinning him forward on a path that was not of his own choosing. He had seen Leela's powerful intuitions at work before. She was rarely wrong, though there was always the hope that this would be one of those times.

"Anyhow, that's one drive I won't have to put up with much longer," Gita said, as Mukunda pulled up one of the rattan chairs that were placed against the wall.

"What do you mean?"

"Oh, I didn't tell you, did I? I'm moving into the ashram this weekend—Lao Tzu dorm, second-story single room with a gorgeous view of the canyon."

"You're moving into the ashram?"

"Uh huh," she said, nodding her head slowly. "I asked Leela about it a few weeks ago. She set up an appointment with Madalasa and that was basically all it took. I gave notice on my apartment last week... you look surprised?"

"I am. It's a little hard to picture you living up here in the hills—cut off from society, so to speak. You don't think it's going to feel a little bit like living in exile?"

"I don't plan on making a prison of it, Mukunda. I have my car. It's not like I'm renouncing the world and moving to a monastery. It was just time for a change, and for now I'm convinced that the ashram is where I need to be."

"So what inspired you to make the move, exactly?"

"Well, George Bush, for one."

"George Bush? What do you mean, George Bush?"

"Do you know how I spent most of March and April, Mukunda?"

"No."

"Glued to my TV set, like most of middle America, watching state-sponsored terrorism by the world's number one rogue state—courtesy of CNN and the gang of criminals who run the White House. It was like a two-month nightmare, only I was awake and it was on my television. Technically, I could have shut it off, I suppose, but you know how far that goes. Not that that would have helped—I still had my share of honest-to-God nightmares during that time—all those horrible images in my mind. You know what I figured out? The best way to hide atrocities from the conscience of the people is to turn it into Hollywood. We've become so desensitized about images of violence, thanks to the movie and television industries, that now when we tune into an actual war—a genocide, in this case—we react to it in the way we've been trained to react: like it's a movie—instead of real people, innocent people, being slaughtered in front of our eyes, or maimed for life; our moral sensibilities gets suspended. Myself included, though at least I was aware of it. I remember, I was watching this general—I forget his name, the guy who was addressing the media over there in the command center, I think it was, where they held the daily media briefings—he was describing some satellite photos taken earlier that morning of a smart bomb, the same morning that one of those smart bombs targeted a bomb shelter. He was lauding the technology, pointing out how precise they were, how they not only helped the military to minimize its casualties, they also helped to prevent 'collateral damage'—as they somehow insist on calling it when they're blowing up defenseless men, women, and children. Talk about desensitization! Meanwhile, the photos from the bomb shelter were splattered all over the international media: mothers with dead children in their arms, old people with their legs blown off, blood and body parts everywhere. So a reporter asked him about it, and he stood there, calm as day, like it was just another question, nothing special, and told her that their intelligence indicated it was actually a military installation, but they were looking into it, just in case—and then he added how proud he was of their efforts to avoid collateral damage, though unfortunately it was impossible to completely eliminate it in a 'conflict' of this kind. I don't know if he actually used the word 'unfortunately'; I may be giving him too much credit. Naturally, the reporter didn't bother to tell him that it would have been easy to do, child's play: don't launch an illegal, unjust invasion against an innocent nation. You know, just once, I'd like to see them admit that these are actually human beings they're slaughtering—not that that will ever happen—or that their 'conflict' was actually a war of aggression, or that their so-called reconstruction is actually holocaust cleanup, a holocaust they engineered to promote US economic interests. Why not just come out and admit it? It's not like it's a secret; it's not like anybody's going to punish them for their crimes if they do—they already have total impunity. But then, they're trained to lie as a matter of course. They have to play the good guys and make sure we know that it's the bad guys they have their guns pointed at—it is a movie after all, right? A Hollywood script?

"God, it makes me so angry: these poor Iraqi people, after all they've suffered, now they have to try to survive in a literal living hell! Do you have any idea what life is like there now for the ones who've managed to survive the bombs? And it's only going to get worse; you can count on this administration for that. You know, I literally threw up one day when I saw some of the footage. God's truth. I couldn't take it. And I wanted to throw up every time I saw that smug smile on Rumsfeld's face. It got to a point, I realized I couldn't go on like that. The whole thing was making me physically sick. The worst part was knowing that there was nothing I could do about it—or that anyone could do, for that matter. I mean, I took part in the protests, of course, I even sang at the protest in San Francisco; and I went up on the pulpit during my gigs to rage against the machine, but these people just laugh at public opinion. It's a joke to them. This was the first time in history that there were massive worldwide protests against a war before that war even started, and Bush joked about it on national television. I don't think there's been any time in the history of this country when popular opinion was so openly mocked on a national stage. But of course they can do that; they're the masters of the world; they do what they like. At least as long as the great beast is securely in its cage."

"The great beast?"

"It's what Alexander Hamilton called the public. With the exception of Jefferson, most of the founding fathers considered the public a dangerous commodity, if it ever woke up and was let out of its cage. How's that for contempt for democracy? It was built right in to the founding of the country. As far as they were concerned, the main purpose of government was to protect property and the rights of the wealthy from the masses—Madison's own words.

"Anyhow, I realized I needed to get away from it all, to go someplace where I could gain some real perspective—not only on what's going on in the world but also on what's going on inside me. It's gotten to the point that I actually truly hate these people, and I don't think you can sow peace through anger and hatred—even when it's directed at war criminals like Bush and Rumsfeld or sociopaths like Bin Laden. I don't want to end up being part of the problem, even if I'm on the right side. I want to be able to act from a place of peace and compassion, no matter what I have to face, and to do that I have to cultivate those qualities inside myself. Thus the ashram. Sometimes you just have to quarantine the patient. Especially when they're as far gone as I am. You know, a few days ago when I went on morning walk with Gurudeva, I got so high, it was like I could finally see, plain as day, the bliss at the heart of the universe, as Gurudeva calls it. Like I was finally cured of all my insanity, finally at peace with myself and the world. But then I went home and like a fool I turned on the TV, and there was the news of the bombing in Saudi—thirty-four people dead, the war goes on, nonstop and in living color. And I lost it, just like that. All that peace and insight was gone in an instant. The whole madness came rushing back in, the anger, the hopelessness, all of it. You know what I did then? I went next door to my neighbor and asked him if he wanted my TV set. He came right over and carted it away. Simple as that. I wasn't planning on bringing it with me anyway, but I didn't want it in my apartment for a single second longer. So you see, you can thank George Bush and company. They've just sent you another spiritual recruit. Who knows, if things go on like this, maybe the people will get so revolted there'll be ashrams springing up like mushrooms everywhere you go."

"Well, that would be one way to change the world. But I hear what you're saying. I couldn't watch the TV at all during the war. It was too revolting. Thank God I live in the ashram. It's not like we're immune from what's going on, but we're protected. Like you say, it's a different perspective you get when you're up here."

"That's why I'm here. I need to drink the Kool-Aid. Forget about the war criminals who are running the country for a while."

"You've come to the right place, though I don't know if I would go so far as to call Bush and Rumsfeld war criminals, or compare them to Bin Laden…"

"No, you're right. That would be unfair to Bin Laden. He's not in their league. He's just your typical sociopath slash religious megalomaniac. History is full of those. These guys are downright Orwellian, on a scale that's never been seen before. It's uncanny. They portray themselves as champions of peace while they wage an unlawful and immoral war; they use the pretext of anticipatory self-defense for a war of aggression by a country who lost its only credible enemy when the cold war ended; and they use the phrase 'tough love' for domestic economic policies that are designed to concentrate wealth in the top two percent and drive down the real wages of the overwhelming majority. Talk about doublespeak. So yeah, you're right. I have no business comparing them to Bin Laden. Big Brother would be closer to the truth. Unfortunately, this is not a novel, especially if you live in Iraq or elsewhere in the developing world. This is real life. But as for being war criminals, well, what other words would you like me to use? I know you don't pay close attention to these things, Mukunda, but just to set the record straight: the original modern definition of war crime was handed down to us from Nuremburg. And what is the granddaddy of all war crimes, according to Nuremburg?"

Mukunda shook his head.

" 'To initiate a war of aggression is not only an international crime, it is the supreme international crime, differing from other war crimes in that it contains within itself the accumulated evil of the whole.' That's a quote and it was punishable by death. It was upheld in the 1996 War Crimes Act, passed by Congress, and again carrying the death penalty. And don't think they aren't aware of that in the White House. What was Gonzales's advice to Bush when they started planning the war, regarding the Geneva convention?"

"Gonzales?" Mukunda said, again shaking his head.

"Come on, Mukunda. Albert Gonzales, the president's counsel. He communicated to the president the Justice Department's contention that the president had the authority to rescind the Geneva Convention—the supreme law of the land according to the US constitution—and he recommended that the president do so. And why did he recommend that? In his words, to reduce the threat of criminal prosecution under the 1996 War Crimes Act. So they knew exactly what they were doing when they were planning this war—not that the US has ever paid any serious attention to the world court, but just in case, they made plans to protect themselves. And by the way, the last I heard, Iraq has yet to attack the US, so there is no other word for it but war crimes. And who is the enemy in this case, the monster of Bagdad? The same guy we supported for the better part of two decades, supplying him with the military aid he needed to carry out genocide against the Kurds, head of a regime that everyone knows is absolutely no threat to the US, except that he controls the world's second-largest oil reserves and he's getting out of line. That's a threat, but it's a threat to US business interests. The suits at Standard Oil are getting antsy, so you send in the tanks and all that oil is ours."

Gita sighed and shook her head. "I'm sorry, Mukunda. I didn't mean to go off on a tirade like that. The moment I start talking about these things I get all worked up. You see what I mean when I say that I need to be quarantined?"

"I'm starting to get the idea. Why don't we change the subject? How's your music going?"

"Yes, let's change the subject... As far as the music goes, things are looking up, and I have the ashram to thank. Markandeya gave me the go-ahead a couple of days ago to record an album of my songs on the ashram label, my spiritual songs. I talked to Kamal about it last night and he told me that I may be able to start as soon as next week. He's going to set up the sessions and get the musicians together."

"That's fantastic. Congratulations."

It was the same old Gabriela—more mature, more articulate, far more spiritual, but just as radical as ever. As she starting telling him about her plans to record an album on the ashram label, her excitement showing in the musical leaps of her speaking voice, Mukunda couldn't help but recall the qualities that had set her apart from everyone else he had grown up with: her passionate and vocal distrust of authority; her readiness to rage against whatever apparent injustice begged for her attention; her penchant for precipitous action, often without any reflection at all—or so it had seemed to him at the time; her brashness, her fire, her inflammatory tongue. He hadn't seen many traces of those qualities in her visits to the ashram these past months—perhaps because they hadn't really had much of a chance to talk—but he should have known. Behind the apparently sedate, talented, charismatic exterior still simmered a live volcano, the same subterranean fires he had first become aware of as a child and which had seemed to be raging more or less out of control by the time they got to high school. The volcano was quiet now—relatively speaking—but it was still active. It would be interesting to see what would happen once she was living in the ashram. If she could somehow find a way to turn all that passion inward, toward the Divine, who knows how far she could go, or how quickly? Hadn't Vivekananda said that rebels and converted criminals often made the quickest progress once they turned to the spiritual path, because the spiritual path required tremendous energy and courage and those were qualities the rebellious character had in abundance, something that was certainly true of Gita?

Maybe the seeds had been there all along and he hadn't noticed. There had been this one time. They had been fourteen, getting ready to start high school in the fall. He had been walking back home from the cove where he had gone to do some late night meditation. It was a twenty-minute walk from the cliffs to the neighborhood where they lived, a beautiful walk at any time of year, but stunning on an early summer night with a full moon painting its ghostly accents across the fanned leaves of the graceful sidewalk palms, sliding across the second-story balconies and clay-tiled roofs, dipping around the edges of the shadows cast by the hills. He felt intoxicated after his meditation, swept away by his mystic imagination and the palpable stillness that lay draped over La Jolla like a saint's shroud. When he rounded the corner onto his block, he saw her slumped against the trunk of a palm tree with a leather jacket in one hand and a bottle of beer in the other, singing under her breath. He softened his step, hoping she wouldn't notice him, but she looked up as he drew near and waved him over with her bottle, patting the ground for him to sit. He assumed she was drunk or high on something or both, and probably she was, but when he sat down he noticed something in her moonlit eyes that swept away all other considerations: an awareness, that sense of spectator that one rarely comes across in a human glance. She said something about the killer party she had been to, how they should arrest Pinochet now that he was out of office—her usual banter—but then she looked at him for a long moment and said, "Michael, there's something I've been meaning to ask you." "What's that?" "Have you found what you're looking for?" The question startled him; he had nothing to say that could match the solemnity with which it was asked. When he finally muttered that he wasn't sure he knew what she meant, she shook her head and said, "Forget it. But if you ever do find what you're looking for, would you let me know?"

And that had been that. A passing of ships in the night marked by a single exchange that he had never forgotten. Even then there had been something behind the wildness and the fire, a searching consciousness that was perhaps not all that different from his own. It reminded him that all was not as it seemed, that he was a spectator on an inexplicable planet, caught in a cross-section of time and still trying to figure out how he had gotten there.

He noticed now that Gita had stopped talking. She was eyeing him curiously. "Sorry," he said. "I spaced out for a second."

"I noticed. Anyplace interesting?"

Mukunda could feel himself blushing. He looked at her, and as he did, he felt a connection open up between them that caught him totally unawares, an unexpected meeting on the rickety bridge that spans the chasm between human beings. Despite his many friendships in the ashram, it was a feeling so rare that it threatened to overpower his understanding. For a fleeting instant he caught a glimpse of the walls that lurked like shadows in his mind, unnoticed, and unchallenged for that very reason, their presence revealed by a momentary shaft of light. Suddenly there was nothing standing between him and the woman seated on the couch in front of him but the air they were breathing—a woman he had known all his life without ever really knowing—as if he had been given a temporary and exhilarating reprieve from an isolation he had not been conscious of. Gita said nothing but she was also looking at him strangely, wonderingly, as if it were a spell that had fallen over them both. But then the door opened noisily behind them and the spell was broken. In stepped Leela and Madalasa in the middle of their own animated conversation, followed a few moments later by Abhay, the tall, taciturn Texan who had been with Gurudeva since the beginning and who presided over the ashram publications. Leela's gay accents brought Bhishma from his room, still groggy from his afternoon nap. Mukunda shared a conspiratorial glance with Gita and then joined the general conversation. A few minutes later Markandeya arrived with the KTTV reporter and her cameraman, and it was time for Mukunda to inform Gurudeva that they were ready for him.

Mukunda found the master in his room reclining on his bed, a simple wooden cot covered with a thin mattress. A blanket was spread over the mattress and over that a hand-printed cotton batik sheet with a design of the Buddha seated in meditation. Gurudeva eased himself into a sitting position, not unlike that of the Buddha beneath him, and nodded his head sagaciously. "Now, Mukunda, you will get a lesson in the art of modern diplomacy. We cannot be quite as blunt as Mullah Nasruddin. The game has become much more complex in our day and age. It is no longer wise to laugh at the Sultan, nor to be so direct with the scribes, but it will amount to the same thing in the end."

Mukunda remembered the story Gurudeva had told a few days earlier over breakfast, but he had no idea what he meant by his remarks, other than that something interesting was about to happen. It was something he was used to. Gurudeva's cryptic comments were often next to impossible to decipher without the benefit of hindsight.

He led Gurudeva down the stairs and retired to a corner while Markandeya introduced the master to the reporter and her cameraman. Her name was Lisa Lamont, feature reporter for KTTV's evening cultural magazine and one of the most recognizable faces in the industry. It wasn't hard to see why, especially up-close and in person. She had that slightly hard-edged, accomplished beauty that always seems destined for success wherever it goes, and she obviously took great care to see that it had all the trimmings: the perfectly coiffed light-henna bob, a stylish pantsuit with a white silk blouse, and just the right touch of jewelry to set it off. More importantly, she had a presence, a kind of artful intensity that most people found engaging, if not arresting, both on camera and off. But not Mukunda. His basic impression was that of a person who clearly didn't meditate—and unless a miracle happened, never would.

Lisa reached out to shake Gurudeva's hand during the introductions; he accepted her hand with a playful expression on his face. In a child-like manner, he asked where he should sit and followed her instructions implicitly as she positioned him on the chair and attached the necktie mic. Meanwhile her cameraman adjusted the tripod, which held a large Betacam. Once he was satisfied with the positioning of the camera, he picked up the handheld and fixed it on Lisa while Gurudeva looked around the room with a mischievous grin and rubbed his beard. Lisa waited for the cameraman's signal that they were ready; when she had it, she launched right into the interview.

"Gurudeva, you have a beautiful place here. I want to thank you for having us and for being kind enough to agree to this interview."

"It's not often we get people of your stature here," Gurudeva replied. "I always like to make sure they feel welcome."

"Well, you've certainly succeeded. Just walking through the grounds from the gate to your house gave me such a peaceful feeling. It was almost as if I were no longer in LA but in some mystical part of the Orient. Can you tell us what prompted you to leave India and set up an ashram in California?"

"Should I look directly into the camera when I speak?" Gurudeva asked with an innocent expression on his face.

Lisa waved her hand. "No, no, just look at me. Just like you were doing. Try to forget that the camera is even there."

"If you say so. To answer your question, all parts of the world are the same to me, whether it is India or America. The same Divine Entity has transformed itself into the different atoms and molecules of this material world, so wherever I go I see only him. But from the material point of view this relative existence of ours is filled with inequality. India, for example, is a very poor country, materially speaking, while America is a very rich country. But India is rich in spirituality while America is poor in spiritual wealth. A simple Indian villager is happier in his day-to-day life than the rich Americans who have their million-dollar homes just down the street from this ashram. There is an imbalance and it is begging for a cure. I have the medicine, the real medicine: meditation and yogic practices. My mission is to bring these practices to America where they are most needed, but it is also my hope that one day my disciples from America will go to the East and use their technological know-how and other skills to help the East overcome its poverty and material difficulties."

Lisa tossed her hair carefully to one side and asked her cameraman softly how it looked. He held up his thumb and winked.

"Well, we are certainly fortunate to have you, Gurudeva. A lot of young people today are leaving the church and their traditional religious teachings and searching for alternatives such as yours. What would you say it is that sets your teachings apart from traditional religion? What does your medicine have to offer that, say, Christianity doesn't?"

Gurudeva adjusted his robes and smiled directly into the camera. "The traditional religions of today, both East and West, have become spiritually bankrupt. Once there was a conference on the death of God. Religious leaders from different traditions were sitting around the conference table discussing the decline in interest in their respective religions and what could be done about it. After much discussion, one of the guests, a psychologist, stood up and put a question to the panel: 'The founders of all your different religions have talked about a certain mystical or spiritual experience that transformed their lives beyond all recognition. Is there anyone here, sitting at this table, who has had this same experience?' Everyone was silent. No one spoke a word. 'There you have your reason, gentlemen,' the psychologist concluded.

"Now this is what I have to offer, that transformative mystical experience. Not only have I had that experience, but I can transmit it to my disciples if they are willing to put in the necessary effort. This is an entirely different kind of medicine from anything that traditional religion can offer."

"Then let us talk for a minute, Gurudeva, about the preparation your disciples have to go through to make themselves ready for the higher dimension you offer. Many of the spiritual groups I've encountered require from their members a certain self-surrender to the will of the group or the guru. This has become a cause for concern for a lot of people, from parents to social workers. They see many young people abandoning their families and their society to join a cult; there is a fear that if they get in too deep they may not be able to extricate themselves, even should they want to, for a variety of different reasons."

"That may or may not be true with some spiritual cults, as you put it, but it is not the case here. I don't ask anybody to come, and I don't ask anybody to leave. Everybody is free to go and come as they please. All I ask is that while they are here they lead the ecstatic life. What those same people who are afraid of cults don't want to admit is that they are slowly poisoning their children with their materialistic ideas. So when their children come here and breathe free air for the first time, it's no wonder they don't want to return. This is the real reason behind whatever bad press we may have gotten in the past. It is a combination of fear and people's unwillingness to look their own demons in the face. Our way of life works. Naturally, some people are afraid of it because it highlights the fact that their way of life doesn't."

"I see," Lisa said, nodding her head. "A few years ago there was an incident in Rancho Santa Fe, Heaven's Gate, where thirty-nine people committed suicide because their guru, Marshall Applewhite, told them they would be transported into a higher realm. When it was investigated afterward, the evidence pointed toward the lack of latitude given the followers of that cult to think for themselves. Isn't there always a danger, as some people claim, of something like that happening in any kind of spiritual cult where you have a charismatic guru figure at the center?"

Mukunda stiffened. The reporter's saccharine tone and practiced smile contrasted strangely with the rather pointed implication of her question, but Gurudeva continued smiling benignly as if he hadn't noticed.

"Not if the guru is a true spiritualist. The leader of the Heaven's Gate group was no more a true spiritualist than Charles Manson or Jim Jones. Being able to talk the talk does not mean that you can walk the walk. In such cases you find nothing but empty words and misguided or delusional actions. But just because there are charlatans around to misguide the gullible is no reason to be afraid of the real thing when it does appear."

Gurudeva leaned forward and the look in his eyes grew more intent. "If you want to find people who aren't able to think for themselves, you don't have to look any further than your typical man or woman of your modern society. Nearly everyone likes to pride themselves on their independence, but if you look deeply and honestly into the matter you will find that nearly everyone is a slave to the currents of social imposition. Throw a few commercials at the average man or woman, and you will find them running after a better car, a better house, or a better job with a bigger salary. Examine the typical conversations of the average person, and you'll find the exact same phrases parroted over and over again. Most people simply drift along blindly with the current ways of thinking without ever questioning them. Almost no one ever actually thinks for themselves, especially those so-called concerned citizens who make judgments about things they know absolutely nothing about.

"To think for yourself in this age of unconscious conformity is an act of real courage that you rarely come across, at least outside of this ashram. Each and every one of my disciples has to perform that act if they want to call themselves my disciples. That's why I encourage them to forget all the social conventions they have been taught and follow their deepest, most authentic impulses, the ones that society has made such a point of trying to snuff out. This is the first step on the road to freedom, and what I have to offer is freedom. Real freedom, not the freedom to conform with what the Joneses are doing, or the Jim Joneses, but the freedom to step beyond that into the unknown. Anything else is nothing more than life in a gilded cage, and I don't want any parrots here."

Lisa glanced over at her cameraman, who shrugged his shoulders. "No parrots. I see. Well, I'm sure some of the parents who will be watching our show will be relieved to hear that." Lisa removed a piece of paper from her pocket and fumbled with it for a moment or two while she consulted what was written there. Mukunda smiled, enjoying the fluster in her movements. He was waiting to see what would come next, her thrust and Gurudeva's parry. It was clear now that he was watching a real life performance of Mullah Nasruddin and the scribes.

"But there are times when our deepest impulses present a danger to society, in one form or another," Lisa said, seemingly abandoning the written script.

"Precisely. And in that danger, as you call it, lies the key to all real human progress. Look at all the great spiritual teachers of the past, the great thinkers and the great artists. What did they all have in common?"

Lisa looked flustered; clearly, she wasn't used to being put on the spot during an interview. "I, ah..."

"They were all considered dangers to society, disruptive influences. Your own Jesus Christ was crucified because he posed too great a threat to the established order. What society considers dangerous and what I consider dangerous are two entirely different things. For society, whatever flies in the face of business-as-usual is considered dangerous; if it inspires people to take their heads out of the sand, it's dangerous; if it teaches people to think for themselves, it's dangerous; if it turns people toward real spirituality and away from the insane worship of commercialism that is the real religion of this society, then it's dangerous. Dangerous to whom? Dangerous to the ones in control, the ones who want to keep everything business-as-usual. You're a journalist. You should know better than anyone what a stagnant cesspool this world has become.

"Do you want to know what the real danger is? The real danger is going along with the Joneses. Not the Jim Joneses, the Dow Joneses. That's the real dry rot that's tearing at the foundation. But then one day a breath of fresh air comes along. Some brave soul shows it all to be the nonsense it really is. And what does society do? Condemn him, crucify him, criticize him in public and in private, throw him to the tabloids."

Gurudeva winked at Lisa and beamed his broadest smile.

"So can we consider you one of these people?" she asked. "One of these disruptive influences that change the course of history, if I can put it in that way?"

"I also have my place in history, but I will let the history books pass judgment on what it is. If you wish to find out, then you will have to exercise patience and be blessed with an extraordinarily long life, but by then your audience will have grown tired of waiting for the news."

Lisa forced a weak smile. "Fair enough. We'll let history be the judge of that." She smoothed her hair and adjusted her collar, taking another glance at her paper before continuing.

"One thing people are always curious about is how a big spiritual organization like yours supports itself financially. It can't be easy to run an ashram as large and as luxurious as this one in Southern California—you have no less than twelve Mercedes-Benzes registered to the ashram, I'm told—especially not as a non-profit organization, which I believe you are? The Mormons, we know, are required to give ten percent of their gross earnings to their church. Do you have a similar system in the ashram?"

"I don't ask my disciples for anything, and if I find any of my full-time volunteers soliciting donations I ask them to stop. I used to live under a tree in a forest in India before my disciples started pestering me to start an ashram, and I was as happy under that tree as I am in Topanga Canyon. If anything, happier. No one ever bothered me for an interview when I lived in the forest. It was my disciples who wanted an ashram. They brought me here and built this place. As long as they want it, as long as it makes them happy, then I am happy. If one day they decide they don't want it anymore, then I will go back to my tree. In the meantime they take care of all the mundane details, and by the grace of the Supreme everything runs smoothly."

"Even despite the IRS audit? I believe that was three years ago, if my research is correct."

"What charitable or spiritual organization has not had the pleasure of an IRS audit? It seems to me they pick organizations like ours from time to time just to get some relief from the greedy lowlifes they normally have to deal with. When they come here they get nice vegetarian food, good music, good company, some peace of mind. Wouldn't you rather audit us if you were an IRS agent, rather than say Ross Perot or Enron."

"Well, I suppose I would," Lisa said with a barely audible laugh. Mukunda couldn't tell whether she was amused or annoyed or a little of both.

"Gurudeva, I was reading an article about you the other day in one of the yoga magazines; they claim that you have certain spiritual powers and that a lot of people have witnessed this. I assume it has helped your disciples to develop faith in your teachings. I was wondering if you could talk about this and perhaps give a small demonstration on camera. I'm sure our audience would find it fascinating; it might convince some of the people who will be watching the interview to visit the ashram and give your teachings a try."

Gurudeva threw back his head and let out a long, hearty laugh. Then he shook his index finger at the pretty reporter in mock admonishment. Lisa laughed uneasily and glanced around quickly from side to side at the other people in the room.

"Excuse me for laughing, but I do love a good comedy. However, let me answer your question on a more serious note. It's a fitting question for the occasion.

"The spiritual powers you are talking about are more properly called occult powers. When Christ raised Lazarus from the dead or restored the sight of a blind man, he was using his occult powers. Every true guru has them and also many people who are not gurus but who have achieved some elevation on the spiritual path. And you are quite correct when you say that ordinary people are fascinated by them and will flock after anyone who openly displays them. You see, people always want something for nothing. That's human nature. They think that if they can get the blessings of such a man, then he will take away their sins or cure their disease or help their son get into a good college or help them to make lots of money. But in the spiritual world you can't get something for nothing. A great man can bless you with riches, but your scale will be balanced somewhere else.

"I'll tell you a story in this regard. Once there was a man who was given a boon by a spirit guide. The spirit guide told him he would grant whatever three wishes he asked, no matter what they were. The man wished for a million dollars. Immediately there was a knock at the door. When he went to open it, there was an insurance agent standing there with a check for a million dollars made out in his name. The man was overjoyed, but when he found out that the check was a life insurance payment for his son who had met with a fatal accident, his joy turned to grief. In his anguish, he used his second wish to ask for his son back. There was another knock at the door. This time it was the skeleton of his dead son. Terrified, he cried out, 'Take it away, take it away.' The spirit guide made it vanish, thus fulfilling his third and final wish. He got his million dollars, but he lost his son.

"This is the nature of the world. Foolish people run after these kinds of supernatural powers, but actually they are meaningless. Only a true guru knows how to use them properly, and a true guru never uses them for show, nor for personal gain. He uses them in certain cases for the benefit of his disciples, and even then he never does it in public; otherwise, it would set a bad example and encourage people to run after something that has no real intrinsic value.

"That's the first point. The second point is that if an ordinary person develops occult powers and indulges in them, there is always a danger that his ego will grow, and ego always leads to a person's downfall. This is an inviolate law of nature. Let me give you an example."

Gurudeva paused for a moment and looked intently at the reporter and then at her cameraman. When he resumed speaking, the tone of his voice was softer but graver.

"Let us say you have the power to read other people's minds. You're sitting and talking with a couple of colleagues from your station, say another reporter and another cameraman. Suppose you invade the privacy of their minds, and you find out with your occult power that this reporter falsified her application form when she joined the station. Say she bought her diploma without actually taking all the journalism classes she claimed to have taken. Not only that—let us suppose she falsified several stories while she was working her way up the ladder and even collaborated with her cameraman to stage shots for those exposés that had nothing whatsoever to do with the truth. Now, if this ever came to light, both she and her cameraman would certainly lose their jobs and be discredited in the industry; who knows, they might even face the possibility of a jail sentence."

Lisa's face and that of her cameraman had gone red with concern. Lisa cocked her head and motioned to the cameraman as unobtrusively as possible to shut off the camera. A picture of the two scribes flashed in Mukunda's mind, but this time one of them was wearing a cream-colored pantsuit and had reddish hair, while the other was busy tending to his camera, trying his best not to be noticed. So this is the lesson in modern diplomacy, he thought.

The camera was turned off, but Gurudeva went right on speaking in an ebullient voice, obviously enjoying the drama.

"Now, if an ordinary person had the power to read someone's mind, he might fall prey to ego. He might go ahead and expose these two scoundrels, convinced that they deserve to be caught. And this will make that person's ego grow. A vindictive action, justifiable as it may be, can lead to the development of vindictiveness. A true guru, on the other hand, only uses his powers for the welfare of others, and he knows where and when to apply them. He will be able to see that these two persons are really good persons, deep inside, behind all the ambition and the lies. They have just become a little misguided. He will use the knowledge he has gained from his occult power to try and help them. He will point out to them that dishonesty never pays, that they should always be just and fair to everyone they come in contact with, no matter what the cost, that they should consider justice to be a sacred journalistic trust. And if he thinks they need a little pressure to help them move along the right path, then he will apply it. He can let them know that he is ready to blow the whistle on them at any moment if they don't toe the line.

"Is it clear, Ms. Lamont? Or do I need to be more explicit?"

Somehow the hitherto unflappable reporter had suddenly developed a nervous tic in her eye. Her cameraman was busy studying the tops of his shoes. Though neither one of them said anything, she shook her head emphatically both times to let Gurudeva know that she did indeed understand.

"Good, very good. It's always a pleasure to see such bright young people. I trust you have enough material for your feature?"

Again Lisa nodded, her downcast eyes mirroring those of her cameraman.

"Very good. I shall be looking forward to seeing it. Looking forward to it very much indeed." Gurudeva glanced at Mukunda and nodded, a signal that the interview was over. As he got up from his chair, he thanked the KTTV crew with the same childlike innocence with which he had welcomed them and asked Leela to take them on a short tour of the ashram so they could get some additional footage for their feature. He asked Mukunda to bring him a copy of his latest book of discourses and presented it to them as a parting gift.

Once they were gone, Gurudeva sat down on the couch and gathered the remaining disciples around him.

"This attractive young reporter that you brought to see me has been planning an exposé of spiritual cults and charlatans who poise as spiritual masters to exploit the gullible. It seems she had gotten it into her head to make us the centerpiece of her story."

Madalasa scowled. "I knew it. I didn't trust her from the moment she set foot in the room. What should we do now?"

"Nothing at all. We don't have anything to worry about. I have seen to that. Our Ms. Lamont is not stupid. She may be more than a bit crooked, but she's an intelligent crook. She's not about to jeopardize everything she's worked to achieve up until now."

Madalasa started laughing and everyone else joined in.

"You see, in this modern age a yogi needs to be the master of diplomacy as well as the master of spirituality. If you live in a cave then you can escape the need for diplomacy, by and large, but the days of yogis living in caves or in the deep forest have disappeared for all intents and purposes. Even the most remote villages in the Himalayas get visits from CNN from time to time or serve as backdrops for Hollywood movies. In the old days you could live up in the mountains, do your meditation, and no one would bother you. Now, even if you do find a cave that hasn't been turned into a spiritual resort, sooner or later you will have the spiritual tourists trooping up to see you with their video cameras and their backpacks, once word gets out that a saint is living there."

"It certainly must have been easier back then," Ganesh said from a corner of the room.

"You can say that it was easier, and you would be right in a certain sense, but you can't say that it was any better or any worse. It was simply different. The fool complains while the wise man adjusts. Remember that. We live in an age of complex political maneuvering, but never forget that the age is made for the yogi, not the yogi for the age. The yogi is the master of all situations. You can't escape political machinations in the modern era, whether you're in the White House or part of a spiritual organization. Politics is everywhere. It's like the cold virus: we breathe it in constantly and if we're not careful it makes us sick. Diplomacy is the art of successful politics. So since we can't entirely avoid the game, we might as well play it better than everyone else. Krishna granted Dhrona a boon that he could not be killed either by day or by night. Everyone knew it; moreover, everyone knew that Krishna's boons could not be broken. Even Krishna himself couldn't undo it. Thus everyone considered Dhrona invincible. So what did Krishna do when he drove Arjuna's chariot into battle to face Dhrona? He arranged for Dhrona to be shot at sunset, during those few moments when it was neither day nor night. Krishna was the world's first great diplomat."

As if on cue, Gurudeva got up from the sofa, saluted his disciples with folded hands, and went back upstairs to his suite. One by one, the disciples began to disperse. Gita was the last to leave. "I guess Gurudeva didn't want a bhajan after all," she said with a mischievous grin, as Mukunda saw her to the door.

"I think Gurudeva had sufficient spiritual entertainment for one afternoon, dealing with that reporter. Still, any excuse that gets you in for guru darshan is a good excuse. Did you enjoy the show?"

"Immensely. There is a whole lot more to Gurudeva than meets the eye, that's for sure. Well, I'll be back on Saturday morning with my stuff. I guess we'll be seeing a whole lot more of each other after that. Sort of like the good old days when we were in pampers."

They both laughed. Mukunda remained in the doorway until she had passed through the gate. What a difference, he thought, between this girl whom he had known all his life and the glamorous reporter who had left a few minutes earlier. Lisa Lamont was more beautiful, more stylish, and far more successful, but what the surface hid, the smile revealed. Gita harbored depths that would have drowned the red-haired reporter. She might be misguided in her passions, but her heart was in exactly the right place. There wasn't an ounce of greed in her, no self-serving ambitions, no manufactured smile. She was determined to help the people who needed it most, and even if the path she took had often seemed reckless to his eyes, the fire that drove her came straight from the heart. Those who pass through the walls of the ashram to stay leave their past behind, Gurudeva had once told him, and what was true for Mukunda must also be true for her. It was time for him to forget their past, to suspend his judgments and accept her for what she was: a fellow disciple and a new friend on the path who was also, paradoxically, his oldest friend. Only time would tell how good a friend she would become, or how intricately the bonds of karma would tie them together, but whatever their karma, it couldn't be bad. He knew that in his heart now, as surely as he knew anything, and the knowledge made him lightheaded. It took him a few minutes before he recognized the feeling as joy—perhaps because it had been a while since that particular lady had paid him a visit.

Strange that it should be Gabriela who had invited her back.

4

Gita emerged into the clearing at the center of the small pine grove and followed the gently curving stone path to the entrance of the meditation hall, a spacious cedar octahedron that could comfortably seat over five hundred people, with polished wood floors and a girdle of six-foot-tall windows that gave its occupants the feeling that they were meditating in the open forest. She left her shoes in the shoe racks outside the open sliding glass doors and padded in her bare feet to the side of the dais where the microphones were set up for the bhajan players. A few scattered devotees were already seated on their meditation cushions; others were stretching their limbs in various yoga poses, waiting for the morning practice to begin. As she was tuning her guitar, Rakhal, the ashram's resident tabla player, sat down in front of the tablas and began tuning them with a small metal hammer. She waited another few minutes until the clock on the wall behind the dais struck five. Then she flipped on the sound system, announced the page number of the bhajan in the ashram songbook, and began singing.

The morning practice—forty-five minutes of devotional singing followed by forty-five minutes of meditation—ended with the traditional chant from the Guru Gita. It was followed by a one-hour asana class, but Gita couldn't stay. Kamal had scheduled her first recording session for nine thirty and she wanted to do some vocal exercises before breakfast and run through the songs she would be recording. As she headed for the door, she was surprised to see Madalasa getting up from a meditation cushion in the back of the hall. Gita had not seen her take part in the collective morning or evening practice during the week that she had been living in the ashram—nor any of the senior disciples, for that matter. Both programs were optional for ashram residents, but she still found it surprising.

The collective practice was one of the main benefits of ashram life in her opinion. It was so much easier and so much more enjoyable than meditating or doing yoga on one's own, though perhaps after years of living in a spiritual environment they no longer needed the extra help.

Gita was just starting down the path toward her dorm when Madalasa caught up to her, wheeling a seven-speed Schwinn mountain bike. As always, her voice was suave and self-assured.

"The bhajans were exceptionally beautiful this morning, Gita. I don't often join in the morning practice, but when I heard that you'd be leading the bhajans this week I couldn't stay away. It's such a blessing to have a world-class bhajan singer in our midst. It was one of the first things I thought about when you told me you were interested in moving in. How are you liking it, by the way, living in the ashram?"

"I love it," Gita said, trying not to blush at the compliment. "I've only been here a week and I'm already starting to drag my feet whenever I have to go into the city."

"I feel exactly the same way. Apart from going on walk with Gurudeva, I hardly make it into the city anymore. It's not often I have any real reason to. Everything I need is here. By the way, I've been meaning to ask you, I'd like to put you on the registration desk for the retreat. It's a good way to get to know the disciples—everybody has to register—and it'll help you to familiarize yourself with how the ashram works. A behind-the-scenes look, so to speak."

"Sure, I'd be happy to."

"Good. There's a few details we'll need to go over; it'll only take a few minutes. Why don't we meet up for breakfast?"

"Okay."

"How about the Buddha Café, eight o'clock? My treat."

"Sure. Eight o'clock. I'll be there."

Madalasa jumped on her bicycle and pedaled off in the direction of the Rumi Hills, the secluded heights on the other side of the ashram where the inner circle of senior disciples had built their houses, an area of panoramic vistas and chic ecological dwellings that reminded Gita of a mini-Malibu. Maybe if she had a house in such an idyllic setting, she thought, she might also prefer to stay home for meditation. But that was not her style, nor would it ever be—not in this life anyway. This was one aspect of the ashram that was not to her liking, but she had no time to think about that now. She needed to get her practice in, and she knew it would not do to be late for a meeting with Madalasa.

The Buddha Café was the ashram's favorite hangout, serving everything from herbal teas and snacks to gourmet meals prepared to order in the adjoining kitchen. It was housed in the same building as The Tao of Shopping, which carried not only the ashram's books, CDs, and DVDs, but just about every bit of esoterica that a New Ager in Southern California could wish for, from designer yogi pants and Gurudeva sunglasses to authentic Tibetan prayer bowls, Ayurvedic brain tonic, and yarrow stalks for throwing the I Ching. Gita normally took her meals in the ashram cafeteria, which was better suited to her budget, but like most of the ashram residents she had developed the habit of paying daily visits to the café, either to satisfy her sweet tooth or to chat with the other devotees over a cup of herbal tea or a fruit smoothie.

When she arrived at the café, Madalasa was already seated at one of the outdoor tables, sipping from a tall glass of green juice—a Spirulina, wheat grass, and assorted vegetable-juice blend that went by the name of "Emerald Isle." She was wearing shorts and a tank top now, revealing a well-toned athlete's body that made her look far younger than her nearly fifty years, though in many parts of California this was an achievement that had become commonplace. With her deep tan and dishwater blond curls, she looked every bit the champion surfer she had once been, though Gita was sure it had been years since Madalasa had been up on a board.

Gita took care to order a light breakfast, nothing that would interfere with her singing, and listened attentively while Madalasa explained her duties during the upcoming retreat. The older woman had always seemed rather aloof to her, almost grim at times, and decidedly business-like the few times they had talked, but on this occasion Gita found her surprisingly affable. As promised, the briefing didn't take long. When Madalasa was done, Gita took advantage of the relaxed mood and the leftover minutes to ask her what it had been like in the early days, when she had first met Gurudeva.

A hint of nostalgia showed in Madalasa's eyes as she pulled her legs up into a cross-legged posture on her chair. "It was very different in those days, I tell you. We had Gurudeva practically to ourselves, me and Markandeya. I spent almost three years in India with Gurudeva, just about the time you were being born, I would think—'75 to '77. We used to hang out with him all day long in those days; we even meditated with him. He used to guide us personally in everything—not just our meditation or our yogic practice. He taught me how to wash clothes by hand, how to spice Indian food, how to make herbal medicines and how to prescribe them, even Vedic astrology. If we had any problem, any problem whatsoever, we'd bring it to him and he would solve it for us. One day, for instance, I was upset with Markandeya over some silly thing, I don't even remember what it was, but I remember Gurudeva sat me down and explained to me exactly how to handle him. And it worked, too, like a charm. He was not only our guru, you see, he was our in-house psychologist, our confidante, and our best friend, all rolled up into one. He wasn't famous then, a hundred disciples at most, and only two Westerners, Markandeya and me, so there were no restrictions like there are now. You could go right into Gurudeva's room, sit down next to him and talk, just about any time you liked. Then Abhay showed up; let's see, that was about a year after I got there. He was a friend of Markandeya's from school. But still it was only the three of us camped out in a little house on the outskirts of Benares with the master and a couple of Indian disciples who took care of most of the cooking and cleaning. Gurudeva was the same as he is now—same sense of humor, same twinkle in his eye, same fountain of infinite wisdom—but everything else was different. No ashram, no KTTV reporters, no IRS audits, no guard at the gate, no list of who can go on walk with him that day. Fifteen or twenty family disciples would come to see him on the weekend, maybe a few more, but the only time it ever really got crowded was during the holidays. Most of the time it was just us and Gurudeva in that tiny house—sleeping on our blankets, eating rice and dal, walking to the market to buy vegetables, buying milk from a neighbor's cow, listening to the master's stories, working on our practices, getting scolded by him whenever we slipped up in our discipline—in other words, paradise."

"Wow. What a blessing that must have been. I can only imagine. How did you find out about him?"

"From Markandeya. One day he showed me two plane tickets and told me we were going to India to meet his guru. I didn't even know he had a guru. All I knew is that I was head over heels in love and wherever he was going, I was going. That was April '75. We'd met in February. I was in a local surfing competition and he was in the audience. He introduced himself in the morning, just after I had ridden the winning wave, and by afternoon I'd been set up and tumbled like a set of ninepins. But if you'd met Markandeya back then, you'd know what I mean: rich, sophisticated, charming, drop-dead good-looking—everything a working-class girl from Silver Lake could hope for. I didn't stand a chance. So when he showed me the tickets I packed a bag and got on the plane. Best decision I ever made. I didn't know a thing about spirituality or yoga or meditation back then but it didn't make a difference. Gurudeva saw to that. He started training me personally from day one. He even said it was better that way, no bad habits to break. Then in '77, Markandeya bought this property, registered the ashram as a non-profit foundation, and we convinced Gurudeva to come to California with us. Not that it took much convincing. He was like a child in that way, an enlightened child, but still a child. Eventually my relationship with Markandeya went south, but I had Gurudeva so it didn't matter. He's all I need, and at this point all I want, though I wouldn't mind taking a time machine back to 1975. It can get old sometimes, having to share him with so many other disciples. But what can you do, right?... We'll always have Benares."

Madalasa winked and finished the last of her juice. "By the way. I was talking to Leela the other day. She tells me you and Mukunda grew up together, even played together when you were children?"

"Right from the cradle, pretty much. Our parents were best friends."

"You don't say? Hmm... You must have some interesting karma together. I've always had a soft spot for Mukunda. He was only nine when he first started visiting the ashram. But I guess you know that. He's quite special, don't you think?"

For some reason, Madalasa's question put Gita on alert. She made a noncommittal remark—something about it being nice to have a trusted friend in the ashram, especially being new like she was—making an instinctive effort to keep any telltale emotion from her face or her voice. There was nothing in Madalasa's tone to warrant this and her question was innocuous enough, but nevertheless Gita remained on guard. For whatever reason, she felt reluctant to say anything that might reveal her true feelings to this woman, especially after she thought she detected an extra measure of curiosity in the senior disciple's eyes. She was relieved when Madalasa glanced at her watch and said that she needed to go change and get ready for morning walk.

Gita arrived at the ashram studio a short while later, brimming with excitement. Kamal had not arrived yet but the door was open. She went into the control room, closed the door behind her, and stood there for a few minutes soaking in the atmosphere. It was a small studio but well equipped. Her eyes lingered fondly here and there as she glanced around at the racks of recording equipment on either side of the digital mixing board with its dazzling array of buttons, knobs, and meters. She peered out through the large double-plate glass window to the live room on the other side of the soundproofed partition, her eyes stopping at the single microphone stand set up in the middle of the room, conscious of its significance in the midst of all that empty space. None of it was new to her or unfamiliar. She had been in recording studios before, and this was one of the first buildings she had visited after moving in. It was more a matter of letting an old magic seep into her, the soft stardust that floated in the air of every studio she had ever been in. As with most musicians, the recording studio was more of a temple to her than a workplace, an alchemist's chapel where the artist's ephemeral musings were pressed into a shape that would last for eternity. The staccato soundings of a guitar, the sharp transients of a drum, the wavering soprano flight of a human voice—all saved from their essential impermanence by the magic weavings of microphones and mixing boards, to be given a place in the sacred pantheon of mankind's artistic works. They would be reproduced on CD players and on radios; be heard in living rooms, on beaches, and in the back seats of cars flying down freeways. From there they would leap into the hearts and minds of a people and become part of their culture. And now it would be her voice they would soon hear. Today would mark her entrance into a world that she had been waiting to enter for as long as she could remember.

 Solemnly and deliberately, almost as if she were participating in a sacred ritual, she slid the high-backed armless engineer's chair out from the mixing desk and sat down. She removed her guitar from its gig bag, tuned it with an electronic tuner, and set it down in a free guitar stand to the side of the mixing desk. The telephone rang. She hesitated for a moment, then picked it up. It was Kamal calling to tell her that he and Rakhal would be a little late, but that they should be there within half an hour. She should just relax and warm up her voice. Gita was glad for the delay. She could use a few minutes to calm the sense of anticipation she felt. Though she had already warmed up her voice, a few minutes of scales would help to settle the tension in her stomach.

 She found the power switch for the keyboard controller and selected a grand piano patch. Then she turned on the powered control room monitors and began going through her scales, softly and slowly at first, then picking up the pace and increasing the volume. After fifteen minutes she stopped, feeling calmer now and confident in her voice. She picked up the guitar and started playing one of her songs, but soon she was noodling, letting her fingers travel across the fretboard as they wished. As her mind drifted, her fingers picked up the threads of her emotions and started weaving them into chordal colors and improvised melodies that reflected the changing directions of her thoughts. It was a reflex with her, this subconsciously improvised music, like a set of clothes that she put on to suit her prevailing mood. Soon she was back in the Buddha Café, replaying her conversation with Madalasa, but this time with the addition of a personalized soundtrack. Up until now Madalasa had seemed a bit of an ice maiden to her, cloistered in a citadel with her master, a citadel she watched like a hawk to make sure no one entered without her approval. Their easy conversation had taken Gita by surprise. But when she remembered Madalasa's remarks about Mukunda, an unruly wave shook the chords of her guitar, drawing forth a dissonant music that crested in her subconscious like the aftereffect of an unnoticed and unrecorded undersea quake. Within moments she was going under, her emotions pulling her down into the green salt depths of the sea. Why had she reacted so suddenly and so strongly? It didn't make sense, unless she admitted to herself that her heart was sliding into something she had very little preparation for. Falling in love was one thing. She had done that many times and never taken it all too seriously. She loved the dizzy sensation of falling off a cliff into a dense mist, knowing she would wake up at some point safe in her bed. But this was different. She hadn't fallen in love at all, as near as she could tell, but then why did she feel so protective of her sentiments? Why did it feel like everything connected with Mukunda took place somewhere near the center of her heart? Was it simply that their story went back to their childhood, making him more deeply rooted in her psyche than anyone other than her parents? She didn't think so. And in fact, it had been years since they'd really connected, except for a couple of conversations, one in the Bungalow just before she'd moved in and one under the tamarind tree after her first Sunday darshan. Then why did she feel bound to him in a way that mere romantic attraction could not explain? Her feelings were a mystery to her, and they were reflected in the jazz-inflected harmonies that bodied forth from her guitar, modulating through unfamiliar keys that she rarely visited.

The muted turning of a doorknob failed to register in Gita's underwater reverie, but when the clarity in the room suddenly increased with the opening of the door, she was summoned from her thoughts. Kamal and Rakhal strode in with infectious grins and an animated "Sorry we're late." She felt a momentary sense of disorientation as she struggled to undo her mind from its moorings, but within moments the anticipation she had been feeling most of the morning flooded back in. She would have plenty of time to think about Mukunda later, but the recording of her first album would have only one beginning and it had finally arrived. She surrendered the engineer's chair to Kamal, who cheerfully went about turning on the rest of the recording equipment and preparing the control room for stage one of the recording session, while Rakhal took his tablas into one of the two isolation booths set in either corner of the live room and began tuning them and positioning the microphones.

Gita watched quietly as Kamal deftly went about his business: checking levels, testing the talkback mike, setting the room EQ. He was a tall, dark, and lanky Gujurati whom Gita had admired from the moment she first met him for being that rarest of breeds: a consummate musician who displayed absolutely no visible sense of ego about his own considerable talents. He looked like a typical Indian film star, right down to the dark dress slacks, the loud silk shirt open at the chest, and the gold chains around his neck—one with an om pendant, the other with a small picture of Gurudeva inserted into a locket. But there the comparison ended. He could sing Indian music better than any Hindi pop star she had ever heard but showed no interest whatsoever in making a name for himself. Though he was constantly sought after by the expatriate Indian community up and down the coast for weddings, concerts, and recording sessions, he limited himself to dates that didn't conflict with his involvement in the ashram, where he was the soul of its musical life and had been ever since Gurudeva had initiated him ten years earlier, already the most respected Indian bhajan and kirtan singer in Southern California. He played sitar well enough to command double scale for recording sessions in town and had written songs for several Bollywood films. The fact that he would be producer and engineer for her first record was something she considered a blessing straight from the gods.

When the levels for the tablas were set, Kamal told Rakhal to go ahead and warm up until they were ready to start on the first track. He swiveled around in his chair, flashed Gita a conspiratorial smile, and asked her if she were ready for him to take her levels and EQ her voice and guitar. Kamal took down a pair of microphones from a locked box on the wall and accompanied her into the live room. There he set up a stool, a boom for her nylon-string guitar, and the two microphones. While he returned to the control room, Gita adjusted her headphones and sang a few exploratory notes into the large-diaphragm Neumann U-87 microphone. She had used a U-87 once before, while recording a demo of her songs in a San Diego studio, and again she was surprised at how warm it sounded. Kamal added a little reverb, making her voice sound better in her headphones than it had ever sounded on its own. Her excitement mounted. Just being seated in front of the microphones in a real studio with a guitar in her hands was a pleasure by itself that rivaled the best of her memories, but the fact that she was seconds away from the beginning of her career as a recording artist brought a welcome moisture to her eyes. She had been waiting for this day for nearly as long as she could remember.

A sudden flourish from the tablas sounded in her headphones. She looked over at Rakhal, who was grinning at her from the isolation booth. Then she heard Kamal's voice in her ear asking her if she had decided what song she wanted to start with. She had. It was the bhajan she had played for Gurudeva the previous week. She had chosen it to invoke the master's blessings and assure an auspicious beginning. It was also easy on her voice: no sudden leaps and a conservative range. She knew from experience to leave her more demanding songs for later when her voice would be better up to the challenge. She played it through once while Kamal listened with his eyes closed and his chin cupped in his palm, a model of serene contemplation. When she finished, he remained in the same posture for more than a minute, swaying gently too and fro as if he were still listening to the music, still digesting it, absorbing the inner spirit embodied in the lyrics and the melody. Finally he opened his eyes and put a graceful finger to his lips, appearing to take a decision.

"I have a couple of ideas how we could treat this track. Shall we give it a listen?"

It was Gita's first experience working with a producer, and she didn't know quite what to expect. Kamal turned to the keyboard, ran his fingers lightly over the keys for a few moments, and effortlessly launched into the chords of her song, humming the melody as he played. It was a different rhythm than the one she had played, more syncopated, more upbeat, freer flowing. It only took her a few moments to realize how much it transformed the song. She felt a surge of excitement as the subtle electricity of the keyboard's rhythmic pulse started feeding her with energy. By the end of the first chorus she was convinced that this was the song's true heartbeat—what she had played had been a temporary stand-in. When Kamal stopped she felt like the air had just been sucked out of the room.

"So what do you think? Is it worth a try? Or would you like to go for a different feel?"

Gita made no effort to hold back her enthusiasm. She already considered Kamal a model for her own budding life as a spiritual musician.

Every time she heard him sing or play, every time she put on one of his CDs, her appreciation for his gifts widened. But this was a side of him she had not seen, and it began to dawn on her how much a good producer could mean to the shaping of a song. Gita felt herself surrender almost worshipfully to his musical judgment as he suggested a rhythm for her to play on the guitar that would compliment what he was playing on the keyboard. They ran through it a couple of times until she felt comfortable with it. Then he told Rakhal what rhythm he wanted him to play on the tablas. They ran through the song a couple of times more with Rakhal until the three musicians started to enter a zone, hanging on each other's rhythms like they had been playing together all their lives. She could feel the music beginning to take flight—somehow, this simple bhajan, whose melody had appeared in her mind one morning after meditation, became transformed in her headphones into a spiritual jazz anthem that made her want to do a soft-shoe shuffle right there in the live room. She could already picture it playing on the radio, and she had to fight the desire to let her imagination run away from her.

With each succeeding pass Kamal made some suggestions. He added space for an intro, doubled the chorus the second time through, and marked off sixteen measures for an instrumental solo. A half hour later they had settled on its structure, and everyone felt comfortable with what they were playing. It was time to record.

They closed their eyes for a few moments of spiritual ideation and invoked the presence of their guru with a resounding "Jai Gurudeva." Then the red light went on and they began laying down the rhythm track. On the third try Kamal was satisfied. Rakhal went to join him in the control room while Gita stood her guitar in its stand, stretched her body, and prepared herself mentally for the lead vocal. It was the moment she had most looked forward to. When she was ready, she gave a signal and closed her eyes. The rhythm track began playing in her ear, the steady, syncopated swing of the intro adding a sense of motion to her interior space, a pulsating landscape into which she began pouring the liquid colors of the lyric. She felt herself calling out as she sang, calling to the Lord she had yet to see, the Eternal Self whose veiled footsteps seemed to echo just beyond the edges of her awareness, as elusive as a whisper in a distant valley. Though the rhythm track surged inexorably forward, time seemed to draw to a standstill. The room around her disappeared and with it all sense of where she was. Soon she was lost in the open vistas of her mind, chasing a presence that seemed to be everywhere and nowhere at once. Borne along by the surging currents of her song, she raced after it, the longing in her heart rising into her voice until she could feel the tears welling in her eyes. When she came to the end of the last chorus and the music in her headphones fell silent, she felt a familiar sense of loss, an oft-repeated frustration, as if she had come within hailing distance of the temple heights where her beloved awaited, only to fall back again, dragged to earth by her own inertia.

She took a deep breath and opened her eyes. Kamal was smiling at her through the glass. He leaned forward into the mic, and she heard his voice sounding softly in her ears.

"Beautiful. I think we're on our way. I do have a few suggestions though."

It was his way of telling her that they still had work to do. Kamal played back the take and started pointing out subtleties she would have missed if she didn't have his ears to guide her, nuances in her performance that could be improved with a little more attention to detail. Steadily but surely they began going over the different sections of the song. Gita repeated certain phrases over and over again while he coached her until she captured his intent with her voice and her heart. For nearly three quarters of an hour she sang overdubs until he had assembled a complete vocal. When that was done she sang the song through twice more without interruptions. It was a grueling session. When Kamal finally called it a wrap and asked her to come into the control room to give it a listen, she could feel the sweat glistening on her skin. She hadn't realized until that moment how exhausting a recording session could be, how much work was required to turn inspiration into art. But when Kamal played back for her the first take and the last, she could scarcely believe her ears. The differences may have been subtle, but to her they were the difference between a valley lost in shadow and the same valley when the sun crests the mountains and reveals a riot of flowers peeking up through the grass. She was tired but thrilled. The recording was far better than she had imagined it would be, although, as Kamal pointed out, it was far from finished. There were a number of tracks yet to record: additional instruments, a solo, backing vocals. But as far as she was concerned, the song had a life of its own now. It no longer belonged to her. She was ready to pull up a chair by the shore and watch it sail its course, waving goodbye to this miraculous creation as she might to a child setting off on its own for the first time.

Kamal leaned back in his chair with his hands clasped behind his head and a gleam in his eye. "Well, what do you think?"

"It's going to be a hit," Rakhal burst out. "All it needs now is a little window dressing."

Kamal chuckled. "Right, window dressing, like bass, backing vocals, solo instruments, a pad, some additional percussion."

"Exactly. Window dressing."

Buoyed by their enthusiasm, the three musicians exchanged some light-hearted banter until Kamal suggested they start looking at the next song. Gita chose a tune she had composed the previous year, a jazz ballad whose lyrics she had recently rewritten, turning what had once resembled a standard torch song into a cry of longing by the devotee for her Lord. Kamal had heard her sing this song before and already had a good idea what he wanted to do with it. He accompanied her on the keyboard, and gradually the three musicians went through the same process as before, this time in the control room. Kamal settled on the rhythmic treatment he wanted, coached Gita on the guitar accompaniment, and did the same for Rakhal, who overturned the garbage can and did an astoundingly good rendition of jazz tablas on its plastic skin. They sketched out the form of the song right there in front of the mixing desk and penciled in a lead sheet. When Kamal was satisfied, they returned to their posts to begin laying down the rhythm track. Several passes later, they had recorded a dreamy sonic landscape that Gita fell in love with. Kamal's piano accompaniment reminded her of Red Garland in the fifties when he was at the height of his expressive powers. Again she was amazed at the seemingly endless facets of Kamal's musical personality. It was a wonder to her how an Indian musician who had not left his native Haridwar for the US until he was twenty, and who was known principally as a bhajan singer, could have mastered such distinctly different styles of American popular music as he had demonstrated on these last two songs. She would not be surprised, she decided, if she caught him playing a Beethoven sonata with the touch of a concert pianist.

With the rhythm track finished, Gita prepared herself to start work on the lead vocal. When she was ready she closed her eyes, took a deep breath, and gave the signal to roll the music. Kamal's opening arabesque sounded in her ears, a languid, descending contrapuntal stream that led her into the opening major seventh chord with a feeling that she was leaning off a cliff and opening her arms for a slow, graceful fall into a mountain pool. She began the lyric, its lilting carriage sweeping her gently onward. When she came to the end of her musical journey, she opened her eyes and looked expectantly toward Kamal, sure in the knowledge that he would now begin to lead her toward a performance that would have been beyond her without his sure-toned guidance. She was startled, however, to see Mukunda seated next to Kamal and Rakhal in the control room, smiling and giving her a little wave.

"It sounded great, Gita," Mukunda said, leaning over into the talkback mic. "I hope it's okay if I sit and listen for a while?"

Gita gave her cheerful consent, but she wasn't nearly as nonchalant as she sounded. Mukunda was already a major distraction in her life, especially in the life of her imagination where the song she was working on resided. She hoped his presence in the control room wouldn't throw her off by diverting her attention from the emotions of the lyric, so important to creating an authentic performance. It had, however, quite the opposite effect.

At first she closed her eyes and tried to pretend he wasn't there—watching every gesture, every expression on her face, listening to every note she sang. She forced herself to concentrate on Kamal's suggestions, and for a while she was successful. By concentrating on the phrasing and timbre of her voice, adding resonance, relaxing her larynx, trying to maintain good breath support as she sang, she was able to keep Mukunda out of the forefront of her mind. Kamal's voice in her ear helped, a patient, soothing presence that she allowed to lead her from phrase to phrase, almost from note to note, with a surety that would not have been possible had she been on her own. But the more she sang and the more the emotions of the song came to the fore rather than her phrasing or the mechanics of her voice, the more she felt like she was singing to an audience of one. Although she had rewritten the lyrics to reflect a spiritual reality instead of a romantic one, it was still a love song; and at this stage of her life she still had trouble telling the two apart. Both lyric and melody were the cry of a woman giving voice to the separation she feels from her beloved; and despite any effort to the contrary, it was Mukunda's face she pictured as she sang, hoping that it wouldn't be obvious. The longing the song expressed was achingly real to her, a latent lament heightened by artifice; she could hear it in her voice as it wavered under the weight of the emotions that ran riot in her body. When Kamal finally put a halt to the recording and called her into the control room to listen to the final product, she knew that she had emptied her veins into the song. Her deepest feelings were out there on display, captured by the fluctuating electrons on the computer's hard disk for anyone to hear whose ears were sufficiently well tuned. Emotionally exhausted, she went in to face the music.

The moment she stepped into the control room she could feel Mukunda's excitement. Fireworks seemed to be going off in his eyes as he told her how much he loved the song—how devotional it was, how beautiful the melody, how much feeling she had put into it. She wondered how he would react if he knew that he was the object of all that emotion. Straight out the door, most likely. Still, it was exactly what she needed to hear. She had sung for him and he had loved it; that was all that mattered.

The four of them sat back to listen to the final take, and she had her first chance to hear what Mukunda had heard through the control room monitors. When Kamal commented that he had never heard her sing better, she agreed, though she declined to mention where the inspiration had come from.

It was after twelve thirty now, time for lunch. The musicians agreed to meet back at the studio at three for the afternoon session. Moments later, Kamal and Rakhal were out the door and she was alone with Mukunda. An awkward moment passed, but Mukunda quickly filled it with a cascade of questions about her plans for the album and her music in general. Somewhere in the course of her answers she realized that he was a fan. It was a startling revelation, the sudden realization that a door she had assumed to be locked had in fact been open all along. She had never even considered the possibility that he might love her music. She had seen no sign of it these past months, and she knew he hadn't thought much of the "noise" she used to make in high school. As she watched him listen with visible fascination to her description of her creative process, she felt a growing excitement that this might be the gateway to his heart, a far more promising portal than the fact that they had grown up together—as if that by itself was a sure sign of some unspoken karmic debt. Just the night before, she had been beset by doubts that she would ever be spiritual enough for him, that years could pass and she would still be that wild vixen from the old neighborhood. But now he seemed to see her with fresh eyes, and it was the music that had done it.

She eyed Mukunda curiously as they talked, her heart settling into a comfortable rhythm in her chest, lulled back to normalcy by the ebullient conversation. He was no longer rail thin as he had been in high school. In the nine years since their graduation, he had filled out into a strapping, graceful young man whose confident movements seemed to be an extension of his daily yoga practice. Obviously he had gone through enormous changes during this time, most of which she could only guess at. She remembered the first time she had seen him in this setting, this ghost from her past who had reappeared within the charmed aura of the famous Indian sage. She had been amazed at the transformation, instantly aware that this was in no way the same boy who had been such an odd but familiar part of her childhood. But as she started to be drawn into his world, she began to realize that in some respects the more he had changed, the more he had remained the same. He still had the same boyish grin that coexisted with her earliest memories; the same slightly distracted air, as if he were tuned into a reality the rest of the world had missed; and, she suspected, the same stubborn naiveté when it came to the hard social realities and rank injustices that had galled her since she had been old enough to think for herself.

It was an offhand remark that alerted her to this holdover from their earlier days. By this time they were on their way to lunch in the cafeteria—he did not need to be back at the Bungalow until two—and they had fallen into the natural rhythm of catching up on the intervening years. The discussion about her music brought them back to her failed efforts to establish her band in the local rock scene after their high school graduation. Resisting her parents' pleas for her to go to college, she had moved into a loft in National City, situating herself halfway between San Diego, where she was playing whatever gigs she could find—from battles of the bands to weddings to low-paid or even unpaid spots in dimly lit bars—and the border, where a fierce battle was being waged over illegal immigration, a battle she took part in by ferrying illegal aliens across the border in her spare time and by fighting the draconian measures of the recently passed proposition 187, which included denying citizenship to children of illegal aliens born in the US and banning them from the public schools. The whole issue had barely registered on Mukunda's consciousness: he had not even voted in that election, the first in which he was eligible to vote. In fact, he had never voted at all, and even after a couple of somewhat incredulous reminders on her part, he still did not remember what prop 187 was. Worst of all, he had been an incoming freshman at the time on a college campus where it had been *the* inflammatory issue among most of the student population. She had seen this tendency in him when they were young and it had always irked her—though mostly she had chalked it up to his almost superhuman innocence—but now she knew where it came from. In this respect, he was no different from most ashram dwellers, who seemed to think that dirtying their hands with the social issues of the day was something no self-respecting spiritualist should do, as if the ashram were a principality in the hills concerned only with its own affairs and content to look upon all visitors as tourists.

When she chided him for his lack of attention to important political issues, Mukunda rallied Gurudeva to his defense. "Gurudeva says that playing politics is a spiritual disease."

Gita was not prepared to argue with Gurudeva, but she was quick to point out that there was a danger in using the master's words as a way to avoid taking responsibility, especially when they were taken out of context or interpreted too literally. How often had the misinterpretation of a saint's words become a recipe for disaster in the past? "If that's in one of Gurudeva's books then I'll certainly take a serious look at it, but even without having done so, I can tell you that there is a big difference between getting involved with politics and playing politics—especially for a just cause in a supposedly democratic state where it's our civic responsibility to stay informed and participate in the workings of self-government. I'll bet anything Gurudeva was referring to the people who use politics to manipulate the public trust and satisfy their greed—which in our country means the rich and powerful. For them politics is just a tool to insure that the wealth and the power stays in their hands and out of the hands of the people. Sure, in such cases politics is a dirty business and a spiritual disease, no doubt about it. And unfortunately nowadays this means most politics and most politicians. But that's because we have a government of the rich, for the rich, and by the rich. Or as John Dewey put it, 'politics is the shadow cast on society by big business.' But that's not what politics is supposed to be. It's supposed to be a collective effort to organize our collective living so that everyone is guaranteed justice, security, and a decent livelihood—in other words, so that everyone is guaranteed the pursuit of happiness, as you may remember from Mrs. Daly's fourth-grade civics class. The ideal may have gotten distorted beyond all recognition, but things are never going to be put right if we don't get involved. That's just giving license to business-as-usual, to borrow a phrase direct from Gurudeva's mouth."

"I don't deny what you're saying, Gita, as far as it goes, but if we are going to talk about the pursuit of happiness, then we have to understand where unhappiness comes from; and in the final analysis it doesn't come from tying up proposition 187 in the courts, like you were explaining—though I agree, that was a terrible injustice fueled by ignorance and intolerance. Fundamentally, the root cause of suffering is our own desire—our attachment to our bodies and our egos, and the sense of separateness that results from that attachment. If we really want to help people, then we have to help them to liberate themselves from the bondage of the ego. Only spirituality can do that. It's not that I don't care about social justice—you know I do—it's just that I know that despite whatever we may or may not be able to do to eliminate injustice—and realistically that's not much—it's still not going to free people from their suffering. They will still be chained to the wheel of birth and death. They will still be just as far away from real freedom as they were before."

By now they had passed through the buffet line with their trays and paid the cashier. Gita had limited herself to a salad with a tofu dressing and a small helping of the banana soufflé that she could not resist. Mukunda, unbound by any restraints on his singing voice, had gone straight to the spinach lasagna, causing Gita to cast an envious eye on his well-stocked plate.

"Mukunda, how do you expect people to even think about spirituality when they're worried about putting food on the table for their children because this country's economic policies have put 80 percent of the collective wealth into the hands of 2 percent of the population and left the working class struggling to survive? Or when they're worried about their kids' safety because the inner city has become so dangerous that half the students in Crenshaw High are more concerned with getting through school alive than they are with getting into college? Some day—not today—I'll tell you some stories about what I've seen with my own eyes, and not very far from here, either. You ignore what's around you at your own peril. We're all in this together, the yogis and the gangbangers."

The argument went unresolved, but she was satisfied that she had gotten his attention. Gradually they slid back into sharing stories from their college days. She saw no need to tell him any more about the year she had taken off after high school to pursue her thankfully aborted career as a hard rocker-activist—no mention of how she had slipped into a vicious cycle of hard drugs that had threatened to spiral out of control; the lost nights of no memories and unknown partners, waking up in rooms she didn't recognize; the various brushes with the law that she kept from her parents except when their help was absolutely necessary. Nor did she share how her music had saved her at a point when she had become sure she would go the way of the gangsta rap she was listening to day and night, how her musical genie had reasserted itself in a primal, redemptive impulse that drove her back to her parents, ready to take up their offer to put her through UCSD, because she did not want to waste a gift she knew she had no right to waste. She didn't share any of these things, only that she had enrolled in the music department, moved back in with her folks, and almost immediately discovered a passion for jazz and an appreciation for classical that rekindled what had been her earliest dream: to become a great artist, someone who could move people to tears and to joy and to meaningful action through the magical gift of being able to connect with an inner fountain that had resisted all her unconscious efforts to dam its waters. This and her assorted tales of student activism, tamer by comparison with her earlier days but no less passionate. And she listened to his stories of being a yogi on campus and laughed as she pictured him going through UCLA exactly as he had gone through high school: this ultra-eccentric, ultra-innocent throwback to some pre-Adamite era whom everyone made fun of behind his back while secretly envying his eerie, unshakable calm and his felt access into some faraway mystical world. Their conversation took them right up to two o'clock, but she made sure to get in a final dig before he had to go. "Mukunda, I have to commend you for your ability to spend four years in a hotbed of student activism and still manage to be almost totally unaware of what was going on. Not that I'm accusing you of sticking your head in the sand or anything, although if I'm not mistaken that does seem to be sand you have on your collar." She reached over and flicked a piece of lint off the collar of his white long-sleeve Indian kurta, and they both laughed, as they had been doing for some time.

As they stepped out of the cafeteria and back into the open air, Gita was momentarily stunned by a glorious mid-afternoon clarity that felt as wide as heaven after a day spent almost entirely indoors. The sun was suspended almost directly overhead in a cloudless, soft-hued sky, streaking the treetops with an amber glare. Mukunda turned to her and smiled.

"You always were the rebel with a cause, Gita. You haven't changed a bit in that respect."

"Nor have you, my dear; nor have you."

What she left unsaid, though she hoped it would linger in the air like some faint reverberation from their long conversation, was that he would. She would see to that. Those beautiful green eyes of his were speckled with stardust, and she could not deny their charm, but she couldn't let them continue that way forever. There was too much at stake.

5

Once Gurudeva was safely napping, Mukunda got Bhishma to cover for him and headed over to the meditation hall to get a look at Manju's mural. It had arrived late that morning along with the temperamental artist from her beachfront studio in the garret of her parents' house in Malibu. This had become an established ritual at the ashram, her "unveiling" of the mural that would serve as the backdrop to the dais during the ashram's biannual retreat. She had been painting them for several years now in four-by-eight sections that she refused to show anyone until she brought them to the ashram, generally only hours before the retreat was scheduled to begin. The only concession she made was to show her preliminary sketches to Madalasa, but her murals were spectacular and not even Madalasa could complain.

As Mukunda stepped into the hall, the mural instantly caught his eye, looming behind the dais in the glow of two muted spotlights. Shiva, the father of Tantra, was sitting cross-legged in the center of the mural, his left hand clutching a trident, his right hand raised palm outward, radiating his blessings. He was seated on the coils of a giant sea-cobra that floated on the surface of a blue-black ocean. The hood of the cobra rose above and behind Shiva's head in a living crown with two blazing eyes like inset jewels. Behind it the night sky was studded with stars. Inside Shiva's body the seven chakras shone forth in the form of lotuses running from the base of the spine to the crown of the head, bright focal points in an otherwise dark and mystical tapestry.

"Amazing, isn't it, Mukunda?" Phanendra was standing by his side now, speaking with something akin to awe in his voice. "Check out the detail in those chakras. Every petal has its seed syllable carved into it in Devanagari script. See how the contrast pulls your eyes upward, toward the seventh chakra? It's almost as if you can feel his kundalini rising. How cool is that? See how detailed the snake is? The scales are perfect, the fangs, the eyes, everything. It has everything you expect from Tantra—mystical, mysterious, foreboding, energetic. Gurudeva's gonna love it."

Gurudeva would indeed love it. It was a fitting backdrop to a retreat that the disciples had been buzzing about ever since the master had announced the title some two months earlier: "Only the Madman Smiles: The Way of Tantra." Tantra was in fashion these days. The esoteric bookstores were filling up with titles like *The Art of Everyday Ecstasy* and *Tantric Love Secrets*. Self-appointed Tantric gurus were charging outrageous sums of money for seminars that promised enlightenment through the cultivation of sacred sexuality. This uniquely Western blend of mysticism and sexual passion, unrecognizable to any authentic Tantric practitioner from India, was tailor-made for a society where making love had long since been raised by Hollywood to the status of a holy sacrament. Nearly everybody in the New Age community was fascinated by Tantra, and Gurudeva had promised to reveal its true essence as it had never been revealed before. Mukunda was curious to find out just how Gurudeva was going to approach this controversial subject. With the master's flair for the dramatic and his love of controversy, he was sure it would be both provocative and entertaining. The master loved to challenge his disciples' fixed ideas about the world, enabling them to break through to a deeper understanding of existence. And there was nothing like a good controversy to provide material for his playful sense of humor. But Mukunda's curiosity would have to wait until tomorrow when the master gave his first official discourse. As always, the retreat would open in the evening with collective practices and dinner, followed by the immensely popular Friday night cultural program on this same dais, a longstanding tradition that featured musical performances, dance recitals, and short dramatic skits. As one might expect in LA, many of the devotees were involved in the performing arts in one way or another, and the list of performers was always crowded with talented artists happy to be up on the ashram stage. At the end of the evening, the sound system would be turned over to a DJ and many of the disciples would stay and dance until the wee hours of the morning.

Phanendra interrupted his thoughts by pointing to the flower arrangements. The birds of paradise that Phanendra had placed on either side of the dais in three-foot porcelain urns were indeed beautiful, as were the rest of the decorations under his experienced hand. The hall had been cleaned the day before from top to bottom, and the ropes for the reserved-seating sections and the aisles were in the process of going up. More than five hundred people had signed up for the retreat, and when it came time for darshan the place would turn into a zoo if they didn't take steps to preserve order. Everyone wanted to sit up front, as close to Gurudeva as possible. In the early days this had been a recipe for chaos. Mukunda hadn't minded as a boy. He had liked the sense of wild abandon that such an atmosphere fostered; it had taught him that passion was also a part of devotion, however oddly it expressed itself. By his teenage years, however, the senior disciples had instituted a system: they roped off the areas up front for themselves and the principal ashram residents, and created aisles down the middle and on either side so people could move about the hall without stepping on their fellow spiritual seekers. The rest of the seating was first come, first serve. The doors opened an hour before darshan. Those who were waiting in line could then file in and claim their spots, laying down their blanket or cushion or meditation seat to mark their territory. Though a certain amount of chaos was inevitable whenever you brought together a large crowd of devotees and a charismatic spiritual master, the chaos had proved manageable.

By the time the darshan hour approached on Saturday morning, the energy was swelling like a rising tide. Outside the Bungalow the devotees were chanting the opening stanza from the ashram *arati: jai shiva shankara, prabhu, jai gurudeva shankara*. They had started almost in a whisper more than an hour before, as if they were calling to the master from a great distance, willing him to appear with this softly rising music. From there the chant had steadily gained in force. Now it rose in tone as well, letting Mukunda know that the crowd was just as aware of the hour as he was. Nine forty-five. Madalasa, Markandeya, Leela, Abhay, and Bhishma were waiting by the door. It was time.

When he got to the top of the stairs, he could see the master through the open door to his bedroom. He was lying supine on his cot with a towel over his head, his usual position whenever he took a short nap during the day. Mukunda crossed the parlor and stepped softly into the bedroom. He hesitated for a moment before saying anything, aware that Gurudeva did not appreciate being woken when he was napping but knowing that if he let him sleep any longer he would be late for the program. His hesitation was interrupted by the lilting resonance of Gurudeva's voice filtering through the towel.

"Mukunda, I am not sleeping. I am preparing my mind for the morning program." Gurudeva pulled the towel down from his face, revealing a broad smile. "When I was a young boy, before my formal *sadhana* began, I used to have all kinds of spiritual experiences in this position. Whenever I took a nap during the day I would have some kind of vision or another: sometimes of saints, sometimes of places or events that I was destined to experience later in life. Since that time, whatever planning I do, I do in this position. Or rather, whatever planning happens, happens when I am in this position. Just now, the whole retreat flashed in my mind: the questions they will ask, the answers I will give them, the whole scenario."

Gurudeva sat upright in one fluid movement. "So, you've come to tell me that the hall is ready and my presence is required."

"Yes, Gurudeva."

"Okay, go downstairs and tell them that I will be down in five minutes."

Mukunda did as instructed. Exactly five minutes later Gurudeva descended the stairs. When he reached the bottom of the stairway, the senior disciples prostrated in front of him. He waited until they stood up again and blessed them by laying the palms of his hands on the crowns of their heads. When he was done, he chanted the sacred syllables *hari om* thrice and started for the door while the disciples followed him out. As soon as Gurudeva appeared in the doorway, the crowd in front of the gate started shouting "*Gurudeva ki jai, Gurudeva ki jai*," victory to Gurudeva. He folded his hands to his chest in greeting and started walking down the path to the gate, accompanied by his small entourage. The chant now changed to *om namah shivaya*, the ashram favorite. As Gurudeva passed the gate, Bhishma, Mukunda, and Abhay started shooing some of the more overeager devotees off the path that led to the meditation hall, so that the master could pass undisturbed. Markandeya positioned himself a few feet in front of the master with his video camera and began walking backward, filming Gurudeva as he walked.

What was normally a six- or seven-minute walk took twice that long. The ecstatic crowd pressed in as close as they could without inciting the ire of the senior disciples. Those who were close enough reached out their hands so that the master could touch them as he passed. On several occasions he stopped to greet a familiar face or pat a cheek. When they at last made it to the steps of the meditation hall, Gurudeva stopped on the threshold. Leela reverently slipped off his sandals and sprinkled rose water on his feet. She lifted the *arati* tray, from which streamed white plumes of perfumed smoke, and started tracing slow, deliberate circles in front of Gurudeva's motionless figure. As she performed the ritual movements, she began intoning the melodious ancient verses in praise of the guru: *jai shiva shankara, prabhu, jai gurudeva shankara, brahma vishnu sadashiva ardhangii dhara, jai gurudeva shankara*... The rest of the disciples, both outside and inside the hall, joined in. Bhishma and Madalasa kept time with hand cymbals and Markandeya blew the conch at the end of each phrase.

When the *arati* was over, Gurudeva started moving down the center aisle, keeping his hands folded to his chest. He reached the dais and sat down cross-legged on a large brocaded cushion encircled on three sides by an intricate floral arrangement. Markandeya adjusted the microphone for him and then made his way through the crowd to the mixing board and video equipment in the center of the hall, where he would remain for the rest of the program, capturing footage for his popular series of darshan videotapes and Gurudeva DVDs. The other senior disciples fanned out on the dais, Madalasa and Leela closest to the master on either side and Mukunda just behind him. A pitcher of mineral water was waiting behind the master's seat. It was Mukunda's job to make sure that the glass that rested on the ground to the side of his cushion remained full.

As soon as Gurudeva settled in, a hush fell over the crowd. He looked around the hall for the better part of a minute, sweeping his head ever so slowly from side to side, every devotee feeling for at least an instant that the master had looked directly at him. Then, with a slight inclination of his head, he signaled to Kamal and the other musicians seated in front of the dais. Kamal closed his eyes and leaned into the microphone, his fingers running over the keys of the harmonium, introducing the melody of Shankaracharya's famous hymn "Bhaja Govindam." Gita added the harmonies on her nylon-string guitar. As Mukunda closed his eyes and began to listen to the lyrics of this thousand-year-old bhajan that Gurudeva loved so much, he could not help but see Gita's face as her voice soared alongside Kamal's, accompanying him in the lead vocal, the subdued pulse of her guitar bridging the gap between the sharp rhythmic accents of the tablas and the hypnotic drone of the tamboura. Mukunda felt a joyful wave pass over him. The devotional depths of the lyric, the drama and expectation of the moment, the swift tug at his heart as he felt Gita's presence inside him becoming part of the song he had learned to love many years ago—all combined within him to lift him above the swaying crowd, freeing his heart from its narrow confines. When the song ended, Mukunda could feel the tears in his eyes. He wiped them with his fingers while the lights were lowered for ten minutes of silent meditation.

His contemplation was soon broken by the sonorous sound of Gurudeva's voice intoning the Sanskrit verses with which he began every darshan: "*Asato ma sat gamaya tamaso majyotir gamaya mrityor ma amritam gamaya....*" The devotees took up the chant in a reverential whisper, echoing the low tones of their master's voice. When the final note of the concluding *om shanti shanti shanti* faded out, there was a solemn hush as the hall seemed to reverberate inaudibly with the mystic spirit of the mantras. For a moment, Mukunda felt as if he had been transported back into the forgotten past of the forest ashrams that had given birth to those timeless utterances from the Upanishads, to a seat under the bowers of a spreading banyan tree, listening to words of changeless wisdom from the lips of an ancient sage. The words that followed were in English, but the spirit behind them was older than the hills in whose shadow they were sitting.

"I bow down to the transcendental spirit that dwells within each of you. Please accept my deepest salutations. Welcome. This retreat is a chance for us to come together in truth for an extended period of time, and I am sure that if you open up your hearts during the two days we have together, then the miraculous will take root inside you and shower its blossoms on us all.

"The title of this retreat is 'Only the Madman Smiles: the Way of Tantra.' Many of you must have been wondering in the days and weeks leading up to the retreat, what exactly does Gurudeva mean when he says that only the madman smiles? And what does this have to do with the ancient and highly misunderstood cult of Tantra? Does he actually mean to say that if I smile, then I must be mad? If only the madman smiles, then it follows logically that I must be a madman when I smile. Or does he mean to imply that the smile that most of us smile is not really a smile at all, that only the smile of the madman deserves to be called a smile? Either way it sounds preposterous. Well and good. Because the preposterous, as we shall soon see, is one of the key building blocks in the foundation of wisdom. The sages who have brought us this wisdom, down through the ages, have all been considered mad from the point of view of an incurably sane society.

"Let us begin by taking a few minutes to look at where this mysterious apparition we call a smile comes from. There are two circumstances under which all human beings—in all cultures and at all times—smile: when they feel joy and when they appreciate humor. In both cases there is a spontaneous feeling within us that lights up our face. Have you ever looked closely at a face that is smiling with joy or with humor? Sometimes we say that the person is shining, and it is the literal truth. If we had instruments subtle enough to measure it, we would discover that there is a subtle luminescence that emanates from the eyes and the face of a person who laughs or smiles. Eyes can also smile, you know. This is not simply a poetic conceit. That sparkle in the eyes is just as much a smile as the grin on our face. A smile is something internal that expresses itself externally; for this reason a real smile cannot be faked. Anybody can turn up their lips and pretend to smile, but that is no more a real smile than a plastic orange is a real orange. And if we are even a little bit sensitive we know it right away."

There was a brief silence while Gurudeva looked around the room, scanning the faces in the crowd. He had once told Mukunda that before every darshan he took one or two minutes to look into the minds of everyone present in the hall. When he spoke, he addressed his words to the precise needs of the devotees, answering their innermost questions and giving them the direction they needed at that moment in their lives. It was for this reason, he said, that he never planned any of his talks. They were spontaneous creations, a divinely guided response to the master-disciple connection. As he watched Gurudeva pass his gaze over the crowd, Mukunda wondered if this was what he was doing now, penetrating the thoughts of his disciples, taking stock of their collective mind before delivering the exact teaching they needed.

When Gurudeva resumed speaking, his words reverberated in the silence of the hall like a pebble dropped into a deep well.

"When we talk about a smile, what we are really referring to is this spontaneous outpouring of joy or humor that can come to us in the oddest of circumstances. And who is it who smiles?"

Gurudeva paused again, looking briefly from one side of the hall to the other.

"It is the madman within us. Not the sane man, not the social man who is so careful not to overstep the bounds of socially sanctioned behavior. Such a man is too busy judging himself through other people's eyes to be able to feel real joy or real humor. It is only in the moment when we forget ourselves and the ties that bind us that we feel the profound joy or the sense of the preposterous that give rise to a real smile. And the one who oversteps those artificial boundaries is, by social definition, mad. He is the man who accepts no rules other than those that spring spontaneously from the source of his being, the man who is his own master. Society can never understand such a man, because that man is beyond the bounds of society. He is a free man."

Gurudeva inflected his voice for this last sentence and slowed his cadence, an effect that was not lost on the crowd. There were murmurs of appreciation, and here and there an excited shout.

"We have all gathered here this weekend for a reason, a single, unitary reason. Mr. X may think that he is here for one reason and Mr. Y for another, but the fact is, we are all here for the same reason. Whether or not we are conscious of it, we are on a quest, a quest that has lasted many lifetimes, a quest for bliss, for peace, for truth, for love, for God, for enlightenment. Whatever you choose to call it doesn't matter. We are searching for something that is beyond words, yearning to complete the journey back to the source of our being. And when we touch that source within us, the spontaneous self that is beyond all boundaries, we realize that all social constraints, all social rules and regulations, manners and mores, traditions, religions, and intellectual philosophies, are preposterous by their very nature. The Infinite cannot be confined to this rule or that commandment. If you say x then the Infinite will say y, just to confound you. That is why, for everything I say, I make sure I contradict myself somewhere along the line. Just to remind you that all models and all conceptions bind us to the illusion of a limited life. They are what stand between us and freedom. They are the blindfold that keeps us from the light.

"When you enter into that limitless joy you see in a flash that your conceptions of reality, all your fixed and oh-so-clever notions, are nothing if not preposterous. The moment you try to confine the Infinite, it will turn the tables on you. The very attempt to do so is nothing but sheer folly. And that is the real source of all humor, this sense of the preposterous, which is nothing more than a divine appreciation of what the sages call maya. And the outer expression of this inner realization is that mysterious emanation of inner light that we call a smile. As all great sages have known, only the madman smiles, because once you go beyond the constraints and limitations of this world and enter the realm of the Infinite, then you have left silly sanity behind."

Ripples of appreciation passed through the crowd, nods and murmurs of assent that crisscrossed the hall like waves in a crowded pool. Gurudeva turned his head from side to side, slowly and rhythmically, drinking in the appreciation of his disciples.

"Now, in the history of spirituality on this planet, there is one great tradition that is the very essence of this divine madness, and its name is Tantra. We can't call it a philosophy because it is really the opposite of philosophy. In fact, it is better to call it the death of philosophy. Tantra says: Throw off your chains; don't listen to anything society has taught you. It is all rubbish, all conditioned thinking, right down to the most elaborate philosophies and religious teachings. The truth is within you, in the fountain of your own existence. It cannot be described or pinned down. Throw off your shackles and dive into that fountain. Wake up. Be alive, be present, as present and as abiding as the sky and the sun and the moon. Taste the joy of who you really are and light up your face with a smile."

Gurudeva lowered his voice and leaned into the microphone.

"When the ancient Tantric masters took this bold and fatal step of revealing the truth behind man's spiritual existence, they did not stop there. They took advantage of the opportunity to expose the conspiracies of the priests who had been trying—and are still trying, even today—to pass themselves off as spiritual intermediaries. Since time immemorial the priests of all religions have been telling their flocks to give up the world, that it is a sin to enjoy the pleasures of the senses; and it is no coincidence that whatever the people give up goes directly or indirectly into the coffers of those same priests. Tantra says 'bah and humbug' to those peddlers of religion. In fact, Tantra is quite comfortable in this world. It declares that everything is an expression of the Divine, that everything is holy and sacred, not just what the priests tell us is, and that the best way to experience the sacredness of life is to embrace it in all its multiplicity and paradox. Naturally this flies in the face of organized religion. 'Disregard all rules, all social conventions, written or unwritten, spoken or unspoken, conscious or unconscious, and plunge directly into the essence of the great mystery.' This is scary stuff for those who have staked their life on the system. In one unguarded moment you have undermined everything they stand for. They see the huge smile on your face and it seems to tell them, 'Look, you've missed the boat; you've lived your entire life without ever learning what a real smile is.' This brazenness incensed the Brahmin priests in India thousands of years ago, and it has the Catholics muttering curses and practicing exorcisms today. It has given nightmares to a long line of popes and a whole legion of Shankaracharyas. In the old days the priests would warn parents to keep their children off the streets if a Tantric was in town. Nowadays they call them hedonists and label Tantra a dangerous cult, but it's nothing but the same fear in modern clothing. Now do you understand why Tantra has gotten the reputation it has?"

From one side of the room to the other the devotees nodded or voiced their assent.

"Yes," he continued, drawing out the *s*, "Tantra has been vilified for centuries. Parents have kept it from their children and gurus from their disciples. Because even the gurus, the so-called gurus, have something to protect. They have their prestige to uphold, their precious teachings and philosophies, and Tantra would have you throw all that away and drink directly from the source. Let the society call you mad, but throw off your conditioning and taste freedom. That is the reason you have all come here today. To learn how to become madmen. Before these two days are over, you will have a taste of this divine madness. If you are ready and willing to part with your sanity, then I will do my part to see to it that you all leave here on Sunday evening as inspired madmen."

Gurudeva turned his head to Mukunda, who handed him the glass of water. He took a long draft and handed it back.

"Now, how do we go about freeing ourselves from the chains of our conditioning so that we can experience the freedom we are seeking? The great Russian mystic George Gurdjieff once said that before someone can escape from a cage, they must first realize that they are in a cage. We want to be free. First we must be aware of our predicament. We must be able to see our cage. And what is this cage? The cage is our ego, the false sense of self that keeps us separate from our eternal source. It is the ego that imprisons; it is the ego that binds us in irons and tosses us to the lions of misery and desire and death.

"In the beginning stages the ego is rooted in the body. You will find some people so completely identified with their bodies that their lives center around physical pleasure and pain. They spend their lives running after pleasure and away from pain. This is the most primitive stage of human development. When our physical desires are satisfied, we're happy; when they're not, we're not. In the next stage we start becoming more mental than physical, but even then this identification with the body continues at the subconscious level. We say, 'I am hurt, I am dying,' when in fact it is only the body that feels pain or dies. The mind suffers because it is identified with the body. This identification is the real source of our suffering. So in the first stages of Tantric practice we must learn to break this identification, by hook or by crook. There is no other way. We can go on repeating 'I am immortal, I am the atman, I am one with the universe' from here to eternity, but as long as we continue to identify with our bodies, then we are no better than a parrot repeating a phrase over and over again that its master has taught it. You may understand intellectually that you are more than this body. You may even be fully convinced that you are eternal spirit, but that knowledge is as good as useless if it remains at an intellectual level.

In India you will see many priests who preach the highest truths of the Upanishads and then go home and get annoyed with their wives because dinner isn't ready. Tantra will have nothing to do with such hypocrisy and pretension. As long as you are identified with your body, then be in that body. Be honest about it. But use your identification with the body to break yourself of that identification.

"Now this may seem like a paradox, but only to the limited logical mind. There is a principle at work here: take anything to its extreme and it will ultimately be transformed into an entirely new existence that functions at a higher level—the old structure dies and a new, more evolved, structure takes its place. The ancient Tantrics understood this, and so they taught their disciples who were trapped at this stage—what they called *pashu jivan*, the animalistic stage, because we share this total sense identification with the animals—they taught them to plunge into their bodily experience so deeply that they would completely lose themselves, and in doing so, go beyond their ego. They understood that the moment you completely lose yourself in your experience, *you* are no longer there. Only your body remains, only the Divine manifesting itself in one of its myriad expressions. Your ego becomes extinct—temporarily, of course. What remains is the miracle of creation.

"The crux of the matter, the reason why we do not ordinarily experience this extinction of the ego through our senses, is that no matter how identified we are with our physical existence, we also live in mortal fear of that existence. How many people really plunge into the waters of their physical life? Ask yourself this. The answer is: almost no one. From the cradle to the grave, all of the world's religions have been teaching us that we have to escape from our physical bondage so that we can attain some heaven in the seventh sky. Sex is taboo, intoxication is bad, too much enjoyment will leave you damned for seven lifetimes to come. We learn this right from our earliest days, and slowly it instills in us a fear of living in our bodies, of really living in them, of embracing and accepting them. Look at little children. They don't experience any shame. They are still at peace with their physical existence. It is all they know; they haven't yet learned that it is somehow wrong to be who they are. Then look at those same children a few years later, after they have started to imbibe that fear, and see how that peace begins to disappear. As we grow older, we learn to be afraid and distrustful of our physical existence. This is the real original sin. We live in our bodies but we are not at home there.

"Now, what Tantra says is the opposite of the traditional religions: Don't be afraid of your physical existence. On the contrary, go into your incarnation as fully as you can. Go into it so deeply, accept it so completely, become so one with your body and its experience in this world, that your ego disappears in the process. This was what the surrealist poets like Rimbaud tried to do instinctively. They tried to overload their senses until they forgot themselves, and it enabled them to write some of the greatest poetry ever produced in the Western world. 'The road of excess leads to the palace of wisdom,' Blake wrote. He was instinctively practicing Tantra without realizing it.

"Now, the key to this paradox is one of the great secrets of incarnate life. It is this very fear of our physical existence, this unwillingness to embrace our physical incarnation, this inability to accept the divine nature of our sojourn on this planet, that keeps our ego alive and rooted to the body. It is what sustains our sense of separateness, which is the essence of the ego. But if you can go deep enough into any physical experience, so that you become merged with that experience, then you eventually reach a point where you automatically abandon your social conditioning—or rather it abandons you—your mental constructs of who you are, your place in this world, everything that serves to prop up this so-called 'self' that you have constructed so meticulously out of the materials that society has handed you. The moment you become merged with your experience you lose yourself, and in that loss you discover the freedom that lies beyond the ego. 'Whosoever would save his life must lose it,' Christ said, 'and he that loses it shall find it.' Instead of pushing away our physical existence, Tantra teaches us to embrace our experience, and in that embrace we set ourselves free.

"Contrary to popular opinion, however, this practice of Tantra requires the greatest discipline. From the outside it appears easy. What could be easier than to abandon oneself to the life of the senses? But there is a trap here, and countless are the would-be Tantrics who have fallen into it. And what is that trap? The trap is that it is just as difficult to lose oneself fully in one's sensual experience as it is to entirely escape from it, which is the path of total renunciation. The Tantrics will say that theirs is the sane alternative, that theirs is the blissful path, while the path of austerity is dry and summarily difficult. And they are right. But what they do not tell you, until it is too late and you are already fighting for your life, is that it is just as rigorous a discipline.

"What happens when a person decides to embrace the Tantric ideal and lose himself in his physical experience? There is always some part that tries to hold back, the part that is afraid of what other people will think or say, of what will happen to his reputation or his future or his marriage. These are all reasonable fears, very reasonable indeed, and that is what makes them so pernicious. Because this very reasonableness is the greatest weapon of the ego. It is the ego that is afraid to take the plunge, because it knows that by doing so, it will put its very existence in jeopardy. So it invents a thousand and one reasons why it should not do so and invests them all with a carefully crafted, totally sound, perfectly airtight reasonableness. To completely let go and abandon yourself, to drop all socially conditioned models of who you think you are, to plunge in naked—well, that is tremendously difficult. Our natural tendency is to cling to the last vestige of our ego as tightly as we can. The great challenge of Tantra consists precisely in letting go of this final attachment.

"As most of you know, society has always accused Tantrics of being hedonists. It has been doing this for thousands of years, even before the word *hedonist* existed, and it's still doing it today. And of course, society is right. Tantrics are pleasure seekers but pleasure seekers of a different order: the pleasure they seek is the bliss of the enlightened state, the state beyond the ego. And what is a hedonist anyhow but a Tantric who has fallen off the razor's edge. He may not have known he was a Tantric, but instinctively he was. That is why it has been said that Tantra is not only the quickest path but also the most dangerous. If you give up halfway you will find yourself so mired in your ego, so surfeited with the pleasures of the world, that you will likely never escape. This is why the Tantras have placed so much importance on the guru. Without an experienced guide, this path is so dangerous that no one should try it. If you take the path of extreme austerities and you fall off, you will, in all likelihood, be no worse off than when you started, and in many cases, better off. The austerities you've practiced will have some lasting benefit. But fall from Tantra and you will be in a world of trouble with no way out. Let's say you go off in search of treasure, and you hear of two such troves. One is in a cavern at the bottom of a lake; the other is at the top of a mountain. If you can reach the cavern then it is a much better, must faster option. It will take much longer to climb the mountain, and you will have to suffer the cold of the higher altitudes. Furthermore, there is always the chance that you won't have the stamina to make it all the way to the top; you may end up settling for some scenic spot in the foothills to live out your days. But once you dive deep enough into the lake then you're completely committed. If you try to go back you drown. If you fail to reach the hidden cavern then you also drown.

"So in Tantra the importance of the guru is paramount. No one should practice Tantra without a guru, and no one who has a guru should practice Tantra without that guru's permission. These are the ground rules. If you don't follow them, then you can't hold anyone responsible for what happens to you. Is everyone agreed?"

A collective murmur of assent swept through the hall.

"Very well then. You all have my permission to practice Tantra, as long as you follow my directions strictly. No one should make any changes to their practice without consulting me first.

"Up until now we have been talking about the initial stages of the journey. Breaking this identification with the body is absolutely necessary before one can undertake the journey to absolute freedom, but it is only the beginning. Let us follow the story even further. Because the ancient Tantrics embraced their incarnate life, instead of trying to escape it, they were able to uncover the mysteries of the human body. You know, if you want to find the truth out about anything, you have to embrace it; you have to become familiar with it from the inside. You can't remain on the outside looking in and expect to find the truth. You can't be strictly an observer; you must be a practitioner. Because those Tantric yogis accepted the divine nature of their bodies, they were able to discover its secrets. They discovered that everything in our bodies, and indeed everything in this universe, is a play of energy. What we see as matter when our divine sight is veiled, we see as energy when we remove that veil. They mapped out this play of energies in the body and gave us what we now refer to as the seven-chakra system, basic yogic physiology. In other words, they gave the world what is essentially a roadmap of human spiritual evolution.

"When we look at this roadmap, we see that the spiritual energy of the human being is sleeping at the base of the spine in the first psychic energy center, the first chakra. The Tantrics named this spiritual energy *kundalini*, and they realized that until it is awakened the human being will remain forever mired in ignorance. Thus they started developing powerful techniques to awaken that energy and send it up the spine to the seventh chakra, the seat of the soul. Remember, heaven is not somewhere beyond the sky. Heaven is sleeping inside you, in a fathomless reservoir of unlimited spiritual energy, which in Sanskrit is called *kunda*. It is sleeping in the base of the spinal column, curled up like a fetus, waiting to be awakened so that it can make its journey home to the crown chakra.

"So the Tantric yogi, instead of searching for God in some mythological heaven, goes into his own body and awakens that dormant force. When it awakens, he finds the entire energy of the universe coursing inside him. This is the greatest of mysteries: the whole of the macrocosm is contained in the microcosm. It is not a metaphor and it is not a joke. When you begin playing with the kundalini energy, be aware that you are playing with more than fire: you are playing with the atomic reactor that powers the universe.

"As the ancient Tantrics went deeper and deeper into their existence, they discovered that their breathing opened a door for them into the cosmos. They found that the rhythm of their breathing contained within it the rhythm of the universe. The deeper they entered into their breathing, the more they found themselves sitting at the heart of the cosmos, breathing in and out galaxies and solar systems. Through this exploration of the power of their breath they were able to awaken the energy sleeping within the spinal cord. They breathed life into their kundalini and entered into the ecstasy that lies at the heart of existence. It is at this point that we begin our practice in this retreat, with the breath, just as the ancient Tantrics did thousands of years ago in their forests and their caves.

"Now I want everyone in the hall to sit comfortably with their eyes closed. Those who want to stand can stand; those who want to sit can sit. The only rule is that no one should be touching the persons next to them. Leave some space between you and your neighbor. If anyone feels like they need more room, they can go out onto the veranda or on the lawn outside the hall. My voice is amplified, so you won't have any problem hearing as long as the doors and windows remain open. Take a minute to get comfortable... Okay. Now I want you to start paying attention to your breathing. The breath is the wheel of life. We are alive only so long as it keeps turning. Turn your full attention to the breath as it enters your body. Feel the vitality filling the pores of your lungs, spreading through the bloodstream to the cells of your tissues and vital organs. Become one with that vital force. Feel it coursing through you, entering with the physical breath and spreading throughout your body as it turns into the inner breath, filling you with life. Follow the breath as it goes out as well, carrying your life force out into the world, merging with every exhalation into the great void. In and out it goes, the wheel of the world, the *prana* riding in on the waves of your breath, filling you to bursting with the energy of the cosmos, and then riding out again, carrying your life force out into the universe, becoming a part of that which it has never left. This is the eternal dance, a continual merging with the world, every molecule and atom of your existence cavorting with the Supreme Partner, the two dancing until the two become one.

"Breathe deeper now, deeper and deeper. Fill every inch of your lungs. Be aware of the air as it enters. Concentrate on that sensation until you become the breath. Again and again, deeper and deeper. Feel your capacity expand until you feel like heaven itself can fit inside you. Now, start speeding up your breathing, little by little... deeper and deeper... faster and faster. Find a rhythm and enter into it. Feel the air beginning to burn inside your lungs. Your breath is becoming a fire inside you, burning hotter and hotter. If you feel yourself becoming lightheaded, surrender to that feeling, but keep breathing—as deeply as you can, as fast as you can, as rhythmically as you can. If you need to sit then sit, but don't open your eyes. Keep all your attention focused within. Merge with your experience. Feel yourself becoming the breath, and the breath in turn becoming the body. You are this great living machine, breathing in and out the universe....

"Bring your whole energy to your breathing now, so that it starts rising from the depths of your being, from your *kunda*, the infinite reservoir within you. Breathe with all your might and all your attention. Watch as the energy begins to awaken, surging up your spinal column and through the nerves into every cell of your body. Feel the storm within you breaking loose. Let your roots shake. Summon forth that sleeping energy. Abandon yourself to it more and more completely with every breath. Feel the electricity pouring into every cell of your body."

Mukunda could feel Gurudeva's voice propelling him inward, into his breath, each hypnotic syllable leading him further and further away from the cage of his ego. Though it was not his intention, his eyes closed and he started following the master's instructions. As PA, it was his duty to remain alert in case Gurudeva needed anything; this precluded his joining in the collective practice. Gurudeva had coached him carefully in this regard, and this was already his fourth retreat since becoming PA, but at this moment he was immune to the weight of responsibility, to the voice inside him that cautioned him to open his eyes and be attentive to the master. A little practice wouldn't hurt, he thought, just this one time.

"Keep breathing, deeper and deeper, just a little longer...." The master's voice continued in its hypnotic pulse. "Abandon yourself... don't hold back... let everything go. Now, when I give the signal, I want you to stop your rapid breathing and allow your body to do what it wills. When I give the word, let your body take over; let go completely. Ready... now. Stop the breathing exercise and let your body become the master. *You* are no longer there. Your body alone exists and it will do as it wills. If your body wants to jerk, then let it jerk. If it wants to get up and dance, then let it dance. If it takes strange positions, or mudras, let it take those mudras. If it shakes, then let it shake. Don't hinder it in any way. This is your body's time to do what it wants—no constraints, no social barriers, no do's or don'ts, no input from the judging mind. No mind, just body. Let the body know what the body knows. Let the body say what the body says. Let the body do what the body does. Don't hesitate or hold back in any way. When the energy inside you rises, your body may shake or do strange things. Don't interfere. If it sits, let it sit. If it stands, let it stand. If it cries or shouts, let it cry or shout. Let the energy express itself any way it wishes."

Mukunda felt a momentary jerk, though he had only been doing the breathing exercise for several minutes. He began to feel a tingling sensation underneath his skin, like electricity searching for a conduit. When it moved, he could feel his body react as if it had a mind of its own. He was tempted to fully abandon himself to the process, to allow his body to carry him into the Tantric abandon that Gurudeva had so beautifully described, but he knew he mustn't. Reluctantly, he opened his eyes, frustrated by the knowledge that he was not allowed to experience what everyone else was. Throughout the hall the previously sedate collection of disciples had become transformed into a strange menagerie of disparate human shapes metamorphosing from one moment to the next, creating a frenetic kaleidoscope of hands and feet and limbs and torsos. Some of the disciples were dancing, whirling in place like dervishes; others were jerking uncontrollably; many were weeping or laughing like madmen; several people were curled up into fetal balls and were rolling on the ground. One rather corpulent, longhaired man in his late forties had removed all his clothing and was running around the room doing a rather poor job of avoiding the obstacle course set out before him. Through it all, Gurudeva sat serenely on the dais, a slight smile stretched across his lips, watching his disciples as impassively as he might have done had they been plunged in silent, motionless meditation.

The scene continued for nearly fifteen minutes, until Gurudeva gave the signal for the gong to sound. Instantly the hall went quiet. Everyone appeared stunned while the reverberations of the gong seeped out through the walls and the windows and then slowly died away. There was an unusually deep silence, unbroken even by the usual sound of birdsong and rustling branches filtering in through the open windows. The devotees remained where they were, motionless, regardless of whether or not they had been there when the session began.

"And now let there be silent meditation. Let the meditation begin wherever you are. Let it begin from the body and swallow you up so completely that you are sure you will never find your way back. Let the silence engulf you, the eternal emptiness at the heart of all form. You have become one with form. Your body did that for you. Honor your body, thank it, and then let the form die. Go, disappear, and do not come back until I tell you."

When the meditation was over, Gurudeva explained how the first asanas, or yoga postures, arose spontaneously during deep meditation and trance states. It was in this way that the relation between certain states of mind and different postures was originally discovered. Even many types of dance, he explained, arose spontaneously out of meditative states; it was this that the disciples were experiencing when they let their bodies take over at the end of the breathing exercise. He gave some additional instructions for the retreat—how to best take advantage of the afternoon workshops and the period of silence, and how to prepare for the evening session when everyone would receive *shaktipat*. Then he left the disciples with a final admonishment:

"We have repressed so much in this modern society of ours that the masks we wear have completely hidden our real faces. We have become so frightened, so suppressed, so crippled, that we are unable to laugh or cry spontaneously. We are unable to dance without being afraid of what others will think. Instead, we have bolted our doors and windows from the inside and become prisoners in our own house, afraid to let the madman out. During these two days I want you to let yourself go completely. Nobody will mind. The pine trees will not object. There are no neighbors to pass judgment. We are all sharing this experience together in a protected space. Let yourself go. Let the madman within you smile as only the madman can."

Once again Gurudeva folded his hands and intoned the sacred mantras with which he had begun the darshan: "*Asato ma sat gamaya*...." Then he got to his feet and started heading majestically up the center aisle with his retinue while the devotees filled the hall with their thunderous cries: "*Gurudeva ki jai, Gurudeva ki jai.*" Mukunda followed just behind him, feeling the surge of energy from the ecstatic crowd. As soon as they left the hall, the devotees poured out behind them and quickly ran ahead to line both sides of the path leading to the Bungalow. They continued shouting "*Gurudeva ki jai*" all the way to the master's house, a spontaneous outpouring such as Gurudeva had been calling for during his talk. Despite his lingering frustrations, Mukunda felt overwhelmed by the scene. Surely, he thought, there could be no better place in the world to be at this moment than walking in the wake of the great master, at the center of a surging sea of devotion-maddened disciples. Only someone in his shoes could possibly understand what it was like to be so close to such a fountain of spiritual energy. Whatever sacrifices he had made, whatever disappointments might be weighing on him, he knew they could never begin to outweigh such good fortune.

Gita strained her neck and tried to catch a final glimpse of Gurudeva as he entered the Bungalow gate, but it was practically impossible to see anything through the several hundred massed bodies pushing and jockeying for position. It was one of those times when it didn't pay to be short. Being female didn't help either, she thought. The female devotees significantly outnumbered the males—as seemed to be true in every spiritual community she had seen in the brief time she had been interested in such things—but there were these occasional moments when it paid dividends to be taller and stronger. Thankfully, they were few and far between. If things worked out, her guitar and her voice would get her closer to Gurudeva than any of the disciples who were now blocking her view.

And to Mukunda.

Once Gurudeva disappeared into the Bungalow, the crowd quickly dispersed, most everyone heading for the cafeteria where an outside dining area had been set up under an awning to accommodate the overflow. Gita decided to pass on lunch. She wasn't very hungry and she wanted to follow Gurudeva's advice to eat as lightly as possible in order to gain maximum benefit from the retreat. Instead, she found a shady spot under the tamarind tree and sat down to do a little meditation.

What a morning it had been! This was her second retreat, but she had been too new during the first one to fully appreciate it. Nor had it been quite this wild. The morning session had been like a trip to the San Diego Zoo, with half the people in the hall making strange noises, jerking around like they were having a fit, or dancing like—dare she say it?—madmen. Nothing of the sort had happened to her. She had felt some strong energy during the breathing practice. Her senses became more alive; her body felt lighter; for a few minutes she felt as if she were going to float away. But when the breathing ended, all she wanted to do was to sit there and enjoy the afterglow. Instead, she spent most of those fifteen minutes watching the other people in the hall as discretely as she could manage. From the standpoint of pure entertainment it was priceless. If part of what Gurudeva was after was to create a living sense of the preposterous, he had certainly succeeded. She smiled as she pictured someone off the street witnessing what she had witnessed. Surely they would think they were all mad. How could they think otherwise? But that was exactly what Gurudeva was after, wasn't it? To free the madman in his disciples under controlled conditions? The "why" she was still a little unclear about, but she supposed it would come clear in time.

After the silent meditation, she had spent the remaining minutes watching Mukunda on the dais behind Gurudeva, half hidden by the flowers. He seemed so integral to the scene, so at one with his place on stage, it was as if he were the master's shadow. It was an aspect of him she had never really noticed before, though it had been right there in front of her eyes all along. This was Mukunda's life. Whatever remained of the boy she had once known, it was submerged in the yogi who lived to serve his master. For all that she might think she knew him, she did not—not unless she understood this simple fact. This was not a stage he was passing through, a temporary role that would later give way to his real destiny. This was what he lived for, and with him she knew there could be no half measures. If she wanted to make a life with Mukunda, then she would have to make this her life. She would have to go all the way or not at all.

Suddenly Gita opened her eyes, startled by her thoughts, any pretense of meditating gone. Had she really just thought of making a life with Mukunda? It was the type of idle fancy that could pass through any girl's mind—what it would be like to be married to this man or that—a thought that would be forgotten within moments, edged out by the other idle fancies with which we occupy our time. But in the same instant she knew it wasn't. This was not a bit of mental fluff or even a brief infatuation. This was something that had been brewing for some time, steadily gathering force in her subconscious until it was ready to present its case to her conscious sensibilities. This was not a passing what-would-it-be-like—this was more like the certainty she had felt when she had realized that she wanted to devote her life to music, a certainty that had rescued her when far more perilous desires had spiraled out of control. It was something that lived far closer to the center of her being than any of the thousand passing fancies that had lit her imagination for shorter or longer periods of her life. She could not even say for sure that she had fallen in love (an odd idea to even entertain, considering how long they had known each other). No, that was too ephemeral a feeling. Something inside her was convinced that they were meant to walk their road together, to share the steps and the stones that would carry them to their destiny. In fact, it did not seem to be romance that her subconscious was concerned about at all but companionship, though perhaps love was lurking somewhere in the shadows. And the moment she thought this, she knew it to be true.

She fastened her eyes on the Bungalow gate through which Mukunda had disappeared less than half an hour before. Her mind became vacant, almost numb, harboring only this feeling of certainty that canceled out the possibility of any other thought. For at least ten minutes she sat there without thinking, minimally aware of the slight breeze at her back, the encroaching sun probing the canopy of leaves, the azure stillness edging the hills behind the Bungalow, the distant sound of kirtan from the cafeteria loudspeakers, muted but insistent. Finally her thoughts began to revive and encircle her, as if the resting wheel of a gyroscope had been tapped back into motion. This time, however, there was no surprise and no confusion, none of the vague reflective lights that had lit her consciousness a few minutes earlier. In their place was a feeling of acceptance, a willing surrender to feelings that would only laugh or be roused to anger if she tried to deny them. So this was it then? She wished—with all her heart, as near as she could see—to wed her destiny to Mukunda's. He was the one—if he would have her. And if he would, then there would be no turning back. This would have to become her world as well.

She looked around her. Some twenty meters away she saw a pair of devotees sitting on the grass, meditating, oblivious to the early afternoon sun. Two hundred meters farther on, a medley of sound was coming from the dining area, an off-kilter blend of a hundred different conversations against the backdrop of an ethereal but captivating kirtan. It was a beautiful place, so rich in experience and so full of challenges, so different from the world she had known, the world that had been simply *the* world before she had begun to realize that the world could be many things at once. Since she had begun living in the ashram, each day seemed to be brimmed with the passionate intensity she remembered from her childhood, before the colors of life had gradually started to dull from the force of familiarity. But she was still a visitor here in so many ways, trying to make sense of what was often a perplexing confusion. This was as clear to her as the sky above the hills, and it was just as clear that it would not change overnight. Her long history was as much a part of her as Mukunda's dedicated sojourn in his master's footsteps. The possibility of closing the doors to her past was unthinkable. But what if this was what was required of her? She shuddered at the possibility, but a minute later she relaxed. Yes, even this was possible, if her destiny demanded it. She had never lacked courage, after all. Why falter now? As her eyes focused once again on the Bungalow and then rose to Gurudeva's second-story window, the prospect suddenly seemed almost exhilarating, as well as unnerving. Especially knowing that she didn't really have a choice.

Shortly after dinner, Mukunda ascended the stairs to inform Gurudeva that it was time for the evening session. He found the master lying down on his cot reading a magazine. Gurudeva sat up and motioned for Mukunda to sit down in front of him.

"It says here that a group of scientists in Japan claim to have discovered proof of the existence of the chakras. They have been measuring the magnetic currents within the body with newly developed instruments, and they've discovered specific concentrations of magnetic energy at the precise points along the spinal column where the chakras are located."

He passed the article to Mukunda.

"It sounds like a real breakthrough," Mukunda said, glancing briefly at the pictures of magnetic imaging that showed definite concentration densities at the points along the spinal column and the brain where the chakras were depicted in the yogic literature.

"Nonsense," Gurudeva replied. "They are as much in the dark as they were before. The chakras are psychic centers; they will never be measurable by any kind of physical instrument. What they have managed to do is to find a correlation between the body's magnetic energy and the chakras, but like most scientists they run wild with their speculations and declare that they have discovered the chakras—that the chakras are actually concentrations of magnetic energy in the body poetically romanticized by ancient mystics who didn't have the advantages of modern science to guide them. There will be a big buzz and a hullabaloo about it for a few days; and with all the uproar and congratulations no one will notice that they haven't actually discovered anything at all. These concentrations of magnetic energy are no more the chakras than light reflecting off a river is the sun. They think they have discovered the 'truth,' but all they have really done is to cover up the truth by fostering complacency. This is the typical rut that science falls into. Scientists think they've discovered something, and then they sit back with their arms crossed and a smug smile on their faces and think that their work is done. Until someone else comes along and demonstrates that it was just another illusion that they were passing off as the truth. If they want to know about the chakras they should ask an adept in Tantra or yoga. We would be only too happy to point them in the right direction."

Gurudeva chuckled at his own witticism, and Mukunda took advantage of the pause to remind him that it was time to leave for the program. In fact, it was past time.

"Patience, Mukunda, patience. You can't hurry the weather and you can't hurry a realized soul either. Everything happens in its own time. The difference between you and me is that I know when that time is and you don't, not yet. The universe has decreed an exact moment for me to leave this room in accordance with the collective karma of everyone gathered to meet me, and until that moment comes I will remain sitting right here. Now, get up and get ready. The moment has come."

It had been several years since Gurudeva had last given shaktipat to the devotees. For the newer disciples it was something legendary. The older disciples would tell wild stories about their extraordinary, life-changing experiences: how Gurudeva had placed his hand on their heads and transmitted the divine energy; how they had felt it flow into them and overwhelm them, sending them into various states of ecstasy. Gurudeva had explained in his talks how an enlightened being could literally serve as a conduit for the descent of the divine energy, if he so wished. Only an egoless being could do this—his emptiness allowed him to serve as a cosmic passage. Once Gurudeva had let it be known that he'd be giving shaktipat during the Tantra retreat, the news had passed through the ashram community like wildfire; within a few days the retreat had been booked out.

As the senior disciples took their seats on the dais and the opening bhajans began, Mukunda could feel the sense of expectation mounting. The energy had been building all day, in fact, and later, when the shaktipat session actually began, it would be primed to explode. But first Gurudeva would conduct a session of questions and answers followed by an hour of dynamic breathing and meditation.

Markandeya got the microphone ready and passed it to the first questioner, a young blond in her early twenties.

"Gurudeva, could you say something about the practice of sexual Tantra and how it relates to what you were saying this morning about abandoning oneself completely to one's experience as a path to liberation?"

Gurudeva smiled and a few laughs were heard here and there.

"First of all, let me start by saying that there is no such thing as sexual

Tantra, per se. What goes by the name of sexual Tantra in the West is, for the most part, nothing more than a clever means of disguising a lust for sensual pleasure behind a veil of spiritual romanticism. In most cases, the driving force behind these practices is not the desire for liberation but the desire for pleasure. As such, they only become the cause of greater bondage. Real Tantra means death to the ego, but this kind of so-called sexual Tantra is generally nothing more than ego-gratification.

"However..." Gurudeva paused and raised his finger. "It is a fact that sexual practices have been a part of Tantra for as long as the race can remember. And they will remain so, as long as the sex act remains the primary means of procreation. As far as Tantra is concerned, every expression of this cosmos is sacred, and every action can be used as a means to liberation, provided it is done in the right spirit. The answer to your question lies precisely in this right spirit, as I will now explain.

"The eyes of Tantra see the Divine in every expression of this cosmos. Meditation is sacred, going to the bathroom is sacred, eating is sacred, and therefore sex is also sacred. The taboos we have all learned regarding sex are social constructs, and Tantra would make sure that you are not a slave to social constructs. Social constructs have their place in social life, no doubt, but they must not be allowed to become our masters.

"So, first of all, be natural. Don't allow socially imposed ideas or taboos to stand between you and your goal. You are in search of your self, but social conditioning acts as a barrier to separate you from your self. How so? Because it instills fear into our mind, and as long as we are governed by fear we can never move ahead. We will remain cowering in a corner, afraid of our own shadow. Our fears are the shackles around our ankles that keep us from advancing. If we want to progress, then we have to throw off those shackles and march ahead in the quest for truth. Only then can we know what it means to be natural. There is an old Zen saying: chop wood, carry water. It refers to the natural state of being where one is in harmony with the universe; in that state everything flows of its own accord. But this state of harmony can only arise when the mind doesn't get in the way. Once the mind interferes, it muddies up the waters. The goal is to have 'no-mind,' as it is called in Zen, the state of oneness when our thoughts and our actions are in total harmony with the universe. That is what is meant by the phrase 'be natural.'

"So when it comes to the celebration of sex, as with anything else, we must first learn to be natural. Everything in this universe is guided by the principle of attraction, and behind this attraction is the desire for union with the Supreme Self, the desire to lose oneself in the All. Sex is nothing but the expression of this innate desire at the biological level. Freud said that if you look deep enough into human motivation you will find sex at the root of everything. In a certain sense he was right, but only about the biological level. There is something behind the sex urge, something far deeper, and that is the desire for union, the longing to lose oneself into something that is both beyond oneself and within oneself. Biology is not the motivating factor. There is something that is motivating biology, a greater principle that causes biology to flow in a certain direction. That principle is the attraction of the Supreme. God is attracting every expression of the cosmos toward himself, toward union; and at the biological level this is expressed as the sex urge.

"So first of all, Tantra teaches us that the sex urge is divine; it is nothing to be afraid or ashamed of; it warrants no mental complex. It is simply the manifestation of the desire for liberation expressed at the cellular or biological level. And we are just as much biological beings as we are spiritual beings. We exist on all levels at once, and we must honor all levels of our existence. The further we wish to grow, the deeper we have to throw our roots. This is a fundamental principle of spiritual growth. If we want to send our branches into the sky of consciousness, then we have to throw our roots deep into the soil of our material existence in order to furnish those branches with the sustenance they need. There is a saying in the Upanishads: 'Those who follow only the material fall into darkness; those who follow only the spiritual fall into even greater darkness.' If you follow only the spiritual without honoring your physical or biological existence, then it is like a tree trying to grow without roots. You are doomed from the outset. You will be blown away by the first strong wind.

"Not only is the sex urge divine, it is also symbolic. It is a reflection of something greater than itself. One of the mysteries that Tantra has revealed is that the macrocosm is reflected in the microcosm; spiritual realities are reflected in material realities. The universe is the play of Shiva and Shakti, consciousness and energy. In the microcosm the divine energy, Shakti, is sleeping in the first chakra in the form of kundalini. The dance of human life revolves around the elevation of kundalini up through the spinal cord, through the different chakras, until it reaches the abode of Shiva, or consciousness, in the seventh chakra. There Shiva and Shakti merge in divine union; the human being becomes one with God; he attains enlightenment. In the physical plane this dance of Shiva and Shakti is reflected as the dance of man and woman. That is why in Hindu mythology Shakti is always depicted as a woman and Shiva as a man, and their spiritual union is symbolized by the union of man and woman. Now all symbols, when they are made fully conscious, reveal the spirit of what they symbolize. Being aware of this, the ancient Tantrics elevated the sexual act to the status of a sacred rite. By cultivating this symbolic awareness during the sexual act, they attempted to awaken awareness of the spiritual union that this symbolic biological dance reflects.

"And so, the ancient Tantrics developed certain rites and rituals through which the sexual act was transformed into a means to free the practitioner from ego consciousness. Instead of performing sex for sensual pleasure, they practiced it as a way to elevate their minds. Those practices required tremendous discipline and ruthless honesty. They were not a license to have a good time. They used those rituals to help free themselves from their conditioned behavior and conditioned thinking and enter into a radically new consciousness. To the extent that they were successful, they were able to attain the no-mind; and attaining the no-mind, they gradually left those rituals behind. They began to realize that this experience is present in every expression of nature. The ecstasy of union is there in the blossoming of a flower, in the movement of the sap through the veins of a tree, in the passing of a cloud across the evening sky, in the rain, in the lightening bolt, in the soil that the rain washes away. It is everywhere and everything at once. And that is when the method starts to drop away. Because the sex was only a means to get at this experience, one of many doors, and when you begin to realize that everything is a door to the same experience, then the need for the method drops away. That is when you begin to chop wood and carry water from the well. Everything happens as it is supposed to happen, within the flow of nature. And you are nature. You are a whorl, a pattern in the universal flow. At that point there is no longer any illusion of a separate self to get in the way.

"So, as you see, these are stages in a process, and these stages apply not only to sexual practices but to all aspects of our physical existence. In the afternoon workshops you were working with sound, color, music, and body movement. After the meditation we will work with pure energy through shaktipat. But it is all part of the same process: passing beyond our social conditioning and allowing the natural flow to come through, and then merging with that flow until we experience the ecstatic union that is the true source and the goal of all our movements. Once you understand the essence of the Tantric process, then you can apply it to the different arenas of your life. Not only to your sexual life but to all your life."

An older devotee now stepped to the microphone. He was a businessman from Santa Barbara in his late forties or early fifties, quite successful but always stressed with the demands of work and family.

"Gurudeva, as you often tell us, much of our spiritual work consists of unlearning behaviors and ways of thinking and models of the universe that society has taught us. We have to throw off our conditioning, as you were just saying. Can you say something about the dynamic between having to work in the world, having to be in that environment twenty-four-seven, and at the same time trying to get out from underneath it?"

"This is a very important question, Govinda. There is a saying that if a saint walks down the street, a pickpocket will only see his pockets. We all see the world according to the models we have in our heads. A pickpocket sees everyone as a potential source of income. That's the plane of reality he lives on, so he reduces everyone else to that plane. Now, it is a fact that if you walk down a typical street in any city or town of the world, you are unlikely to run across a single saint. What to speak of a saint, you may not even run across a single person who is doing spiritual meditation. There are over six billion people in the world, and only a small fraction of these six billion are true spiritualists. And most of those cannot be found in the society. True spiritualists have always made it a practice to live more or less in seclusion—in caves, in forests, in monasteries, and in ashrams, though nowadays they sometimes live unnoticed in quiet suburban houses in places like Santa Barbara. This has been the tradition since time immemorial, and it will continue to be so. The question is, why?

"C.W. Leadbeater once claimed that when we live in a city or a town only 50 percent of the thoughts we think are our own. The rest come from our environment. Leadbeater was only partially correct. Actually, for most people far more than 50 percent of their thinking is absorbed from the psychic environment in which they live. Listen to the typical conversation between two people on the street or in their living room. Record it, if you can, and analyze it. See how many of their sentences you have heard somewhere before. And not just once or twice but hundreds of times. 'Now how about those Dodgers? If they only had some hitting.' 'Young people nowadays just don't know how to behave anymore.' 'All I'm asking for is a little appreciation.' You will hardly ever hear an original thought. Original thoughts have become so rare that you can sometimes go for days in a typical city without hearing one. Now consider for a moment how difficult it must be to be spontaneous or spiritual in an environment where everything you hear, everyone you come in contact with, reinforces just the opposite. The odds of success in that case become astronomically small. For this reason sincere spiritualists since time immemorial have either left the society completely and went to live in nature, or else formed their own society, the ashram, where instead of getting negative reinforcement for their practices, they get positive reinforcement. If you can get the right environment, then half the battle is already won. The rest is easy.

"So when you ask about the dynamic between living and working in the world and at the same time trying to throw off your social conditioning, what you are really asking is, how can we create an island in the middle of the madness? Society will never leave you alone, unless and until you get off the mainland. That is why I advise everyone who can live in the ashram to do so. It is an island, a safe haven that will guarantee your rapid progress on the path. Often people who have come to live here tell me that when they first arrived they let out a big sigh, as if they literally felt a weight fall from their shoulders. This is a common experience. As long as you are here, you have the protection you need to rise above the muck and mire of the world. I advise those who live nearby to spend as much time here as possible. Even a few hours a week in a spiritually charged environment can mean the difference between being swallowed up by maya and making it safely to the other side. But not everyone can live close to the ashram. For those who live farther away, I encourage them to get together with the other disciples in their area and form their own communities. These communities then become a refuge. But if you don't have other disciples nearby with whom you can spend time, you can still make your home into a safe haven. Sanctify it with your spiritual vibrations, so that whenever you come back from the wars of the world you can leave them behind you and get back to what is lasting and true. And when you must be out there, do your best to steer clear of the illusion. Do what you have to do, but try not to become too involved or preoccupied with what is going on around you. Let it be like a foreign country where you don't speak the language. All kinds of things are happening, but because you don't understand the language you are not aware of them. They might be preparing for an invasion or getting ready to host the world cup, but you go blissfully on your way with no unnecessary distractions.

"Take politics, for example. Everywhere you turn, you see people getting lost in one political drama after another, from national politics right down to family politics. What is politics, actually? Politics is how you play the game of separateness and turn it to your advantage. It is mainly concerned with manipulating situations and people; as such, it is one of maya's most insidious traps. As long as the mind is caught at this level, it is impossible to see the unity behind the creation. Rather, you go on reinforcing your separateness and your ego until your ego or your group ego becomes your object of worship. Why is the political arena filled with crooks and scoundrels and cheats? Because that is the nature of the game. Once you allow yourself to get sucked up in it, you can't help but be affected. Power corrupts and absolute power corrupts absolutely.

"Don't allow yourself to fall into that trap. Only fools play with fire. Try to pass through this world leaving as little trace as possible. Let your footprints be like the tracks of the birds in the sky. When you can learn to do this, when you can learn to leave the world alone, then and only then will the world leave you alone. This is the real meaning of asceticism. Look at the life we lead in the ashram. We have the best of both worlds. We enjoy our physical existence to the fullest, but at the same time we enjoy all the treasures of the spiritual world. The muck and mire of materialism is safely locked outside our doors. But you don't need to live in the ashram to do this. Make it your daily practice and your own home will become your ashram, whether you live in a upscale residential neighborhood in Santa Barbara or in a rundown apartment in downtown Hollywood."

A man in his mid-thirties whom Mukunda had never seen before now stepped to the microphone. He was dressed more conservatively than most, in tailored slacks and a cardigan. The moment he began formulating his question in a peculiar, high-pitched, almost whiny voice, Mukunda knew he was a newcomer.

"I would like to know what you think of Martin Luther King's contention that the real problem in the world is not the clamor of the bad people but the silence of the good people. Was he right in thinking that it is the responsibility of morally minded, spiritually minded people to speak out against injustice and take an active part in trying to create a better world? And does this not accord with the bodhisattva ideal to renounce liberation in order to free all living beings from their suffering?"

Mukunda was annoyed by the question, though he was unsure whether or not the speaker meant it as a challenge to what Gurudeva had been saying. From the murmurs in the hall, it seemed he was not alone in his reaction. The master, however, was his usual tranquil self.

"First of all, I would have asked Reverend King to take a good look at the world he lived in and then look back through history. Could he say that the amount of suffering was any less for the average person, the unenlightened person, during his time than it had been a hundred years before, or a thousand years before that, or five thousand? Martin Luther King was not only a compassionate man; he was an intelligent man. He would have had to admit, just as any honest person must, that the amount of suffering the average person has to face in their life has not really changed, not at any time in the long history of the human race. People still get sick and die. They still lose their loved ones, fight with their friends, and feel depressed because they can't find meaning in their life. The nature of that suffering may have changed with the advancement in technology, it may be less physical and more mental, but the incidence of suffering remains the same. This has been true since human beings took their first steps on this earth, and it will remain true for as long as they live here, no matter what you or I try to do about it. The desire to change the world is a noble one, but it's still a desire. And if you look into the heart of this desire you will find the same old enemy, ego, albeit in snappier clothes. Who are you to think that you can change the world? Who am I to think it? The one who made this world is doing just fine, and he will go on doing as he sees fit, regardless of what you or I have to say about it. In essence, the belief that we can change the world is a subtle form of egotism, a kind of blasphemy, in fact, since you are in effect telling the Supreme Being that you don't like the way he is doing things. What you are saying is that were it up to you, you could do a better job. Is it not?"

Murmurs and nods of assent passed through the crowd, but the man at the microphone remained silent.

"Personally, I don't have any expectations of making the world a better place. This world is already a paradise, a masterwork beyond human comprehension. You are new here, so perhaps you are not familiar with the teachings of the sixth patriarch of Zen, Hui Neng. I doubt that Reverend King was familiar with his teachings, either. The sixth patriarch once said that the great way is easy for those who have no expectations. A man who is at peace with himself, a man fulfilled, has no expectations. He doesn't want anything. If you want something, it implies that something is missing in your life. If you have expectations, it means there is a hole inside you waiting to be filled, but you will never fill it until you give up your desires and your expectations, for there is no end to them. That is the nature of desire. You satisfy one and another immediately takes its place. This is the wheel that has the world in thrall. Give it up and you will find that the world is, and has always been, perfect. God does not make mistakes.

"You see, it is not by changing your external circumstances or your environment that you can gain freedom from suffering but only by changing yourself. As the Buddha said in his four noble truths: the very nature of incarnate life is suffering; the root of suffering is desire; the cessation of desire leads to the end of suffering; and the spiritual path is the means by which we can extinguish desire. The Buddha came to teach that spiritual path, and I have come for this same reason."

"But what about the ideal of the bodhisattva to forego liberation until all beings are liberated?" the man countered. "How do you explain the work of saints like Mother Teresa or Sri Aurobindo?"

"There is nothing to explain. The example is sitting here in front of you. Why am I sitting here if not to serve as a vehicle for the alleviation of suffering? Which can only be achieved through spiritual liberation, not through politics or putting a Band-Aid on social ills that cannot be eliminated as long as people continue to be trapped in their egos. The bodhisattva dances in the world of form so that the people who seek him out can learn how to dance the dance that carries them beyond form, beyond both pleasure and pain. The bodhisattva doesn't play politics; he doesn't get caught up in a game that leaves everyone right back where they started from. If you go through the history of the great bodhisattvas who have come to this world, you will find them standing outside of that confining circle and calling to the captives within: 'Leave the muck and the mire; come join me and I will set you free.' "

As he said this, Gurudeva raised his hands and made a beckoning motion. A chorus of affirmations rose up from the crowd.

"As for Mother Teresa, she was a noble lady, but she was no bodhisattva. Aurobindo was a revolutionary, no doubt, but he was only a revolutionary until he began his spiritual practices. Once he began his *sadhana* and had a vision of Krishna in his jail cell, he gave up politics forever and retired to Pondicherry to build his ashram.

"Now, let us have one final question."

A tall sandy-haired young man stepped to the microphone. "Gurudeva, could you say something about the importance of the spiritual guide in Tantric practice?"

"I'm glad you asked that question, Chaitanya. It is a very important question.

"The relationship between master and disciple is unique and unparalleled. It cannot be compared to any other relationship on earth. In this relationship the master is searching for the disciple, and the disciple is searching for the master. Both are searching for each other, and the object of their search is one and the same. They are the same being, and it is that being they search. The only difference is that the master knows this and the disciple does not.

"When a disciple goes in search of a master, he is really going in search of his own self, but he does not yet realize this because the light of his inner self has been covered by the shroud of his ego. Even if the disciple is intellectually convinced that the truth is within him, he cannot recognize that truth until he first meets it in the external world. When he meets the master, the one whose inner being is not veiled by ego, he feels the touch of consciousness, and through that touch he begins to awaken. This divine touch comes from outside and he calls it the master, but the simple truth is that the master is nothing but the disciple's own inner self reflected in a mirror. I have just said that the master is also in search of the disciple. In fact, the master is nothing but the disciple's inner being coming in search of itself.

"Do you understand? The spiritual guide is nothing but the inner spirit of the disciple taking an external shape so that the disciple can meet his self, talk to his self, and one day come to know his self. The master's sole responsibility is to reveal the disciple's inner being. He can do this because he is fully conscious of himself as consciousness, as the innermost being of every one of us.

"Now, as to the relationship between the two who are really one, the essential quality is one of listening in silence to what is not said and not heard. The guru may say so many things. He may guide his disciple; he may scold him; he may joke with him. But it is not through his words that the master reveals the disciple's inner self but through what lies between and beyond those words, in the spaces where nothing is spoken and nothing is heard. It is there that the master exists in the full awareness of his being. And this is the only thing to be communicated. If you have it, then you have everything. If you don't, you have nothing. You may have volumes upon volumes of words, of sage counsel, of enlightened teachings, but without the being behind them they are as vacant as an empty shirt fluttering on a clothesline. From a distance they may give you the illusion of life, but if you get close enough you see how empty they are.

"Thus, the only requirement for a true disciple is to listen to the song of the master's being. To do this you must become quiet, for any noise, any noise at all, will drown it out. If you are quiet enough, then you will hear the master's song communicating to you the existence of your inner self. Of course, I use the word *communicate* advisedly, because the reality is that nothing is said and nothing is heard. In the silence that exists between master and disciple, the white noise of the disciple's ego disappears. What lies beyond is freedom.

"Is it clear, Chaitanya?"

"Yes, Gurudeva."

"Good. Then let us taste of that silence that exists between you and me. Let us now begin the meditation."

For the next hour Gurudeva led the gathering in dynamic breathing and meditation, as he had done in the morning. Then the moment arrived that everyone had been waiting for: shaktipat. The hall attendants quickly began clearing the space down the right-hand aisle. Instructions were given over the loudspeaker and the devotees began lining up. Madalasa and Leela positioned themselves at the head of the aisle to ferry the devotees onto the dais one at a time. It was Madalasa's duty to make sure they understood the instructions, while Leela handed them a Kleenex to wipe the sweat off their face and hands. Mukunda was to remain by Gurudeva's side, ready for whatever he might need, be it water or a towel for his face or help with an overly zealous disciple. Bhishma had deputed three assistants, all trained in karate, to guard Gurudeva in case anything got out of hand. The four of them positioned themselves on either side of the master. Abhay and the other senior disciples formed a semi-circle at the front of the dais. Their job was to take care of the devotees once they received shaktipat and to remove them if need be to clear space. In front of the dais the ashram band had begun playing kirtan; they would keep playing for the rest of the night, until everyone had a chance to go in front of the master, a process that would last for several hours.

When everything was in place, Gurudeva gave the signal. One by one the devotees started approaching. As they reached the front of his cushion, they kneeled down. Gurudeva laid his hand on their heads, recited some mantras, and looked them directly in the eyes for ten to fifteen seconds. The look on his face was as intense as Mukunda had ever seen it, as if fire were pouring from his eyes into the eyes of his disciples. Several devotees screamed when Gurudeva touched them. Many wept. Others started to jerk uncontrollably, as if they were having a seizure, or else began spontaneously assuming various yogic asanas or mudras. Still others passed out or went into trance, overwhelmed by the energy. These had to be carried off by the senior disciples and laid down safely in some free spot near the dais.

All over the hall, people were experiencing strange sensations and manifesting yogic *kriya*s, the involuntary movements that often accompany the movement of spiritual energy. People were throwing their hands in the air, watching them move to a will that was not their own. Bodies snapped backward and fell to the floor, while others stood up and wobbled and creaked. At the back of the room Govinda, the businessman who had asked a question, started assuming poses from classical Indian dance, weeping as he turned and turned in his spot. The energy in the room became so intense that virtually no one was left unaffected. And throughout it all, the music pulsed and reverberated through the hall, surging like stormy waves in a tight coastal bay.

When the last person had received shaktipat, Gurudeva raised his arms and started chanting a verse from the Guru Gita: *nityam shuddham nirabhasam.* . . . At that moment the wind started picking up. Pieces of paper started to swirl in the hall. Moments later a few heavy drops started thudding against the open windows. The hall attendants rushed to close them; no sooner had they done so than a fierce rain started pelting the panes of glass, followed almost immediately by brilliant bolts of lightening and powerful thunderclaps that rattled the windows. Mukunda was sure that the sudden storm was no coincidence. Gurudeva had served as a conduit for more than the subtle spiritual energy that had passed into the bodies of the devotees. He had channeled the energy of the skies as well, unleashing this unforeseen storm to serve as a symbolic close to what had been an extraordinary night.

It was after one thirty in the morning when Mukunda finally made it back to his room. He tried to meditate for a few minutes before turning in, but he found it impossible to concentrate his mind. His thoughts were flying around like leaves in a windstorm, the emotions rolling like tumbleweeds. Though he had not received shaktipat himself, his body was buzzing when he entered his room, as if he had stepped out of a high-speed jet after a long flight, a contact high that was slow in wearing off. But as the excitement gradually waned and his weariness mounted, a sense of frustration rolled in like a wave, washing him onto his rolled-out sleeping bag from where he stared up at the ceiling.

For reasons he could not fathom, he felt as if he were going backward. When Gurudeva made him PA it had been the high-water mark of his life, but somehow it seemed as if it had been all downhill from there. He had been the master's protégé since his childhood, part of the inner circle before he even knew there was one. Meditation had been easy for him. He had gotten high on mantra before his childhood friends could boast of having tasted their first beer. He was still in grade school when he had his first experience of shaktipat, and by the time he was a senior in high school he was teaching yoga and meditation to adults three times his age. All his life he had been flying down the spiritual path at breakneck speed with nothing on the horizon that could keep him from his ultimate goal of liberation in this lifetime—until the last two or three years when his meditation, and by extension his life, had fallen into a glutinous rut. What had been effortless and blissful slowly turned mechanical and dry. A sense of disquiet began taking root, as if he were gradually becoming aware that he was headed in the wrong direction, despite all the signs to the contrary. When he first became aware of this, he tried to dismiss it as an unavoidable low-water period, a test of his determination such as those he had read about in his spiritual books. He stepped up his efforts and dedicated more time to his meditation, determined to defeat his uncooperative karma with a surge of spiritual heroism. And for a time he thought he had succeeded. When Gurudeva made him PA it was a sign not only that the master was pleased with his efforts but that his destiny had spoken. No temporary malaise, no matter how long it lasted, could derail him from his lifelong quest. But when his euphoria wore off and he settled into the daily routine of caring for the master's needs, he found that he had less time than ever for meditation and more nagging doubts.

The first day of the retreat had been a perfect example. While most of the disciples were enjoying powerful spiritual experiences, he had been left out of the loop. People who had been meditating for a couple of years at best had fallen into trance right in front of him during shaktipat, while he had watched them with a sense of dull envy, aware that he felt nothing, suspecting that he still would have felt nothing had he been in their place with Gurudeva's hands on his head. As the night wore on, the same doubts assailed him that had grown more frequent in recent months: Was he not an impostor in a yogi's guise, the master's right hand but no closer to being a sage than the students in his yoga classes? At one point he had even wondered if he had any right to be there at all. He had shaken it off, of course, but now, as he lay down, waiting for the thankful oblivion of sleep, the feeling returned. He had been granted extraordinary privileges in his life, finding the spiritual path as a child and drawing near to a realized master, as near as a disciple could get. There was nothing more to wish for, other than a continuation of what he already had, until his boat could safely find the shores of the endless sea, and yet dissatisfaction had taken hold of him like a niggling virus. The solid ground of his interior life had begun to give way, and there seemed to be nothing he could do to stop it.

The last thing he remembered before he fell asleep was Gita sitting with the band by the side of the dais, filling the meditation hall with her angelic voice and her cobalt eyes. The image of her smile lifted the clouds from his mind and reminded him that he was letting his ego run amok. Life was a mystery—had he forgotten that?—and his own destiny was simply one facet in that ever-revolving jewel. He could not fill it with preconceived notions and expect it to respond to his desires. Just look at how she had streaked back into his life like an unheralded comet, undetected by scientists until it became visible to the naked eye. He could never have predicted such an event, could never have even imagined it in his long years as a self-absorbed yogi, but now that she had appeared in his nighttime sky, he was learning lessons he might never have learned otherwise. His spiritual aspirations might be dissolving into chimera at this moment, but there was much to be thankful for. The sure hand that had guided him all these years was guiding him still. He just needed to be more attentive to its whispers.

6

They were well into the morning session when Gita started to suspect that Kamal had not asked her to come because he needed her input, as he had told her, or because he wanted her to feel she was a vital part of the post production of the record, as she had assumed (in other words, out of politeness), but because he wanted to teach her the craft. Perhaps he saw in her some potential that could be developed to the ashram's future benefit, or perhaps he just enjoyed teaching what had hitherto seemed to her an interesting but tedious part of the recording process; whatever the reason, it was clear from his professorial manner and his craftsman's enthusiasm that he had invited her as a prospective protégée. She not only felt flattered; she felt as if he were showing her a facet of her artistic destiny that she had entirely overlooked.

They had finished recording her final vocals for the ten songs three days earlier. He had told her that he would call her when he was ready to mix, but she had never expected to become such an integral part of the process. They had been at work on the mix of her first song for just over an hour when it dawned on her that she was going to be spending even more time in the studio working on the post production of her songs than she had spent recording them. They started off with the basics: the panning of the instruments and the addition of reverb and EQ. "First we have to locate each instrument in space," he told her, pointing to the sound room as if the musicians were physically present, tuning up their instruments and waiting for their cue. "As you probably already know, we do this through a combination of panning, reverb, and EQ. Panning, of course, moves the sound from left to right, reverb from front to back, and EQ separates the sounds from each other so that we can tell them apart properly. There's a little more to it than that, but it's a good way to think about it while you're learning. You'll pick up the nuances as we go along. The goal is to give each instrument its own unique space so that when you listen to it your ear is tricked into thinking that the musicians are right in front of you. You want your listeners to hear each instrument just as clearly as if they were sitting in a performance hall with perfect acoustics. Which hall is up to us to choose. It can be anything from a warm little backstage room to a huge cathedral, depending on how intimate a setting you want. For now we'll keep it warm and private, especially for this song. Let's put the lead vocal front and center; that's you, Gita one. We'll put your doppelgängers, the backing singers, more toward the back and fan them out. We'll put the guitar there, keyboards over there, put Rakhal right next to you...."

Gita watched and listened in fascination as each instrument, including her voice, gradually and distinctly began to occupy its own space, unique and inviolable, yet always acting in concert with the other instruments. When Kamal was done with the preliminary mix, he went back over each step, showing her how each sound processor worked, explaining its strengths and weaknesses, giving practical demonstrations of the different reverb settings and how they affected the ear, showing how he used EQ to bring out the unique qualities in each instrument. In just under two hours she learned more about mixing and sound engineering than she had learned in all her years as a musician, and yet it was clear to her that she was just beginning to scrape the surface, that this was her first classroom session in what could easily amount to a doctoral degree that might take her years to complete. But what was far more exciting was the unexpected discovery that she loved it. This was not some esoteric technical discipline, she realized, more the province of engineers than of artists; it was the perfect blending of technology and art, the chance to shape sound into the living expression of the artist's dream, a chance to take the raw material of music and work on it as a sculptor works on stone, one chip at a time, until the finished product is capable of producing in the listener the exact effect the artist dreamed of when she first composed the song, never thinking that she could actually attain it. If giving external, perceptible shape to the insubstantial leanings of the imagination was art, then this was just as much art as sculpture, painting, or musical composition.

They had just started on the preliminary mix of the second track when the flautist arrived. It had been Kamal's idea to add flute to the opening track, both for the instrumental solo and to double the arpeggiated guitar figures that he had added to the verses and the chorus, writing them out for

Gita to play. As Kamal took the flautist's levels and EQed her instrument, he continued his detailed introduction to the basics of sound engineering, schooling Gita in the subtleties of EQing a transverse flute. Once the track was ready to roll, however, his attention at once became absorbed by the musician on the other side of the glass. Gita relaxed and sat back to watch Kamal at work. It was her first chance to be a spectator while he was working with an artist, and she was able to recognize subtleties in his craft that she had missed when she had been on that side of the glass, intent on trying to follow his directions. She was smiling to herself over a bit of dialogue between producer and musician when the door to the control room opened and Mukunda stuck his head in.

"Is it okay if I come in and listen for a bit? The red light wasn't on."

Kamal waved him in but continued his dialogue with the flautist as if he were barely aware of the interruption. Mukunda pulled up a chair next to Gita, on the other side from Kamal.

"How's the session going?" he whispered.

Gita was pleased at the unexpected surprise. The preliminary mix was sounding wonderful to her ears—although her sole input had consisted of agreeing with Kamal's suggestions and trying to soak up every bit of information she could. She had just been thinking that she would love to be able to play it for Mukunda and point out all the subtleties that Kamal had pointed out to her. And there he was.

"Kamal's been teaching me sound engineering," she answered, also keeping to a whisper. "I never thought something so technical could be so fascinating. Here, he's going to roll the track again."

Gita would have preferred that Kamal play the song all the way through for Mukunda, but all they got was the sixteen-bar instrumental section and another solo by the flautist, followed by a discussion between producer and musician as he played sections of the solo to illustrate his points.

"What do you think?" she asked, as Kamal continued his discussion with the flautist.

"It sounds great, so far. When do you think the record will be ready?"

"No idea. It all depends on Kamal. Soon, I hope."

Gita was excited to have Mukunda there but not too excited to notice that he didn't have his usual aura of quiet, jovial grace. "Is there something bothering you?" she asked.

Mukunda shrugged and then nodded. "It's probably nothing, but I am a little worried about Gurudeva."

"Really? Do you want to take a walk or something? "

"Do you have time? I don't want to interrupt your session."

"No problem. Kamal, is it okay if I step out for a little while?"

Kamal swiveled around in his chair and beamed a smile. "Sure, go ahead. This may take a while. Why don't you come back after lunch. I should be finished recording her by then and we can start mixing it in."

Since the retreat, Mukunda and Gita had started taking their own morning walks while Gurudeva was out on his, the only free time Mukunda was assured of during the day. He had invited her unexpectedly the day after the retreat. Since then she had made sure she hung around the gate on mornings that she didn't have to be in the studio, just in case he thought to repeat the offer. Mukunda had taken the hint. They usually struck off for the walking trails in the canyon behind the Bungalow, tracing a leisurely round trip that brought him back in time to welcome Gurudeva from his walk. This was neither their usual time, however, nor his usual mood, which always seemed to dispel whatever clouds might be hanging over her mind. She asked him if he wanted to sit and talk, and he readily agreed. They found one of the many secluded benches that dotted the picturesque walkways of the ashram, this one beneath the overhanging branches of a young sycamore, and took a seat in its shade.

"So what's going on?" she asked.

"Markandeya and Madalasa took Gurudeva to the doctor's this morning. That's the second time in less than a week. I'm a little concerned about it."

"Did they say why?"

"Not a word. Yesterday afternoon Markandeya called me and told me to cancel morning walk for today since Gurudeva had a doctor's appointment at eleven thirty. Usually I go with him to the doctor's, or on any special trip, but Markandeya made a point of saying that I'd be free this morning."

"He didn't say anything else?"

"The first time they took him he told me it was just routine. This time, when I asked him about it, he said that Gurudeva was over seventy, there are always things breaking down at that age but it wasn't anything serious, I shouldn't worry about it. That was all I could get out of him."

"He's right, you know. Gurudeva is over seventy. He may be a realized soul but he still has a human body. He probably has some nagging little geriatric ailment that requires a few extra visits. It's perfectly normal for his age."

"I know. It just struck me as a little odd, the whole business."

"Odd that Markandeya and Madalasa would take advantage of the opportunity to have a little extra alone time with Gurudeva? From what I can see, that's just about par for the course. I'm surprised they don't do it more often, actually. And who knows, did you ever think that if Gurudeva does have some nagging little ailment, they might not want his baby-faced PA blabbing it to all his friends?"

"What, you don't think I'm discrete?"

"Well...I did notice that you wait for everyone to clear off before we take our walks. I suppose that counts in your favor. But you'll never be as tight-lipped as Madalasa or Markandeya. Anyhow, I'm sure there's nothing to worry about. If it were anything serious, they would have told you about it. You're Gurudeva's PA. You're the one who takes care of him every day; you have to know these things."

"Exactly. Although Markandeya and Madalasa don't always see it that way. They still treat me like I'm ten years old sometimes."

"Yeah, well I wouldn't count on that changing anytime soon. They're always going to be a lot older than you—and a lot wiser, I suppose."

Gita tried to keep her voice as deadpan as possible. For a few seconds it worked. Mukunda flashed a look of indignation, but a few moments later he broke into a sheepish grin—one of his most endearing traits, though an all-too-rare occurrence—and she could no longer suppress her laughter.

It was almost noon. Markandeya had told Mukunda not to expect them back before one at the earliest, so they decided to head over to the Buddha Café and grab an outdoor table. Gita didn't have to protect her voice and she had been thinking all morning about the superlative vegan cheesecake that the café served. She decided to appease her body with an avocado salad and reward her mind with the cheesecake.

Mukunda's mood brightened considerably. As they walked over, she sang him snatches of a new composition she was working on. She was thinking of calling it "City of Quartz; City of Angels," a Dylanesque (both Bob and Thomas) rock bolero that she hoped would bring out the contrast between the city's underbelly, with which she was all too familiar, and its vibrant spiritual culture, which she had only recently come to appreciate. Once they had their food and had taken their seats, she asked him what he thought of the unfinished lyrics and if he thought the ashram residents might like the song.

"Well, I'm no music critic, and even less of a poetry critic, but I think it's pretty uplifting. I think people will like it. I don't know how it will fit with the ashram label—that's up to Kamal and Markandeya to decide—but there has to be a place for songs that take a spiritual look at what's going on out there. Like I said, I'm not a music critic, but it seems to me that if you can evoke compassion at the same time that you elicit tears, then you've really accomplished something, and I think you've done that. I expect it will open up some eyes."

Again the sheepish grin that she wouldn't mind seeing more often. But this time it was backing up words she wouldn't have expected from him a few weeks ago. Were their talks getting to him? She liked to think so. She had been making a conscious effort in that direction, and it was nice to think that she was making inroads, but there was a tone of conviction in his voice, self-conscious and hesitant as it was, that she knew had nothing to do with her. It was entirely his own, and it made her wonder if she were merely watering seeds that had already begun to sprout before she'd arrived on the scene with her dreams and her watering pot.

"I didn't tell you that I used to work in South Central, did I?"

"No," he said, looking surprised.

She nodded. "For almost two years, from the time I left San Rafael almost up until the time I first came to the ashram. That's where the lyrics came from. They're things I've seen with my own eyes ... unfortunately."

Mukunda was barely picking at his food now. It was a comfortable feeling, knowing that her words were falling deep into the wells of his eyes. It wasn't often that she had a chance to converse with someone who was so fully present. Either he was growing in this quality over these past weeks, or she was only now starting to appreciate how fully present he could be.

"San Rafael was great for my music. I got to study the world's oldest and most advanced musical tradition with some of its greatest masters—Zakir Hussein, Nikhil Bannerjee, Swapan Chaudari, and of course Ali Akbar himself. I learned more about music from them in eighteen months than I might have learned in a lifetime had I remained in San Diego. There is no way I'd be the musician I am today if I hadn't gone there. Plus, that's where I started getting interested in spirituality. Just being there changed my whole way of looking at the world. Well, you know as well as anyone, the whole Indian musical tradition is based on spirituality; it's like a spiritual practice for them. They didn't talk about it much but just being around them started opening me up to that side of myself. So pretty much any way I look at it, it was a fantastic experience. But I didn't much like living in San Rafael. It was too upper middle class for my tastes, too comfortable, too Anglo ... too much like La Jolla, actually, in many ways. So when I finished the course I couldn't wait to get out. I wanted to get back to the struggle, get back to fighting for the people, which was always as much or more important to me than the music. It was almost like I had been in exile for a year and a half and it was time to go back home, time to reconnect with my roots—minorities, working class, the poor—time to start hanging out with the oppressed again instead of schmoozing with the privileged. I know that must sound pretty strange, coming from a third-generation middle-class Latina from La Jolla, but I felt like that was the direction I had been moving in all my life and I was getting away from it. Do you know what I mean?"

"I think I do."

"Anyhow, I felt like it was time to get back to who I really was. I never considered going back to San Diego, though. There was only one place I could go: the city of angels, eye of the hurricane. You know, when I was in high school I used to imagine sometimes that I was living in Compton or South Central, taking on the man with my music, stirring up the people. Part of it was all the gangsta rap I was listening to. I was totally into the whole inner-city thing: the language, the voice against injustice, the take-no-prisoners attitude. That was the place where the revolution was going to begin, at least that's what I thought at the time—even though I was about as far from the inner city as a girl could get. Even the year I lived in National City, when I was slumming it with my homeboys, it was still light years from South Central. More like a third-rate knockoff. I found that out quick enough once I started living there. Well, not living there, exactly, but working there. When I got to LA, I found an apartment right above a gay bar in West Hollywood—probably the most politically enlightened place in all of Southern California, by the way, which I really liked—but after about a month I found exactly what I was looking for: a job at the Midcity Youth and Family Center on Vermont, right in the heart of no-man's land between Pico Union and South Central, the Mara Salvatrucha and the 18th Street gang on one side and the Cripps and the Bloods on the other."

"Really? That's pretty serious. What kind of work were you doing?"

"I was working as a counselor and assistant social worker for unwed teenage mothers—70 percent Latina in Los Angeles County, by the way. Almost all of them were involved in one way or another with the gang culture. Either their boyfriends were in a gang or they were in a gang or their brothers were. There was almost no way to avoid it. It would have been like going to France and trying to avoid the French. Good luck. The gangs were why there was such an outbreak of teenage pregnancies in the first place. When you think about it, it makes perfect sense. Why not have a baby at fifteen if there's a good chance your boyfriend won't be alive by the time you're seventeen? Add to that the fact that sexual exploitation of women is an accepted way of life in the hood. That was one part of the songs I never liked, but it was another thing altogether to see it with my own eyes... death and sex. Those were the main presences in a young person's life down there. Especially death. Everybody I worked with had seen their friends die; they'd all attended too many funerals. For them it was just a fact of life: nothing they could do about it, so they might as well live as much as they could in the short time they had. And that meant sex and drugs and the adrenalin rush that comes from having a loaded gun in your pocket and knowing you're ready to use it. At least having a baby is a way for some part of you to live on if you don't make it. I think in some ways it was like being in a permanent war zone, or what I imagine a permanent war zone would be like. The rules change. When you're fighting for your survival any kind of conventional morality goes out the window. Those girls would laugh at you if you even mentioned it, or look at you like they didn't know what you were talking about. They were good Catholics—at least that's the way they thought of themselves—but a lot of things that might seem obvious to you or me just didn't make sense to them under those conditions. If life is going to be that intense and that cruel, then what choice do you have, other than to harden yourself and try to get what you can while you can? Ninety percent of gang members in Pico Union and South Crenshaw are either dead, in prison, or on parole by the time they're twenty. Statistical fact."

She had managed to finish her avocado salad, but she was too unsettled to start on her cheesecake. The memories were too painful, the reality too close to home. She might be living behind the protected, almost enchanted, walls of the ashram, but she could not forget that a few short miles away young women and men that she knew, that she had tried to counsel while they made their way through the minefields that were laid out for them, were still struggling under the same appalling conditions that she had shared with them for a few hours each week. Some of them might be dying as they spoke. Some, she knew, were already dead, having seen their obituaries in the LA Times, it being the first section she turned to when she read the paper, always afraid to see what she might find there but never surprised when she saw a name she recognized. Writing the song had been difficult for her; it had stirred up memories that were still hard to accommodate, but it had been cathartic as well, a way to cast those experiences in a different, wiser light, to infuse them with a spiritual understanding that might one day be the difference between an early death and a dignified life—but only if it was the society at large that was lit with that understanding, for she knew better than anyone that these young people were not at fault for the nightmare they had been born into. It was a product of larger forces that were blind to the victims they created.

"There was this one girl I was working with, Mariana."

"Mariana? That's the same name as the girl in your song."

"That's because it's the same girl.

Mariana had been barely seventeen when Gita first met her, a scarred but determined young woman who was in many ways far older and far wiser than she was. At that age Mariana already had two young children and one dead boyfriend, the father of her second child; he had been killed in a drive-by while entering a 7-Eleven in what cops from the Rampart Division CRASH unit—thought by many to be the biggest and baddest gang of them all, responsible for its own enviable share of murder, mayhem, and terror, as well as hundreds of false arrests—labeled a "random retaliatory attack." The boy had been with him at the time. From the testimony of eyewitnesses, he had tried to shield the child from the automatic weapon fire but the one-year-old had taken a bullet to the face. He survived the operation, though they couldn't save his eye or reverse the partial facial paralysis, but Mariana sometimes wondered aloud if it wouldn't have been better had he died, considering what he had to look forward to: early recruitment by his uncle into the 18th Street gang and a justifiable lifelong hatred of the Mara Salvatrucha, who had left him disfigured and his father dead. And nothing she could do to shield him, short of fleeing everything and everyone she knew for a life of grinding poverty on some unknown city street.

"Mariana was one of my first clients. She taught me how to see the world through her eyes, about as painful lesson as I've ever had, but I had to thank her for it. She made me give up a lot of my illusions and that made me a better person. After I got to know Mariana, the cause stopped being 'the people' and started becoming actual people, Marianas and Cecilias and Patricias and Pacos, people I cared about and worried about. It wasn't easy, having to see what they had to go through every day just to stay alive and keep their families together. Mariana lived in this rundown little tenement, just south of Pico—her and her mother, her three younger brothers and sisters, her own kids, and a cousin. One bathroom, a tiny kitchen, and barely enough room for everyone to lie down at night. But she never complained about it. All she talked about with me was what she could do to help her family... that and the terrible things she'd seen. That girl had more courage and more street sense in her little finger than I'll ever have in my lifetime. What advice could I give her? Tell her to take her kids to Mendocino County and live on the street? I did what I could to help, of course, but there was only so much I could do, for any of them—help them get food stamps, maybe a job referral or daycare for their kids, or just a shoulder to cry on when they needed one. At the time I didn't have the spiritual perspective that I have now. I wish I did. I think I could have helped a whole lot more. That's what I was thinking about when I started writing the song. I was thinking that maybe she might hear it one day and it would help her look at her life in a way that made sense, and maybe some of the other girls as well. I guess it was a kind of catharsis, a way to somehow go back and give her what I couldn't give her then. But as I was working on it, I started wondering if maybe I couldn't help other people to see the world through her eyes, like she'd taught me to do. Then maybe they would also want to help. Maybe they would realize that her eyes are also our eyes, that we're all in this together, and if one of us suffers like that, then we all do. I don't know, I just wish we could find a way to put an end to all that unnecessary misery."

"Maybe your song will help."

"I would love to think so, Mukunda, but from where I sit it looks a lot like trying to take down a mountain with a plastic shovel. This country is rolling in money. Just look at the Fortune 500 and their profit ledgers. The rich have so much money they literally don't know what to do with it. The one thing they do know is how to keep it out of the hands of the people who really need it. That they've been practicing all their lives, and their fathers and grandfathers before them, and they're not going to stop now because some crazy little do-gooder's song comes on the radio. One stroll down Crenshaw Boulevard will tell you that much. The one thing I've always wanted to do with my music was to open up people's eyes and hearts to all the injustice that's going down on this planet. The people who live in South Central aren't responsible for the conditions they live in. Society is responsible for that, specifically the people who control society, the rich and the powerful. They're the ones who are really responsible for what Mariana has to go through each day. Her brothers and cousins may be gang members and criminals, but what are their crimes compared to the crime of treason against humanity that men of wealth and political power commit every day all over the globe while they pretend to be the guardians and benefactors of the human race? Answer me that. These people who play with millions of dollars every day like it was paper money, like it's some game they're playing, while mothers like Mariana a few miles down the road are worrying how they are going to feed their kids or clothe them or send them to school, a school where they are as likely to be assaulted as to learn how to read. Where is the justice in that? Where is the humanity? It would be nice if people like you listened to my song and if it meant something to them, but after everything I've seen, I'm convinced that the only way my music could make any real difference at all is if it somehow got into the boardrooms and the chauffeured limousines. That is, provided the people who ride in those limousines actually have human hearts."

"It could happen, Gita. All it takes is one corporate executive with an iPod and a conscience; who knows if your song doesn't convince him to make a donation to some foundation that benefits hundreds or even thousands of people. Art can do that. It can be that powerful, you know. And you never know, it may well be the people who come to the ashram and who listen to your music who will take it into the boardrooms—or at least the sentiments you stir up in them."

Gita looked at Mukunda in surprise. She had always thought of him as forgivingly naive, too starry-eyed to see the world for what it was but too good-hearted to be blamed for it. And yet what he said made perfect sense. Didn't someone once show that if you added up all the contacts that one person had with other people, and then all the contacts that each of them had with other people, you were only six persons removed from every other person in the world? Perhaps the emotions stirred by a song could send ripples that would then send out other ripples. She had read in one of Gurudeva's books that artists were at the vanguard of all the great social upheavals, right behind the great spiritual masters. She had always believed that, or at least had wanted to believe it, though she had never felt herself to be in the vanguard of anything—closer to a voice crying in the wilderness, heard only by people just as lost or as marginalized as she. But maybe those crying voices, when they were added together, could raise a cry that could make itself heard in the city, that could remind people that there was no greater wilderness than concrete and glass when you failed to take care of the human beings who lived there. One thing she must not do, however, was let herself get as starry-eyed as Mukunda. She had warned herself about this more than once these past weeks, as she felt the growing allure of his beguiling optimism, and she felt the need of warning herself once again.

"You may be right, Mukunda. I hope you are. But for now, as long as

South Central and Pico Union continue to be the South Central and Pico Union that I know, then nothing we do up here will have any lasting significance. Nothing we do anywhere will, anywhere on the globe. As long as people are forced to live under inhuman conditions, robbed of human dignity by a society that is supposed to nurture them, then we have nothing to congratulate ourselves for. Doesn't the spiritual philosophy say that we are all one?"

"It does."

"Then we are all responsible for Mariana; we are responsible for what she has had to go through and for what her children will have to go through. Until we put an end to that kind of oppression, we have nothing to be proud of. We can only be ashamed."

Mukunda didn't say anything but he didn't need to. She could see it in his eyes, in the suggestion of a tear that caught the reflected light of the midday sun. She had never seen him so thoughtful, and it made her grow even more reflective. He had to return to the Bungalow but she remained there, nursing the last morsels of her cheesecake. She could not enjoy it as she had hoped to. The sorrows and hardships of the young people she had counseled had left a bitter taste in her mouth that no dessert could remove. She hummed again the melody of the chorus she had sung for Mukunda, reminding herself through her own words that there was a divine purpose behind everything, a benevolent hand at work even in the underside of life, a turning toward the light that time could only postpone but never annul. Maybe Mukunda was right. Maybe she would do something for Mariana before she was through. Maybe even from up here in these hills.

7

When Markandeya phoned Mukunda to tell him that he wouldn't be going for morning walk but that he did need to talk to him while Gurudeva was out, Mukunda's first reaction was disappointment: he knew right away that he would likely miss his walk with Gita that morning, and their walks had become the highlight of his week, alongside Gurudeva's Sunday darshan and those rare, unexpected moments with the master when he forgot for a few minutes that he was PA and could fall back into simply being a disciple. But when he began to wonder why Markandeya wanted to talk to him, a sense of disquiet overtook him. It continued through breakfast while Markandeya waited for him in his room, the older man insisting that there was no hurry—he should eat his breakfast first and then they would talk.

When he returned to his room a few minutes later—more of an office really, where he kept his clothes, his sleeping bag, and his yoga mat—Markandeya was sitting behind Mukunda's desk, thumbing through some of the books from the adjoining bookshelf. Open on the desk were several spiritual classics, *The Gospel of Sri Ramakrishna* and Gopi Krishna's *Kundalini* among them; in his hand was Swami Rama's *Living with the Himalayan Masters*. Markandeya put the book down and swiveled the chair around while Mukunda set down a glass of orange juice on the desk and pulled up the spare stool he kept in a corner.

"So, Mukunda, I suppose you're wondering why I wanted to talk to you."

"Does it have anything to do with Gurudeva's visits to the clinic this week?"

Markandeya looked surprised, but he followed with a smile, a rather wan smile that did nothing to lessen Mukunda's sense of foreboding.

"That's very perceptive of you, but then I suppose I should have expected no less. Yes, it does have to do with his doctor's visits this past week. First of all, I don't want you to get alarmed. It's nothing life threatening or anything like that, but Gurudeva does have a medical condition that is going to bear watching from now on. As his PA, you need to be properly informed about it; you need to know what steps are going to be necessary to maintain Gurudeva's health."

Markandeya paused, but when Mukunda didn't say anything he continued.

"About a week after Gurudeva's checkup, Bruce Remmler called. As you probably know he's an old friend; we get together from time to time to play tennis. He wanted to talk to me about the results of the checkup. Do you remember that sinusitis problem Gurudeva had a while back? Well, as a precaution, Bruce had an MRI done to get a look at the soft tissue in the upper sinus cavities—one of the reasons I started bringing Gurudeva to him some years back, other than him being a top-flight physician, is because his clinic is so well equipped; you have an imaging center right there in the same building. Anyhow, when the MRI came back it showed what looked like a growth on the surface of the brain behind the sinus and eye cavities, on the meninges, to be exact. Bruce sent the results to a friend of his at Cedars-Sinai, Ralph Mordicai, and also to another friend at Harvard Medical—both of them top-rate neurooncologists, specialists in exactly this type of growth—and they concurred with his initial diagnosis: what they call a meningioma. Technically, it is a type of tumor, but it's almost always benign. Malignant meningiomas, in fact, are quite rare. So then Bruce set up an appointment with Ralph at Cedars-Sinai for further testing. That's where we took Gurudeva on Thursday."

Mukunda felt himself grow numb. A brain tumor? How could that be? He tried to steady himself, but he could hear his voice cracking as he asked Markandeya if the doctor at Cedars-Sinai had given a prognosis.

"I know it's a shock, Mukunda, but like I said, there's no reason to be alarmed. None at all. Yesterday we met with Dr. Mordicai and Bruce at Bruce's office. The tests they did at Cedars-Sinai confirmed Bruce's original diagnosis: it's what they call a medial sphenoid wing meningioma, in effect, a benign tumor. Dr. Mordicai gave us a good deal of literature on it, and I've been doing my own research these last few days. It was a shock for me, too, believe me, when Bruce first called, but I feel a lot better about it now that I'm better informed. The mortality rate for this kind of tumor is less than 1 percent. Okay? And that's when surgery is indicated. There are a certain number of people that never have to undergo surgery at all, and there's a good chance that Gurudeva will fall into that category. I'll try to explain it to you as they explained it to me and then you can read the literature."

Markandeya took out a small sheaf of papers and some pamphlets from his satchel and set them down on the desk.

"First of all, benign meningiomas are not cancer. They're more like a cyst that grows on the surface of the brain, though they don't really know why or how they start. A meningioma is a little different from a normal cyst because the brain is involved. If it continues to grow, it can end up compressing the brain tissue because the cranium doesn't allow it any room to expand outward. This can obviously lead to neurological problems; it can even prove fatal if it's left untreated. Fortunately, in those cases, as long as the meningioma is accessible—as it is in Gurudeva's case—it can easily be removed, and with the advances in microsurgery and radiosurgery the success rate for this type of meningioma resection is now about ninety-nine percent.

"Now, that's when surgery is indicated. In Gurudeva's case he's asymptomatic. They won't know what the growth rate is until they've had a chance to monitor it for a while, but in his case it hasn't gotten to the point where it's started to cause any observable symptoms. Because of its location, right near the orbital cavity, the first symptoms are usually visual problems. In more severe cases it can cause edema in the nearby tissues—a fluid buildup—and that can lead to other types of neurological problems, even seizures, but as I said, in his case there are no symptoms, and there may never be. Dr. Mordicai is considered to be one of the leading experts in the treatment of meningiomas, and he says that as long as the patient is asymptomatic or has only mild symptoms, then the recommended course of action is to keep him under careful observation until such a time that surgery becomes necessary. He wants him to have a monthly checkup and MRI. For now that will be at Cedars-Sinai, but eventually he'll be able to have his checkup at Dr. Remmler's office, once they have a good idea of the growth rate of the tumor—six months, a year at most. After that he can go to quarterly or even biannual visits. As long as Gurudeva stays asymptomatic, and as long as there's no significant growth of the tumor, then there's no reason to operate. According to Dr. Mordicai, these meningiomas can be very slow growing; it's not that unusual, he said, for an asymptomatic patient of Gurudeva's age to never need an operation. Fifteen, even twenty years can go by and the person dies of old age in their bed without ever having to have an operation, especially patients who have a healthy, low-stress lifestyle. And no one has a healthier lifestyle than Gurudeva. We're going to need to be careful, but the chances are he'll never need anything more than a few visits each year to the clinic for an MRI."

Mukunda had recovered by now from his initial shock. The idea that Gurudeva could have a brain tumor still seemed almost incomprehensible, but the fact that he was in no immediate danger, and might never be, was enough to help him calm his rampaging emotions. His first question for Markandeya was to ask how Gurudeva was taking the news.

"Gurudeva? As you can imagine: no change whatsoever. You should have seen him these last two visits. He was joking with the doctors, talking about how meditation affects the brain, discussing neurooncology like a medical savant, giving them a crash course in Ayurveda—how the ancient Ayurvedic doctors invented surgery, how they treated similar conditions, what they attributed the causes to for brain tumors and a score of other conditions. They were enchanted with him. The nurses, the receptionist, everyone."

"I could have guessed. So now, tell me, what do you need me to do?"

"Well, first of all, Dr. Mordicai emphasized that the two most important factors in assuring a positive outcome are maintaining a stress-free lifestyle and an optimistic outlook. We don't have to worry about an optimistic outlook, obviously, but we are going to have to limit any external stressors. I had a long talk with Dr. Mordicai about Gurudeva's daily lifestyle. The two things he was most concerned about were his public programs—retreats especially, but also Sunday darshan and morning walk—and any administrative burdens he might have. We called an emergency board meeting two days ago and we've already taken steps to relieve Gurudeva of any administrative stress. You don't have to worry about that. But we will need to start scaling down his regular routine. I think the days of Gurudeva giving shaktipat to five hundred disciples are over, and in general we're going to have to scale down the retreats, at least his participation in them. Dr. Mordicai said it would be better to eliminate any long or strenuous walks, so we'll need to sit and go over the venues for morning walk. For instance, the hiking trails at Griffith Park—we'll need to cut them from the schedule. He can still go on morning walk but he shouldn't be climbing any mountains. We'll also need to limit the time he spends for Sunday darshan. No more two-hour talks."

"How are you going to do that? Do you really think Gurudeva is going to accept these restrictions?"

"Leave that to me, Mukunda, to me and the rest of the board members. We'll talk to Gurudeva about it and we'll make the necessary arrangements. You'll just need to keep on top of it, that's all. Remind him whenever necessary, especially if one of us is not there. There may be some occasions when it gets a little difficult, but you'll just have to be firm. I'll be counting on you for this. We'll all be.

"Now, here's a list of possible symptoms should the tumor continue to grow and press on the surrounding tissue. Memorize it and keep a close eye on Gurudeva. From time to time ask him about his eyesight and so on. We'll also be keeping tabs on him, but you're the one who is closest to him during the day. If you notice anything, anything at all, call me or Madalasa immediately and we'll schedule an exam.

"The next thing is that you'll need to call the senior disciples—here's the list—and tell them that Gurudeva has summoned them for an extremely important meeting this Sunday at three. You should get on it right away so they have time to make their plans. Many of them are already aware of the situation, but if anyone asks what the meeting's about, tell them to contact either myself or Madalasa for more information; don't volunteer anything. As far as the rest of the disciples are concerned, Gurudeva doesn't want anybody else to know about his condition until he is ready. Okay? If anybody comes to you and asks about Gurudeva's health, or tells you they've heard something, you don't know anything. If they want to, they can talk to me. Until Sunday it's business as usual. That means no long faces, nothing out of the ordinary. Go about your business as if you hadn't heard a thing."

Mukunda didn't see how he was going to do that, but he didn't mention this to Markandeya. After the senior disciple had left, he sat in the chair behind his desk and stared out the window. A pair of sparrows was sporting among the hanging plants on the veranda, but their restive frolic barely registered on his consciousness. All he could think about was how one conversation could so radically alter his life. Nothing had changed except his perspective. Gurudeva's tumor had been there yesterday, had likely been there since before he had become PA, but he knew that from now on nothing would be the same. From now on there would always be a hint of mortality in the air, an awareness that his time with the master was limited, that it would one day come to an end—if not today then tomorrow. Reluctantly he reached for the phone and started dialing the first number on the list, conscious that a few devotees had begun singing once again outside the gate. He was nearly finished with the list when he heard the shouts of "*Gurudeva ki jai*" that signaled the master's return.

A few minutes later, after he had accompanied Gurudeva to his room and brought him a fresh pitcher of water in preparation for lunch, Mukunda worked up the nerve to broach the subject of his condition.

"Yes, I asked Markandeya to brief you this morning," Gurudeva said, seemingly paying little attention to the question. "So, what has Ganesh prepared for lunch today?"

After Mukunda related what was on the menu, he returned hesitatingly to the subject. "Gurudeva, I was thinking that maybe we should limit morning walk to one or two days a week."

Gurudeva looked surprised. "Limit morning walk? Why?"

"I just thought…"

Gurudeva smiled and a gleam came into his eye. "Here, Mukunda, sit down. No, here, beside me. Now listen. I have always been aware that my stay on this earth was only temporary. There is nothing remarkable or tragic about that. I will walk tomorrow morning as I walk every morning, as I have walked every morning since before you were born, and as I will continue walking every morning as long as my body is physically able to walk. Nothing has changed. And anyhow, I am not going anywhere, not just yet. Remember one thing, Mukunda: nothing is ever as it seems."

Mukunda felt part of the cloud lift from his heart. Gurudeva's smile was the same as it had always been: it still sent a sliver of pure sunshine straight through him. Nothing *had* changed. Though he might not yet be able to see it that way, he knew that Gurudeva would make him see it that way eventually.

"Now you go see to my lunch. We'll have no more of this talk and no long faces. Markandeya has given you your instructions. Follow them. Have you called the senior disciples and informed them of the meeting?"

"Yes, Gurudeva, all but a few."

"Then go and finish your work. You still have twenty minutes before you need to serve my lunch."

The following morning everything seemed exactly as it did on every other morning. Gurudeva left for morning walk with his regular coterie and the half dozen other disciples that Mukunda had added to the list for that day; when the remaining disciples dispersed, Gita was waiting by the gate, her guitar leaning against the iron trellis where it would be watched by the gatekeeper. He smiled what he hoped was his usual smile, and they took off for the hiking trails behind the Bungalow, a circuit they normally completed in just over an hour, bringing him back in plenty of time for a late breakfast before Gurudeva's return. His smile, however, was not nearly as disarming as he'd hoped, for no sooner had they reached the edge of the initial descent into the canyon than Gita asked him what was wrong. He wasn't surprised. In the last few weeks an intimacy had sprung up between them that had surpassed any of his other relationships. He had shared with her things he had shared with no one else—up to and including the sense of spiritual frustration that had clouded so many of his moments these past months—and she had shared with him feelings so intimate he felt sure that she had bared her soul to him as she had bared it to no one else. Their friendship had come upon him so suddenly and progressed so rapidly that he felt disoriented by the changes, almost giddy at times, but he had only to remind himself that he had known her all his life to remember that this was also part of the unseen but perfectly choreographed pattern of his life.

And so, whatever reservations he had about maintaining secrecy were quickly swept away by his need to share with her this happening that had altered the ground on which he stood. As they descended into the small canyon and then up into the hills beyond, Gita listened silently and attentively—listened, he felt, as much to the timorous whisperings of his heart as to the words that conveyed the outward facts of Gurudeva's condition. The few questions she asked were delicate and perceptive enough to show how complete her attention was, and it wasn't until she asked him if he wanted to sit for a few minutes—as they were cresting a grassy knoll just before coming in sight of the Bungalow once again, a place where they had halted once or twice on previous walks—that she shared with him her own feelings.

"I wouldn't dare claim to know the reasons a realized being does what he does, but I can't help wonder if maybe Gurudeva isn't using this, or is going to use it, as a way to remind us how ephemeral life is—and for that reason, how precious every moment is. While you were talking, I think I felt some of the same feelings you felt yesterday: shock at first, then a realization that I can't take anything for granted anymore—like there's no guarantee how long Gurudeva will be with us, so I'd better not waste this opportunity I've been given?—and maybe a little fear about my own mortality mixed in as well. It's so easy to forget how temporary everything is—how momentary, you know? But if everything is so temporary, shouldn't we use every moment as wisely as we can and appreciate it as fully as we can? Isn't that a big part of what it means to become spiritually aware? I wouldn't be surprised at all if Gurudeva means to use his condition as a teaching tool. I wonder if that wasn't what he was hinting at when he said that nothing is as it seems. Didn't you say that he had a special gleam in his eye at that moment?"

"He did. In fact, afterward I was convinced that this was part of some special plan he has that he wasn't ready to tell anyone about yet. But that wasn't enough to get rid of the sinking feeling in my stomach."

"I know what you mean; I feel the same way. But maybe that's just a sign that we need to be more mature about the whole thing. I was reading in one of Gurudeva's books the other day that a devotee should treat everything that happens to her as a lesson from the Divine. I know it's a truism, but once we get over the shock, shouldn't we be trying to understand what he's trying to teach us and do our best to learn it?"

How many months had Gita been meditating? Seven? Eight? How long had she even been interested in spirituality? Not a whole lot longer. Yet despite the gulf between his experience and hers, she had reminded him of something he knew but had managed to forget. Rather than feel piqued in any way, he felt a glow of pride, almost as if by this she had justified their sudden, disorienting friendship. She might have only been meditating for eight months, but he could see now that she possessed an innate spiritual understanding that he had completely overlooked. She was a special soul. Her charisma was not merely in her voice or her musical talent; it was in the spirit that breathed life into the notes she sang, a spirit that was perhaps only now reawakening to a long-submerged but never completely hidden spiritual sensibility. He felt proud of her, proud that she was his friend; for the first time he wondered if perhaps there was a reason why they had been born two months and two houses apart, a reason that he had been too blind to see, that maybe they were picking up where they had left off an unknown time ago.

At a quarter to three on Sunday, the senior disciples began trooping upstairs to the master's sitting room. Mukunda had repositioned Gurudeva's recliner against the far wall, just beside the door that opened into his bedroom. He had cleared the other pieces of furniture from the room and draped a large batik bedsheet over the TV and sound system. He had also brought extra cushions from the main hall and a spare harmonium. Satisfied that everything was ready, he took up his position by the master's door and watched as the disciples took their seats, thirty of them in all, including the eight board members who oversaw all aspects of ashram administration and made whatever executive decisions needed to be made, except on those rare occasions, such as this one, when Gurudeva called for a meeting with all the senior disciples and asked for their input. Gurudeva was the board chairman, the ninth member, but he never attended board meetings, being content to read the minutes afterward and give his input when he met individually with the different members, as he did regularly every week or two.

At one minute past the hour, the door to the master's room opened and Mukunda escorted him the few feet to his chair. The disciples began filing past one by one to touch the master's feet and receive his blessing. When they were settled once again on their cushions, Gurudeva called for a bhajan, which Kamal sang with what Mukunda perceived to be an unusually poignant air. Thereafter they closed their eyes for a few minutes' meditation, until the master filled the silence with his confident basso drawl, intoning the traditional Sanskrit verse.

"It has been some time since we have all been gathered here together, you and I," he began, after surveying the faces in front of him with his usual serene smile and faultless composure. "You are my elite disciples, the ones I have chosen to assist me with my work and to carry it on when I am gone. Thousands of devotees come to this ashram. They come and they go, but those of you sitting in this room are the one constant in this endless flow, the first faces I see whenever I give darshan. So it is only fitting that what I have to say today is said in front of you and not in front of the general ashram public. It is you, after all, that it concerns most.

"First of all, I think you are all aware of recent developments concerning my health. The way news travels in this ashram, I suspect some of you knew even before I did. Nevertheless, I will ask Markandeya to give a short summation."

Gurudeva chuckled lightly at his own joke and leaned back in his recliner, resting his arms on the armrests, his feet hidden under the folds of his tunic. Markandeya rose and went to stand by the side of Gurudeva's chair. He briefly described the master's condition and related the prognosis given by the doctors. There were a few barely audible whispers among the disciples that died down again as soon as Gurudeva resumed speaking.

"So that is what the doctors say. But what does Gurudeva say? First of all, I am going to be around for a long time yet. You will not be free of me so soon. However, this development is a signal that my mission has reached a critical juncture. We are entering a new phase in our work together. This is a day that I have been waiting for and planning for, for a long time. A very long time.

"The other day on morning walk Rajeshwar asked me a question, a very pertinent question. He asked me if the world would remember me in a thousand years. I told him that the world would not only remember me in a thousand years, the world would remember him in a thousand years. For the better part of three decades I have been building up this ashram and guiding all of you in your spiritual life. However, if any of you thought that my only purpose in being here was to lead my direct disciples to enlightenment, then it is time for you to reassess your thinking. My relationship with my direct disciples and my commitment to their eventual enlightenment is a significant part of my mission on this planet, but it is only one aspect of that mission. There is a greater purpose for which I have been building up this ashram and training all of you with such single-mindedness. A new age is about to dawn. The darkness of the Kali Yuga, the age of materialism and spiritual decline, is drawing to a close, and the light of the Satya Yuga, the golden age, is getting ready to flood the horizon. This ashram and my disciples will play a major role in laying the spiritual foundations of the coming era. A new spiritual consciousness is in the process of being born that will sweep away the skeletons of the past and bring fresh life to humanity. You will be the midwives in the birth of this new consciousness, the vanguard of the sweeping changes that this planet will soon witness, the ones humanity will remember centuries from now when everyone else has been forgotten."

Murmurs passed through the room as the disciples looked at each other and back again at Gurudeva.

"Rajeshwar also asked me why I didn't have more followers, why we were still relatively unknown compared to the organized religions or the Sai Babas of the world. The simple answer is that they belong to the past and I belong to the future. The past cannot understand me; only the future can. I have come to put an end to the past; and you have come for that same reason, to be my instruments in this monumental work.

"Think for a moment. Why is it, that out of the more than six billion people on this planet, you are with me at this moment, in this room? I want you to reflect on this for a minute, reflect on just how miraculous it is. Six billion people on planet Earth, but you, specifically, are the ones chosen by fate to be sitting here with me at this critical juncture in time. Why have you had the great fortune to receive my teachings and be receptive to them while the rest of humanity continues to labor in the dark? There is a mystery here. You may not be able to unravel that mystery at this time, but a day will come when you will. For now, all I will say is that each of you has agreed to play a particular role in the unfolding of this drama, a role that I have chosen for you. You should remember this and cherish it, because of all the countless souls wandering this planet, you alone have been chosen; otherwise, you would not be sitting in this room today.

"From now on, the focus of our work together will start turning toward the future. Though I will be with you for quite some time yet, my stay on this planet is, nonetheless, temporary. This has always been the case, whether or not you were fully conscious of the fact. The events of the past couple of weeks have only served to bring this into relief, to imprint it on your consciousness. You must prepare yourselves to carry on my work when I am gone. If you had not been thinking about this before, then it is time to start doing so. You must be ready to pick up the banner and carry it forward. This will be the focus of our time together in the coming years. Think of today as the first step on that road.

"Now, since you are my elite disciples, those of you in this room and those who are waiting in the wings, you will have to learn to work together. You must learn this now, while I am still here, so that you do not break apart when I am gone. You are a team, and as with any team, each one is of equal importance, each one has a different role to play, but no team can ultimately be successful unless everyone plays their role and plays it well. Every team must also have a leader, a captain, someone who can coordinate its efforts and make a final decision when final decisions must be made. For the time being, I am the captain of this team, but someone will have to take over when I am gone. That person will be my successor. When he or she gets older they will choose their successor, and in this way the mantle will pass from generation to generation, long after we have all become figures in the pages of history. Next Sunday we will meet again here in the afternoon, and in that meeting I shall name my successor. After that I will begin training him or her to take over for me when I am gone and carry the work of the ashram into the future. But before then I want to emphasize one thing: You are a team. One person will lead after I am gone, but you will all be of equal importance. I have chosen all of you for this work, and I will be depending on all of you to work together to bring about the birth of this new spiritual consciousness. I have come on a mission, but it will be you, all of you, acting in concert, who will fulfill that mission. This is my hope and this is my promise."

For more than a minute an unearthly silence reigned in the room. Everyone seemed stunned. Finally Gurudeva broke the silence by asking if anyone had any questions. His voice was playful and his smile as mischievous as Mukunda had seen it, despite the seeming gravity of the situation. At first everyone seemed hesitant, but after Abhay voiced a question it was like a spigot had been turned on. The discussion continued for nearly an hour but Mukunda only half listened to the animated interchange between the master and his disciples. Throughout that time his mind continued to swirl with the revelation of Gurudeva's words.

Mukunda had heard the master talk many times about the Kali Yuga. He had advised the disciples in his discourses that humanity had reached a point of maximum spiritual degeneration. He had assured them that this age of darkness would be followed by the radiant dawn of the Satya Yuga. But he had never revealed so clearly the purpose of his incarnation. Never had he admitted that he had come to usher in this golden age of spirituality—nor that he had come with his team. If Rajeshwar would be remembered after a thousand years, what did that say about him, the master's PA? Or about Leela, Markandeya, Madalasa, and the rest? Those who had brought Gurudeva to the West and those who had come to occupy the principal places by his side. It was a revelation that was difficult to assimilate. For a moment he tried to think of his own place in history, but his mind balked at the thought. It was simply too hard to picture himself as a historical figure. But Gurudeva? Yes, it made perfect sense. There was no greater spiritual figure on the planet to his knowledge. His coming to America? Again it made perfect sense. Where better to begin the spiritual revolution than from these heights overlooking the city that had come to dominate the American consciousness, the cultural center of the one country more than any other that held the world's fate in its hands. His mind began to reel with images of the future, some of them with Gurudeva still among them, most of them further into the future, the master's picture by then a symbol of the teachings that were leading humanity into a new era, an era of spiritual understanding and human cooperation, an end to the wars, to the grinding exploitation, to the poverty and oppression that so affected Gita's spirit and sparked her aspirations with thoughts of a long-overdue revolution. It was dizzying to think about; and so the better part of Gurudeva's conversation with the disciples passed him by unnoticed.

The final question was again Abhay's. He wanted to clarify one aspect of Gurudeva's instructions for how they should prepare the rest of the disciples for the following Sunday when the master would announce his successor during the evening darshan. Mukunda paid attention for a few moments but again his mind drifted. Whomever Gurudeva chose to be his successor, it did not seem of much importance to him at that moment. Whoever it was, whether Markandeya or Madalasa or any of the other senior disciples, it was not going to change anything. Gurudeva was going to be around for a long time yet, as he himself had affirmed; and as long as he was physically present he would be pulling the strings. As he had hinted at during his talk, he had come with a plan that only he was privy to. Mukunda was confident that the rest of them would continue to remain in the dark for a long time to come. But even this did not matter. For the dark was always followed by the light; in this case that light would reveal the purpose of their lives, the hidden reason why they had been born into this world, the buried jewel of destiny that he had been searching for as long as he could remember.

8

Gita watched from the shade of the tamarind tree as the last of the three cars disappeared out the main gate. The third car had been added a couple of days earlier to accommodate the influx of senior disciples who were staying at the ashram for the week. Despite the unsettling news about Gurudeva's condition, there was an aura of excitement in the air. The uncertainty about the master's health, the buzz about his announcement that he would choose his successor on Sunday, the crowd of senior disciples that seemed to be hovering perpetually in or around the Bungalow—all added to the feeling that momentous happenings were afoot, happenings that would decide the future of the ashram and thus play a smaller or greater role in the destiny of each disciple. Unfortunately, the whirl of motion around the Bungalow also meant that Mukunda was far busier than usual. They had yet to take their regular walk this week. She had managed to talk to him a couple of times in the aftermath of morning walk, but that was the only time they had spent together. She was hopeful that today would be different, but if it wasn't, she knew that everything would settle down after Sunday. Then they could have that conversation she had been putting off.

She glanced over at Mukunda. He was standing by the gate with a harried look on his face, talking to a group of senior disciples. Poor guy. Everybody wanted a piece of him. She doubted he'd had a moment's respite all week. No, this was not the time, even if he could get away for a short walk. Better to wait until Monday, or maybe Tuesday, after everything had calmed down. Then she could tell him how she felt and see if her feelings were reciprocated, though she was sure they were, no matter how different ashram culture might be from the rest of the known world. They had reached a level of intimacy these past few weeks that she had never experienced before—it still amazed her that there was nothing physical about it (so far, at least). In fact, it was precisely that aspect of their relationship, strangely enough, that she found most gratifying. Even her best and longest-lasting relationship—with a jazz guitarist she had met at UCSD and then followed to San Rafael—had gradually disintegrated when the romance and the sex no longer proved sufficient glue to keep them together. Somewhere along the way they had come to the common realization that what had kept them together after the romance had simmered down was equal parts habit and convenience. Whatever that deeper connection was that could exist between two people, it was clearly missing. She had once thought of it as "love," but that wasn't the word, at least not by itself. If anything, it was more a sense of shared destiny, a sense that the sum of two intertwined paths would prove far greater than the disparate fates that her relationship with Carlos had devolved into over time. With Mukunda there had been no chance to set a match to whatever mutual passion was fermenting below the surface, but even in its absence—or perhaps, in part, because of its absence—she had seen that sense of shared destiny flower into an intimacy that had opened doors she had not known were there. Together they had visited places inside her psyche that she had never visited before, places she could not have reached without his presence as a catalytic agent, and she could sense that the same was true for him. The fact that they had gotten there without the catalyzing impetus of passion was not only an unexpected and gratifying achievement—it made their relationship feel as solid and as lasting as the earth beneath her feet. There were no illusions to be wary of, no leaning on sensual bliss in the hopes that it would one day blossom into a deeper kind of intimacy. They had already crossed that bridge and they had done it alone and unaided. The passion would ignite one day, she was sure of that, but there was no need to hurry it along, especially when she knew there was always a risk it could burn away the foundations they had laid. Who knows, maybe by then the passion would only be an afterthought, a bit of sweet, ethereal smoothness for the palate—like the Buddha Café's otherworldly cheesecake—after a substantial and nutritious meal that was all a body really needed. For a moment, the thought crossed her mind, as it had many times before, that this could still be just another fantasy, but she immediately brushed it away. The disciples had dispersed by now and she could see Mukunda smiling at her from across the drive. His smile was her invitation to the dance and more than enough to banish any lingering doubts.

"I'm glad you waited," he said, as she crossed the drive and met his obvious pleasure at seeing her with an equal measure of her own. "It seems as if I'm actually free this morning—for once—although I'm sure I won't be if I hang around here any longer than necessary. What do you say we take a walk up Topanga Canyon Boulevard? That way there's less chance anybody can find me while I'm gone."

Gita smiled and nodded in reply. Nothing could have pleased her more. "It's been really crazy, huh?" she asked, as they headed toward the gate.

"It hasn't stopped since Sunday. Gurudeva's been meeting with the board members and the other senior disciples from morning till night. I've been spending most of my time waiting outside his door in case he calls for somebody. If I can't get them on the phone, then I have to go run and find them. When I'm not doing that, I'm bringing refreshments, taking notes, sending messages, you name it. This is the first time since Sunday that Gurudeva or Markandeya or one of the other senior disciples didn't give me some assignment to do while Gurudeva was out on walk; and if I wait around I'm sure somebody will find something for me to do. I've never seen it so hectic around here, not even close. On a normal day Gurudeva will give one, maybe two private audiences in the afternoon. Three or four nights a week he'll meet with a board member or two. If one of the senior disciples is staying the night he'll usually fit him in also, but it's always totally relaxed. But as soon as the doctors say he has to take it easy, he revs up the engine to full speed. With Gurudeva you can never predict what's going to happen. There's no use in even trying."

They had passed the gate and had started heading up the hill. They crossed the arch bridge that spanned Topanga Creek and continued up the road, careful to keep an eye out for the intermittent traffic. By now Mukunda's face had lost its harried expression. He seemed to grow freer and more relaxed with each step.

"I used to love walking up here when I was young," he told her. "I bet I know the Santa Monica Hills better than anyone who lives on this road. God knows how many hours I've spent on the hiking trails around here. It was like my own private paradise when I used to come up here as a kid; once I got off the road and into the hills I hardly ever ran across another living soul. When I think about it now, though, I wonder why more people don't come up here. LA probably has more tons of poured concrete than any city in the world, and this is one of the few places in striking distance where you can get away from it all, but no one ever comes here. Strange, don't you think?"

"I think a lot of people aren't even really aware that Topanga Canyon exists. If it weren't for the ashram, it would probably still just be a name on the map to me."

"Speaking of the ashram, how is the proletariat taking the news? The only people I've had a chance to talk to this week are the senior disciples."

"Everybody's concerned about Gurudeva's health, of course—by now everybody and their mother seems to be an expert on medial sphenoid wing meningiomas. From what I've heard, the prognosis is good. Gurudeva will likely never need an operation. But if he does, there is a 90 percent probability, by popular reckoning, that he will use his spiritual power to cure himself."

Mukunda laughed. "Well, that's good to hear. I hadn't actually heard that."

"I also heard something about Rajeshwar becoming famous one day, and some of the other senior disciples. Does that include Mukunda?"

"Well, of course! I shan't deny it. But let's keep it between you and me. I want to preserve my anonymity as long as humanly possible... Here, let's cross the street. You see that sycamore there? There's a cool hiking trail that starts just behind it. If you follow it for about twenty minutes you come to a hidden canyon where I once found the nest of a California condor."

"You're kidding!"

"God's honest truth. I was twelve years old and it was the greatest discovery I had ever made—after meditation, that is. Come, I'll show you where it was. We have enough time. It's a great place to sit and talk, or just be quiet; the view is spectacular. We can hang out there for a little while, if you like, and still make it back in time for Gurudeva."

As they walked up the trail, disappearing into a solitary wilderness of chaparral and sage, all the more stunning to her eyes for being so close to the gaping maw of Southern California's runaway civilization, Mukunda started recounting stories from his childhood: his first visits to the ashram; his early efforts at meditation; his many wanderings in these hills on weekends when his father would drop him off, let loose on the border of two youthful paradises: the wilderness of the Santa Monica Hills and the enchanted world of the ashram that nestled in its shadows.

When they reached the edge of the canyon, Gita held her breath for a moment. It was a stunning vista, a recondite discourse of natural interiors lit for its lone spectators by the glory of the late morning sun. Mukunda pointed to where the nest had been, at a time when the California condor had become all but extinct. Just a few months ago, in February, she had read that the last known female condor to be born in the wild had been shot by a poacher, a great matron with a ten-foot wingspan who was thought to be more than thirty years old. What a treasure Mukunda had found and what a shame he hadn't told anyone about it—though maybe in the end it was best he hadn't. It saddened Gita to think of the caprices of human beings. Too many tragedies at their hands, regardless of what kind of creature you were.

They sat down on a bed of California oat grass and remained silent for several minutes, muted by the natural beauty that surrounded them but glancing at each other from time to time to acknowledge with their eyes how powerful the presence of nature could be. Gita picked up a stalk of dried grass and spun it between her fingers.

"Ah, Mukunda, I wish I could have known about all of this when I was young. I have a lot of lost ground to make up."

"All of what?"

"The ashram, Gurudeva, meditating in these hills."

"But you did know about it. I told you, remember? More than once, as I recall."

"I know... but at the time I was convinced you were a little crazy. Nice, but crazy. Turns out you were the sanest guy I knew."

"Well, you're here now. That's what really counts."

"I guess... So, tell me, who do you think Gurudeva is going to name as his successor? Do you have any inside information?"

"None whatsoever. I could make a guess but it wouldn't be worth much. I'm sure you've heard a lot of opinions already."

"That's for sure. They're even taking bets; there's an ashram pool going."

"You're joking."

"I kid you not."

"So who's winning the pool? Any idea?"

"The smart money is on Markandeya. Madalasa is a close second, and Abhay a distant third."

"Well, that's about what I would expect. But there are some other highly elevated senior disciples that most people don't know about because they're not around so often. Personally, I think there's a chance Gurudeva may pick one of them. Anyhow, we'll know for sure in three days' time. No sense overheating our brains about it now."

"There's a rumor going round that Gurudeva said we were on the verge of entering a new age—the Satya Yuga, right? Isn't that what it's called? Is there any truth to that?"

Mukunda looked surprised, but then he smiled and began summarizing for her what Gurudeva had said in the meeting with the senior disciples, most of which the master had left out of his evening discourse in the main hall. Gita had heard a scaled-down version that had made its way through the ashram community, a version that was nowhere near as direct or as categorical as what Mukunda related for her. A year ago she might have suspected Gurudeva of hubris, but she had lately come to the conclusion that if anyone could see into the future it was Gurudeva. Still, given the world they lived in, it was difficult to see just how such a golden age could come about anytime soon. Mukunda had his own ideas that he had obviously been mulling over for some time.

"I think there will be some kind of worldwide crisis that will force everyone to completely rethink how they look at life, something that makes it obvious that the old ways don't work anymore. Some people think there's going to be a sudden evolutionary shift, a sudden leap in consciousness; I've heard people talk about a pole shift as a possible cause, or even stuff as wild as alien intervention, but I don't think it has to be anything so esoteric. A worldwide crisis could have the same effect. We've already seen an increase in natural disasters the last few years. Say that accelerates—it could get to the point that it throws the whole world into chaos and confusion, especially if a majority of the planet is affected. A world war would do the same thing. Or else, if the economic system collapsed, for whatever reason. You know how nothing unites people more than a crisis? Well, if it happened on a worldwide scale, it might be enough for people to reject both religious dogma and materialism—if they got to a point where they realized how destructive they both are. Then if there was a group of people, spiritually minded people, preaching and practicing something that actually made sense, they could step into the void. We just need to reach the tipping point, the critical mass when people are finally ready to listen. In the meantime, as I understand it, Gurudeva is preparing us to be ready when that moment comes, ready to unite with all the other people in the world who are thinking along the same lines. And there are a lot of those. We may be scattered and disconnected now, but it won't always be that way. All we need is the right conditions for people to finally pay attention to what we're saying. Once they do, that might be all it takes."

It sounded plausible, in a utopian sort of way, certainly more plausible than the worldwide workers' revolution that she had dreamed of when she was younger, but there was still that little problem of all the power and the wealth being concentrated in the hands of a tiny elite that was in no way going to give up its power or its privileges unless it was shorn of them, whether through natural occurrences or through forceful dispossession. It was certainly true, as Mukunda claimed, that there were a lot of conscious people in the world, and maybe, as Gurudeva had hinted at, their numbers would soon be rapidly increasing, but even so, what chance did they have against the power brokers of the world and the governments they coerced into doing their bidding? She said as much to Mukunda, but she could see that he had missed her main point. Maybe it was her invective-laden dismissal of "the Bushes and the Rumsfelds of the world" that distracted his focus.

"I'm not blaming everything on the government, Mukunda. Government is just a tool in the hands of the rich and powerful. By itself, it has the potential to do great good as well as great harm—which is what makes the powers-that-be so careful to not let it get out of hand—but as long as it is controlled by people who do not have humanity's best interests at heart but only their own, it's never going to be free to promote the welfare of the people. I agree with you that we need a change in consciousness more than a change in government, but as long as the dominant governments of the world continue to serve the people who hold the real power in their hands—economic power—they'll never permit that change in consciousness to happen. At the very least, they'll fight it tooth and nail all the way to the bitter end. They've always understood this. That's what's enabled them to hold on to power for so long. Just look at history; it will tell you all you need to know."

"What do you mean?"

"Do we have time for a quick history lesson? Okay. Then let's start at home. You remember the constitutional convention, when the so-called fathers of the nation got together and decided what kind of government we were going to have, now that we had thrown off the yoke of British tyranny? Well, during their debates, James Madison—he was the main voice at that time, the central architect of the constitution—he said that the primary responsibility of government was to protect the minority of the opulent against the majority. He warned everyone of 'the danger of the leveling spirit of those that labor under the hardships of life and secretly sigh for a more equal distribution of its blessings.' And everyone agreed with him. The only one who would have objected was Jefferson and he wasn't there; he was in France. They specifically designed a system to protect the rich against the poor, and they were perfectly up-front about it. Go and read the documents. They wanted the wealth to stay in the hands of the wealthy, so they devised a system to ensure that. It wasn't anything new. Governments have always been devised and controlled by the wealthy in order to protect their wealth and their position, all the way back to feudal times. They were just continuing that tradition. In defense of Madison, he sincerely believed that the wealthy would be benevolent statesmen. He said that 'power must reside in the hands of the wealthy, the more capable set of men,' but he thought they would devote themselves to the welfare of the people. Well, we know how that turned out. Even he realized that later on. In the early 1790s, when he saw how business interests had taken over the government and were making life miserable for the people, he was revolted. He lamented what he called 'the daring depravity of the times,' and talked about how business had become 'the tools and tyrants of government, overwhelming it with its combinations and bribed by its largesses.' We've been suffering those tyrants ever since.

"If you examine virtually every governmental policy from the 1780s until today, you'll find that they were all designed to maintain the existing power structure, to see to it that the wealth and the power remained concentrated in the hands of an elite minority. Wealth creates power and power perpetuates wealth; that's the governing principle. Any social impulse that goes against that principle has to be put down. Look at the nineteenth century. What was the leveling force, as Madison called it? It was the labor movement, the unions. Study the history of the labor movement and you'll see that the business oligarchy did everything they could to crush it. In the nineteenth century it was mostly through violence, fear, and intimidation, but also through the legal system, blocking any kind of workers' rights legislation. Early in the twentieth century they had to start shifting more to propaganda tactics because it wasn't so easy any longer to rely on brute force. Have you seen any movies from the twenties, or read the books, or seen the commercial press from that time? They paint this cozy picture of a carefree, blissful, opulent society. But what was the reality? The reality was that the rich had to hire guards to protect their parties from the angry people outside in the street who were getting paid slave wages to work in their factories, when they had a job at all—no rights, no benefits, millions of people struggling just to put food on the table or keep a roof over their head. The stock market was making a handful of people rich beyond their wildest dreams, but the vast majority of people were worse off than they had ever been. Even the British right wing press in those days couldn't believe how badly the working class was treated in America. The labor movement by then had been totally crushed. And the business class was thrilled about it. They talked about having reached the 'end of history,' the perfect society: total control.

"Think about that mentality for a moment. Why would business interests even want to break up unions in the first place? Why would they go to such extreme and inhuman measures as soon as anyone tried to organize: killing them, throwing them in jail, burning down their houses, demonizing them in the press?"

"Because they didn't want to pay their workers more money."

"Exactly. That's the one and only reason. Greed, pure and simple. Greed for money; greed for power. Accumulate all you can and to hell with everybody else. That's the essence of capitalism, always has been. Back in the 1850s the labor movement had a slogan for it: gain wealth, forgetting all but self. It's the exact opposite of spiritual consciousness: pure selfishness, materialism at its worst. At that time the labor movement was mostly factory girls and artisans, people like that. They weren't sophisticated people. They weren't leftists or radicals. They were just simple people trying to make a living, but it wasn't hard for them to see how degrading the system was. They considered it no better than industrial slavery.

"So then we get to the depression. Everything falls apart—that's your crisis for you, though not on the scale you're talking about; people start protesting right and left, and in the thirties the working class finally starts gaining some rights; they pass the Wagner Act; life actually starts getting better for the majority of people. They were still trying to crush the unions but times had changed; they couldn't openly use violence anymore as their main weapon, at least not on the scale they could before. So what happens then? The business community became hysterical. They were afraid that their whole system was going down the tubes. The people were fighting for their economic rights, and they were scared to death about it. So they initiated this massive propaganda campaign. They started talking about the need to 'indoctrinate people in the capitalist story in order to win the everlasting battle for the hearts and minds of men.' That's straight out of the propaganda literature. The campaign was interrupted by the war, but as soon as the war ended, it went right into full gear again. That's basically how the public relations industry, as we know it today, was born. I bet you don't know that history, either? I didn't think so.

"The public relations industry didn't even really exist until the 1920s; there wasn't any need for it before then. It only got going once business realized that the old repressive methods weren't going to work anymore. A guy named Edward Bernays wrote the standard manual in 1928—a book called *Propaganda*, interestingly enough. Nowadays he's referred to as the father of public relations. In the beginning of the book, he says that the conscious and intelligent manipulation of the habits and opinions of the masses is the central feature of a democratic government. He also says later in the book that we must regiment people's minds as efficiently as armies regiment their bodies. And that's exactly what they set out to do. In the late thirties, business got together and started developing a far more sophisticated plan for fighting labor, and most of their ideas were taken straight from the public relations manuals. They started flooding the media and the educational system and the entertainment industry with the capitalist story. It got interrupted by the war for a few years, but after 1945 they went all out. To give you an idea, by the early fifties, 30 percent of educational materials at the elementary level were supplied directly by business. They also concentrated on the churches, especially fundamentalist churches, for obvious reasons: religion is a great means of keeping people quiet. Has been ever since feudal times. The essence of their strategy, as you can read for yourself in their literature, was to create a false picture of social harmony—harmony was the big buzzword—the happy working-class family where the wife hands her husband his lunch in the morning and stays home to take care of the kids; the hard-working executive who's devoted to the people who work under him; the friendly neighborhood banker, always ready to help you out with a loan; the smiling policeman who is there to protect your family. Total fabrication, of course, but that was the point. You want people to buy into a dream, the so-called 'American dream.' And then you have the outsiders: the labor organizer, the communist, the criminally minded minorities, whoever doesn't fit with this picture. The idea was to convince people to blame these outsiders for their problems, to learn to distrust them, even hate them. 'To protect our way of life.' Anybody who looked a little different was an easy target, not hard to find in such an ethnically diverse country like ours. In other words, anything to keep people unaware of what was really going on, of who was really responsible for their problems. This was all totally conscious, completely planned out. Do you remember the movies from the fifties?"

"God, how I used to hate those movies. They were always so phony."

"Exactly. People didn't realize it but they were watching formula propaganda drawn up by big business. But it wasn't just the movies and television. It was the educational system, the advertising industry, the commercial mainstream media, the recording industry, and on down the line. And all backed up by the unquestionable authority of the churches. The point was to make people docile, to get them to accept the status quo. Not just accept it, but be happy about it, as if it were divinely preordained. There was a reaction to it in the sixties, of course, but they were able to get that under control by the mid-seventies. The rest you know: Reaganomics; the steady decline of real wages over the past thirty years and the increasing concentration of wealth in the hands of the top 2 percent; the blatant marriage of government to business and corporate power right through the Bush and Clinton years; the increasing marginalization of large segments of the population; and finally the triumph of globalization across the board—in effect, the victory of corporate tyranny. Corporations, of course, are the ideal totalitarian system, completely unaccountable; their decision-making is totally hidden from the public eye, even from their own employees, and because they're transnational, they're basically free from government interference. If labor gets out of hand, or if they don't get the subsidies or the tax breaks they demand, they just move their operations to a different country that will offer them what they want. Nowadays, they don't even have to move. All they have to do is threaten to move. That's what globalization boils down to: the total domination of corporate power. And in the meantime, we're so indoctrinated we don't even notice what's going on. It's the same old formula, it's just been adapted for the times. Just look at almost any TV show, any commercial movie, any mainstream magazine or newspaper, any bit of ad copy. Can you imagine a sitcom ever dealing with any real social problem, say life in South Central or the plight of the working class or the rise of religious fundamentalism or the marginalization of minorities and the poor? Anything that might stir up the people, motivate them to struggle against injustice? Of course not. It's all designed to put you to sleep."

Mukunda looked at his watch and flashed a look of contrition. "I hate to interrupt, Gita, but I have to be getting back."

"I'm sorry, Mukunda. I got carried away again. As usual."

"No, it's okay. We'll make it in time. With all the extra people going on morning walk, Gurudeva's been getting back later than usual. We're fine. But we do need to get moving."

"I hope you weren't too bored. I know I have a tendency to get up on the pulpit sometimes; I forget that not everyone finds this stuff as interesting or as important as I do."

"I wasn't bored at all. Actually, I found it kind of fascinating. We can talk as we walk. I want to hear what you think has to happen if we are going to somehow make it to the Satya Yuga."

They started heading back down the trail at a brisk but comfortable pace. Gita knew she had let herself get carried away, but she couldn't help herself. She felt too strongly about these things. It was impossible for her to sit back and keep quiet when it was so painfully obvious how bad things had gotten and how unaware most people were about it, though she knew they could not be blamed when they had been force-fed their passivity since birth. Nor did she regret having gone off on that particular tangent. It was an important part of who she was, and she wanted to share her whole self with him, not just the parts they both found agreeable. In fact, she was glad they had gotten into this discussion now rather than later. She could sense that the sober look on his face and his lack of words did not stem from any reluctance on his part but from the full attention he was giving to her words. That quiet attention buoyed her spirits as they walked and spurred her to imagine what a new age would have to look like for it to be not only new but worth the pains of getting there.

"To me, the essence of a golden age would have to be the recognition that we are one family; it's not us against them, as we've been trained to think, but just us. And not just us human beings, but all living beings and the environment. One family, one planet—I think you have to start there. Did you ever read Chief Seattle's letter to the president in the 1850s? In the letter he asks, 'How can you buy or sell the sky or the land? The earth does not belong to man; man belongs to the earth.' The Native Americans, and most native cultures for that matter, would just shake their heads in disbelief if you talked about 'owning' some part of Mother Earth. How can anybody own nature? We're part of nature, in the same way that a tree or a bird is. In that respect they were infinitely wiser than we are. If God created everything, then it stands to reason that if it belongs to anyone, then it belongs to everyone equally. We're all equally part of his creation. But of course it doesn't belong to us. It belongs to him. We're blessed to be able to use it, that's all. At best we can say that we're custodians of a common patrimony. Can you imagine a family where one brother hoards all the wealth and the others starve? Of course not. It's inhuman. Or where a brother treats his sister like a slave? Not if they care for each other as members of a real family do. To me, that's the essence of a spiritual outlook: one family of living beings who love each other and take care of each other. And that includes being ready to sacrifice what we have, if necessary, so that our brothers and sisters don't have to undergo any unnecessary hardship—and our brothers and sisters include the animals and the forests and the soil and the water and the mountains.

"If somehow everybody's consciousness evolved to the point where we all looked at life that way, then that would be the end of social problems. If it were somehow psychologically impossible for one human being to exploit another, or to destroy the environment, or to mistreat animals, then I'm sure our social institutions and policies would automatically change to reflect that reality. And maybe we will get there someday as a race, but I don't think it will be anytime in the foreseeable future. So in the meantime, if we want to make the transition to a golden age before our collective consciousness evolves to the point that it happens naturally, then we have to somehow make sure that our social institutions and policies reflect that spiritual outlook, even if everybody in society hasn't reached that level yet. And to do that, you have to ensure that the people who make those policies and run those institutions subscribe to that outlook. As it stands now, the people who control society, both economically and politically, have the exact opposite outlook. So it only stands to reason that they have to be removed from power and separated from their wealth, and a system has to be put in place that not only makes it impossible for this kind of exploitation and inequality to exist to any significant degree but also educates people in the kind of values that will insure it won't happen again. Which means, of course, that capitalism has to come to an end. Think about it. As a spiritually minded human being, is there any way you can justify a system in which some people are rolling in luxury while others are starving?"

"Absolutely not."

"But that's the essence of capitalism. It's the effort to accumulate physical wealth, and physical wealth is limited—as long as some people have more, there will always be others who have less. And anyhow, the whole idea of running after money in the first place is a kind of mental disease."

"No disagreement there. That's basic spirituality. People think they will be happier if they have more money, a nicer house, a better car, and so on, but of course it's not true. If anything, the wealthier a person becomes, the unhappier they get, because their attachment grows, their greed grows, they lose the ability to appreciate the joys of a simple life. It's what every spiritual teacher has taught since civilization began: happiness can only be found within. Looking for it in the external world is a kind of delusion."

"But how many people actually understand that? Hardly anyone. And why not? Because the capitalist system is predicated on increasing our hunger for material wealth. One out of every six dollars in this country is spent on marketing—talk about wasted capital—and 100 percent of that goes into propaganda specifically designed to create artificial wants, whether it's a new car we don't need or the latest fashion. Our culture is based on the illusion that these things will make us happy, and everybody buys into it because that's what they've been fed since the cradle—through television, advertising, the media, the entertainment industry, popular novels—and all of it financed by the business sector. How many people ever stop to think that the richer they get, the poorer somebody else gets—inevitably, by the laws of physics? Though that somebody is usually far enough away that they don't have to be reminded of it, whether she's down the hill in South Central or struggling for her next meal in Sub-Saharan Africa. The irony, of course, is that what really makes people happy, as you were saying—intellectual and spiritual wealth—is unlimited. You can accumulate as much as you want and it only makes the people around you better off. The better person you become, the more everyone around you is benefitted. Of course, *we* know that because we are meditating and practicing spirituality. We belong to the lucky few in that sense. But most people are so conditioned by the educational system, the media, the entertainment industry—all of it designed to perpetuate the dream of materialism—that they don't even realize what's happening to them. The system is sowing misery on all levels—materially for the have-nots, who are in the majority, and emotionally, intellectually, and spiritually for everyone else—but no one even sees it. So, one way or another, capitalism has to go."

"I doubt there is any truly spiritually minded person on the planet who will disagree with you, Gita. You're a lot more educated about these things than I am, obviously, but even I can see what's going on out there. I don't know a single disciple who wouldn't welcome an end to capitalism. I know for a fact that's part of what Gurudeva means when he talks about the coming Satya Yuga. I've heard him talk about the evils of capitalism more than once, though perhaps I didn't paid as much attention as I should have. The question then becomes, what do you replace it with?"

"Honestly, Mukunda, I think that's the easy part. The hard part is getting people to agree that we are one human family, with equal rights to the earth's blessings and equal responsibility to make sure everyone shares in those blessings to a more or less equal extent. The institutions, economic structures, political structures, that we would need to ensure a just and conscious society have been pretty well mapped out by the leading social thinkers in the past century and a half."

"Such as?"

"Well, first of all, you have to put an end to private ownership of business, including private corporations, except on a very small scale, like a neighborhood grocery store. The production and consumption of goods has to be managed through cooperatives. Even nineteenth-century factory girls knew that. They knew the mills they worked in should have rightly been owned and run by the workers. It's just common sense, really. Then you have to put a ceiling on the accumulation of wealth. For example, you set the maximum yearly income at two hundred thousand and the minimum at fifty thousand, to allow some scope for natural human desires; you just have to cap those desires. No more insane salaries for CEOs or athletes or pop stars, no more business magnates accumulating ungodly amounts of money, no more speculation on financial markets. Then you have to gear up the educational system to teach spiritual and universal humanitarian values to the children. Turn the media and the entertainment system into public institutions and use them to promote universal welfare. Start instituting economic decentralization and political centralization—one legal system, one penal code. And so on. We know what we have to do, if we ever get the chance to do it. That, and design the system so that there's no returning to the dark ages, so that even if unscrupulous people tried to, they couldn't turn the system to their advantage. If you're interested, there's any number of books I can recommend. But like I said, it's easy to know what to do; the hard part is actually doing it."

"Well, it's going to require a monumental change in the way we do things on this planet; I know that much. A change for the better, of course. But if Gurudeva says we're going to get there, then I have faith we will. One way or another."

"I'd like to think so. But it has to start with me and you."

By now they were turning in the gate, Gita was half out of breath from all the verbal exercise and uncomfortably aware that her words were falling over each other in her headlong rush to get as many of them out as she could before Mukunda had to disappear back into the Bungalow. But as awkward as she felt, Mukunda's attentiveness and the warmth in his eyes made her feel that none of her verbal stumbles mattered. She felt sure that he saw straight through them and into her heart.

"Why don't you make up a reading list for me? Not too big a one to start off with, though; I'm not the most patient of readers... It seems I have a lot of catching up to do in this area."

As they approached the crowd outside the Bungalow, a couple of voices called out in unison for Gita to lead the bhajans. Mukunda smiled and went to fetch her guitar from the gatekeeper. As she watched him go, she was careful not to let her own smile overflow its borders, just in case anybody was watching with undue curiosity. It took a conscious effort on her part. Every step she took with Mukunda now was a step down a road that left her breathless with excitement. Whatever might be the fate of the ashram going into the future, whatever direction Gurudeva chose to take during the time remaining to him, she knew now that she would be there by Mukunda's side, working with him to materialize a dream that she hoped would one day become a common prayer. Maybe they would even have something to say about what that direction would be. It had been her lifelong aspiration to do something to shake the world from its sleep and lead it to a wiser, more just, more compassionate future. But lately she had been struggling with a growing sense of helplessness, if not hopelessness. For years she had fought for different causes that she knew to be part of one great cause, but the more she struggled, the more society seemed to be falling apart at the edges. She had begun wondering if her efforts would be of any lasting value at all—if a better society, a better world, was really possible in the face of such overwhelming odds. But from where she stood now, everything looked radically changed, as if she had crested a forested mountain after laboring up a dark trail and suddenly seen the landscape flooded with light. Maybe this was what she had been waiting for all along, to reach the ashram and discover that the missing ingredient in her struggle was spirituality. And now she was not alone. Together they *could* really do something—if not to usher in a golden age of human harmony and justice, then at least to help secure the foundations of that coming day. The thought was enough to fill her heart with joy—that, and the thought of Mukunda by her side.

9

From his perch in front of his computer, Mukunda could smell the rice pilaf and curried vegetables that Ganesh was preparing in the kitchen, the pungent aroma of the Indian spices as familiar to him at this time of day as the sun climbing overhead in the late morning sky. Outside, the music was rising in volume, in preparation for Gurudeva's return from Sunday morning walk, the crowd far larger than usual. Indeed, it was almost like a retreat atmosphere, with disciples thronging to the ashram in anticipation of Gurudeva's historic announcement. The master had even scheduled a special bhajan session for his walk that morning, and had requested both Gita and Kamal to attend.

Mukunda took one final look at the list of books Gita had emailed him the day before—he had ordered three of them from the online catalogue of a used bookstore—and then returned once again to the text that followed. It was short, but that didn't stop him from reading it again several times, lest he miss any hidden message she might have left there. Her words were understated, but they left no doubt that their walks had become as important to her as they were to him. She had used the word "comfortable" twice, each time—as he interpreted it—to underscore the providential nature of their developing relationship. And though she had apologized for letting herself get carried away, he could tell from her tongue-in-cheek tone that she was just as comfortable with that part of herself as he was. The fact that she was so passionate about what she believed in was part of what he found so attractive about her. There was nothing superficial about this woman and no half measures. When she gave herself to something, she held nothing back. There were not many people he could say this about, and it made him consider what it would mean to enjoy the lifelong love of such a woman—a woman who was reintroducing him to a side of himself that had long lain fallow. But what surprised him most about her was the depth and the maturity of her spiritual understanding. This was not something that could be achieved in seven or eight months, even by the most diligent of souls, if it had not been there in one form or another all along. She might have arrived at the spiritual path comparatively late, but it didn't mean she was far behind. In fact, the more time they spent together, the more the gap between them seemed no wider than the space that had separated their bodies while they'd gazed at the canyon that had been his secret boyhood wonderland.

Suddenly, Mukunda noticed that the chanting outside had picked up in intensity. He sprang from his chair and hurried to the Bungalow door. By the time he reached the gate, Gurudeva's car was already pulling up. He ran to the car door and opened it for the master, while two of Bhishma's assistants emerged from the crowd and took up positions on either side of him. As soon as Gurudeva got out, he held his folded palms in the air and turned a slow circle to greet the devotees. The master remained there for more than ten minutes, chatting with the disciples who crowded around him, obviously enjoying their exuberant energy. Then he gave them his *namaste* and disappeared through the gate with Mukunda close behind.

When they reached the foot of the stairs, Gurudeva asked Mukunda to come up with him; he had something he wanted to tell him. Mukunda was expecting instructions regarding the arrangements for the afternoon meeting, and perhaps a mention or two about lunch, but when Gurudeva sat on his cot in formal meditation posture and asked him to meditate in front of him, he knew it wasn't simply a matter of routine instructions. When Gurudeva asked him to open his eyes five minutes later, he was surprised at the formality in the master's expression.

"Mukunda, do you remember when we first met? You couldn't have known it at the time, but I had gone there to put you to a test. When your aunt called and told me about your unusual dream, I suspected right away who you were, but I had to be sure. Do you follow?"

Mukunda shook his head, baffled by the master's cryptic statements.

"Do you remember the end of that conversation, just before we went back inside, when I touched you on the forehead?"

For a moment nothing registered in Mukunda's mind. Then something began to surface, a hazy image of that morning on the back deck of his childhood home. He remembered that when he was about to get up from his chair he had seemed to black out for a few moments, as if from a sudden flight of vertigo—it must have been then that the master had touched him. Afterward he had felt strangely disoriented.

"When I touched you I put you into a brief trance; while you were in that trance I made sure of who you were. Do you understand now?"

"Not really," Mukunda replied, with a growing sense of strangeness.

Gurudeva smiled, the first time he had done so since he'd begun talking. "Long before I came to this country I had a vision of a young monk who would wear these robes after me. I knew it was a vision of my successor, the one who would take over my mission when I was gone and carry my work into the future. You were only nine years old when I first met you, but while you were in that trance I confirmed what I already knew the moment I saw you coming down the stairs: you were the one I had been waiting for. Since then I've been watching over you, training you, preparing you to accept this responsibility so that I may be free to leave when the time comes. Your training still has a long way to go, but fate has ordained this day for me to name you as my successor. Henceforth, Mukunda, you are no longer a child. It is time for you to leave the dream behind and step into your true role in this life."

Mukunda was stunned. The master continued speaking, but Mukunda felt as if the sound in the room had been turned off, as if he were observing himself as he might a character in the reel of a modern-day silent movie, muted by the cameraman's love of the distant past. His body grew rigid and the thoughts seemed to crawl in slow motion across his mental canvas. Had he heard correctly? Could the unthinkable have just happened, his life so changed in this slowly moving fraction of time that it no longer appeared to be his anymore? Though he had once nurtured dreams of becoming a spiritual teacher when his beard turned the color of Gurudeva's, that possibility now seemed so far beyond the realm of his present-day experience that his mind failed to make sense of what he was hearing. For several minutes he remained in this hinterland of consciousness. Then his normal awareness began to return. Gurudeva's hypnotic voice started filtering in again among his thoughts, giving shape to the words his mind had failed to comprehend.

"...Normally the sannyasi oaths are taken in a private ceremony, but in some special cases that ceremony is held in public. Since you will be my first sannyasi, I will conduct the ceremony during evening darshan on your return from Del Mar. During that ceremony you will take a formal vow of celibacy; you will receive your orange robes and a new name that will end in *ananda*. The new name symbolizes that you have broken all ties with your former worldly life. In the old days, in India, once a yogi took the sannyasi oaths, he would break off all contact with his worldly family and retire to the forests or the mountains, or else travel around visiting different pilgrimage spots, always careful never to allow himself to become attached to any particular person or particular place. However, times have changed, and furthermore, this is not India. In your case, I want you to maintain a cordial relationship with your family. Following that tradition here in America would only lead to unnecessary problems for the ashram. Traditionally, novitiate monks also shaved their heads, as a further aid to taming the ego, but I think we can dispense with that custom as well.

"Now I want to make one thing clear, Mukunda. You will be my first sannyasi. This is a special distinction that will always be yours. But you will be the first among many, and all will be deserving of your respect. I have been planning the creation of a monastic order for a long time now, but I had to wait for the right conditions. First I had to build up the ashram and prepare a cadre of disciples who understood my teachings and were completely committed to them. Most of these were necessarily family people—stable, responsible members of the society who could set an example for other family people. That part of my mission is now complete. The next phase will be to disseminate my teachings throughout the globe. As my teachings spread, they will help to create the revolution in consciousness that the world has been waiting for. But for that to happen, a core of monastic disciples will be indispensable—young, energetic, idealistic men and women who can dedicate their full time to this work, disciples who don't have family responsibilities to hold them back. They will carry my teachings to the far corners of the globe; and you will guide them, just as I am guiding you now. Of course, this is still well in the future, but your training needs to begin now so that you will be ready when that day arrives."

Mukunda's mind grew giddy under the weight of Gurudeva's words. As a teenager, one of his heroes had been Vivekananda, the Hindu monk who brought the teachings of yoga to the West for the first time. Vivekananda had dazzled his youthful imagination, as he had dazzled the imagination of so many others for more than a century, his fiery personality and prescient wisdom blazing across the spiritual skies of this planet like a rare and magnificent comet whose appearance becomes a source of legend for generations to come. Now he saw visions of himself in those same orange robes, marching to distant lands as Vivekananda had once done, inspiring a spiritual renewal in an age of materialist decay. He felt his body tremble and tears well up under the urging of his youthful dreams and the spell of his guru's voice. But at the same time, his insecurities and doubts wrestled for a place in his attention. Their voice became more and more insistent, until he felt forced to confess that his meditation was not progressing well, that he felt far from enlightenment these days, so far indeed that he was afraid it would be nothing but a sham if he became the spiritual head of the ashram.

"Mukunda, it is the guru's job to know when the disciple is ready, not the disciple's job. Leave that to me. Enlightenment is a matter of one second to the next. It is already inside of you; you just don't realize it yet. One turn of the key and you will have it, but for the moment the key remains in my pocket. However, you are right about one thing: it is a great responsibility and not to be taken lightly. Nowadays everyone wants to be a master; no one wants to be a disciple. But before you can be a true master, you must first be a true disciple. This requires that you surrender your ego to the master, that you give him full power of attorney. Very few people are ready to do this. Most would rather hide their ego or polish it up a little rather than surrender. Real discipleship forces you to become naked before the master, to expose each and every one of your shortcomings and defects so that he can go to work on them. That is a painful and difficult process, not at all to the liking of most disciples. They are too busy thinking about becoming a master one day to take the trouble to become a real disciple. This is one thing that separates you from the rest, Mukunda: the fact that you have never had any desire to become a master is the first requisite for becoming one."

The next few hours were difficult ones for Mukunda. Despite Gurudeva's assurances, he did not feel in any way ready for the monumental responsibility that would come with being named the master's successor. He drew some comfort from the thought that any real responsibility would still be years away. The master was still here, and he had promised to be around for a long time yet. But there were other considerations as well that weighed on his mind. As he discharged his midday duties, helping Ganesh to serve the master's lunch and preparing for the afternoon meeting, he was acutely aware that the attitude of his fellow disciples toward him was about to undergo a radical change. He suspected that some of the senior disciples might well resent him for having usurped an honor that should have rightfully been theirs, that they might consider him too young and too green to be their leader, no matter how far into the future that day might be. Nor could he blame them. He might have felt the same had he been in their shoes.

And then there was Gita. She came rushing back into his mind the moment the master finished his lunch and went into his room to rest. In these last few weeks she had gone from being a perplexing reminder of the La Jolla youth he had long since left behind to becoming his best and truest friend—with the promise of becoming more than just a friend rushing at him like a swift and swollen river, threatening to carry both of them off in its fateful current. What would it mean to their fledgling relationship were he to become a sannyasi? Could it in any way survive a sannyasi's vows? And if not, was he prepared to sacrifice the tumultuous promise of these last weeks for a greater good? He had not asked for this honor, but it was his by Gurudeva's command and the force of his own karma. In three weeks time he would become a celibate monk.

As the hour for the afternoon meeting drew near, the consequences of his destiny began to close in on him, the weight of history falling heavily on his shoulders; sadly, he knew it was a burden that she would also have to share. He had read accounts of monks who had lost their way because of their feelings for a woman—something he could not allow to happen, not with the fate of the ashram upon his back—and of women who had lost their inner spark because of their love for a man whose vows did not permit him to requite that love. He hoped Gita would not be among them—the mere thought of that possibility pained him—but looking back on their dizzying descent into an intimacy he had never known before, he did not see how she could escape that suffering. Could they not somehow harness the powerful current of their feelings for each other and continue their friendship into a radically different future, whatever the limitations forced upon them? It seemed unlikely. Those monks he had read about who had permitted themselves to harbor anything more than a brotherly love for a woman had ended in either suffering or dishonor, and often both. Such stories existed in the spiritual literature as a warning against the dictates of passion, a fatal detour on the road to enlightenment. The great teachers had always taught their disciples to rise above those feelings, to sublimate them so that the kundalini could be free to rise upward without being tethered by the coils of unfettered desire. It was a teaching he had accepted unquestioningly, but he had never had to face it in the flesh. Could he be equal to the task, he wondered, especially if he was having so much trouble accepting that this was what he really wanted? The thought flashed in his mind that this could be a test the master had arranged for him, a final, terrible litmus to prove his worthiness, demanding a sacrifice greater than any he had ever made. The thought tormented him for several minutes, frightening him with its mythic perception of the universe's obscure designs. But soon it was swept away in the whirl of warring emotions that had taken possession of his mind.

By a quarter to three, the senior disciples had gathered in the master's sitting room. An aura of anticipation surrounded the gathering, a glowing, rippling energy that was very nearly visible to the naked eye. Outside, underneath the banyan tree, some devotees had gathered to sing bhajans, drawn by the historic significance of the occasion, as if they were waiting outside the Vatican for a plume of white smoke. Mukunda was positioned by the side of the master's door, knowing that once it opened, another door would clang shut on the life he had known, imprisoning him in a future weighted with responsibilities from which there would be no escape. His uneasiness continued until he heard the master's muted footsteps and saw the door open. He accompanied him to his chair and then sat down on the floor beside him and resigned himself to his fate, sure that he could hear the echoes of that other door closing behind him, one relentless reverberation after another separating him from his past.

After Kamal's bhajan and a few minutes' meditation, Gurudeva wasted no time in announcing him as his successor. Mukunda saw looks of surprise sweep across the room, but the two persons who should have been most surprised—Markandeya and Madalasa—were grinning as if he were the guest at a surprise birthday party. Madalasa looked as if she were doing her best to stifle a laugh at the expression on his face; she even winked at him. Gurudeva began recounting Mukunda's past for the disciples, starting with his boyhood dreams and their first encounter on the deck in back of Mukunda's house. As he talked, Mukunda could feel the disciples taking his measure, sizing up this young boy who would one day be the leader of their community. It was only when Gurudeva announced the creation of a monastic order that the mood began to change. The master spoke for nearly an hour about the future of the ashram, its place on the world stage, and the key role the monastic disciples would play in this work. He made it clear that his successor would be the first among equals, and so it would remain as the mantle passed from generation to generation over the coming centuries. The monastic order as a whole would embody Gurudeva's teachings and carry them throughout the globe, just as Buddha's monastic disciples had done twenty-six centuries earlier. They would be supported in their work by the lay disciples. Together the two groups would work hand in hand to be the catalyst for the coming transformation of human consciousness. Mukunda would be the first to take the sannyasi vows, but in the near future more would follow, some of whom were present in that room. Finally, he called on them to lend Mukunda their full support as his successor, for it was only in unity that they would be able to bring their glorious mission to fruition.

It was nearly six o'clock before Gurudeva ended the meeting and returned to his room. As soon as the disciples began to disperse, Madalasa, Markandeya, and Leela surrounded Mukunda with hugs and congratulations. When he tried to protest that he thought it should have been one of them, both Markandeya and Madalasa told him that Gurudeva had asked each of them for their recommendations during the week, and they had each recommended him. Most of the other senior disciples also offered their congratulations before they made ready to go to the main hall. It was six thirty before he was left alone again in front of Gurudeva's door. One ordeal was over but another was set to begin. Soon he would bear the scrutiny of the entire ashram community. From then on, he would have to live with the knowledge that all eyes would be watching him to see if he measured up to expectations he couldn't possibly measure up to, to see if he would prove worthy of being the leader that Gurudeva had marked him out to be. There was one set of eyes, though, that he knew would not judge him in that way, but that was no consolation. Indeed, they would be the most difficult of all to face.

An hour later Mukunda was in his usual place behind Gurudeva's cushion on the dais of the main hall. When Gurudeva intoned the chant to end the opening meditation, Mukunda opened his eyes and abandoned his unwieldy efforts to rein in his mind. The master began his talk with a humorous story about the squabbles between Swami Shivananda's disciples when he was nearing his end and had yet to appoint his successor. The analogy was obvious and the story brought huge peals of laughter as Gurudeva poked fun at his own bevy of good-natured senior disciples. When the laughter died down, however, his tone grew serious.

"There is a tradition in spiritual life that before an individual can receive higher initiation he or she must undertake a special interior journey. In the Native American tradition this is known as the vision quest. The vision quest has been around since the beginning of human civilization. It marks the passage of the individual into spiritual maturity, and in the higher spiritual traditions it has evolved, in its different forms, into a necessary component of the individual quest for freedom. It is the great test by which a spiritual aspirant proves himself worthy of accepting the mantle that is about to be passed to him. If you investigate the history of the great spiritual traditions, especially the history of the great masters of those traditions, you will find that each has undergone his own particular brand of vision quest before his final achievement. You have read about how Jesus went into the desert to meditate for forty days and forty nights, how he was tempted by his internal demons, how he vanquished them and then returned from the desert as the world teacher. You have read about Buddha, how he sat under the Bo tree and resolved not to get up until he achieved enlightenment, how his internal demons came to do battle with him, and how he emerged victorious. If you haven't read about it, then I'm sure you have at least seen the movie."

Gurudeva paused until the laughter died down.

"Though it may take many different forms, the vision quest is an important stage in the life of every dedicated spiritual aspirant. Those of you in this room who aspire to spiritual greatness will also have to undergo it one day. For many of you, that day is still a long way away. It will come when I am no longer in my physical body, although I will still be there in subtle form to guide you through it. For others, that time is rapidly approaching; I have been preparing you for it without your knowledge. But for one of you that time has already come, and that person is Mukunda, who I am officially appointing today as my successor once I am gone. I think you all know Mukunda."

Mukunda got up and prostrated in front of the master. When he rose to a kneeling position, the master placed the palms of his hands on the crown of his bowed head and intoned a stream of Sanskrit mantras. Then Mukunda returned to his place behind the master's cushion amid a smattering of muted approbation. As he looked out at the assembly, all eyes trained on him, he felt a sudden surge of pride. All his life he had been dreaming that he would one day become a great yogi, a modern Vivekananda, a disciple worthy of the master's attentions and capable of preserving his teachings for future generations. Could it all be coming true? Had the dryness of the last few years simply been a preparation for the next leg of his journey, a journey that would eventually transform him into one of the planet's leading spiritual teachers? It was difficult to believe, but the hundreds of shining eyes that stared at him on the dais, reflecting the soft lighting of the meditation hall, assured him it was so.

This was his destiny. This was what he had been born for. It was time for him to accept it—humanity was waiting.

"Tomorrow morning Mukunda will begin his vision quest. I am sending him to our hermitage in Del Mar where he will spend the next three weeks in seclusion and meditation. What will happen during these three weeks, no one can say, except that the Mukunda who returns will not be the Mukunda who leaves here tomorrow. The outer shell will be the same, but its contents will be changed forever. Something that he has been waiting for his entire life will enter and something else will leave. In that loss there is freedom, though the form it takes will only be known to him—for the journey of the vision quest is unique and inexplicable, as you will each discover when it comes time for you to undertake that journey. It is then that you will come to fully understand your role in the universal drama, a role no less important, no less dignified, and no less mysterious than Mukunda's. To see you all here today and to be able to see what is coming brings a smile to my face. For it is my privilege to watch over the destinies of all my disciples in the theater of this mysterious and beautiful world—for as long as I am here, and even after I am gone."

There was murmuring throughout the hall and several cries of "*Gurudeva ki jai*." When the commotion died down, Gurudeva began to delineate his plans for the future, as he had done for the senior disciples that afternoon: the formation of the sannyasi order and the role his monastic disciples would play in the coming revolution of consciousness.

"When Mukunda returns from his encounter with the unknown, three weeks from today, we will celebrate his initiation into the ancient order of *sannyasa*, here in this very hall. I will give him the orange robes of the yogic monk and a new name. From that moment on, he will be my spiritual son in flesh as well as in spirit, to be honored as the next spiritual leader of our community once the time comes for me to leave behind my earthly existence. I hope you will all be able to attend what is sure to be a historic day in the ongoing history of our movement."

Gurudeva folded his hands to his chest and intoned the ritual blessing with which he ended every evening darshan. As Mukunda rose to follow him out of the hall, he looked over at Gita, who was standing with the other musicians, clinging tightly to her guitar. She was at least ten meters away and separated from him by a crowd of surging disciples, some of them seemingly as interested in him as they were in Gurudeva, but he thought he caught a glint of tears in her eyes as they exchanged smiles. It was difficult to tell with the muted lighting, but his heart told him it was so, the same tears he had struggled with that afternoon. He wondered if he would have a chance to talk to her before he left. There was so much to say and so little time remaining in which to say it. But perhaps it would be better if he didn't, not just yet. Maybe when the tears dried and they both had time to listen to the songs of their separate destinies, they would know better what to say and where to go from there. Gurudeva had promised that he would return a different man. What he meant by that, Mukunda had no way of knowing, but it occurred to him that it might also be a different Gita he would return to. The weight of history would also be on her shoulders these next three weeks, and only time would tell how she would emerge from that test.

10

Ordinarily Gita would have followed Gurudeva to the Bungalow with most of the other disciples, but on this night her feet felt rooted to the spot. At first, when she heard Gurudeva announce Mukunda as his successor, she couldn't believe her ears. She even nudged Kamal and asked him if she had heard correctly. As Gurudeva talked about the vision quest, her surprise gradually turned to pride. Her Mukunda was going to be the head of the ashram one day? She could scarcely believe it, but in many ways it started to make sense—his childhood dreams, his lifelong dedication to the spiritual path, Gurudeva appointing him as his personal assistant at such a young age. The spiritually precocious youth that she had grown up with was going to become a well-known spiritual leader one day! The thought of it made it almost impossible for her to pay attention to what Gurudeva was saying; her mind began to spin with images of the future and the role that she would play by Mukunda's side, his companion and confidante, a shield from the outside world whenever he needed one—whatever it took to be the wife of a spiritual leader. But when Gurudeva let it be known that he would become a monk, the first in the new monastic order, her attention was wrested back again, disoriented by images of Mukunda in orange robes, until the words that made her stomach knot and her eyes cloud over: "a vow of celibacy."

When the hall was empty, except for a few attendants who were cleaning up, Gita sought refuge in the one sanctuary that had always been open to her: her music. She sat back down in the area reserved for the musicians, glanced up at the dais where she had seen Mukunda accept the honor that now promised to divide their destinies, and began fingering the strings of her guitar. Her fingers quickly sought the chords of a song she had begun composing the day before, a love song for the man with whom she hoped to share her fortunes—or had hoped until half an hour earlier. She had tried to write lyrics subtle enough that anyone who heard them would think they were an ode to love itself, the spiritual overture of a young woman's longing to know the infinite, but nuanced enough, for the one man who would know how to read the signs, to make clear the powerful torrent of her feelings. Now it seemed unlikely he would ever get to hear it.

For nearly forty minutes, Gita let her fingers play among the unfinished stanzas, adding a word here, a phrase there, wandering through its landscape as if she were wandering through ancient ruins, the visible reminder of what had once been a towering monument to mankind's grandest dreams. A new tenor crept into the melody as a major chord turned to minor, adjusting to the weather of her heart, fastening its notes to the shifting winds until the air in the now-empty meditation hall became fragrant with sadness. Having taken birth as a declaration of her feelings, her song now became a lament for a love that had once been, the bittersweet nostalgia for a time that had been carpeted with dreams—only to see those dreams reveal themselves for the illusions they had always been. The rich scent of rapturous memories melded with the sobering recognition of their loss, and as always, when she was able to transform her sorrows into art, her heart began to lighten under its burden, to taste the elixir that she had long ago learned to distill from the wine of sadness. It was not enough to free her from her sorrow—in fact, it made her all the more conscious of it—but it was enough to remind her that her sorrow was not to be run from but embraced, willingly subsumed into the many-faceted canvas that was her life.

By the time Gita returned her guitar to its case and made for the door, the tears had dried on her cheeks. Her eyes were still moist but the languidness in her limbs had begun to dissipate. As she pulled her sandals from the shoe rack and reached to shut off the lights, she was startled to see a figure sitting in the shadows on a bench a few meters away.

"It is not often we see stars like those."

The musical Irish brogue was instantly identifiable, despite the hushed, almost reverential tone. Gita crossed the few paces to the bench where Leela was staring off into a sky that was as clear and as cloudless as Gita had seen in a long time, though she wouldn't have noticed had Leela not brought it to her attention.

"It makes you realize sometimes just how small this planet is," Leela continued, still gazing up at the sky. "A spinning speck of cosmic dust revolving round a sun that is one star among millions, and a small one at that. A sobering thought, especially with music like that in the background. I couldn't hear the words, of course, but the melody seemed quite sad, and getting sadder all the time. Here, have a seat."

"You've been sitting here the whole time?"

Leela nodded. "I was waiting for you."

"For me? Why?"

"I thought you might need a little company. Or maybe it was I who could use the company. Either way, it's been quite a night. I haven't seen a night like this in a long time."

Leela was looking at the sky again, her voice wistful, as if the muted radiance above had thrust her back into memories she had long forgotten. For a moment, Gita wasn't sure if she were talking about the stars overhead or the evening's events in the meditation hall. It was only after a few moments' silence, when Leela resumed speaking again, that her meaning became clear.

"I suppose the last time anything came close was when Gurudeva took Madalasa and myself into the canyon behind the Bungalow and taught us an advanced form of meditation. He told us something about our past lives then and something of what the future would bring. I didn't understand it at the time, but today it all came clear. The two of us have enjoyed growing into old maids together in Gurudeva's shadow. It's been fun. It seems, however, that we may soon be trading in our yogi whites for robes of a different color. But today was not about us. It was about Mukunda—Mukunda and you."

Leela fixed her eyes on Gita now. There was not a trace of wistfulness in them, only a powerful sense of presence that seemed to be commanding her to speak.

"Mukunda and me? What do you mean? Did Mukunda say something?"

"He didn't need to."

Leela seemed to be willing her to continue. Gita tried to think of something to say, something that might enable her to avoid having to disclose her hidden feelings. But even in the darkness she could see from Leela's eyes and the focused tilt of her smile that the older disciple was all too aware of exactly what she was feeling. For a few seconds she fumbled with her words. Then she made an admission that was also a final attempt to remain alone with her sorrow.

"I am happy for him, Leela. I really am. He deserves this."

Leela's smile widened at the edges. "I'm sure you are. But that doesn't mean *you're* happy. It may be dark but those are not tears of joy streaking your face."

Gita let out a sigh and shrugged her shoulders. "Well, what can I do? That's life, right? I guess it wasn't meant to be." She felt the tears starting to well again but she made no effort to restrain them. Suddenly, she was glad that Leela had stayed behind to keep her company.

"Have you ever seen *Brother Sun, Sister Moon*?" Leela asked.

"No."

"It's an old film. I'm sure few people your age have ever heard of it, but it's really worth seeing. It's from my day, 1972. Franco Zeffirelli. Beautifully filmed, stunning scenery—the quintessential spiritual love story. It's the story of St. Francis of Assisi and St. Clare, filmed on location—sort of like Romeo and Juliet for the spiritual set but without the tragic ending. They fell in love as teenagers and were betrothed to be married, but Francis felt the call to become a mystic and a celibate monk. Clare loved him so much that she decided to adopt the same life. She became a celibate nun and eventually a saint. Most people know that he started the Franciscan order, but not that many know that she founded her own order also, what eventually became the Order of St. Clare."

"Are you saying that I should become a nun?"

"Janie Mac! That voice of yours was not meant to be shut away in a cloister. What I am saying is that there are many ways that two people can love each other, and not all of them fit into the Hollywood format. I doubt there has ever been a man and a woman who loved each other more than Francis and Clare. Hollywood may make the myths we accept as our romantic ideal, but in the real world it is the saint who knows how to love best and love deepest. Just look at Gurudeva. In the end, both Francis and Clare became saints, and their love for each other may still be the single greatest example of love between a man and a woman that the world has ever seen. And they never slept together. They didn't need to. They knew that love was something that is communicated from one soul to another, from one heart to another. To be honest, Gita, more often than not the body just gets in the way."

"So what are you trying to tell me, Leela?"

"I'm trying to tell you, in my outdated Irish manner, that if you really love Mukunda—and I'm convinced you do, whether you admit it or not—then I wouldn't let a little thing like a vow of celibacy stop me."

"Don't you think Mukunda might have something to say about that?"

"Child, nothing and no one can stop you from loving Mukunda—not even Mukunda. You might not be able to choose the way in which you express that love, but the only one who can stop you from loving him is you. And I'll tell you another thing: most of what we imagine is going to happen never does, so there's not much sense in wasting a lot of mental energy over it. If the love in your heart runs as deep as I think it does, then be true to that and let Gurudeva take care of the rest. You know that old saying, 'it's better to have loved and lost than never to have loved at all'?"

"Sure."

"Well, love can't be lost, not unless you close your heart. As long as you keep your heart open, it's yours for the duration. Now, give me a hug. It's time for me to get my old maid's rest."

The two women got to their feet and embraced. As Leela was turning to leave, she added what seemed to be an afterthought. "Oh, by the way, I heard Madalasa say that Gurudeva wants Mukunda to leave by seven thirty, before the devotees begin gathering to sing bhajans. Don't be late, okay?"

Gita watched Leela walk away with a mixture of gratitude and disbelief. Somehow, the hope that had been extinguished while she sang her aborted love song had been brought back to life by the senior disciple's unabashedly candid words. Leela did not want her to give up. She had practically insisted as much. A half hour earlier Gita might have thought her ideas a little daft, or at least beyond her powers of adjustment as a modern, romantically mature woman, but the sense of authenticity she had felt radiating from her words under the reflective sheen of a moonless night had given her a glimpse of a world only known to the spiritual of heart, a world far more subtle and far more powerful than the one she had inhabited for most of her life. There was no doubt in her mind that this woman was far wiser than she was, wiser perhaps than she would ever be. The tingling she felt in her body was a testament to that. The kind of love she had talked about might be hidden among the clouds on some snowcapped peak, but all mountains were scalable. Even Everest had been tamed. If Leela thought that the love she shared with Mukunda still had a future—a love they had never talked about but which was evident to those whose eyes were as keen as Leela's—then she would be a fool not to pay attention to her words. Their rightness sung inside her, just as her love for Mukunda continued to sing, not in the mournful tones of the lament she had sung earlier, but in a defiant, determined, inspired readiness to accept whatever challenges life presented. No, she was not ready to give up, she realized. If it was a mountain she had to climb, then so be it; no one had ever promised her it was going to be easy.

When Gita arrived at the Bungalow gate at seven the next morning, she found it deserted except for the gatekeeper. For a moment, she was afraid that Mukunda might have left already, but a quick word with the gatekeeper reassured her that he was still inside. A few minutes later she saw Markandeya strolling up the drive with his wife, Sarala, a diminutive Taiwanese woman with a quiet demeanor and an iron will, and their thirteen-year-old daughter, Amrita, a budding, spiritually precocious Eurasian beauty who was smarter than any teenager Gita had ever known. Markandeya said a brief hello and then went inside to check on Mukunda, while Sarala and Amrita remained outside with Gita. They seemed to consider it a given that she should be there to see Mukunda off, and the conversation helped to calm her racing emotions. Other senior disciples soon appeared, including Leela and Madalasa. The car pulled up at 7:25, and Mukunda appeared a few minutes later accompanied by Markandeya. Once his bags were in the trunk, the dozen or so senior disciples who had gathered by then each gave him a hug and wished him well on his vision quest. Madalasa handed him a basket of his favorite snacks for the trip, and Markandeya gave him an illustrated collector's edition of Sir Edwin Arnold's *The Light of Asia*. Gita made sure she was the last person to give him a hug before he got in the car, determined that hers would be the last face he saw before he left. Though she was aware of the other disciples' eyes on her, she hugged him as tightly as she could and held on for as long as she thought seemly. "We'll talk when you get back," she whispered as she buried her face in his neck. "In the meantime, make me proud." When she released him, she saw the moisture in his eyes and the almost mournful look that passed across his face, but she smiled her broadest smile and his face immediately brightened. Then he was gone, but not before giving her a final wave from the back seat of the car, a wave that might have seemed as if it were meant for everyone but which she knew was intended for her and her alone.

Part Two

Del Mar

11

ONCE THE CAR PULLED out of the gate, Mukunda informed his driver, Ananda, that he was going to meditate for a while. He wasn't very successful, however. Though he made his usual determined effort to concentrate on his mantra, to distance himself from the parade of thoughts that had been marching in his head all morning, his mind seemed to insist on being left alone to roam as it willed. He could still feel Gita's embrace, wrapped around him as if she had yet to let him go, and her whispered words in his ear, reminding him of her continued presence in his life. The warmth of her body accompanied him backward down the stream of time: walking with her among the Santa Monica Hills, watching her pour her heart into the microphone during one of her studio sessions, their first conversation under the tamarind tree. Other images followed: his frozen surprise when Gurudeva told him he had been grooming him as his successor; the eyes of hundreds of devotees inspecting him on the dais, knowing that her eyes were among them and likely filling with tears. One after another they competed for his attention while his mantra faded into the background like music from a distant valley growing fainter with every passing minute, until his turbulent memories segued into the disjointed tapestry of a fitful sleep. And still they continued, a discord of images that tossed him from one moment to the next. In one of these dream fragments he found himself sitting in Madalasa's kitchen, sipping one of her green-vegetable-juice concoctions while she pointed to his birth chart, spread out in front of her on the kitchen table, and explained to him how the aspects formed by his natal Jupiter and Saturn to his Sun foretold a monumental change in his life when he reached the cusp of his Saturn return, a dangerous crossroads that could spell either glory or ruin, depending on the choices he made. She then drew a thick tome of astrological esoterica from a bookshelf that magically materialized by her rack of sprouting jars and began perusing it for some sign of the road his destiny would take, the frown growing more and more pronounced on her face, while all the while he felt the cold shivers of impending doom mixing with the unpleasant, bitter residue of wheat grass and watercress on his tongue.

When Mukunda awoke, the first thing he noticed as his head jerked up from his chest was the row of palm trees in front of Oceanside Pier and the sun slanting through the opposite window, burning through the last of the morning haze. An Eric Clapton CD was playing on the car stereo, a soulful blues-inflected line at the end of the second chorus of "Knockin' on Heaven's Door." The familiar sights and the lilting rhythms acted like a balm on his spirits. He was back in San Diego County! Within moments his warring impulses and conflicting hopes receded into the distance, as if by crossing the county line he had stepped back into the safety of his old life. Three weeks of freedom! Three weeks that no one would be sizing him up to determine if he were fit to be their future leader; three weeks that he would not have to find the words to let Gita down lightly, knowing that those same words would not be so kind to him; three weeks that he would not have to live with the weight of history and a beautiful woman's dreams on his shoulders; three weeks to forget the world with all of its problems and dive into the depths of his being in search of that elusive fountain of bliss that had evaded him so facilely these past years. Never had he been so thankful to be away from the ashram.

Twenty minutes later the car pulled up to the entrance of the Del Mar hermitage. The electronic gate opened before Ananda even had a chance to press the button and announce their arrival. He eased up the gravel drive to the main house where Mukunda found the caretakers, Lakshman and Sujata, waiting for them at the door. After a round of hugs and congratulations, Lakshman carried Mukunda's luggage to Gurudeva's suite and left him alone to embark on his quest.

Once Mukunda had put away his things, he parted the curtains and opened the sliding glass doors to the back patio. The house was a smaller version of the Bungalow, a single-story Spanish revival-style ranch house with white stucco exteriors and a red-tiled roof, but it was what lay beyond the house that Mukunda found so enchanting about the Del Mar property. The back patio was separated by a small strip of lawn and a low row of hedges from the chiseled edges of the Del Mar cliffs, one of the world's most compelling ocean vistas. Mukunda walked to the edge of the carefully trimmed hedges and looked out over the escarpment at the sonorous music of the sea, spilling its roiling foam onto the sands some thirty meters below. Far out on the horizon he caught a glimpse of sails heading southward and beyond them the azure tint of the sky curling over the edges of the world. Some of his most rewarding hours with Gurudeva had been spent by these cliffs, meditating on the lawn with the master during his rare visits to the hermitage, walking through the grounds with the other disciples and listening to the master's informal discourses. Now he was alone here—alone with his destiny, gazing out over the ocean toward the horizon where his future was waiting for him to prove himself worthy of the honor he had been given. Still unsure what he would find there, he turned his gaze from the horizon and began a circuit of the familiar grounds—three acres of Torrey pines interspersed with beautifully manicured gardens, gravel walkways, sculpted fountains, fish ponds, and beds of the colorful desert flowers unique to that sun-drenched but water-stingy land—as aesthetically refined a setting as a yogi could wish for, designed by its previous owner, a renowned local botanist.

After his walk, he sat down in the shade of the lone tree between the house and the hedges, a gnarled old lemon tree that offered just enough shade for three or four people to sit comfortably. He closed his eyes and began meditating. This time he felt no trace of sleepiness. The crashing of the waves on the beach below and the sharp, tangy ocean aroma heightened his senses and helped him to concentrate his mind on the mystery they were doing their utmost to hide. His retreat had begun! The greatest challenge and the greatest opportunity of his life! A sannyasi had no past and no future, he recited to himself. His life belonged to the present, and his present was clear and incontestable. He was alone in this spiritual oasis, ready to set his sights on the highest of all goals and launch his mind like an arrow toward its target. He would do now what he had longed to do all his life but had never had the chance or the stamina to attempt. He would shut out the outside world and disappear into his meditation like the Buddha beneath the Bo tree. For three weeks he would not let anything stand in his way, no inner conflict or outward distraction, no weakness of mind or faltering of his body. The Buddha had sat under the Bo tree and vowed not to leave that spot until he attained illumination. He would take a similar vow. He would raise his standard like a warrior preparing for the ultimate battle and set it to wave on the shores of the infinite ocean for the gods of his inner world to see. The sun by day and the stars by night would pay witness to his struggle; and when the sun came up on his final day at the hermitage, twenty days hence, he was determined that it would shine on the first hours of a newly awakened life.

Over the next few days Mukunda settled into a routine that would have done justice to any Himalayan sage. Each time he sat, he forced himself to continue until his legs ached and his mind quavered from the strain. Soon he was meditating twelve hours a day, weary from the effort and proud of his determination to let nothing stop him in his quest. He left his room only for long walks after his morning and evening practice, when his body cried out for movement and fresh air, and his mind for some sight of a landscape beyond its borders. Sujata brought his meals to his room at fixed hours, just as she did for Gurudeva whenever he was in residence. Other than a brief exchange with her at mealtimes and an occasional glimpse of Lakshman working on the grounds when he went for his walks, the young yogi had no contact with other human beings, no chance to break his external silence and escape from this unrelenting encounter with the self.

His first few meditations had their moments of true exhilaration. At times his mind elevated almost effortlessly, stretching its wings and gliding over an ocean far more expansive than the one whose salt spray floated up from its landing on the beach below. The heavy stagnancy that had dogged his efforts over recent months seemed to have been blown away by the constant breeze that swept in over the cliffs. He rode that breeze while it lasted, but the easy weather soon turned—as he had suspected it might. All his life Mukunda had been an avid reader of spiritual biographies, and he had never come across a saint or yogi who had not had to undergo severe trials along the road to illumination. He knew his own inward odyssey would not be so easy, that eventually it would require the kind of effort he had read about but never made. Sure enough, as one hour bled into the next and the days rolled back, he began to realize how arduous a journey it was. His body was young and strong, honed by countless hours of yogic asanas—he could sit for twelve hours a day and longer and fight the fire in his legs and back without giving in—but his mind was not prepared to face itself for such long hours without having anyplace to turn for refuge. The more he meditated, the more he began to find himself both spectator and participant in a pitched battle, the reluctant witness to a rebellion that he was having increasing difficulty putting down. The easy optimism with which he began his retreat gradually gave way to the grudging realization that if he wanted to make it to the Promised Land, he was going to have to walk through fire to get there. The more he struggled to concentrate, the more his mind mocked him, dangling his many desires in front of his closed eyes as if to show him up as the impostor he refused to admit he was. He tried to ignore them, to concentrate on the light beyond, but they pulled at him like a swift undertow, carrying him further and further away with every stroke. The fond distractions of recent memory clouded his vision, and when the clouds receded, a swarm of forgotten impressions rushed in to take their place. Every mistake he had knowingly committed and then conveniently forgotten, every bit of sloth and greed and selfishness, came back to sneer at him and shake the foundations of his confidence. He had hoped for a journey into the empyrean lands of his deepest consciousness, a journey limned with the bright rays of the breaking dawn; instead he found himself waving a paper sword at shadows in the dark, stepping over bodies that he had piled in the cellar long ago and then erased from his memory.

As his meditation grew more difficult, Mukunda took increasingly to sitting in the garden during his morning walks, reading from his illustrated copy of *The Light of Asia* in front of a small fishpond filled with brightly colored tropical fish. For the first time in his life, he began to truly appreciate the frightening earnestness of the Buddha's heroic fight with the demons on the eve of his enlightenment. The beautiful but ferocious color plates of Mara and the other demons bore an uncanny resemblance in feeling and tone to what he was experiencing in his daily practice. This was no mere allegory, no mythic fantasy with which to while away the idle hours. This was deadly serious business, as real and as unforgiving as the jagged clusters of feldspar that ringed the outskirts of the fishpond. The Buddha had faced the fires of his inner netherworld and emerged scorched but triumphant. But for every Buddha that had walked the earth, there were many more whose courage had failed them or who had settled for the easy pleasures of a comfortable compromise, exchanging the painfully won temple interiors for the pale but easily accessible light of the lamppost outside.

It was comforting to feel that he was not alone in his struggles. Even the greatest of masters, the Buddha himself, had faced what he was facing, but that comfort only lasted as long as it took him to walk from the garden to his room. Each time he returned to his meditation seat, the battle resumed, and there the poetic images of the Buddha's achievement could not help him. His frustration mounted and his faltering confidence slipped steadily toward self-doubt, the very obstacle Gurudeva had warned him about and the one he most feared. The unworthiness he'd felt when Gurudeva had told him he would be his successor came back like a brush fire whose sudden swift march defies all efforts to put it out. Was he really so foolish as to imagine that he could duplicate the Buddha's efforts, what to speak of his accomplishments? Did he honestly think he could become the leader of a spiritual community in truth as well as in name? Was this not delusion? Was it not false pride laid bare by his failure to harness his rampaging mind? He had no answers to these questions and no means of putting them aside. They were as insistent and as omnipresent as the sound of the waves beating in the darkness while the city of Del Mar slept. They crashed against the edges of his soul and left him dizzy after his practice, to the point where he sometimes had to lie down before he could get up and do his yoga postures or go for his walk.

At times he turned to Gita for solace in his struggle, conversing with her in his mind as he conversed with Gurudeva, reaching for the connection that had sprung up between them as if it were a lifeline at sea, but it didn't take long for him to realize how dangerous this was. Though the mere thought of her was often enough to buoy his spirits, as if he could tap into her natural confidence by telepathic transmission, the heightened sense of energy that ensued only made him even more acutely aware of the attraction that had been building these past weeks, an attraction that their physical separation could do nothing to stem, rising like the ocean at high tide and threatening to sweep him from his moorings. His book had a painting of Kama, the king of passion, whose promise of heaven in a glance and paradise in a soft embrace had melted into the void before the indomitable will of Siddhartha; it made him wonder how his own will had become so weak. Was it from disuse, or had its existence only been a well-fed illusion? Or could it be that the attraction he felt had nothing to do with passion at all, but instead emanated from the unexplored regions of his soul where his destiny lay in waiting? At times her presence in his mind was so strong that he was afraid to close his eyes, either in meditation or in sleep, knowing whose image he would see there when he did. When this happened he would reach for his book and reread the verses where Kama sends the image of Yasodhara to tempt the Buddha, who would not curse "a form so dear" but knew her for the shadow she was and sent her into the void. It was not Gita who was appearing in his mind, he told himself, but his own desires taking the shape that could best turn him from his resolve, but even then there was a part of him that refused to accept that such a powerful magnetic force could be an emissary of anything but the Divine, calling him to the road that had been marked out for him since his earliest days.

Each morning before his meditation, Mukunda lit incense in front of Gurudeva's picture on the night table and asked for guidance with these dilemmas that seemed insoluble to his youthful eye. During these few minutes, while he readied himself for another day of heartache and effort, he could see the master's smile changing from one moment to the next—sometimes light and playful; at others, serene and unfathomable. The strength that seemed to pour from the photo gave him courage to face what he knew would be coming, another league onward into the dark night of his soul. Once Gurudeva had taken some couplets from Saint John of the Cross's masterpiece and used them as the basis for his Sunday discourse. The poetry of the saint's verses and the revelatory way in which Gurudeva made them intelligible to the disciples' twentieth-century sensibility had moved Mukunda to tears, although the suffering that Saint John described had seemed more mythic and romantic to his youthful imagination than the stuff of real-life human emotions. Now Gurudeva's words came back to him and took on a new meaning. The master had asked the gathering when it was that God finally appeared to the devotee. Was it when they put forth their most intense efforts and cleared away all confusion from their mind by the force of their own will? The devotees had all cried out in unison, "Yes!" Gurudeva had paused and then answered in dramatic fashion: "No! He comes when you feel like your entire existence has been wrung dry and the only moisture that remains is your tears." He had fallen in love with the master's answer, but only now did he realize how literal it had been.

On the night of Mukunda's seventh full day of practice his self-doubt reached its zenith. The thought of giving up and simply playing out the string appeared for the first time in his mind, insidious but attractive. He could simply go through the motions, meditating a few hours each day and spending the rest of the time on the beach with a few good books. He had two weeks to go. Why not treat them as a vacation and enjoy the time that was left to him? What was the point of all this effort if he wasn't going to get anywhere in the end? Why put his body through such an excruciating test of endurance if his mind were simply going to treat it as an opportunity to flay him for every mistake he had ever made and taunt him with his own inadequacies? Though he knew that this was the voice of Mara, he also knew that he needed some kind of a respite; otherwise, that voice might soon appear so reasonable that he would yield to its entreaties.

A full week of nothing but looking at his own face in his mental mirror had worn his nerves to the nub. He needed a chance to get away from himself and replenish his depleted stock of inspiration.

It was after ten. Mukunda opened his eyes and stepped to the sliding glass doors, the surf pounding inside his head, beating against the hollow interiors with the resolute force of an invading army. He slid the doors open and stepped through, the sound of the surf rising in volume like an abrupt crescendo in a runaway symphony. For the next hour he walked up and down in front of the hedges, stopping occasionally to gaze out over the inky black waters toward the dimness of the horizon but mostly keeping his eyes on the ground in front of him, too wired to sleep, too frustrated to concentrate on his mantra, too caught up in the webs of his thoughts to appreciate the hypnotic beauty of the night sky, studded with the lights of a thousand stars like so many gemstones cut into the fabric of eternity. He invoked Gurudeva's name and cried out to the Lord of his heart, shaking his fist at him as he had read about Aurobindo doing whenever he fell down on his spiritual journey, putting all the blame where it belonged—on God for being the puppet master in this roadside carnival. When he stopped to listen, however, the only answer he received was the whisper of the breeze brushing against the hedges, almost inaudible against the ever-present backdrop of the Del Mar surf.

Eventually his mind began to quiet down, wearied and worn out by the motion of his feet. His thoughts seemed to lose the necessary energy to go on thinking themselves into existence. Gaining what he knew was only a temporary reprieve, short-lived but not to be wasted, he went back into his room, unrolled his yoga mat, and curled up beneath his blanket, his head just below Gurudeva's picture. The drapes swayed gently back and forth beside him, stirred by the ocean breezes coming in through the open doors. Within minutes he was fast asleep.

He slept fitfully at first, tossing and turning, vague sentiments rolling through his dreams like wind through a field of tall grass, but he soon settled into the long sleep of the mentally exhausted, a weary, numbing vacuity that took him well into the morning, into one final dreamscape that would trouble him to the point of waking. In this dream he was walking the California desert at twilight, among deserted hills speckled with ragged mesquite and palm trees stunted by the relentless wind and the vagaries of the desert climate. He found a trail that ran alongside a small, stony arroyo and followed it, lulled by the sound of the water splashing over the smooth, unseen stones. He continued on as night fell and the moon rose, a thick crescent shining ghostlike above the nearby hills. The trail ran to the foot of the hills, from which point the stream edged upward, turning into falling water as it climbed. Looking up, he saw the deep shadow of what appeared to be the opening of a cave cut into its slopes, just below the summit. Curious, he began to climb, feeling his hopes rise as his feet picked their way through the rough terrain. Nearing the summit, the stream passed through a thicket of mesquite and creosote that shielded his view. He plunged in, fending off the branches with his hands. When he emerged from the thicket, he stopped dead in his tracks, mute with surprise. There, seated by the side of the stream, a few meters below the mouth of the cave, was the sage who had initiated him into the spiritual path and given him the mantra that had become as familiar to him as his breath. Apart from the setting, everything was just as he remembered it from his childhood. The sage was seated on a tiger skin, his thick matted locks spilling onto his shoulders. His nut-brown body was smeared with ash, and he was naked except for a loincloth and the gleaming silver trident, which he held cradled in his left arm.

Mukunda rushed up to the teacher of his childhood and prostrated himself, tears stinging his eyes as he threw his body on the ground.

"By what right do you come here? Explain yourself!"

Mukunda was shocked by the sternness in the sage's voice and the scowl on his face. As he rose to his knees, he could feel the sage's ire pushing against his chest like the blast from an open furnace.

"I don't understand," he said.

"You took a vow before me once and you have broken that vow. Had you lived up to it, you would have earned the right to be here. This would have been your moment to fulfill your destiny, to meet the Supreme Lord who has been waiting for you for centuries, waiting for you to live up to your promise. This would have been your anointed time. But now you are just a beggar, whimpering for that which you do not merit. There is no room here for beggars. Be gone from my sight!"

Mukunda shuddered, conscious of the implacable nature of the sage's command. Panicked, he cried out, "But you are my guide. How can you forsake me like this? I don't even know what I've done."

The sage scrutinized Mukunda's face. The sound of the falling stream cut through the silence like the rustle of ankle bells falling through stars, while the moon hung in mute witness just beyond the summit of the hill.

"What was the vow you swore in my presence, that night by the river when I agreed to initiate you into the spiritual path?"

Mukunda had to search his thoughts. It had been a long time since he had even thought of the sage, and far longer since he had thought of the vow he had taken. Then it came back to him, like a voice rising from the depths, reciting the forgotten words of its own volition.

"I promised not to harm any other living creature and to dedicate my life to the welfare of others."

"Just see. Now what do you say? Why do you bother me by coming here?"

"But I have lived up to my vow," Mukunda protested. "I've never knowingly hurt anyone, and I've always tried to do the best I could to help others."

The eyes of the sage flashed with anger. "Do not attempt to deceive me, you ungrateful rogue. I have been with you every step of your journey. Behind every thought and every action I have been there, watching you, waiting for you to become worthy of the grace that was showered upon you. The only reason you have not seen me is because you have not bothered to look, so do not play me for a fool. I know what you have become. What have you done for humanity? What sacrifice have you made for those who are suffering? All you have ever thought about is your own liberation. At least have the honesty to admit it."

Mukunda hung his head. It was true. He had not lived up to his vow. He had not even tried.

"If you think you can get liberation by sitting all day in meditation, then think again. Even if you sit all the twenty-four hours it will not save you from your selfishness. I did not teach you these practices so you could pursue your own happiness and ignore the suffering of others. So that you could take from society your comforts and not give anything in return."

The sage stamped the butt of his trident on the ground and pointed his right index finger at the downcast Mukunda.

"You may become a guru in the eyes of the world, but to those who have the eyes to see, you will only be a great egoist. Beware, young master. The closer you get to the top, the farther there is to fall."

Again the sage stamped the ground with his trident. Mukunda felt a wind ruffle his shirt, gusting harder with every passing second. He recognized that wind. It was the same wind that had taken hold of him years before. When he looked up he was already being lifted from the ground. He caught a final glimpse of the sage's immeasurably stern visage before he disappeared into the same fog that had carried him away eighteen years earlier. When his vision cleared, the first thing he saw was a burst of light and a billowing of orange. For several moments, he felt disoriented. Then he realized that he was looking at the orange drapes in Gurudeva's room, shifting in the morning breeze that was slipping in through the open sliding glass doors.

He sat up and looked around the room. Then his eyes lost their focus. An immense sadness opened up before him and pulled him in, rising like the waters of a river during an endless rainstorm, slowly obliterating the fields around it. Tears started flowing, silently and profusely, from the corners of his eyes, the same tears he had successfully held back these previous days, and fresh ones also, running down the sides of his cheeks until he felt their salty-sweet sting on his lips. He saw no reason to stop them now, no reason to even wipe them away, so he let them flow until there was no more water to be had.

And still they came.

12

After breakfast Mukunda went for his usual morning walk, but the once familiar landscape now seemed as alien to him as an untraveled ocean. The previous day he had walked through these grounds as if they were his own private garden. Now he felt like a trespasser ducking under fences for a glimpse of what he would never have and would never deserve. He sat down on the oak bench in front of the fishpond, comforted momentarily by the sight of the plump exotic fish flashing their brilliant colors as they swam lazily about, one eye on their next meal, but he could not bring himself to open his book. His dream had left him reeling, and there was no room in his mind for mythic parallels with the life of a master who was everything he was not. Rather than sharing the Buddha's dedication to the spiritual quest, as his pride had led him to believe, he had merely been cultivating a selfish desire for his own freedom. When he had closed his eyes and reached out to part the veil that had long separated him from the light, all he had seen was the Cheshire grin of his ego. The stinging rebuke of the sage had given voice to what he had suspected to be true all along: he had no right to be here.

And yet...the master had placed his faith in him. Despite all Mukunda's faults, Gurudeva was ready to hand him the keys to his kingdom. There had to be a reason, a reason that was purposely hidden from his eyes. He thought back to the evening in the meditation hall when Gurudeva had announced him as his successor. The master had promised that something unique and mysterious would happen to him in these three weeks, and those words had proved true, but Mukunda had never stopped to think that the mystery might lie not in the mystic reaches of his soul, as he had imagined, but in the muddy shallows of his selfishness and his pride. The irony of the master's words was not lost on him. He had not promised that his experience would be pleasant; there had been no guarantee that the mystery would come clothed in light instead of darkness. He was sure now that the master had foreseen the sage's return and sent him alone and unaided to this encounter, knowing that only in this way could he prove his worthiness. Mukunda had often wondered about the link between his master and the mysterious guide of his childhood—he had even questioned him about it once, but the master had laughed and then added a few cryptic words that only served to increase his confusion—and he knew it was no coincidence that the sage had reappeared at precisely this moment in his life. In some inexplicable way these two beings were working in tandem to test him. And, perhaps, to guide him through that test as well. Could they already see the outcome? Had the master chosen him as his successor because he knew that he would somehow find his way back from the brink, that he would eventually find a way to satisfy the sage and live up to his guru's lofty expectations? He could only hope. What he did know was that he had strayed unknowingly from the path the sage had marked out for him at the beginning of his spiritual journey. A crossroads was looming in the darkness. The encounter with his childhood teacher was not over. He was sure of that. The sage was waiting inside him, hidden but watchful, waiting for some act of redemption that could set his soul right. And the master was right beside him, willing him to choose the fork in the road that his destiny demanded.

Mukunda peered up through the wind-twisted branches of the Torrey Pines that lined the walkway. The sun was resting just above them, its mid-morning radiance burning away the last of the early morning haze. As his glance drifted toward the horizon, he sensed some great joy bearing down on the sky, as the sky bore down on the garden, a vaulted presence so still that the merest flicker of an eye would be enough to shatter the glass. It lasted for a brief moment, an ancient recognition stirring inside him like the memory of a former life when he had looked up at that same sky and felt that same presence awakening. Then he shrugged his shoulders and turned away, knowing that it was out of reach and would remain out of reach until some distant time that he could not as yet foresee.

Rather than go back to his mat and resume his meditation, as he had done each of the previous seven mornings, Mukunda decided to go for a walk along the beach. At the south end of the property, there was a break in the hedges where a steep, rocky path led down the cliffs. Mukunda clambered down the path and hit the sand with a short leap. As soon as he landed he felt his spirits begin to lift. It was the first time he had left the hermitage since he'd arrived, and the first time he had seen another human being other than Sujata and Lakshman. The beach was dotted with bathers stretched out on the sand or strolling by the edge of the water, carrying their sandals in their hands. The few surfers who were left at this late hour were busy paddling out to the next wave. Mukunda kicked off his own sandals and started walking south along the beach, relishing the touch of the wet sand underneath his feet and the stimulating spectacle of unfamiliar faces. For a moment he felt a sense of exhilaration, as if he were escaping from house arrest, but then he remembered that he was bringing his mind with him—"the jailer that never sleeps," as Gurudeva had once put it—and the moment passed. No amount of temporary freedom, he knew, could help him with his trials.

As he walked, he tried to keep his mind on the picturesque summer seascape. He took off his shirt to feel the sun on his back and consciously breathed in the moist salt air, letting his eyes linger on each novel sight, from the cleverly camouflaged dance of a hermit crab inside its shell to the gulls tracing dark gray circles by the edges of the cliffs; but soon he lost sight of the beach and became engrossed again in his internal conversation. Unable to escape from the burden of self-doubt, he called on Gurudeva for guidance and reminded him that he was only there because the master had sent him there. He pleaded with the sage for some indication of what he wanted and reaffirmed to him that he was ready to rededicate his life if he would just show him how to proceed. He felt Gita's presence as well, both comforting and disturbing, and for a while he shared his thoughts with her and listened carefully to her answers, knowing that they sprang from some hidden part of himself that he hoped was wiser than his ordinary mind. He had gone a couple of miles when he shook himself loose from his thoughts long enough to look around. The hermitage had disappeared behind a bend in the shoreline and the sun was nearly overhead. He had gone farther than he had planned. He turned and headed back, quickening his pace. It would be lunchtime by the time he got back, but despite the long hiatus from his practice he decided it was worth it. He had needed a break. He was no closer to a solution to his dilemma, but even so, he could feel some of his natural optimism seeping back in, aided, no doubt, by the healing change in perspective. At the very least he was ready to go on, to continue his efforts while he remained watchful for some sign of what he should do next.

Mukunda was nearing the hermitage when his reverie was interrupted by a gruff voice that took a few moments to separate itself from the ambient noise and register in his consciousness.

"Excuse me?" he asked, suddenly aware of the wizened, weather-beaten old man dressed in second-hand clothes who was stretching out his empty palm, wrapped in the sickly sweet stench of stale wine and unwashed flesh.

"Can you spare some loose change? I haven't eaten anything since yesterday. A dollar would help."

Mukunda winced at the odor but forced himself to be polite. "I'm sorry," he said. "I didn't bring any money with me."

"Even a quarter would help."

"Sorry."

"Okay. Have a nice day."

Mukunda forced a smile and continued walking, anxious to escape the odor. It wasn't often one saw homeless people on the Del Mar beach—or anywhere in Del Mar, for that matter. They were common enough in Hillcrest or in downtown San Diego, especially around Balboa Park, but Del Mar was a world apart, a world of privilege where it was easy to forget the problems that festered in the city. When he reached the foot of the path to the hermitage, he glanced back and noticed the same homeless man shuffling toward what looked like a makeshift shelter at the base of the cliffs, fashioned from cardboard and a few pieces of driftwood. If you had to be homeless, he thought, this wasn't a bad place: Del Mar beach in the summer—clean, picturesque, a regular supply of rich patrons and no competition. He smiled at the thought—until he remembered Gita and her anger over how badly the homeless were treated in LA, all eighty thousand of them. His amusement quickly gave way to shame. In one conversation, she had pointed out how for years the popular media had either romanticized the hobos, depicting them as free-spirited adventurers who refused to be tied down to a home or a job, or else portrayed them as shiftless lay-abouts, living off the toil of honest citizens. Anything to direct the public's attention away from their misery and the role that an unjust society had played in bringing it about. In fact, there was nothing romantic at all about sleeping on a cardboard bed in a back alley with no certainty where your next meal would come from, and virtually no one living on the street who wouldn't sell his freedom for a steady job and a rundown apartment.

Mukunda was halfway up the steep slope when he turned around and began retracing his steps. When he reached the hobo's shelter, he found him sitting on a boulder trying to light the stub of a cigarette. The man didn't seem to notice him. He was staring fixedly at a box of matches as he fumbled with a match, cupping it in his hands to protect against the ocean breezes.

"Need some help with that?" Mukunda asked.

The man looked up at him for a few moments and then turned his attention back to the matchbox. "Nah, I can get it."

"Okay. Mind if I sit for a moment?"

"Free country," he said, shrugging his shoulders but not bothering to look up.

Mukunda wasn't sure how old he was, but from the white stubble on his head and cheeks and the tough, wrinkled hands, he guessed that he was well past sixty. He found the stench from his body repulsive, but he was determined to disregard it.

"You said you hadn't eaten today. Is that true?"

The man shot him a hard glance as he took a puff on the finally lit cigarette stub. "Do I look well-fed to you? You think this is the Del Mar Hilton here? I just order room service and they bring me food?"

"Fair enough. What do you say *I* bring you some food?"

The man lowered his cigarette and trained his attention on Mukunda. "Yeah? What do you got?"

"How about some bread and cheese? I can probably dig up some salad and a piece of fruit. I'm staying up there on the cliffs. I can see what's in the refrigerator and bring something down."

"Bread and cheese sounds good. You got any wine?"

Mukunda laughed. "No, no wine. There should be some juice though."

"Juice is okay. Juice is good. Anything to wash the food down with."

"Okay. You wait here. I'll see what I can find and I'll be back in ten."

Mukunda hurried back to the house where he found Sujata in the kitchen putting the finishing touches to lunch. She looked surprised to see him, but when he told her he wanted to bring some food to a homeless person on the beach, she quickly got together some leftovers from the refrigerator and put them in a bag with plastic utensils and a bottle of juice. He thanked her and hurried back to the beach. The hobo was waiting for him with some old newspaper that he spread out on the sand. He took out each item, inspected it, and then laid it down neatly on his makeshift dining table. When he got to the casserole, he pried open the top of the plastic container, crinkled his nose, then shrugged and put it next to the other items. It didn't take long for Mukunda to realize how famished he was. He ate as if he were in a footrace, kicking hard for the finish line. Mukunda cautioned him to slow down and enjoy the food, but the man merely smiled and continued tearing into his meal as if it might disappear at any second. Mukunda barely had time to catch his breath before the last bit of casserole slid down the man's throat, his head tilted back as he tapped the container to make sure he got the last thick drop. When he was done eating, he opened the bottle of juice and took a long, satisfied swig; then he let out a loud belch.

"Pardon, I don't mean to be rude. In Japan, you know, it's a sign of politeness for the guest to belch after a meal. It tells the host they enjoyed the food."

"Glad you enjoyed it."

The man patted his belly. "It's all the same once it gets down here. But if I had my druthers, I wouldn't have gone for a lentil casserole and a salad. A nice T-bone would have done me just fine—with onions on top, if you know what I mean."

"Not much of a chance of finding a T-bone in my house, I'm afraid. We're vegetarians."

The hobo fished a toothpick out of his upper coat pocket and started cleaning his teeth. "So I gathered. Half of this damn state is some kind of vegetarian or another. Not that I have anything against vegetarians, mind you. It's just not my cup of sake, so to speak.

The man reached out his hand. "Name's Joel. I am obliged to you. That was right nice of you."

"Happy to do it," Mukunda replied as he shook the man's hand. "My name's Mukunda."

"Mukunda? What kind of a name is that? Arabic or something? You don't look Arabic."

"It's Sanskrit."

"Sanskrit? So how come your parents gave you a Sanskrit name?"

"They didn't. My guru gave it to me when I was a kid.

"Oh, I see. You belong to one of those cults, then? Think a big spaceship is going to swoop down one day and take you all up to paradise, do yah?"

Mukunda gave him a disapproving look, but he didn't say anything.

"Just joking, just joking. Whatever works for you, that's what I always say."

"We practice meditation and yoga. There's no superstition involved. It's actually very scientific. You learn how to calm your mind and discipline your body. You learn how to be happy and at peace no matter what your circumstances. There's nothing more worthwhile than that."

"Sure, meditation and yoga. I know. I have a friend who's into that. Jamal. We were staying together in Balboa Park for a while, in the canyons back of 28th, until somebody ratted us out to the police and we got moved along. That's when I headed for the beaches. I thought the ocean air would do me some good, and I was right about that, but I rarely manage to make it more than a day in one place; they don't take too kindly to bums in these beach towns... Yeah, I used to see him meditating at night sometimes. He liked to hang out in the library and read books about meditation and that sort of thing. I used to go with him every once in a while. He was a vegetarian, too. Didn't help him stay healthy, though. He came down with a case of AIDS. Dirty needle, no kinky stuff. Too bad, too. He's a nice kid. But that's what happens sometimes. The ones who least deserve it are the ones who get it. Life can be a bitch."

The gruffness was gone from the old man's voice and his face had relaxed into an almost eager smile. It wasn't hard to see that he loved to talk, and Mukunda was happy to indulge him. After a few minutes' conversation, Mukunda asked him how long he had been on the street.

"About three years now, off and on. I had a job for a few months last year—working as a bagger in the checkout line at Ralph's; I even laid off the booze for a while—but for some mysterious reason they up and fired me." Joel laughed as he said this.

"You couldn't find anything else after that?"

"You try finding a job with no fixed address and no place to take a proper bath. They can spot a bum a mile off, and I ain't met too many people willing to give a job to a homeless guy. Anyhow, it's only temporary, just until my social security kicks in. In the meantime, I'm okay. It's a whole hell of a lot better down here than it was in LA. Now that was the pits. I spent some time living on skid row there. That was a dangerous place, I tell you. This is like paradise by comparison."

"Because of the cops?"

"The cops, the psychos, the addicts, the other bums, even the tourists. You know, I got maced by this Japanese guy once. Yeah. I wasn't even panhandling. I was just going to say hello to the guy, ask him how he liked California, and he whips out this can of mace and douses me. I was lucky, though; it didn't get in my eyes. I wasn't that close to him. But that's what it's like there. You're lucky if they just shoot you a dirty look. You know? You've got these gang kids running around, beating up on the bums for sport. All the drug addicts, ready to knife you if they think you've got a buck. Everybody's running scared, and for good reason. It's way more laid back down here. They may not give you any money, but at least they don't look at you like you're Jack the Ripper if you ask them for a quarter and then scream for a policeman. Even the cops are pretty laid back compared to those LA cops, as long as they don't catch you sleeping in the Gaslamp Quarter or making a nuisance of yourself when you're panhandling. And anyhow I don't panhandle; I leave that to the schizoids and the addicts. I asked you, but that's only because I'm up here for a few days. When I'm downtown I make enough recycling bottles and cans to get by. Twenty bucks every two or three days, if I work at it. And I can usually get some food at one of the missions. Plus there's a few people who know me there. I can usually count on them for a quarter or two without having to ask. It's not too bad. As long as you stay out of people's hair, they mostly leave you alone. That's what I like about San Diego. That and the weather. Imagine sleeping on the street when it's ten below like those poor bastards in New York. Now that's my idea of hell.... "

When Mukunda finally said goodbye to the old man with a promise that he would return in the evening with dinner, he was glad he had taken the time to stay and talk. He had felt the old man's loneliness gradually soften and give way as he talked of his life on the street, of the thousand daily injustices that his aging eyes had chronicled over the past few years, how the color of rage had faded from red to green until it became indistinguishable from the color of the leaves in the park where he sometimes slept. As Mukunda climbed the hill, he felt the sting of indignation sharpen his senses, and it did not exclude him as a target. The guy might have had a drinking problem, he may have made some poor decisions in his life, but he didn't deserve this. No one did. And Joel was better off than most. Nearly half the homeless people in San Diego and LA were mentally ill, with no access to even inadequate treatment and no chance of fending for themselves. Another goodly portion consisted of drug addicts and alcoholics who were losing the fight against their addiction with no safety net to catch them when they fell. The rest were an odd assortment of downcast souls who were losing what Evelyn Waugh had once called "the unequal struggle with life." As he thought about it, he could find no justification for a world that could harbor such injustice with such brazen indifference, but even more galling was his own failure to recognize the hardships that so many people were forced to suffer through. He had a lot to think about when he finally sat for meditation that afternoon, and while his meditation bore no resemblance to the luminous vistas and oceans of peace that he had read about in his books, it was just what the sage had ordered. By the time the sun started going down and he got ready to bring the old man his dinner, he could feel a sense of purpose growing inside him, a rising flame that seemed quite independent of the thoughts that crowded his head.

Early the next morning Mukunda stepped back into the same desert dreamscape that had treated him so rudely the previous morning, a land that was instantly familiar to him. He sought the same path he had stumbled on before and strode it resolutely toward his destination, lit by the same wrought-iron flame that had hied him up the hermitage cliff and into a long chain of thoughts that he had had no wish to undo. The sage was waiting for him by the mouth of the cave, the same implacable scowl etched into his face.

"So, you are back again, you miserable excuse for a yogi. Sitting all day, doing nothing. Just misusing the time, abusing the time. Do you think feeding one hungry person is going to win my sympathy?"

Mukunda kneeled, touched his head to the ground, and then sat up and looked unflinchingly into the sage's eyes. "No," he answered. "I am not asking for your sympathy. I am asking for your guidance. I have taken a vow and I will fulfill that vow. I ask only that you show me the way to do so."

The sage looked long and hard at Mukunda, who stared back with an air of defiance, fueled by the fire he felt inside him.

"Very well then. You will have your chance, but it will not be handed to you. You have squandered the grace that was given you. You will have to discover for yourself the way to earn it back."

Mukunda bowed his head. It was all that he could have wished for, and more than he had expected.

"Now, be gone from my sight, and do not come back until you have earned the right."

The wind began to gust and within seconds he could feel himself being lifted from the ground. The last words he heard before he disappeared into the darkness were "Remember, I am watching."

A few moments later Mukunda awoke. He pushed aside his blankets and sat up. The first sound he heard was the surf drumming its ancient rhythms on the compacted sand of the beach below. He could feel the heaviness in the air and sense the quiet stretching out past the city and into the nearby desert in the hour before dawn. Gradually, he became aware of an inseparable connection that bound him to the vast panorama that he could sense but not see. To the surf and the beach; to the stars still visible in the sky and the glittering lights of the city to the south that flickered like a distorted reflection of those stars; to all the countless human beings, no different than he, asleep in their beds or awake, gazing at the encroaching sky and trying to hold back their tears. Years of meditation and he had never realized such a simple truth: he and Joel were bound by a single thread that would never let them go. There could be no liberation for one if there was no liberation for the other.

He sat there for a long time watching the light inch forward outside the sliding glass doors. Then he walked out to where he could see the first surfers bobbing up and down like seals in their black bodysuits, greeting the dawning day with their borrowed island ritual that now seemed to be a form of worship he had never understood before. Their voices against the surf sang out like a distant *arati*, an ancient invocation of the powers that come from over the ocean to guide us. Mukunda raised his arms to the sky and lent his own mantras to their melody. Then he sat down on the grass to perform his meditation.

Strangely, for the first time in weeks, his mind was quiet.

13

The next morning Joel was gone and so was his temporary shelter. Mukunda spent some time searching for him up and down the beach, toting the old man's breakfast in a paper bag, but eventually he called off the search and returned to the hermitage. Joel had been evicted; he had no doubt of that. All it would have taken was one call by a local—if the police hadn't already moved him along or arrested him for vagrancy—and Joel was quite right in his observation that the residents of beach towns like Del Mar didn't take kindly to transients on their shores. Mukunda was disappointed. Joel had been his only link to the hidden designs of the sage, his window into a world of suffering and injustice that he knew held the key to his redemption, and now he was gone. He may have only been one hungry man, as the sage had said, but a door had creaked open the moment Mukunda turned back and sat down to talk to him; now it was up to him to find out what lay on the other side of that door. If he were to find his way back into his teacher's good graces, he was going to have to embark on a different kind of journey, one that could not remain confined to the four walls of his hermitage room.

After breakfast, Mukunda borrowed one of the hermitage's cars and set out down I-5 toward the city. He had no plan, other than the vague promise the sage had given him that he would have his chance, and the faith that if he could only remain alert then Providence would steer him to his path. The only clue he had was Joel. As he pondered the meaning of their encounter, barely noticing the familiar scenery slipping past his window, he remembered Joel's friend Jamal, the AIDS patient who practiced meditation. Something stirred inside him, and he seized on this feeling as a traveler would a sign pointing to the next village. Could Jamal's brief mention have been planted purposely by the sage in Joel's conversation, the next fractured piece in an interlocking jigsaw puzzle? There was something about it that had caught his attention. Perhaps it was only the natural kinship he felt for a young man whom he had never met but who seemed to share his spiritual ideals, a man whose suffering must be overwhelming. The idea of looking for Jamal seemed to make sense to his groping mind, if only as a place to start—when a man was trying to climb out of the dark, he welcomed whatever handhold he could find. Satisfied with his decision, he bowed mentally to the sage and asked for his guidance. Then he tried to imagine what it would be like if he were in Jamal's shoes: living in the park, ravaged by a terrible disease. Would he be able to meditate? Would he be able to accept the possibility of his death with the equanimity of the great sages whose life stories sat on his bookshelf—alone and deprived of the protective environment that had sheltered him all his life? He doubted it. This was a kind of courage he had never been called upon to show. What then must Jamal be going through? The thought of it nearly turned his stomach, but perhaps there was something he could do to help.

When he reached Balboa Park, he left the car on a side street off 28th, near the north end of the golf course, and headed for the canyons. He had walked past them numerous times as a teenager. He and his friends would periodically make the trip from La Jolla to attend events in the city, and much of their free time on those trips had been spent visiting the park exhibits and hanging out to watch the passersby. Once he got his license, he started going down to the city on his own, and the park remained one of his favorite haunts. He saw concerts there, an occasional theater production, and spent time in each of the various museums, but most of all he loved to go to the planetarium, see a show with stars in it, and then go to the botanical gardens to meditate, or to the lily pond or one of the other, more secluded garden spots. He remembered seeing signs of campers at the bottom of some of the ravines, the kind of useful trash he had always associated with the homeless, and it had seemed unnecessarily ugly to him, a desecration alongside the beautifully manicured gardens where he loved to spend his time. Now he felt ashamed of his youthful indifference, conditioned though it was, ashamed of upper-middle-class America, wheeling their strollers down the beautiful cobblestone paths only a stone's throw away from where their fellow citizens were trying to make it to the next day without shivering in the cold or getting run off or going hungry.

As he scrambled down the side of a vaguely familiar ravine, attracted by some muffled noises near the bottom, he could feel an old fear rising, the fear of unknown places and dangerous people, but he fought it back with a sharp and sudden distaste. Fear was not a guide worth listening to, much less trusting. At the bottom of the ravine, he found a scraggly path and followed it in the direction of the voices he'd heard until he came upon the kind of encampment he was looking for: a small clearing under a pair of eucalyptus trees, littered with the survival gear of the down-and-out: strips of cardboard arranged as bedding and as shelter; a pair of shopping carts crowded with worn blankets, old clothes, pots and pans, and knickknacks; the remains of a series of makeshift meals—some blackened stones in a tight circle, empty cans and bottles and paper cartons strewn haphazardly on the ground nearby. A couple of scruffy-looking men in their mid-forties were sitting under one of the trees, one black and heavyset, the other a short and sturdy Hispanic. They were nursing cans of beer and talking softly as they watched him come up the path. Mukunda approached cautiously, heedful of the broken glass on the ground, and called out a greeting.

"Hi guys. How you doing today?"

The two men exchanged suspicious glances before the black man answered Mukunda in a gruff baritone.

"We're doing okay. So what you want, Homes?"

"I'm looking for somebody. I was hoping you might know where I could find him."

"Yeah? And who that be?"

"His name's Jamal? Young guy about my age? Kind of sick?"

"You a social worker?"

"No. He's a friend of a friend. You guys know Joel? Older guy, in his sixties maybe? I met him up in Del Mar."

The Hispanic fellow let out a snort. "Sure, homey, we know Joel. I've been wondering where he got himself to. So you're looking for Jamal?"

"Yeah. Do you know where I can find him?"

The Hispanic man nodded. "Yeah, as a matter of fact, I do. I heard he got into St. John's, in Hillcrest. You know the place?"

He didn't, but the two men gave him some rough directions and then hit him up for a few dollars that he made them promise not to spend on alcohol or cigarettes—not that he held out much hope of that. A few minutes later he was in his car, happy that he seemed to be heading in the right direction.

St. John's Village consisted of a sprawling 1920s mansion and a trio of adjoining cottages at the end of a quiet cul-de-sac just north of the park; it had been converted into a nursing home and hospice facility for the homeless by the Catholic Diocese of San Diego, with the help of a generous donation from San Diego's most prominent philanthropic family. The property was fronted by a row of thick, high hedges that concealed all but the second story of the main building, and if it were not for the small sign by the side of the driveway, Mukunda would have mistaken it for the sheltered hideaway of some old-money San Diego mogul. It was run by the Sisters of Mercy and the motto inscribed on the sign read: "We can never love enough."

From the reception desk, he was sent down the hall to the director's office where he was told he would find Sister Martina Karlsberg. The door to the office was open. Inside, behind the desk, was a small, plain-faced woman with short-cropped sandy hair. She was in her early-to-mid-fifties and wore a white doctor's lab coat, not exactly his image of a Catholic Sister. Above her head there was a wooden carving of Christ on the cross and below it a painting of an Irish nun that he later came to find out was Catherine McAuley, founder of the Sisters of Mercy. He knocked on the open door.

"Excuse me, are you Sister Martina?"

"Yes. How can I help you?" The woman spoke with a soft but distinct Bavarian accent, and her smile was as genuine and as welcoming as Mukunda had seen in a long time.

"I was hoping to be able to visit a patient of yours, Jamal?"

Sister Martina looked pleasantly surprised. "I see. Please, come in. Have a seat. Are you a friend of Jamal's?"

"Not exactly. Not yet, at least."

The sister's eyes lit up with a look of bemused curiosity. Mukunda sat down and started explaining how he had met Joel on the beach and how it had led him to look for Jamal in the park. He went on longer than he wanted, but he found it difficult to stop. The genuine interest she expressed and the spirit of generosity she radiated seemed to draw out the storyteller in him, to the point that he even shared with her his hopes that he could be of some help to the people who needed it most. Sister Martina crinkled her freckled nose and laughed under her breath as he spoke, as if she were listening to an entertaining tale with all the time in the world at her disposal—though she was obviously a very busy woman—but when he was done, her words left no doubt that she appreciated the seriousness of his undertaking.

"I wish there were more young people like you in the world, Michael.

From my experience, it usually takes most people until my age before they start learning the value of compassion—if then. It's too bad. People would be a lot happier if they did. What most people don't realize, I think, is that compassion does even more for us than for the people we help. It's through compassion that we discover our humanity. Without it, I don't know if anybody can really be happy. But here, let me take you to Jamal. I want to warn you, though. He's very weak at the moment. He's just coming off a bout of pneumocystis pneumonia; it was touch and go there for a few days. I don't know how long he will be able to talk, but I do know that he will be very, very happy to see you. Just try not to tire him out too much, okay? And do me one favor, if you could. When you're done, stop by and see me on your way out."

She led him out the back door of the main house and into a small room in one of the adjoining cottages where a gaunt young black man was propped up on a raised hospital bed, wheezing softly while he watched television. "Well, young man, I hope I'm not interrupting anything important," she said cheerily as she walked up to the head of Jamal's bed. She asked him if he were feeling any better and took a towel that was hanging from the railing of the bed and dabbed some beads of sweat that had collected on his forehead. The affection that existed between them was obvious from the subtle timbre of concern in her voice and the brightness that appeared on Jamal's face. It was just as obvious that Jamal was not doing well. He looked very weak, barely able to sit up on his own. His eyes appeared glazed over—whether it was from the drugs or the failing resources of his body, Mukunda could not tell—and he was having noticeable trouble breathing. But when he spoke, there was an echo of innocence in his voice that would have surprised Mukunda no matter where he met it, but which in this place and under these circumstances seemed to be something of a minor miracle.

"I have somebody here who's come all the way from Del Mar to meet you, Jamal," she said, catching Mukunda by the arm and drawing him to the bedside. "You and he have a mutual friend, but I'll let him tell you about that. Why don't you two gentlemen have a nice talk; I'll check back a little later and see how you're getting on."

Jamal reached out his hand and smiled. Mukunda could feel a slight tremor in his hand as he shook it and was dismayed to realize how much effort even this simple gesture had cost him. He began the conversation by recounting how he had met Joel on the beach and how it had led him to come and pay him a visit.

"Joel told me you were interested in meditation and yoga?"

Jamal's glazed eyes glittered at the reference. "Yeah. I'm kind of a fanatic, you could say."

"Me too. I've been meditating since I was a kid; I'm also a yoga teacher."

"Really! Here, let me shut off the TV." Jamal seemed to gain energy as he used the remote to shut off the television and fumbled with the bedside controls to change the bed to a more upright position.

"So, what kind of meditation do you practice?" Mukunda asked as he helped him to reposition his pillows.

"Different kinds. Mostly Vipassana, a little Zen. I learned from books, mostly, but I've been to a few *satsangs* here and there, picked up a few things along the way. I wish I could be more disciplined, though."

"That'll come. I do mantra meditation myself. I teach yoga up at The Ashram in Topanga Canyon. Have you heard of it?"

"Sure! I've heard of it. I read an article about Gurudeva in the *Yoga Journal*. I think it was last year, or maybe the year before. I've always wanted to go up there and see him, but I never had the chance. I don't suppose that's in my karma now."

"Who knows? Karma's a funny thing. You never know what's going to happen next. So, you got any good books to read while you're in here."

Jamal motioned to his night table where there was a meager collection of spiritual books. From their tattered condition, they looked as if they had been traveling the streets with him for quite some time.

Mukunda thumbed through the books and placed them back on the night table. "You know, Jamal, I was thinking of going over to Controversial Books a little later. I could pick something up for you, if you like. Have you ever read *Living with the Himalayan Masters*?"

"No, I haven't. Is it good?"

"It's great. It's one of my all-time favorites. It's about Swami Rama's adventures in the Himalayas when he was young, all the great yogis he met. It's got some amazing stories. You'll love it...."

They continued talking for the better part of an hour, drifting from one spiritual topic to another. Mukunda almost felt like he was back at the ashram, talking to one of the newer devotees or a student from his yoga classes. Only when a student intern came in to give Jamal some medication did he lose the feeling that he was in a spiritual sanctuary, safe from the intrusions of modern-day society. By this time it was clear that Jamal was tiring and needed to get some rest. Mukunda promised to drop by again when he got time and went in search of Sister Martina. He found her in her office giving instructions to a couple of staff members. He waited in the hall until they were done and then ducked his head in to say goodbye, but she waved him in with both hands.

"Don't run off yet, Michael. Come in, have a seat. Why don't you shut the door so we can have some privacy. As long as the door's closed no one bothers me, unless it's an emergency, or something close to it." She took a last glance at one of the documents on her desk and tossed it in a filing tray. "So, how did it go?"

"He doesn't look too good, to tell the truth. It's really a shame. He seems like such a nice guy."

"One of the nicest you'll ever meet, Michael. He never complains, and God knows he has a right to. His immune system is almost completely non-functional. We're doing what we can but... well, there's only so much we can do."

"I heard he has AIDS. Is that true?"

"Unfortunately, it is. Like many young men in his position he's had to struggle with a substance-abuse problem. Somewhere along the way he ran into a dirty needle. It's a lot more common than you might think."

"What about the new drugs they use for treating AIDS nowadays? Is he not responding or something?"

"I have Jamal on antiretrovirals, but unfortunately they are not very effective in the later stages of the disease. By the time Jamal was diagnosed—that was at St. Vincent de Paul—the virus had already debilitated his immune system. That's why I admitted him into St. John's. At this point there is only so much we can do, medically speaking, and most of that is palliative care. If we had gotten him earlier, things would have been different, but that what happens all too often with the homeless. They fall through the cracks and get swallowed up."

"I see. How long do you think he has, if I can ask?"

Sister Martina shrugged her shoulders; a look of futility appeared briefly on her face. "With advanced AIDS patients it's very hard to say. Their immune system is unable to fight off other diseases; they can contract something that would hardly bother you or me, and it can kill them in a matter of days, even hours sometimes. You just never know. And then again, sometimes they react positively to the drugs and they can survive for quite some time. There's simply no way of knowing. In Jamal's case, he's fighting a rather aggressive B-cell lymphoma and a few other complications as well. It's not a good situation... Anyhow, that's not exactly what

I wanted to talk to you about. Do you know much about the hospice movement?"

"Not really."

"Well, we're a nursing home and hospice for the homeless, those who can no longer take care of themselves and have no place else to go, and those terminally ill patients that no one else will take. Our main focus in hospice care is the emotional and spiritual well-being of the patient. We have excellent medical treatment, but with terminally ill patients the focus is on palliative care; in other words, we do whatever we can to give them the best possible quality of life during the final stages of their illness, physically, mentally, and spiritually. We have social workers assigned to each patient, a psychiatrist who comes twice a week, and a chaplain—which in this case is me; I'm both the chaplain and the head physician, as well as the director. A lot of hats, I know, but with our hospice patients it all comes to the same thing. One thing I've learned here over the years is that we have to learn how to heal our spiritual pain before we can heal our physical pain. With the homeless that's especially difficult since so many of them are cut off from their families, cut off from society, marginalized, outcast, however you want to put it. So much of the healing process, both spiritually and emotionally, has to do with our relationships, whether it's with our families or our friends or with society at large, or with God—seeking forgiveness, dealing with broken relationships, finishing unfinished business, coming to peace with our past so that we can be free to move on—and many times with the homeless there's no way of repairing those relationships. In most hospice facilities you work directly with the family, but we rarely get that chance. In Jamal's case we haven't been able to get in touch with his family at all. We tried, but he wasn't able to give us much information and the little he did proved to be a dead end. He's been here a little over a month and you're the first visitor he's had. No friends, no relatives, no one. His social worker drops by once a week, we get other visitors from the diocese, and of course the staff does all it can—we're mostly staffed by student interns from the different nursing schools—but in cases like Jamal's one real friend can make a world of difference. I've seen it happen, time and again. Someone who doesn't work here, who's not sent over from an agency. Someone who's here just to see him, to spend some time with a friend... What I wanted to ask you was if you might consider visiting Jamal from time to time. I don't know what your personal situation is, of course, and I know it's a lot to ask, but it would make a big difference to him, a very big difference. More than you can imagine, I dare say. I know how much your visit today meant to him. I could see it in his eyes. We do all we can but we're underfunded and understaffed. We can't give him the time and attention he deserves. Anyways, I'd appreciate it if you'd at least think it over; it would be a real service."

Mukunda had no need to think it over. He didn't need to measure her words in the balance scales of his intellectual understanding. The mere thought of the sage, watching and waiting in the moonlit landscape of his dreams was enough to free his mind from doubt, leaving him as malleable as a blade of grass bending in the wind.

"Sure. If you think it would help, I'd be happy to."

"That would be wonderful, Michael. I knew I wasn't mistaken about you. I knew it the moment you stepped in the door."

"Actually, I have a few hours before I need to head back. If there is anything else I can do, I'd be happy to volunteer. Anything at all. Cleaning, mopping floors, it doesn't matter."

Sister Martina's smile widened and her eyes sparkled with a girlish gleam. "I'm quite sure we can find something for you to do. If there's one thing there's no shortage of around here, it's work. I'll take you to Sister Rita. She's in charge of the volunteer staff. You can help them with their rounds. How does that sound?"

"Sounds good."

A few minutes later, Sister Rita was introducing Mukunda to the volunteer staff with her musical Irish brogue. He spent the afternoon accompanying two volunteers from the SDSU School of Nursing on their rounds. He learned how to give sponge baths, empty bedpans, and assist the non-ambulatory patients with their bodily necessities. Most of the patients had special needs, depending on their condition, and as he learned how to assist them he started to get a sense of who they were. It was not glamorous work or easy. Some of the patients were quite difficult to deal with, especially the hospice patients, and it was easy to understand why: many of them were dealing with a lot of pain and fighting the effects of the drugs without which the pain would have been unmanageable. All of them were coming to terms with the undeniable fact that they would be dying soon, that St. John's was the last place on earth they would ever see. A good number of them were clearly dealing with mental illness as well, as were some of those whose principal ailment was old age. Mukunda experienced firsthand what Sister Martina had told him about the hospice patients. They were all reaching out for solace, each in his own way, reaching out through their anger or their forced attempts at laughter, through their sullenness or their garrulousness or their confusion, reaching out for understanding and a hand to walk them through the dark. The longer he worked, the more he could feel their necessity and their unspoken sufferings hanging in the air like a low-pressure system, thickening the atmosphere to the point where his hands and legs seemed to meet resistance with every arc they traced. It wore on him as he could see it wear on the other young volunteers who smiled their way through it but let their exhaustion show each time they took a break.

At one point, he and the two girls gave a sponge bath to an old man whose intestines were being eaten away by cancer. While they were getting ready to bathe him, he called them closer and whispered to them that he had asked the doctor to help him to die but that she had refused. What did she think? Did she honestly believe that her God wanted him to suffer like this? Did she think it was a blessing to drag out his life in this way? All he was asking for was a simple injection to put him out of his misery. Couldn't *they* help him? Sister Rita passed by, overheard, and intervened, but by then the baptism was complete. He could see the old man's question etched in his fellow volunteer's faces, a question that made a mockery of their fragile sense of right and wrong. What kind of a world do we live in? he could almost hear them ask. Mukunda had his philosophy to pacify his intellect—the law of karma to which all beings were subject—but it didn't stop him from feeling the old man's pain as it seeped across the barrier that divided them, a barrier that was growing increasingly porous with every passing minute.

As he smiled his way through the afternoon, Mukunda forced himself to listen attentively to their stories and their complaints. He forced the resistance and reaction from his mind, knowing that they deserved his full attention, at the very least. Slowly he began to understand that it was the quality of his consciousness that mattered most, rather than the little services he performed as conscientiously as he could. As he stooped to change a bandage or help someone eat his meal, he tried to fill the space between them with as much of his fortitude and peace of mind as he could muster, hoping that some of it would bridge the gulf that separated them. What better gift could he give these people in a world where the line that separated the light from the dark was as thin as a spider's silken thread? As the day wore on, he began to feel gratitude for the years of spiritual practice, for the attentions of Gurudeva and the admonishments of the sage—not because of the bliss it promised, not for the liberation he desired, but because it gave him something to share, something they needed far more than any material comfort he could give them. When he took a late afternoon break, his thoughts strayed for the first time to the Del Mar hermitage and his meditation mat out on the grass. The beauty of the ocean over the bluff flashed in his mind and brought a sudden glaze of tears to his eyes. He closed them for a few moments and sent his mind into the spirit from which that beauty arose—not so that he could enjoy it for himself but so that he could share it, looking to catch light in a chalice so that he could pass it around for everyone to sip.

After dinner Mukunda sat for a while with Jamal. He brought him a chocolate bar from the machine in the staff lounge, and the two of them slipped into an easy conversation about reincarnation. Jamal wanted to know if Mukunda believed that we get to choose our next life, or if he thought it just happened automatically according to our karma. Most of all, he wanted to know how he could avoid having to go through so much suffering the next time around, though it seemed to Mukunda that what he really wanted was to feel some assurance that he would get another chance to set it right, the kind of second chance that Mukunda was getting.

"I think only the enlightened masters know the answers to these questions, Jamal, but I can tell you what I believe. I think we do choose our next life, in the sense that every action has its consequences and we have to face those consequences sooner or later, in this life or the next. If we cause suffering to other living beings, then that's the destiny we create for ourselves. We get dealt the hand we deal to others. Conversely, if we cultivate love for God and try to serve him through his creation, then we meet that love in our next life."

"I must have done some pretty crappy things in my last life; you can bet on that, Michael."

"You may be right, but I'll tell you something else. You must have done something right also. A lot right, I'd say; otherwise you wouldn't be on the spiritual path. We wouldn't be sitting here together talking about karma and mantra or meditating together. I'll tell you what I think, Jamal. I think you're paying off a very old debt, something you couldn't finish the last time around, but in the meantime you've been doing everything else right, and that's what really counts. I was talking to Sister Rita, and she tells me you're everybody's favorite patient. Yeah, really. You want to know why? It's because you're always so nice to everyone, no matter what. They can feel the spiritual vibe, just like I do, even if they don't realize that that's what they're feeling. And then I think about the conditions you've had to face: living on the street like you have, having to deal with your disease. Most people would be bitter or angry or clinically depressed or who knows what. But you've kept your spiritual feeling alive and growing. You don't have any bitterness, from what I can see. I think that's remarkable. I think it requires a lot of courage and a lot of surrender. To tell you the truth, from where I sit, I'd say you've lived a pretty successful life. I honestly don't know if I would have been able to face all that adversity and keep my spiritual ideal alive like you have."

"You really think that?"

"I do. You know that old saying 'you can't take it with you'? Well, there is one thing you do take with you: you take yourself, who you are inside. And in the next life you pick up where you left off. Have you ever read the Bhagavad Gita?"

"Sure. It's one of my favorites. I used to hang out in the downtown library a lot. They don't have a lot of spiritual books, but that's one of the ones they do have."

"I don't know if you remember, but there's one section where Arjuna asks Krishna what happens to a man who doesn't reach the goal of yoga in this life, and Krishna tells him that none of our efforts are ever lost. Whatever progress we make in this life, we pick up at the same place in the next one. I always tell myself that, when things are going bad. It helps me to remember that this is a long journey we're on. Whatever difficulties we may be facing right now, they're never really so important, just as long as we keep moving ahead."

Jamal blinked his eyes and looked out the window for a few moments. Then he looked at Mukunda and spoke with an innocence that startled him. "So you really think I'll do okay next life, Michael. You think I can become a good yogi and all?"

"Jamal, I think you're well on your way to becoming a good yogi in *this* life. Hopefully you have a lot of years left. Sister Martina seems like an excellent doctor to me; I don't think she's going to let you go so soon. But whenever that time does come, you can rest assured; you'll be a yogi the next time around. That's how it works. You pay your karma, keep moving ahead, and God does the rest... Unfortunately, I have to be going now, but I'll come by tomorrow and we'll hang out. What do you say we do a few minutes' meditation before I leave?"

Mukunda helped Jamal to straighten his back with the assistance of a couple pillows, and they meditated together for nearly half an hour, far longer than he thought Jamal would have the stamina for. Though it was only a short meditation by Mukunda's standards, when it was over he felt as if he had just climbed a mountain, his head cleared and his spirits lifted by the exertion and the rarefied air. Jamal was looking at him and smiling. Though he was obviously exhausted, there was a quiet laughter in the young man's eyes that was beyond the reach of his body, rendering the rampaging virus powerless to prevent his silent celebration of life. Mukunda could already feel a bond growing between them, as binding as any he had with his fellow devotees in the ashram. He felt a surge of gratitude, not only because he had been given a chance to help another living soul but because he suddenly realized how much Jamal was helping him as well—that compassion lived on both sides of the narrow divide that separated them.

When Mukunda stopped in to say goodbye to Sister Martina, he knew that his retreat had extended its boundaries to include St. John's Village. The walls of his ashram were expanding. They had stretched from Topanga Canyon to the windswept Del Mar bluffs and now to a cluster of buildings on a quiet residential street in the Hillcrest area of San Diego. For whatever reason, he felt sure that the lessons he needed to fulfill his vows to the sage would be found in this place, that the guidance he required would come from the lips of a young man ravaged by a terrible disease and from his fellow outcasts facing the ultimate journey, as well as from the small group of people who had been chosen by Providence to accompany them to the embarkation doors. The hope he felt must have showed on his face, for Sister Martina remarked as he was leaving that St. John's seemed to suit him. It wasn't often she saw a volunteer finish the day looking so much happier than when he'd begun. Mukunda took it as a sign that his heart was in the right place, and that the right place for his heart was here.

14

Mukunda entered St. John's the next morning with a full rucksack and a small box tucked underneath his arm. In them he carried the spoils from an extended shopping spree and a brief canvassing of the Del Mar hermitage. While at the spiritual bookstore the previous evening, he had remembered Jamal saying that he had wanted to visit the ashram but would never get the chance. It had occurred to him that if Jamal could not go to the ashram, then perhaps the ashram could come to him. An hour later he had left the bookstore with an assortment of pictures of different saints and yogis, a collection of bhajan and kirtan tapes, varieties of incense, a hand-carved sandalwood incense burner, some Tibetan and Indian wall hangings, and a compact library of spiritual classics. A short trip through the department store had netted a Sony Walkman, portable speakers, and picture frames; a quick stop at the florist in the morning had completed his shopping. When he explained his idea to Jamal, the young man's eyes lit up. He spent the next half hour directing Mukunda in his efforts. Opposite the foot of the bed Mukunda fashioned an altar out of a small table and a batik sheet that he had found in the hermitage. Several saints, including Gurudeva, found a home there; they were accompanied by twin flower vases and a small bronze statue of Shiva Nataraj, the father of the yogis, absorbed in the eternal dance of creation. Soon the gentle fragrance of incense was floating in the room, tracing delicate white fingers in the air, while Sanskrit mantras from the portable speakers colored the atmosphere with the echoes of eternity. On the wall above the altar, Mukunda hung a verse from the Bhagavad Gita that he had printed out on the hermitage computer and framed: "The soul is never born nor dies; nor once having been, can it ever cease to be. For it is unborn, eternal, everlasting, and ancient; even though the body is slain, the soul is not."

Among the books that Mukunda brought for Jamal were the *Tibetan Book of the Dead* and the *Tibetan Book of Living and Dying*. He had read both of them as a teenager, but at that time death had been little more than a mythic figure whose existence he had acknowledged but whose face he had never seen. No one close to him had died during his short life, and as with most young people the prospect of his own death seemed impossibly remote. But a single day at St. John's had shaken him from his sleep. He had felt death lingering there like an unwelcome houseguest, one who is in everyone's thoughts but whose name no one dares mention. He had seen his presence reflected in the troubled frowns of the dying patients and in the uneasy glances of the volunteers who saw their own mortality in that mirror. Mukunda had picked both books off the shelf at the spiritual bookstore with a certain eagerness, thinking that he needed guidance in his own journey through unfamiliar terrain. His initial thought was that he would read them at night to help him gain some insight into his labors. But as he laid down on his blanket that night and read through the opening chapters of the *Tibetan Book of Living and Dying* while the breeze slipped in through the open sliding glass doors, it occurred to him that Jamal deserved this book far more than he did. It was an agonizing thought, one he was still wrestling with on his way into the city in the morning. His instincts warned him that it might be excruciatingly painful for Jamal to read such a book. For his part, he had no wish to be reminded of death at every second moment, which was exactly what no reader of that book could avoid. How much more difficult then would it be for Jamal, whom death was already tapping on the shoulder to ask for the last dance? But his conscience insisted that death was a teacher whose lessons should not be ignored, and his heart backed him up. So he took the books out of his rucksack with the rest of the offerings, and they were the first ones Jamal turned to once the room had been decorated to his satisfaction.

"Wow," he said, holding up the books and looking at them with wonder in his eyes, "this is exactly what I was thinking about last night after you left. I was thinking I needed some books that could help me prepare... you know... for that moment, when it comes?"

Mukunda's uneasiness began to dissipate. "Are you sure?" he asked, as he pulled up a chair by the side of Jamal's bed. But there was no mistaking the genuineness of Jamal's smile. Together they started looking at some of the chapters, first in one book and then the other. Mukunda showed him some of the visualization exercises that Tibetan practitioners used to prepare themselves for their deaths, and at Jamal's urging they began practicing them. Jamal did the meditations while Mukunda read the passages out loud. They finished their morning session with a loving-kindness meditation in which Jamal visualized himself taking on the sufferings of others and sending them back compassion and light. When Jamal finally opened his eyes, he was weeping silently. Mukunda was so moved he hardly noticed the moisture in his own eyes.

Over the next few days, Jamal and Mukunda settled into an easy rhythm. Each morning they practiced the meditation exercises from the book along with some preparatory chanting, and afterward they discussed their experiences. They repeated the practice again in the afternoon before dinner. Though the sessions were not long, they were exhausting for Jamal. His breathing was labored, and it was obvious that he was experiencing a great deal of discomfort, but he would not consider easing off or stopping his meditations before he reached the limit of his physical endurance. Mukunda was concerned that he might be overtaxing him, but when he mentioned this, Jamal smiled and said that he didn't remember the Buddha taking it easy when he was weak and exhausted. There was such a look of contentment and confidence on his face when he said this that Mukunda felt sheepish for having even brought it up.

As each day passed, Mukunda began to marvel more and more at the young man's courage. Instead of trying to keep his mind on other, happier topics, as Mukunda was sure he would have done had he been in that bed, Jamal was soon spending all his waking hours either practicing the meditation exercises or listening to Mukunda read to him from his books or debating with Mukunda on how best to use his death to help him grow spiritually. His favorite exercises were those in which he visualized himself taking on the sufferings of others in order to help them achieve liberation, thereby cultivating his sense of compassion and lessening the iron bonds of his ego. The single-minded dedication he brought to this endeavor humbled Mukunda. In many ways he felt less the teacher and more the student. Though he was reading from the texts, it was Jamal who was teaching him how to use them. This young man, who was having trouble getting enough air into his lungs to keep his body alive, was staring down a human being's most frightening adversary without batting an eye. As Mukunda sat there on his chair while Jamal went through his exercises, he found himself looking at Gurudeva's picture, begging for the master's blessings to fall on this gallant young man, ever cognizant of the magnitude of the master's serenity despite the presence of a tumor on the surface of his brain. He pictured the sage in his desert landscape and asked him to help guide Jamal in his transition from one life to the next, as he had guided Mukunda in his. And he prayed to both of them, and to whoever else might be listening, to help him cultivate the same courage when it came his turn to leave the world.

Whenever Jamal was resting, Mukunda took time to help the other volunteers with their tasks, doing his best to embody the light of compassion that Jamal was sending forth in his meditations. He noticed how the atmosphere in Jamal's room was starting to have its effect on the rest of the staff. Though none of them, perhaps, would have recognized the word *ashram* had they heard it, they soon started treating Jamal's room as if it were sanctified ground. However animated their conversations, the moment they entered his room or even passed by it they dropped their voices to a respectful whisper. If he was doing meditation they would back out quietly without a word, even at meal time or med time, and come back again later when he was done. When they did talk with Jamal, it was in subdued tones, conscious of the aura of incense and mantra. Some of them even asked him about his meditations and his preparations for the transition that was awaiting him. Mukunda thought he detected subtle changes in their faces as the aura in Jamal's room worked its way outside its walls, slipping unnoticed down corridors and under closed doors, seeding serenity and compassion as it went.

One day Sister Martina called him into her office, her bright eyes seemingly missing nothing in the small universe she presided over.

"Michael, I just wanted to tell you that I think it's really great what you're doing with Jamal. Every time I walk past his door and smell the incense I just want to smile. Although we are a Catholic institution, we are strictly non-denominational within these four walls. We try to help all our patients worship in whatever tradition they feel drawn to. It's such an important part of their process. Before you arrived I tried to encourage Jamal in his faith, but I know very little about meditation or Buddhism or such things. I've always been curious about meditation, but I've never taken the time to learn. That's part of the reason why I was so happy when you showed up. You were exactly what Jamal needed. I've been thinking how nice it would be if some of the other patients could benefit from your expertise while you're here. A couple of them have asked me about it, actually. I was wondering if you would consider teaching them some simple meditation and breathing exercises, some relaxation and stress management, maybe, some of the different things you've been doing with Jamal that could help them with what they're going through... What do you think?"

"Of course. If you think it will help."

"Wonderful. I think it would be a much better use of your time than cleaning bedpans. Even Sister Rita mentioned it. She feels the same way I do. Actually, we probably need it as much as the patients, if not more."

From that moment on, Mukunda found himself serving as a part-time counselor. None of the other patients who requested his help were ready for the kind of discipline that Jamal had taken upon himself, but he was able to find something for each of them. He wasn't as qualified as he would have liked to be, but he had had some great teachers over the years, and those experiences now came to his aid. The courses he had taken with Sarala, Leela's guided visualizations, the thousand teachings he had absorbed in Gurudeva's presence—he drew on each of these and on the books he had read, taking the Tibetan Buddhist exercises and adapting them as the situation suggested or inventing new ones as his inner voice directed him. The response from the patients and staff encouraged him to trust his instincts and gave him confidence that he was responding to the promptings of an unfailing guide. Once again, he found himself humbled by the experience, knowing full well that the help he was giving was not coming from him but through him; that rather than teaching, he was being taught—taught how to open his heart to the Divine and become a medium for its grace, how to open his eyes to the greatness that reflected from every human face and his ears to the echoes of eternity in their fleeting words.

Early each evening, Mukunda returned to Del Mar to do his meditation, tired but satisfied that at long last he was on the right track. As if by way of confirmation, the anxiety that had plagued his efforts earlier in his retreat disappeared of its own accord. Instead of worrying about his lack of progress, he animated each session with the hope that his efforts would make him a fitter vehicle for serving the creation. As his attention shifted from the results of his practice to the sincerity of his efforts, a sense of acceptance took root and flourished. As long as he gave his best, he told himself, he could ask for no more; everything else—and even his own effort—he trusted to the Lord's unerring hands. Surprisingly, though he had less time to meditate, he felt like he was accomplishing more. His mind was far more concentrated than it had been, far more responsive to the whispers of his soul. The day's challenges and the worries that had traveled with him from Topanga Canyon vanished like birds before the hunter, chased away by the purity of his intention, and in their stead he caught glimpses of the ocean he had long been seeking. This newfound clarity lessened his need for sleep, and when he did lay down, usually well after midnight, his sleep was untroubled and profound. Though the sage did not return to visit his dreams, he could feel him keeping watch, and the thought brought him comfort rather than anxiety, knowing that it was the sage's watchful eyes that were guiding his footsteps.

One evening, when Sujata brought his dinner to his room, she hesitated for a few moments in the doorway. Mukunda could see the unspoken question in her eyes. He invited her to come in and keep him company while he ate, a light meal that would not compromise his night meditation. Mukunda was halfway through his salad when she asked him what he was doing each day when he went into town. Was he doing his practices somewhere else? In the desert, perhaps, or at the cove, or in some other favorite spot? Her eyes rounded in surprise when he told her he was helping in a project for the homeless in Hillcrest, but as he related the details of his dream and his encounter with Joel on the beach and then Jamal, her gaze grew thoughtful and quiet. A tear appeared in the corner of one eye and she nodded, as if she could see Jamal reclining on his bed and had recognized in him the sufferings that strip away our masks. When he was done, she asked him if she could send Jamal some food in the morning, her hesitant tone making it seem as if she were asking for a favor instead of offering to help.

From then on, Mukunda left the house each morning with a tote bag full of food that Sujata labored over while he practiced his meditation—not only his lunch and Jamal's but Jamal's dinner as well and an assortment of snacks and sweets. Mukunda could see that this came as naturally to her as smiling, and the warmth he felt as he watched Jamal eat from the dishes she had prepared reminded him that compassion was the essential quality of an open human heart. When Jamal made a simple origami phoenix for her and inscribed his best wishes for her future on the back, Mukunda recognized the same quality in him and knew that it was everywhere, biding its time, waiting for a chance to be awakened. When he brought the phoenix back for Sujata, she put it on the meditation altar in her room and returned to the kitchen to bake a large batch of cookies for the rest of the patients. When Mukunda sat for his meditation, he could smell the rich aroma of the baking cookies sliding in under the door, more fragrant than any incense, more promising than the thought of nirvana at the end of the path. For a moment, he thought he caught a glimpse of the Divine Presence veiling itself in the world of forms, wrapping itself in fragrance and color and sound until it was so finely hidden that not even the sharpest eye could see past the undulating surface sheen. Then suddenly the world turned. A brief moment hurtled by in which he was sure he saw the truth from the other side, a flickering reflection of the diamond's other facet: the Divine was not hiding itself in the world but revealing itself through the world; without the world to serve as a mirror there could be no reflection of the Self's original face, no way to make visible what could otherwise not be seen. The moment passed, and he wondered if his experience had been real, if a door had truly opened and shut, or if he had shaded it into existence with the brush of his imagination. The moment passed and left the world just as it was, except that now he suspected that what he was searching for was not hiding but standing on display in front of him, turning circles in the light and waiting for him to clear the glare from his eyes.

If the diamond top stopped spinning, would he see that it was not a top at all but a gathering of the light?

15

One morning, ten days after his arrival at St. John's, Mukunda passed through the front door carrying several trays of coffee cake. Sujata's desserts had acquired a place of distinction among both residents and staff, ever since the appearance of her first batch of cookies, and Mukunda had quickly gotten used to people eyeing the bundle underneath his arm while they greeted him with their morning hello. This morning, however, the lounge was empty and there was no one at the reception desk. He set the still-warm trays down on a table and headed for the back door, the rich aroma reminding him how much he had enjoyed the three pieces he'd eaten on the drive down from Del Mar. As he walked past Sister Martina's office he ducked his head in. She waved him in and asked him to sit down. As he was taking a seat, he noticed that she looked unusually tired; there were circles under her eyes, as if she hadn't slept.

Sister Martina got up from behind the desk and pulled up a chair next to his. "Michael, there's no easy way to say this, so I'm just going to come right out and say it. Last night Jamal had a respiratory seizure."

Mukunda felt a sudden hot flush in his face and hands. He jumped up from his chair and told her that he had better go and see how Jamal was doing. She got up as well and reached out a hand to restrain him.

"Sit down, Michael. Before you go back there we have to talk."

Mukunda felt the anxiety racing to his stomach. "Just how serious is it?" he asked. "How is he doing?"

Sister Martina reached out and held his hand. "Michael...Jamal didn't make it. He died early this morning. They came for him a couple of hours ago. I was by his bedside when he passed."

Mukunda stared at her, unable to comprehend what he had just heard. After a few moments he became aware of her hand in his and realized that he was gripping it far too tightly. He let go of her hand and slumped back in his chair, fighting the tears that were beginning to form a wet sheen over his eyes.

"Go ahead and cry, Michael. I'd join you, but I'm all cried out. Here, take some Kleenex."

She handed him the box. Mukunda wiped his tears and hung his head as he struggled with his emotions. He closed his eyes and started practicing a deep-breathing exercise, grateful for Sister Martina's respectful silence. When his breathing finally calmed down, he looked up and nodded.

"Do you want to spend some time alone in Jamal's room? I've asked the staff not to go in there until you've had a chance to say goodbye in your own way. I wish we could leave the room just the way it is, but unfortunately we can't. We need to give that space to somebody else. I was hoping that you would take Jamal's things. As you know, we've never been able to locate any relatives. I'm sure he would want you to have them. We all would."

Mukunda nodded. "I'd like to have a chance to meditate in there one more time. I think that would be the right way for me to say goodbye."

"I thought you might. After you're done, come back here and we'll talk."

Jamal's room was just the way Mukunda had left it the previous evening, except for the empty bed. As he sat on his usual chair by the bedside he noticed the *Tibetan Book of the Dead* lying open on the night table. He was sure that it was the last thing Jamal had read before he went to sleep. He would have practiced one or more of its meditations to prepare for a moment that was only hours away. He wondered if Jamal had had any sense that his death was approaching, that he had so little time left to get ready. Then he wondered if it really mattered. Jamal had done all he could during his last days on earth to prepare himself. Mukunda doubted there were many people in his position who had done as much, no matter how much advance warning they might have had. He pulled his legs up into the full-lotus posture and began performing one of the Tibetan exercises for helping the newly departed soul on its journey through the *bardos*. He did not assume that his effort would help in any mundane sense; it just seemed the perfect vehicle at that moment to send Jamal his love and best wishes. They had formed a bond in their days together that could not be broken by anything as pedestrian as Jamal's departure from his physical body; that bond demanded that he offer Jamal all that was in his heart as a parting gift for the journey. After he completed the exercise, he visualized the sage and Gurudeva sitting side by side on a white lotus in the crown of his head, against a backdrop of stars and space. He invoked their blessings and prayed to them to purify Jamal's negative karma, to free him from the bondages of his past actions and lead him to a birth in which he might have a chance to realize the highest truth, and to continue to guide him until his final merger with the Supreme. He saw the two masters smile and visualized the light of their compassion pouring out of them and cleansing Jamal, purifying his soul of its karmic dross, until he saw his friend merge in that blissful, luminous presence. Mukunda felt that same light enter his own heart and knew that for as long as there was a path, he and Jamal would be fellow travelers.

After his meditation Mukunda collected Jamal's belongings, silently thanking Sister Martina for the gesture. Some of them he would keep to remember Jamal by; others he would pass on to people who might need them, knowing that he would be passing on something of Jamal's spirit. He carried them out to the car and returned to the sister's office. There he slumped down in the same chair, part of his mind still following the light that had bathed his memory of Jamal. But where there had been sorrow before, there was anger now, a sudden simmering indignation over what could have and should have been. A remarkable young man's life had been cut short. Why? Because he was poor and lived on the street. Because his fellow citizens had walked past him without noticing he was there—or if they did notice, it was only to turn their heads and look the other way. Modern medicine had the means to allow him to live a long and productive life, but he was not allowed access to those means. Why? Because he was poor and lived on the street. It was as simple as that. He had been born into a world in which he and millions like him, born on the wrong side of a gaping divide, died while those who had money in their pockets did not.

Sister Martina listened patiently while Mukunda vented his frustrations. The grim set of her mouth was like a silent echo falling on his eyes. Jamal had been left behind by the society that had given him birth, as his companions who had shared his hard times on the street knew all too well, for they each had their tale to tell. No matter how different the plot, the story remained the same.

The more Mukunda talked, the more he felt the hard intensity of Sister Martina's gaze feeding his indignation. He realized that he was not saying anything that she had not faced day-in, day-out for years. This was her daily reality. He had merely stepped into it for a brief moment. He fell quiet for a minute, his head reeling from this momentary glimpse into a world where injustice and suffering held sway 365 days a year.

"These people deserve better, Sister."

"Yes, they do."

"So what do you do? How do you cope?"

"What a question! I've been here for thirteen years, since St. John's opened, and I doubt a single day goes by when I don't ask myself that question, or a thousand just like it. Sometimes I wish I could just stop asking, but I'm not built that way. Come on, what do you say we go and take a walk, get out of here for a little while? Get a little fresh air while we talk."

Mukunda was glad for the chance to escape the oppressive gloom that seemed to have settled inside those walls. He was glad to feel the sun on his skin, to feel his legs moving and his eyes forced to take note of what was up ahead instead of what was inside. They walked over to Vermont and up past University Ave to Washington Street, and then up the busy thoroughfare in the direction of El Cajon. As they walked, Sister Martina talked about how the urban landscape in the place she now called home had changed in the thirteen years she had been there, mostly for the worse. She had spent a lot of time walking these city streets, mostly in the Hillcrest and downtown areas. It was her way to get to know the people she was trying to help, an entryway into the mysteries of their daily lives. The walks were good exercise, she said, but a hard education. She pointed out some of the homeless's favorite hangouts, the places they would sleep when there was no shelter to be had, the ins and outs of the many ways they managed to scrape together money for their daily survival, culled from the hundreds of stories they had shared with her on the art of panhandling. Mukunda felt as if a veil were being lifted from a part of town he had walked through as a teenager but never really seen, revealing the subsurface life that went unnoticed by all but the sharpest of eyes. He watched as she pointed out a pair of teenagers selling a bag of crack to the driver of a car that pulled up to the curb for a scant second and then flashed away in the slanting sunshine. "They get started earlier all the time," she said. "It's barely ten o'clock." He would have thought the car had stopped to ask directions if she hadn't guided him how to see, forcing his eyes into a consciousness they instantly regretted. The signs of the homeless and their trials were all around him—their addictions, their confusion, their hunger, their hopelessness—but it took her eyes to make him see the little details that underscored their plight. The city's hidden underbelly was in full view, but if you blinked you could just as easily miss it—unless you knew what you were looking for, and then you would be sorry you knew, for you could never pass by again without seeing it.

They walked for nearly an hour. On the way back they stopped at a donut shop. Mukunda felt weary, not so much from the walk—the exercise had done him good—but more from the effort of opening his eyes to the harshness that the world had hitherto succeeded in hiding from him. He wondered how Sister Martina had managed to keep walking for so many years with eyes so open, how she had managed to survive getting so close to the people she worked with, knowing they were going to die on her, every one of them, often while she sat by their bedside. He had observed her now for ten long days. These people were her family, and many of them were on their deathbed. It seemed a strange place to ask her about it, in a donut shop staring out the window at a city that seemed as impersonal and as impassive as a city of shadows, but he had no choice but to ask.

"You can't stop caring, Michael. I don't think it's even possible. It's just the way we're made. You just have to accept that you're going to get your heart broken, every time... About three years ago there was a girl here for about six weeks, Marcy. She was my age. St. Vincent sent her over with a case of terminal tuberculosis. Tuberculosis, of all things! Here we are, at the beginning of the twenty-first century, living in supposedly the most livable of all American cities, sunny, ultra-modern San Diego, and in walks a woman with terminal tuberculosis. Incredible! Of course, with the homeless the same rules don't apply. We became good friends. I used to sit up with her at night sometimes and talk. We could talk about anything and never get bored. Near the end it got pretty hard for her to talk, so I used to read to her. Sometimes we'd just sit there and look out the window. I was with her when she died. She was in a coma for a day or so. Then about ten o'clock at night she opened her eyes. I took her hand and she squeezed it; then she closed her eyes and she was gone. Her lungs just stopped working.

"I don't know why, but when Marcy died it really got to me. In the ten years I'd been here I'd seen so many patients die. I was used to it. More used to it than you'd ever want to be. But this time I went home and I couldn't stop crying. I cried for two days. I didn't come into work; I just called in sick and refused to answer the telephone. I couldn't see the point. It was the first and only time I ever really seriously questioned my faith. Not my faith, exactly, but the relevance of it in the face of all that suffering. All these doubts kept pouring through my head: Was I really doing any good here, or was I just fooling myself? Had I made the right choice to come to St. John's instead of leading a life of contemplation? Why was I such a poor nun? Why couldn't I be more like Catherine McAuley? Had I done the right thing in becoming a nun in the first place? Was I really fit to minister to these people when I was so full of doubts and fears myself? I tried to find the answers in prayer but it didn't do any good. When I raised my eyes to heaven all I saw there was emptiness and all I heard was silence, as if God were absent or on vacation or simply didn't care. I felt so lonely and so dry, it was the most painful thing I've ever gone through. I just couldn't take it anymore: all the misery, all the suffering, and all of it so pointless. That was the worst part—I couldn't see any reason for it, for any of it... After two days I was so emotionally and spiritually exhausted, I didn't know what else to do, so I got up in the morning and I went to work. When I saw Marcy's bed with someone else in it, it was like getting hit with an electric shock. I felt it physically, in my chest. But then I went and talked to the new patient—he was a seventy-year-old alcoholic with intestinal cancer and a lot of anger—and I realized that he was just frightened, as frightened as Marcy had been when she first came in. So I gave him something for the pain and listened to his complaints and talked to him about God and the mystery that we'll never be able to solve. What else could I do? He was a human being and he needed my help, just like everyone else there. It was as simple as that. So I came in the next day and the day after that. And I began to realize that even though I was suffering, my being there was helping these people to suffer less. Then I remembered that Marcy had been more or less at peace when she died. I was the one who was all broken up, not her. And part of the reason she was able to die in peace was because I had been there for her. And now I had the chance to be there for someone else. That one thought was enough to keep me going. It still is. You remember that line from Shakespeare where Polonius says, 'And this above all, to thine own self be true'?"

"And then it follows, as night follows day, that thou canst not be untrue to any man."

"Exactly. Well, I think it's just as much true the other way around, if not more so. If you are true to your fellow man, then you can't be untrue to yourself. After a time I found that that was the answer to all my questions. So to go back to your question, what do I do? I do what I can, however little it may be, even though I know it's never going to be enough. You changed Jamal's life, and his death. It may not be enough, but it's more than he had before you came. Personally, I don't think there's anything more valuable in this world. I hope you can learn to live with that."

Mukunda could do nothing but nod. What could he say to that?

Sister Martina finished her doughnut and took a sip of her coffee. "It's not just Jamal you've helped, you know. It's the rest of the patients that you're working with and the staff also. Your being here has made a big difference to a lot of people. I hope you'll remember that, Michael. Jamal's gone, but they're still here."

"I have to go back to LA on Sunday, but until then I'd like to keep volunteering, if that's okay."

Sister Martina smiled, though the sadness was still apparent in her eyes. "Finish your doughnut. You're too thin as it is."

When Mukunda returned to Del Mar, he had the unpleasant task of telling Sujata that Jamal had died. Though she had not seen Jamal physically, she had formed her own special bond with him. Every evening at dinner she would ask Mukunda how Jamal was doing and listen avidly to his stories of what had transpired that day with him and the other patients that Mukunda had begun working with. Even the normally taciturn Lakshman had gotten interested and begun sitting in on their late evening chats. So it came as no surprise to Mukunda when Sujata broke into tears upon hearing the news. The three of them were sitting on some old lawn chairs on the back patio, looking out at the stars over the ocean, sharing their stories of how they had found the spiritual path. Sujata asked him how Jamal had enjoyed the coffee cake and that was enough to bring water to Mukunda's eyes. When he finally stammered out the news, Sujata consoled him for a few moments before she burst into tears herself and sought the consoling arms of her husband. Instead of going back to his room to meditate, Mukunda stayed up with them for several hours, talking about the mysteries of life and death and the terrible injustices that seemed to continue, world without end, no matter how many tears were shed or how much people tried to do something about it. Together they shared that ineffably human awareness of being mortal beings in an immortal universe. They sat on the slippery edge of a spinning planet and realized how small they really were, how little their actions, or anyone's, mattered in an endless march where all you could hear was the beat of the cosmic drum. You either fell in step with that rhythm or the whirl of the planet would send you spinning off into space, another speck of cosmic dust to lend some texture to the void.

It was after midnight when Sujata and Lakshman went to bed. Mukunda placed his folded blanket on the lawn, at the edge of the high cliffs that separated him from the ocean and the sky. He sat facing an immense silence that even the crashing of the surf could not dent and tried to meditate, but something in his heart had slipped that day and left him rudderless in the wind, open to every suggestion of every breeze that climbed over the hedges and ruffled his locks. As he closed his eyes he felt strangely empty. The burdens he had been carrying for so long held so little interest for him now that they became weightless and were carried off by the breeze. Wherever he was being blown, it did not seem to matter anymore. There was something else that was vying for his attention, something that had nothing to do with who he was or where he was going. Jamal's life and his death had carved him open and left a space where there had been no space before. He could not put a name to it. It was just space. But something had been waiting for that space to open, something so large that the sky would have to bend to let it pass. And he could feel the sky bending, a section of the stars folding under to make way for an upswell from beneath the ocean floor. He felt himself being blown headlong into the face of destiny, the same destiny the sage had castigated him for not fulfilling, the one he could not call *his* because it was the very effort to make it his that had kept it from his door. It was not his to choose but only to fall into, once the emptiness had been made large enough to hold. Mukunda could not remember any dream that night, but the absence of memory did not fool him into thinking that nothing had happened while he'd slept. When he awoke in the morning he could feel that his heart had slipped even further out to sea. And the winds were still blowing strong.

16

THE NEXT FOUR DAYS tore at Mukunda's heart with a relentlessness that he could not and would not avoid. The quavering knot that lodged in his stomach was exacerbated every time he walked past Jamal's old room, but he refused to look away or to banish Jamal's haggard but luminous smile from his mind. All his life he had been proud of his spiritual detachment—now he was ashamed of it, for he had begun to see that what he had called detachment had merely been a thin mask stretched over his incapacity to feel his way into the heart of another human being. Without realizing it, he had stepped across the boundaries that separate one person from another, past the differences that blind the eye and fool the heart, and stood face to face with another human soul in that clear space where each looks into the mirror of the other and sees his own reflection looking back. It was only after Jamal had vanished behind the curtain that Mukunda fully realized how deeply he cared, how much his own awareness had become rooted in the connection that had sprung up between them. The sadness that came with this discovery was a welcome sadness. It fell like rain watering the fields after a long drought. His heart demanded tears and he gave them willingly, even when they did not show on his face, like a tribute long overdue and well deserved. Behind his tears and behind the sadness he could sense a tranquility waiting, but he knew that before he could reach it he would first have to pass through the sorrow-shadowed vale where the water of the human heart is the water with which all living things grow.

Gradually, he began to discover that what bound him to Jamal bound him to everyone else as well. When Ralph, the gentle, hulking blind candy seller, felled by a failing heart that could not accommodate his simple dreams, complained of the pain in his shoulders and chest and wanted to know when the hell they were going to let him get out of there and go back to his street corner, Mukunda heard the fear of death skirting the edges of his defiance. He acknowledged it as a worthy adversary, but behind it he could see the courage that had sustained Ralph through the long years of fighting the cold nights and the thousand daily indifferences. Mukunda spoke to that hidden strength, fanned it with his respect and his admiration. He looked at Ralph's scarred and stubbled face and saw a being so deep, so mysterious, so complex and unfathomable, that he considered it an honor to be sitting by his side. He listened to his complaints and felt the harshness of being human in an unforgiving world. He listened to his stories and realized that, like him, Ralph had been privileged to walk this beautiful earth and experience things no other human being had ever experienced, that the universe had coalesced in him in order to experience itself, and that the world would never be the same for having felt his footsteps on its back. One day Ralph asked him to let him feel his face. As Mukunda felt Ralph's sure fingers advance across his skin, curious and tender, it startled him to discover that Ralph could see without eyes, that there were other ways of seeing that could pierce even the deepest darkness.

When the voices Wilma heard pulled her into long and largely unintelligible conversations, Mukunda would take her hand and feel himself connected to a wild and tortuous landscape that defied time and space, dipping and twisting through the maze of the past and the uncertain apparitions of the future. Throughout each wild flight he tried to transmit to her his courage, his sense of surrender, and his faith, silently offering whatever the spirit inside her was willing or able to take. He would chant mantras in a low voice to carry them both to safety and gently massage her thin, worn hands, whose skin hung so lightly over the bones that he could feel the striations on their surface. Slowly Wilma would calm down. The tension would seep out of her body, the glistening sweat on her pocked forearms tremble and cool; then her eyes would focus on him, and she would smile a smile that was grace itself, a gift from the formless to the world of form.

As Mukunda moved from one patient to another, finding his way into their suffering, trying to keep his balance as he put his arm around their shoulders and helped them navigate the taut chord that would lead them out of this life and into the next, he began to discover the lineaments of a teaching as timeless and as delicate as a drop of dew on a blossom caressed by the first touch of the morning sun. When he tried to fasten it with his gaze and absorb it into his understanding, it would disappear, like a mirage that can only be seen out of the corner of one's eye, but this didn't bother him. Rather than go chasing it down the corridors of his mind, he kept his eyes open to the persons in front of him, to their sufferings and to the many joys that refused to be held back by the long litany of difficulties that life had strewn across their path. Then a moment came when the river rounded a bend and perfection shone forth for a brief, infinite instant. He saw his patient's face turn into the face of Krishna. What had been a playful, mischievous twinkle of an eye became a cosmic glance, the sound of divine laughter filling his ears and echoing across the room, and the dance they did crossed oceans and filled the cosmos. The moment stole up on him unawares, like a thief through an open bedroom window, and it left just as stealthily. But when it was gone the open space in his heart contained the calling card left behind by his divine visitor.

It was just a moment, but this one moment glittered among the many sadnesses and struggles of his day like a gemstone in a field of tangled scrub, and that one moment led to another and then another. One by one, he picked them up and set them down in the fields of memory, trusting their light to illumine the edges of his path. A sense of wonder began to overtake him, a mute awareness of the mystery that inhabits all living things. It seemed to him as if he had never really looked at a human being before, never followed another's eyes into the infinite spaces behind them, never asked the question "Who is this person?" Now it seemed like the only question worth asking.

Early one evening, as he walked Sister Martina back to the nearby Hillcrest apartment that she shared with Sister Rita—their two-bedroom convent, as she called it—he tried to find words for what he was feeling, not knowing if that were even possible. She remained quiet as he talked but the solemn, thoughtful expression on her face made him feel as if she were extending to every word the sanctity of the confessional. When they reached her building, they sat down on the front steps and watched the sun disappear over the low-rise apartments across the street in a mellow haze of purples and oranges and golds. She pointed to the trees beside the buildings and showed him how they changed the color of sunset by setting it against a field of green. For several minutes they were silent, their eyes fastened to the horizon as dusk settled in. Then she let out a sigh and threw up her hands in a gesture that reminded him of a saint in divine rapture, making him wonder if some of those saints had simply been reeling at the sight of something their mind could not comprehend, overwhelmed by the mysterious like a beach by a forty-foot wave.

"It's so beautiful, isn't it?" she said. "Sometimes I fail to understand how the world can be so beautiful and so cruel at the same time. He takes the colors of creation and dazzles our eyes until our heart wants to burst, and the very next moment he tightens his grip until we can't see through our tears." She shrugged her shoulders. "Sooner or later I always fall in love with my patients. It happens the moment I start seeing Christ in them. And then they die and the pain begins again. There's something Mother Teresa once said: 'I know God will not give me anything I can't handle; I just wish that he didn't trust me so much.' I feel the same way sometimes. It can be a terrible burden—but you know, I wouldn't want to live without it. If it weren't for the tears, I don't think we would be able to see the beauty. We need them to wash us clean. Maybe that's part of what you're feeling."

Mukunda nodded his head. "I think you're right. I think that's exactly what it is. I just hope I don't forget the lesson."

Sister Martina smiled. "There are some things we can't forget, Michael, no matter what happens afterward."

They fell quiet again, watching the horizon deepen and slide into the dark. The lights of the street lamps and apartment windows gradually grew brighter as the dying day gave up its struggle to hold back the night. Mukunda wanted to find some way to tell her how much she had meant to him over the past couple of weeks, but he couldn't think of anything to say that would have done justice to his feelings. Fortunately, he knew it wasn't necessary. Years of working in conditions that force open the human heart had given her the ability to see what words could not express. He knew now where the openness came from that he had sensed in her when they first met. He couldn't imagine how many tears she had cried over these years, but it was easy to see how fertile they had made her heart.

As Mukunda walked back to his car, he thought of all the people who had deserved his thanks and never received them: Joel, who had led him to St. John's and the many lessons that awaited him there; Jamal, who had reached out through the innocence of his smile and opened a door that had long been closed; Gita, who had awakened his mind to the importance of social justice; the many others who had crossed his path, if only briefly, and helped him along his road, often without his being aware of it at the time. Many of them he would never see again, but he resolved that the best way to thank them would be for him to do the same for others, to take advantage of every opportunity that came his way to be of service to his fellow travelers. As he reached the car and fitted the key to the lock, he paused to look around, noticing the slight breeze in his face, the fallen olives on the sidewalk grass, the murmur of the leaves above his head. Silently he thanked the sage for guiding him to this place, and for the blessings he had been given along the way. Before he started the car, he closed his eyes and prayed for the gift of compassion, for a chance to ease the suffering of those he could and accompany the sufferings of those he couldn't. As his prayer filled him with its solemn music, he felt like he was waking from a long sleep to discover that it was night and that those who were still sleeping would need him to be awake in the hours before dawn.

On Mukunda's last day at St. John's, the staff threw him an impromptu going-away party. Although Sujata's Toll House cookies ended up being the main attraction, Sister Martina baked a serviceable pound cake and an excellent batch of brownies; she also put up decorations, including a small banner thanking him for a special two weeks. Mukunda had not expected anything like this, and he had to make an effort to keep his composure. He had gone years without crying, but since Jamal's death his tear ducts had followed the path of his heart. The sense of community at St. John's was, in its own way, as strong as it was in the ashram, and it moved him to see how much a part of their lives he had become. The afternoon was filled with unhurried goodbyes and tearful conversations—however short those two weeks might have seemed to him, he knew they were a universe of time to someone who counted his life in weeks instead of years. Once again he was reminded that it was the quality of our lives that count, not the duration. When evening fell, Sister Martina walked him to his car. She gave him a card that everyone had signed and made him promise to drop by whenever he had the chance. It was one promise Mukunda knew he would keep, no matter what the future might bring.

It was later than usual when he arrived back at the hermitage for his final night in Del Mar. His meditation was short but deeply satisfying, perhaps the best of his retreat, but he barely gave it a second thought. A lot had changed in three weeks. He could no longer meditate without being aware of the vast community of living beings to which he belonged, connected to him by a bond of sympathy that he valued more than the dreams of liberation he had cherished for so long. It was their welfare that mattered to him now, and as the burden of his own drama lightened, he felt a sense of freedom far different than the one he thought he had been searching for—less transcendent, perhaps, but more substantial. He realized that it had been his preoccupation with his own spiritual progress that had held him back all these years. As he watched them quaver and dissolve, he felt lighter, more buoyant, until the ground seemed to grow transparent underneath his blanket and the breeze passed through him without obstruction, whistling through the empty spaces like music through a reed.

After a late dinner and a short conversation with Sujata and Lakshman, Mukunda lay down on his blankets and stared out through the open sliding glass doors to the sky hanging low on the horizon. He listened for the surf, but never before had the ocean seemed so still at this hour. A small cloudbank rolled lazily underneath the stars and continued its vague course while his eyes closed and released his mind from its moorings to the world outside. In the early morning hours the sleeping Mukunda felt the wind rise and carry him gently back to a now-familiar landscape. When the mist cleared he saw the sage seated on his tiger skin in front of the mouth of his cave, the moon sitting higher in the night sky than the last time he had seen it. The sage's eyes were closed. His face was wrapped in a serenity that appeared as if it would outlast the surrounding mountains. The scowl was gone and in its place was a gently curving smile. Mukunda hesitated for a moment; then he prostrated in front of his teacher, his body trembling from the intensity of his emotions. After a few moments he felt the sage touch him lightly on the top of his head.

"Rise," he heard him say. "Sit before me."

Mukunda sat up with his legs crossed, blinking back the tears.

"Now, tell me again, why have you come?"

"To ask for your guidance, so that I may be able to understand what I have been unable to understand and do what I have failed to do."

The sage looked pleased. He remained quiet for a few seconds and then nodded his head slowly.

"All you need to know, Mukunda, is already in your heart, just as I am in your heart. You have simply forgotten. Whenever you are in need, look inside and you will find the answers, even to that which seems to have no answer."

By now Mukunda's tears were flowing in a silent but steady stream.

"Real spirituality cannot be selfish. You will know that you are on the right path when your heart reaches out and embraces all life, when the sufferings of the world become your sufferings and the urge to alleviate them becomes as necessary as breathing. All your practice is for this, and this alone. It is he who has become the world, Mukunda, and it is him you serve when you serve the world. Remember this and you will never go astray. Surrender to his will; make yourself the perfect instrument. If there is injustice in the world, fight it. If there is suffering, alleviate it. When you fight against injustice you fight for him. When you alleviate another's suffering you lessen the Lord's burden. Every particle of this creation is he. If you turn your face from any part of it, then you turn your face from your beloved. If the Lord disguises himself as a beggar and shows up at your door, will you tell him to go away because you have to sit for meditation? No. First please the one on whom you are meditating. Feed him if he is hungry. Remove the injustice that blocks his path. Listen to his sorrows and wipe his tears. Then and only then will your meditation bear fruit. God cannot be found in a dry heart. He would never choose such an inhospitable place for his residence. He lives in the hearts of those who love him more than life itself, who love him so much they forget themselves in that love. To the eyes of such a devotee, every particle of dust in this creation is the face of his beloved and worthy of his reverence.

"Now, come. Follow me."

The sage got to his feet, turned, and disappeared into the cave, using his trident as a walking stick. Mukunda followed close behind. As he stepped inside, he saw the cave open up into a clean, spacious chamber, just high enough for him to stand comfortably. The floor of the cave was smooth and worn, and at the back he saw a tiger skin placed over a folded blanket with a begging bowl beside it. Two torches were stuck into crevices in the wall on either side of the tiger skin, their flickering light leaping and dancing across the small chamber.

"Do you remember this place?" the sage asked.

Mukunda shook his head.

"Think."

Something stirred in Mukunda's mind, a rumble of distant memories that remained shrouded in a deep mist. The cave held some significance for him, he could feel it, but the images seemed too remote, too insubstantial for him to bring to the surface.

The sage nodded his head slowly. "Those memories will return, and so will you. This is your cave, Mukunda. You found God here once on that tiger skin—or rather, God found you. He will be waiting for you here when the time comes, but first you have some work to accomplish. You took a vow here once, an ancient vow, and you have come back to fulfill it. Do you understand?"

The sage seemed to be glowing now in the firelight. The dancing shadows played over his figure like living ornaments, and his presence seemed to fill the space around him. Mukunda had never seen anyone so beautiful. As he stared at the sage, transfixed, he felt an avalanche of forgotten memories threatening to sweep down out of the darkness and engulf him.

"Do you understand, Mukunda?" the sage asked him once again.

"I think so."

"Good, then our work here is finished. Let us go back outside. The cave will be waiting for you when you return."

As Mukunda stepped out of the cave, the wind started picking up. It was time. He turned to say goodbye, but the sage was nowhere to be seen. He peered into the mouth of the cave but saw that it was empty. Then the wind enveloped him and carried him back into the darkness. When he awoke he found himself sitting in lotus posture, unsure how he had gotten there. He could still see the mouth of the cave in front of him, a beckoning ring of darkness more inviting than the night sky outside his room. He closed his eyes and began meditating, filled with the uncanny feeling that he was in two places at once, meditating in both the cave and his room, that there was in truth no difference between the two: in the space between his eyebrows neither time nor place mattered. The past and the future settled into one bright moment, flooding his awareness until all boundaries dissolved and he lost himself in an endless flow of something to which he could not give a name.

He could only say afterward that there was a fountain and that its waters ran everywhere.

17

Mukunda left for LA shortly after breakfast with Lakshman and Sujata. The two caretakers were planning to stay for the evening program and then return to Del Mar the following morning; Mukunda's future was not nearly so well defined. As they passed Oceanside, Mukunda looked out at the palm trees lining the pier and remembered his sleepy-eyed glimpse of those same trees three weeks earlier. He had been as uncertain then as he was now about his future. In that sense nothing had changed, but in truth everything had. As he watched Camp Pendleton appear up ahead, desolate and withdrawn, separating the affluent beach towns of northern San Diego County from the sprawling megalopolis to the north, he knew he was hurtling into a future entirely different than anything he had hitherto imagined. For a moment he felt as if he were not only in the back seat of Lakshman's Toyota but in the back seat of his own life, speeding up the freeway toward his destiny with someone else at the wheel, a divine trickster who refused to tell him where he was going but who did it with so much charm that he didn't mind. Considering his own inept attempts to guide his destiny, he decided that the back seat suited him just fine.

Camp Pendleton was soon out of sight and the first signs of Santa Anna appeared on the horizon. The parched and empty hills gave way to a parade of high-rises under construction and a tumult of rumbling tires. Sleek sports cars and sturdy SUVs weaved in and out of traffic as they jockeyed for position, swarming toward the congested heart of the American West. Mukunda decided to attempt some meditation, hoping to clear the LA of his mind before he arrived at the ashram. He closed his eyes and sought the master among the tumbling artifacts, until he found him sitting serenely in the eye of the hurricane, his powerful gaze willing him to slow the jumble of his thoughts. Using the mantric formula he had learned as a boy, he sought the master's blessing. He strove to empty his heart of desire and focus his attention on the eternal source within, hoping that its silent voice would point him toward the decision that he could no longer put off. At some point Mukunda passed from meditation into sleep. The reins of his attention loosened. The calm meditative flow was lost, and his mind began wandering aimlessly down corridors of the familiar, the heaped images swirling together like strips of confetti tossed into a breeze. He saw Sister Martina and Gita walking together down Topanga Canyon Boulevard, holding hands and laughing through their tears. He watched them walk through the ashram gate and into St. John's Village where Jamal was listening to Tibetan chanting on his CD player. Behind St. John's, Gita's music was spilling out of a radio and onto a beach where Joel was poking for clams. From there his mind returned to the meditation hall. The disciples were gathered together, listening to a dialogue between the master and the sage. A test of wills seemed to be taking place on the dais. As the bearded voices rose in volume, the vague outlines of the hall dimmed and faded. Stars emerged out of the blackness and danced above the heads of the two images of Shiva: the one sitting on the coils of a cobra, his sonorous voice rolling past the edges of space, filling the firmament with its music; the other brandishing his trident and flashing white fire from his eyes. The battle—if a battle it was—continued while time stood still and the universe watched and wondered, until Mukunda felt the walls of the universe shake and the fabric tear. He awoke with a stinging in his forehead. As he jerked up, he realized that his head had knocked against the front seat.

"Are you okay there, Mukunda?" Lakshman asked, without turning his attention from the road. In the passenger seat Sujata was doing her best to stifle a laugh.

"Sure," he replied, embarrassed. "I guess I might have dozed off a bit."

"You think? Well, it's time to wake up anyhow. We'll be there in no time."

The car was on Pacific Coast Highway now, not far from the Topanga Canyon Boulevard exit. Lakshman popped a darshan CD into the CD player and turned up the volume. Mukunda smiled as he adjusted his ears to the sound of Gurudeva's voice, the familiar hypnotic drawl that had provided the sound track for the greater part of his life.

"In one poem Kabir says, *Ab tum kab sumiroge ram; jivada do din ka mehman.* 'When will you start meditating on the Almighty Lord? Remember, you are only a temporary guest here.'

"This is the way of the world. People talk and talk about spirituality, but how many actually take the trouble to sit and meditate? How many even remember that they are on a journey, that they have come here for a purpose? A few days go by and then, when the train of death pulls into the station to pick them up, they suddenly realize that they have wasted their lives running after glass baubles instead of searching for what is real and lasting. But by then it is too late. They will have to come back again, in another body. That is what Kabir is telling us. Don't wait for tomorrow, he says, because tomorrow's sun may not rise on the horizon of your life. Use your time wisely. Keep your eye on your destination, on the Lord who is waiting for you to penetrate his maya. Don't give yourself cause for regret because you allowed your life to slip away in vain.

"*Jhuti kaya jhuti maya akhar soth nidan.* 'The body is illusion; it decays and dies. That is the only certainty.' *Kahat kabir suno bhai sadho do din mehman.* 'So, wise men, says Kabir, do not forget that you are just temporary guests here.'

"This life is like the waiting room in a train station. The train pulls in, you get off and wait in the waiting room with the other guests from other trains, and then your next train arrives and it's time to go. A wise man knows that he is on a journey. He will chat with the other guests while he is there, but he never forgets that he is going somewhere. His mind is on his destination. He keeps an eye out for his train, and when it pulls in, he is ready...."

Mukunda recognized the talk. He had yet to become PA at the time and it had left a great impression on him. For weeks afterward he had felt a great sense of urgency: time was passing all too quickly; if he were not careful, his life would run through his fingers like water.

Two years later, it was still running through his fingers, and faster than ever.

When Mukunda entered the Bungalow, Ganesh was serving Gurudeva his lunch. The master greeted him with a jovial smile and told him to come to his room around two, after he had taken his customary rest. Mukunda was grateful for the reprieve. He still was not sure exactly what he would say, but he knew that no matter what he said, it would not be easy. Again he debated with himself over the wisdom of saying nothing. He could not hide from the master what had happened on his quest, neither the reappearance of the sage nor the fact that he had spent most of his time volunteering at St. John's instead of doing meditation, but he could leave it at that. He could simply recount for the master what had happened and leave his future in the master's hands, as he had always done in the past. As he knew the master would expect. Or else... It was a debate that had been raging in his head since morning, fueled by his memory of the sage's majestic figure and the cave where he had been granted a glimpse of his hidden past. And still he seemed no closer to a resolution than when he'd awoken, sitting upright on his blanket and staring into a place where both future and past ceased to exist.

Instead of waiting for Ganesh so they could eat together in the Bungalow kitchen, Mukunda took a quick shower and went looking for Gita. He found her sitting on a blanket underneath a tree outside her dorm, her eyes closed in meditation. He stopped for a few moments and watched her from a distance, proud of the determined look on her face and heedful of the beauty of her features that seemed to grow more beautiful every time he saw her. He felt a sharp pang as he remembered how much he had missed her, followed by a glad sense of relief, but what he felt more than anything was the need to talk to her, as if the sound of her voice were the only thing that could help him get his bearings, as if by connecting to his past he could find his way securely into the future. Finally he walked over and sat on the grass beside her, thinking to join her in her meditation. He had barely sat down when Gita opened her eyes.

"I thought it might be you. At least I was hoping it was. So you're back?"

"I am," he said, still nervous at the encounter, though no less than she.

"And how was the vision-questing?"

"The normal. Walking in the wilderness, talking with the gods, that sort of thing. What do you say we talk about it over lunch? How does the Buddha Café sound to you?"

"It sounds perfect."

They found a small, semi-secluded table out back and ordered their food. Mukunda insisted on first hearing how her three weeks had gone, his initial nervousness having given way to the joy of being together again.

"It was pretty eventful. The day after you left, Madalasa asked me if I would be interested in working in the office with her."

"Really?"

"Yeah, it really caught me by surprise. I always had the impression that Madalasa didn't exactly like me. Anyhow, I couldn't say no. She was nice enough to let me live in the ashram, and to be honest, I was a little down after you left—I guess I had gotten more attached to our walks than I had realized. I thought it would be a good idea to stay busy when I wasn't working on my music. Less time to think about things. As it turns out, Madalasa was much better company than I thought she would be. She's been like an older sister to me the last couple of weeks. A rather wise older sister. She can be a little controlling sometimes, but she's a real yogi. I've learned a lot since I started working with her."

"I know what you mean. She's taught me an awful lot over the years. It used to make me uncomfortable sometimes how overprotective she was, but later on I started to see the wisdom behind it. There is a lot more to her than meets the eye."

"So I discovered. Anyhow, last week she called me aside for a little chat—that's what she called it, but it turned out to be a lot more than that. First she started filling me in on the history of the ashram, right from the time they bought the land, how the board was formed, how it works, and where she sees everything heading. It was fascinating, but I couldn't figure out why she was telling me all that, until... until she told me that she had been looking for someone she could train to take over her duties one day, to run the office and handle the ashram administration, and... after working with me for a few days she had decided that I was the perfect person."

"You're kidding?"

"No. I'm not. I was totally floored. I couldn't believe that she would think that I would be the right person. You know better than anyone. What was that you called me, a rebel with a cause? Can you picture me running the ashram one day? It's like the exact opposite of the image I've always had of myself. But that wasn't the whole of it. There's more."

"What?"

"That's when she told she was thinking about becoming a sannyasi."

"Madalasa? A sannyasi?"

"Uh huh. Actually she's been thinking about it ever since Gurudeva announced that he was going to create a sannyasi order. She wants to be his first female sannyasi. Now that I know Madalasa a little better, it makes perfect sense. Anyhow, she told me that she has a feeling that Gurudeva is going to eventually send her outside the ashram to spread the mission, which is why she needs to start training somebody now to take over for her in case that happens."

"So what did you say?"

"I didn't know what to say. The whole thing was so out of left field. I asked her for a few days to think about it, but that was mostly to be polite.

I couldn't imagine myself saying yes. But then I got to thinking. You know, after Gurudeva—and maybe Markandeya—Madalasa's probably the most important person in the ashram. Very little happens around here without her approval. I got to see that firsthand, once I started working as her assistant. And the more I thought about it, the more I realized how important Gurudeva's mission has become to me. You know I've always had a passion to change the world—ever since I was a kid—but until I met Gurudeva I never realized that until you can change people's consciousness you can't change the world. It's the quality of our consciousness that determines the quality of our lives, both individually and collectively. Without a spiritual revolution, an economic or political revolution will never be enough. You can't remove people's suffering without transforming their consciousness. Of course, I don't need to tell you that, but for me it's been a revelation. After spending time with Madalasa I understand a lot better now what Gurudeva meant when he talked about the role that the ashram would play in the future. And that got me to thinking about my role in all this. It's not an accident that I'm here, you know, just like it's not an accident that we grew up together. And it wasn't an accident that Madalasa asked me to work with her. It was meant to happen. I just have to learn what my place is in the drama. Of course, I have my music, I always will, and there's a lot I hope to be able to do for the mission through my music, but there's a lot more I can do besides that. What better way to help the revolution along than to be one of the future leaders of the ashram?"

"Are you saying you agreed to do it?"

"I did, a couple of days ago. Between my music and helping to run the ashram, I can't think of a better role to play. Well, yours isn't too shabby, either."

"I don't know what to say, Gita. I'm speechless." Gita blushed at his words but Mukunda wasn't exaggerating. It was so totally unexpected that his mind had drawn a blank.

"To tell you the truth, I feel more at peace with myself now than at any time in my life. It's taken a long time to get here, but it was worth it. You know, I even thought about the possibility of becoming a sannyasi one day. It's just a thought, of course, but who knows, maybe when we're both Madalasa's age and you're officially the guru. It could happen. You might need me around in orange to keep you on your toes."

"Wow, now you've really caught me by surprise."

"I can see that. It caught me by surprise too. But when you think about it, it kind of makes sense. Our parents are best friends. We're born two months apart. We grow up together on the same block. We both become followers of the same guru—a few years apart, I'll give you that, but still...And then at the same time that you go on your vision quest, Madalasa starts training me to take over for her when she retires. When I think about it, it seems like the coincidences are too carefully orchestrated to be coincidences. Doesn't Gurudeva say that there's no such thing as coincidence? Plus, you're going to need help, you know. You're not going to be able to run this ashram by yourself. It will help to have a close friend in your corner, someone you can count on, no matter what."

Mukunda realized that he should have been pleased, that she expected him to be, but though he smiled as genuinely as he could and told her how proud he was of her decision, he simply couldn't picture Gita working in the office, dedicating her energy and her talents to the administration of the ashram, as Madalasa had done all these years. Or was it that he didn't want to picture her there, that he had secretly dreamed of her in a far different role and was now shocked to see that expectation shattered?

They had more or less finished with their meal when Gita coaxed Mukunda into telling the story of his retreat. She had barely picked at her food, as had he, but it was obvious that neither of them was interested in eating. Slowly he began to recount his tale: meditating twelve hours a day during that first week, fighting to go beyond the limits of his mind, meeting the dragons at the gate, how they had led him to Joel and from there to Jamal and St. John's Village. At first he was hesitant, not knowing what she would think, wanting to tell her what an important role she had played in his internal struggles but not succeeding, hoping that she would be able to read between the lines. But soon the elixir of her attention loosened his tongue. He began to talk with passion about his discoveries, about the people he had met and the terrible privations they had suffered. He marveled at the dedication of Sister Martina and Sister Rita, working tirelessly for people the society had willfully neglected, and wondered out loud if he would ever make such a pivotal difference in people's lives.

When Mukunda finished his story, Gita had tears in her eyes. "Now I don't know what to say," she told him, her voice breaking up. "I wasn't expecting this, but perhaps I should have been. You're going to make a great spiritual teacher one day, Mukunda, the kind of spiritual teacher the world really needs."

"I don't know about that," he said, unsure if she was terribly happy or terribly sad or a mixture of both. "But I do know that the ashram is lucky to have you, Gita. Luckier than anyone knows. I hope Madalasa appreciates what she's getting... Unfortunately, I have to go now. Gurudeva asked me to see him after his rest and I'm already late."

Mukunda gave Gita a long hug, a mirror image of the one she had given him before he had left for Del Mar, not wanting to let her go, as he knew she had not wanted to let him go on that day. When he did let her go, his shirt was wet at the place where her cheek had been pressed. As he walked away from the café and headed for the Bungalow, he touched his shirt with reverence and added her tears to his own. She had honored him with her tears, as Jamal had honored him with his smile on the last evening of his life. It was a gift he knew he would treasure for the rest of his days.

Saddened by the unexpected turn of events, Mukunda slowed his pace. His return had turned out to be far more difficult than he had thought it would be on the drive up from Del Mar. He had gone looking for Gita, thinking that now he could finally tell her how much he loved her, how much she meant to him, how much he wanted their roads to run together. The sight of her sitting on the grass had made him instantly feel more alive, more awake, as if her simple presence was enough to bring him fully into the moment. But he had forgotten that she had her own road to walk. Not only had he returned a different person—she was a different person, one whose road had diverged from his at the very time that he had thought their roads were finally running together. Then, while he had been telling her his story, he had realized how powerfully the experiences of the past three weeks had marked him. He had seen it reflected in her tearful eyes and in the passionate feelings he could not hold back as he spoke of the sage and the friends he had left behind at St. John's. He had realized at that moment that he could not be true to himself if he were not true to the people society had left behind, and he could not be true to them if he did not seek the road the sage had marked out for him. As difficult as it might be, he would have to say goodbye to the illusions he had carried with him for so long. One of those illusions he had left behind at the Buddha Café, a parting as difficult as any he had ever made. But he could not and would not interfere with her spiritual life. He would not put in jeopardy the peace she had found or turn her from the path she had taken. Love demanded that he place her needs above his, and it was painfully clear that what she needed did not include being his partner on an uncertain voyage.

So many partings, he thought. And the hardest yet to come.

A few minutes later Mukunda stepped through the Bungalow door. He saw

Leela and Bhishma sitting together on the sofa near the foot of the stairs, reveling in each other's company with a carefree abandon that seemed to him like an alien music that his ears could no longer comprehend. The possibility that he might never see them again stung him afresh with the same pain that had filled his eyes with tears during the difficult walk from the Buddha Café to the Bungalow. He smiled bravely and gave them each a grateful hug, silently thanking them for all the joyful moments he had spent in their company, for Leela's sisterly guidance and Bhishma's cheerful companionship. Then he was up the stairs and in Gurudeva's sitting room, where he found the master in his recliner, watching the news. Gurudeva clicked off the television and asked Mukunda to sit in front of him on the carpet.

"Come, Mukunda, tell me about your experiences in Del Mar. What did you discover in your quest?"

Mukunda took a deep breath and started unfolding the story of the past three weeks. As he narrated his initial struggles in his meditation, Gurudeva smiled and nodded his head, as if he had been expecting it. But when Mukunda described the first appearance of the sage and his obvious anger, the master grew pensive. He furrowed his brow and listened intently without making any other outward expression. As Mukunda narrated his encounter with Joel on the beach, his subsequent dream of the sage, and how that had led him to Jamal and St. John's, Gurudeva sank back into his chair and stared quietly at the empty television screen, rubbing his chin and closing his eyes from time to time. When Mukunda finished his story, the master nodded and returned his gaze to his disciple.

"I had been wondering when the sage would make his next appearance. Or rather, when those memories would surface again and in what form. Now tell me, Mukunda, what have you taken from this experience?"

Mukunda hesitated, unwilling to say what he was about to say but knowing that he had no choice. Perhaps he had never had a choice, not even on that long-ago day when he'd first met the master in the living room of his childhood home.

"I learned that I had been blinded by my own selfishness. In the last two weeks I have taken the first steps toward overcoming that selfishness, but I still have a long way to go. First I have to prove that I can serve the world selflessly before I can think of doing anything else. I have to keep my vow."

"And what does that mean?"

Again Mukunda took a deep breath. "I need to be somewhere where I can be of real service to the people who need it most. I don't know where that is yet, but I don't believe it's here, at least not for the time being." Mukunda paused and swallowed the lump in his throat. "I'm not ready to become a monk, Gurudeva... and I'm not worthy to become your successor. Perhaps someday I will be worthy, but that day hasn't come yet. It would be dishonest of me to accept an honor I don't deserve. And if I were dishonest to myself, then it would be the same as being dishonest to you."

Gurudeva's look grew sterner than he had ever seen it. Mukunda could feel the power of his disapproval and it made him tremble.

"Think carefully what you are saying, Mukunda," he said, raising his voice. "Do you think that I have not taken all this into account? Do you think that I do not know who and what you are? Do you doubt me?"

"No, master."

"Then why this faintness of heart? You have spiritual greatness within your grasp. Will you simply throw it away?"

Unable to meet the master's gaze, Mukunda lowered his eyes and struggled to get out the words. "Gurudeva, I feel like I need to spend some time doing service. I won't get that chance if I remain here and become a monk."

"*Åre!* What greater service can there be than becoming a monk and one day the head of my spiritual mission? Do you think cleaning toilets and handing out medicines is going to do more good than teaching people spirituality. I did not raise you to be a fool, Mukunda. You know better than that. Use your brain. Just think how much more service you'll be able to do when you have an organization at your command. Then you will have the power to do real good. Otherwise, you will give these people a few medicines and they may live a little longer, but they will die as ignorant as they lived. That is not the highest service, Mukunda. It is just a subtle way of giving your ego a good pat on the back."

Mukunda could feel the force of the master's words as if they were a weight on his head, forcing it to the ground. This was his guru speaking, his master, the focal point of his life and the example he had always used to set his course; the logic seemed irrefutable to his ear, and yet he could not stop the words from tumbling out, confused as they seemed to be.

"I wish I could accept, I really do, but I can't. I don't have the realization."

"Realization!" Gurudeva let out a snort. "Do you think a spiritual teacher has to be realized before he can take up the mantle from his guru? Nonsense! If every guru had to wait until his principal disciple was realized before he could name him as his successor, then most spiritual lineages would be broken. Milarepa didn't attain his realization while he was with Marpa. He attained it years later, after meditating for years in a cave in the mountains, and after he had already gained many disciples. In the meantime he maintained the lineage of his guru. The Dalai Lama was only a young boy when he was chosen to carry on his tradition. He accepted the responsibility and in that way he has helped to keep the Tibetan tradition alive. He didn't say, 'No, I won't accept being the Dalai Lama because I'm not realized yet.' That would have been selfish on his part. He accepted his destiny. That is what I am asking you to do. I know what you have achieved, and I know what you will achieve if you have the courage to accept this responsibility. I would not have selected you and spent all this time training you if I wasn't sure that you were capable. Millions of people are waiting to come in contact with my teachings. You want to do real service? Well, there is no greater service than to bring those teachings to them."

Mukunda blinked back the tears and wiped them with his fingers.

Gurudeva's tone softened. "Now, Mukunda, are you ready to give up this foolishness? We won't say another word about it. These moments of weakness happen. Face them with courage and they will vanish."

For a moment Mukunda was torn with indecision. Gurudeva was right; he had always been right. How could he go against his wishes? Then the voice inside him spoke out, strong and steady, almost against his will.

"I'm sorry, Gurudeva. I can't be your successor. At least not now. This is something I have to do."

For more than a minute, silence reigned in the room. Finally Gurudeva nodded slowly and gravely, wrapped in a somber tranquility that Mukunda found impossible to fathom. "I see," he said at last. "Then what will you do?"

"I'm not completely sure. I will go to the city first. I feel like there is something waiting for me there. I just have to find it."

Gurudeva shook his head. "So you will go like a beggar into the streets?"

Mukunda kept silent.

"So be it. Go with God."

Mukunda prostrated at the master's feet and then backed away to the top of the stairs, engraving in his mind's eye the familiar image of Gurudeva with his hands folded to his chest, wearing the same slight, enigmatic smile that he had first seen as a boy. That image was still foremost in his mind when he reached his room and quickly began packing a bag with his clothes, Gurudeva's picture, and those few books that were closest to his heart. When he was done, he looked around one last time at the room that had been his and then slipped out the back door, careful not to let Bhishma and Leela see him leave. A few minutes later he was easing his car out the ashram gate and onto Topanga Canyon Boulevard. He had not said goodbye to anyone, neither to Gita nor to any of the disciples who had been his family for the past eighteen years. He could not have borne the pain. For the first time that he could remember, he was alone in the world. His heart felt heavier than it had ever felt, but his conscience was clear. His car was heading south toward Pacific Coast Highway. From there he would turn east into the city. After that, only the Lord knew. An image flashed in his mind of the sage standing in the firelight of the cave, next to the tiger skin that drew him like a magnet, and then he smiled, a weary, solitary smile.

He could be in no better hands.

Epilogue

As usual, Gita was looking forward with undisguised pleasure to her Sunday morning. It was practically the only leisure time she had all week: no going in to the office, no rehearsals or recording sessions or bhajans to lead, no morning walk—an entire delicious half day all to herself. She thought about some of the misconceptions she had had before she first moved into the ashram and laughed. If anybody thought that ashram life was an easy way to avoid real responsibility, it was a sure sign that they had yet to live in one. Let them step into her shoes for a day; they would soon discover what all dedicated ashram residents knew: building up a spiritual community was no Sunday picnic, any more than walking the spiritual path was a stroll down a tropical beach. The good times were legion, but they were sustained by a lot of hard work and headaches, and in her case by just enough heartache to make her fully appreciate each luminous moment when it appeared.

Today she planned to catch up on her reading and then spend some time working on a song she had begun writing the night before, a slow bossa that reminded her of Johnny Mandel in the sixties, full of that airy nostalgia that made her think of floating clouds and island paradises. She propped up some pillows against the headboard of her bed in the small cottage in the Rumi Hills that she had been living in for the past year and opened up the Sunday edition of the *LA Times* that she had picked up at the Tao of Shopping after breakfast. After a short perusal of the Op-Ed section and a look at the world and national news, she opened the *Sunday Magazine*, deliberately saving the Arts & Entertainment section, her favorite, for last. As she scanned the table of contents, an article caught her eye: "Innercity Yoga: A quiet revolution in South Central." Intrigued, she turned to the first page of the article and paused to study the photo of a large two-story building with an ornately engraved signboard bearing a highly stylized om symbol and below it the words "Innercity Yoga & Cultural Center." She smiled, appreciating the unlikely artwork, and started reading.

John Donne once wrote: "No man is an island... Any man's death diminishes me because I am involved in mankind and therefore never send to know for whom the bell tolls; it tolls for thee." I wonder what John Donne would have said had he lived in Los Angeles at the beginning of the 21st century. Would he have even bothered to pen such lines knowing that his fellow city dwellers could hardly be listening in this age of 1.5-second sound bites and indentured desensitization? Would he have made the 20-minute voyage from Rodeo Drive to Crenshaw and decided that as a writer he had a duty to wake his community up to what was going on? Or would he have just taken a cue, like the rest of us, from that seminal scene in the movie *Grand Canyon* where Danny Glover saves Kevin Kline from the hands of the gang members who patrol that particular turf, and simply never have gotten off the freeway south of the I-10 in what has become famous to the world as simply "South Central."

We've all seen the images on television. We've watched *Beverly Hills 90210*, and most of us have taken off on a Saturday afternoon to walk those fabled streets and stare at the opulence, which, after all, is even more overstated than the show made it out to be. But how many of us, I ask, have taken off on a Saturday afternoon to walk down Crenshaw Boulevard in South Central, other than those who were born there and haven't had the chance to escape? There are no chic shops there with $10,000 evening gowns displayed in the shop window, no glitzy malls, no farmer's markets with $5 peaches wrapped in designer paper—just a sea of liquor stores, auto repair shops protected by rolls of razor wire, and one lone bank fortified like a WWII bunker. Would any of us even recognize that infamous zip code, the 90043, where the median household income hovers around $20,000—fully 1/7th of what it is in the 90210?

And yet there are those who are painfully aware of this divide that rips through the cultural, political, and economic life of our city, a kind of social apartheid that persists in front of millions of closed eyes. There are even people who have dedicated their lives to doing something about it, and not all of them do it because they were born there. Some of them were even born on the right side of the tracks, such as in La Jolla, that all-so-exclusive community to the south that considers itself a Beverly Hills with substance. I experienced this firsthand when a friend told me that if I wanted to recover my faith in humanity, I should visit the Innercity Yoga & Cultural Center in South Central. I was, of course, skeptical, to say the least, as those of you who frequent my offerings in the *Sunday Magazine* can well imagine, but I have yet to consider myself beyond redemption. I went (by day, to be sure—I, too, have seen *Grand Canyon*), and what I discovered there has helped me to reaffirm a faith that had been slipping in recent weeks as I have finally had to come to grips with the reality of living through a "bush administration."

The first thing I noticed as I pulled up in front of the yoga center was how perfectly it fit into its surroundings. The dilapidated exterior with the obligatory graffiti on the walls was exactly what you would expect in this part of the city, and entirely unlike any other yoga center I've ever seen, most of which are far better suited to Rodeo Drive than Crenshaw. But looks are known to be deceiving. Step inside and you enter a world that stands in stark contrast to the bleak and desolate landscape that surrounds it. The inside of what was once a two-story warehouse facility looks like a scene from *Alice In Wonderland*—a slightly surrealist warren of small classrooms and spacious halls tastefully decorated with varieties of artwork and pictures of prominent spiritual and social figures from different traditions and cultures. The decorations and renovations, as I later discovered, are the work of local volunteers and artists supported by donations from the surrounding community. As in any yoga center, you can smell the incense and feel an aura of peace in the air, but that peaceful aura is the backdrop for a bustle of activity that goes on from early morning to late night, seven days a week.

One of the young staff members came up to me in the lobby—no doubt the flummoxed expression on my face identified me as a newcomer. He introduced himself and offered to give me a quick tour of the facility. I accepted and soon discovered (if it wasn't obvious at first glance) that Innercity Yoga is anything but your typical yoga center. There are plenty of yoga and meditation classes to attend, seven days a week, for all levels of participants, but that's where the comparison with any other yoga center in the city ends. As I poked my head into some of the rooms, I found self-defense classes in progress, drug awareness and counseling sessions, support groups and discussion groups of various kinds, job-search seminars, health seminars, small-business seminars, English literacy classes, stress management, Tai Chi—well, you get the idea. Most of the classes are free to local residents (non-locals pay a nominal charge), and all were crammed full of people of all ages, from grade-schoolers to doddering matrons. Pretty soon I found myself expecting the Cheshire Cat to appear around a corner looking for Alice. When I asked if this was all there was (the irony, it seems, was lost in the translation), my guide went on to tell me that the center has organized a local task force to keep the neighborhood clean and a lobby to campaign against local government policies that are adversely affecting the community; they are also in negotiations with the city counsel to open up a homeless shelter and medical clinic down the street.

Enough said?

Apart from reaffirming my faith in humanity, what I saw that morning made me wonder just how such a project could spring to life in South Central, the least likely and most deserving of all places in the city. I asked my young guide and discovered that Innercity Yoga is the brainchild of one rather remarkable young man from (yes, you guessed it) La Jolla who appeared one day in South Central about two years ago (a bit like Alice through the looking glass) with a few changes of clothes in his shoulder bag and a vision of doing something for the people in the city who needed it most. He began by putting up a few posters for a free yoga class in a nearby community center, and the rest, as we writers like to say, is History, this time with a capital "H." I asked my guide if I might be able to meet this mythological-seeming personality, and five minutes later I was shaking hands with Michael Smith-Chavez, the 29-year-old founder and guiding light of a community that is proving to be the most successful vehicle for grassroots change that I have seen in many a year....

The moment the image formed in Gita's mind of a young man from La Jolla entering South Central two years ago with nothing but a shoulder bag and a vision, she felt her breath catch in her throat. She read on haltingly, afraid of what she might find. When she saw Mukunda's legal name in print, the tears began to roll down her cheeks, carrying their salt sting to her lips. All the accumulated heartache and anger of the past two years flooded back in, sweeping away in seconds the flimsy barrier that she had erected with so much care and effort. By the time she reached the small snapshot of Mukunda at the end of the article, with his unfamiliar, neatly trimmed beard, she was unable to contain her sobs. She dropped her head into her hands and struggled to calm the convulsions in her chest. When her breathing settled down, she got up and started turning tight circles in the constricted space of her cottage, torn by the memories of Mukunda that she had only recently been able to put out of her mind.

He had been gone for two full years. Two years without a word, and he had been in the city the whole time! Ten days after he'd disappeared, after he'd closed his email account without answering any of her letters, she'd called his parents, sick with worry and confusion. They told her he was traveling and that he had asked them not to disclose his whereabouts to anyone. They apologized. They couldn't understand why he would want to cut himself off like that, even from a childhood friend, but he was their son and they had to respect his wishes. She was furious. After all they had been through, how could he shut her out like that, without even an explanation? She would have walked through fire for him. He had to know that, even if they had never spoken their feelings. And yet he had left without even bothering to say goodbye. But the anger soon gave way to depression, fueled by the fear that she would never see him again. She barricaded herself in her room to the extent she could and cried herself to sleep more nights than she cared to remember. Some of the other devotees tried to console her, especially Madalasa, though she was no less affected by Mukunda's departure, but time was the only ointment that proved to have any lasting effect. Eventually she got her bearings, chalked it up to karma, and settled into a life that was far more rewarding than she had imagined. But all time had done, she realized, was to slap a Band-Aid over a wound that was far from healed.

As she paced the room, she vacillated between anger and heartache, between the pain of missing him and her resentment over having been left behind without a word of explanation, twin wounds that she had spent the better part of these two years trying to cure. But she was soon overcome by the excitement of finally knowing where he was. Unable to contain her mounting elation, she ripped the article out of the magazine, stuffed it into the rear pocket of her jeans, and headed out the door, making straight for the canyons at the far end of the property. She walked quickly, nervously aware of the article burning in her pocket, hoping that no one would notice her. The *prana* in the air and the magnificent scenery acted like an elixir on her spirits. Before she knew it she was skirting a ridge that overlooked a steep canyon filled with scrub. She stopped, looked around to make sure that no one was in sight, and sat down in the shade of a large laurel sumac just off the trail. She took the article out of her pocket, unfolded it, and read it once again, much more slowly this time, and then a third time. The tears returned to her eyes as she read yet again the reporter's interview with Mukunda, pausing over every word, proud of how he had helped to bring a sense of hope and peace to the lives of people who regularly straddled the hinterland between bitterness and anger. She could feel the fire for social justice in Mukunda's answers as clearly as if she had been the one conducting the interview, could feel the conviction, the compassion, and the dedication, rising from every word like heat from a blaze. She wondered openly how he could have accomplished so much in so short a time, wetting her cheeks with pride as she realized that Mukunda was doing with his life what she had always hoped to do with hers: making a difference and making that difference count.

When she finally put the article back in her pocket and looked out over the canyon at the smoky haze on the horizon, she remembered the shock she had felt when Gurudeva had announced to the darshan audience that Mukunda had failed his test. Later she had overheard some disciples saying that Mukunda had fallen victim to spiritual pride, the same stumbling block that had felled him in his previous life—supposedly Gurudeva had revealed this in a closed session with the senior disciples, though when she brought it up with Madalasa, the older disciple's eyes grew stormy and she demanded to know who was spreading such tales. Gita hadn't believed those stories, but it had hardly mattered to her at the time. What did matter was that he had left her and might never be coming back. But it mattered now. She knew Mukunda. She knew what he had gone through during his three weeks in Del Mar, how his heart had been blown open by compassion in much the same way that St. Francis's heart had been blown open during his illness, scenes she returned to over and over again in her periodic viewings of *Brother Sun Sister Moon*, as she returned over and over again to Clare's smile when she sat with Francis on the grass and said, "People say you are mad, do you know that? When you went off to war you were fine, intelligent, but now you are mad because... because you sing like the birds, you chase after butterflies, and you look at flowers; I think you were mad before, not now." Whatever Mukunda had done, he had done it because it was the right thing to do, and let anyone who said different be damned. She had grown to love Gurudeva and her fellow devotees, but if Mukunda's downfall was spiritual pride—and she could not believe it was—then may we all be sinners, and the faster the better, if it could inspire us to do the kind of work he was doing. Gita felt the rekindling of an old fire, one she had not felt in a long time, and it brought a determined smile to her face. She bolted to her feet and practically ran back to her cottage, knowing exactly what she had to do now, as if her life were a highway reaching into the distance, listening for the sound of her footsteps. Five minutes later she was in her car heading north on Topanga Canyon Boulevard with the article open on the seat next to her, the address of the Innercity Yoga & Cultural Center underlined three times with a red Magic Marker.

It had been three years since Gita had been to South Central, though it had never been far from her heart. As she exited the I-10 and wound her way through the once-familiar streets, she was accosted by memories of her time at the Midcity Youth and Family Center, by the sufferings of her clients and her powerlessness to do anything about it. She felt ashamed for having stayed away for so long, but she promised herself that it would never happen again. She turned off Crenshaw and onto Slausen, and from there down a side street until she recognized the building, its stylized om even more startling in its real-life habitat than in the photo. She found parking a block away, fixed the Club to the steering wheel, and closed her eyes to prepare her emotions for an encounter that she still could not believe was about to happen. After five minutes' meditation, she folded her hands to her chest and hoped that her nervousness would not show.

As she walked up to the building, she was startled to hear her own voice floating out the open front doors. It was a song from her most recent CD, released the previous month. The next thing she noticed, as she stepped into the lobby, was the bustle of activity that the reporter had noted in his article and the calming scent of incense. People were coming in and out in a steady stream, and the energy in the air was unmistakable—enthusiastic and upbeat, but peaceful and relaxed at the same time. She walked up to the reception desk, where a couple of young men were talking, one Hispanic and one black. She introduced herself as an old friend of Michael's and asked if he were around or if they knew where she could find him.

"An old friend of Michael's?" the Hispanic boy answered, eyeing her with a curious smile on his face. "I don't think I've ever seen one of those. He's talking to a couple members of the city counsel right now in his office. If you'd like to wait, he shouldn't be too long."

"That'd be fine."

"There's a sofa here with some magazines and some information about the center. Make yourself at home. If you have any questions, anything you'd like to know, we'd be happy to answer them. My name's Carlos. This is Rashad."

"Gita," she said, shaking hands with each of them.

"Gita?" Rashad asked. "Gita from where?"

"I'm from La Jolla, originally, but I live in Topanga Canyon."

Rashad looked startled by her answer. He pulled her CD cover out from underneath the counter and pointed to it.

"You wouldn't by any chance happen to be this Gita, would you?"

"Actually, I am. That's my CD you're playing."

"Jesus H! You really are Gita! I recognize you now from the photo. Hey, Carlos man, go get Jamie and Roslyn quick and tell them that Gita from The Ashram is in our lobby. Right now. They're going to flip."

Carlos bolted out of the lobby like a thunderstruck rabbit. A couple of minutes later he was back with a small group of youths in their early twenties who crowded around her as if she were a rock star and they were her fan club. Soon she was signing autographs and answering questions about her music. The two girls among them were both budding songwriters, and Gita was astounded to discover that she was their role model as a musician; they had even been up to the ashram once to hear her play. It was the first time that anyone had ever said that to her, and the fact that it came from a couple of South Central girls made it all the more gratifying. After nearly thirty minutes of animated conversation, Rashad informed her that Mukunda was free now and waiting for her in his office. She excused herself and followed his directions to the back of the center where she found Mukunda standing in the doorway waiting for her. They greeted each other with an awkward, tearful hug and sat down in front of his desk on a couple of straight-backed chairs.

"Well, this is something of a shock," he said. "I've been thinking about you a lot lately, but I never expected to see you here."

Gita pulled the article from her pocket and held it up. "I would have thought you'd be expecting a visit or two once this came out."

Mukunda looked at the article in obvious surprise. "Oh, that. Actually, the thought never even crossed my mind. I've just been too busy to think about it, I guess. Well, if anyone was going to visit, I'm glad it was you. So how have you been?"

She hesitated for a few moments, still distracted by the beard, which she had to admit looked good on him. "Well, that's a question. I don't know if I'm quite ready to answer it yet."

"Okay," he replied, looking puzzled. "Then tell me how everybody else is. How is Gurudeva doing? What's been happening in the ashram since I've been gone?"

"Gurudeva's doing pretty well. It's been all good news so far with the tumor. He's not quite as accessible as he used to be, but otherwise he's the same. Inspiring, funny, wise as ever. As far as the ashram goes, it's still the Mark and Madalasa show...."

Mukunda listened with obvious interest as she filled him in on all that had happened in the two years he'd been gone. She was glad to have something neutral to talk about—it helped her to settle her emotions for what she knew was coming next—but she carefully steered clear of how the other disciples had reacted to his leaving. She did explain how Gurudeva had legally constituted the board as a governing body presided over by a president, which for the moment was Gurudeva. The council, as it was now called, would continue to run the ashram, both administratively and spiritually, after he was gone. He had not named who would take over as president after him, but most assumed it would be either Markandeya or Madalasa, who had become the master's first sannyasi shortly after Mukunda left.

When she was done, she asked Mukunda if he ever thought about going back.

"Sometimes, especially in the beginning when it was really hard sledding. But not so much anymore—at least not to live. This is my life's work now. But I'm sure I'll go back to visit at some point—provided Gurudeva lets me. Actually, I don't know how much longer I can put it off. He's still my teacher, even though I went against his wishes and left the ashram."

"He's not the only one you deserted." Gita looked Mukunda directly in the eyes, ready now to say what she had come to say. He didn't answer, but she could tell from his downcast look that he knew exactly what she meant.

"You left without a word. No goodbye, no explanation, no answer to my letters. Two years and you never bothered to contact me. You couldn't pick up a phone or write an email? You knew how much you meant to me, Mukunda. You knew how much it would hurt."

Mukunda met her gaze now, the moisture in his eyes reflecting the sunlight slanting in through the open window.

"I wanted to, Gita, more than you can imagine. Not a day has gone by when I haven't thought about it. But you told me that you had found your mission in life, that you were finally at peace—for the first time in your life, as I remember you saying. You were even thinking about becoming a sannyasi one day. I couldn't interfere with that. It wouldn't have been right. I just thought it would be best for your spiritual life if I made a clean break. Believe me, it was one of the hardest things I've ever done, but sometimes that's the price you pay for doing the right thing."

Gita shook her head bitterly. "For someone who's supposed to be a highly developed yogi, you can be pretty stupid sometimes, Mukunda. The only reason I said those things was because I was looking for a way to still be part of your life. You were going to become a sannyasi, remember? A celibate monk? What else could I have done? I still can't believe you left without telling me. Two years and not a word—and all this time you've been right here in the city."

"I don't understand. Are you saying you didn't actually mean what you said?"

Of course! What do you think? I was grasping at straws for chrissake. Do you have any idea how hard those three weeks were for me?"

"I'm sorry, Gita, really. I didn't know…Anyhow, maybe it worked out for the best in the long run. You seem to have come an awfully long way in the last two years."

Gita glared at him. "Two years of constant heartache will do that for you. Bitter medicine is always the best medicine, right? Isn't that what they say in Ayurveda?"

"Was it really that bad?"

"Worse." Gita paused to let the words sink in. Then she shrugged her shoulders. "Anyhow, I guess I'm cured now. It was a long time ago."

"It was."

"And in the meantime, look at you. Look at all you've done. It's pretty amazing. I couldn't believe it when I read the article."

"It's not just me. It's those kids out there and a lot of other people in the community. They're the ones who are responsible for making it all work. And your fingerprints are there as well. If you remember, you had a lot to do with awakening my sense of social consciousness. I've never forgotten that."

Gita smiled. Despite the beard and the painful memories, she found herself liking this Mukunda even more than the one that had left her in the lurch two years earlier. "Do you remember one time when we were in high school, I was sitting out on the street in front of my house late at night—it had to have been after midnight. You passed by on your way home from somewhere and you stopped to talk for a few minutes?"

"I do, actually. I was on my way back from meditating at the cove."

"I don't know if you remember this, but I asked you if you had found what you were looking for. You didn't really answer me, but you promised that if you ever did, you would tell me."

"I remember."

"So then? Have you found what you're looking for?"

The question seemed to catch Mukunda by surprise. "What a question!... I guess all I can say for now is that I'm not really looking anymore. To explain it any better would take quite a while. How much time do you have?"

"I've got the rest of my life."

Mukunda looked at her oddly and then broke into a slow smile; for the first time she saw that boyish sparkle that she remembered so well.

"Well, I guess there's no rush then. Are you hungry? What do you say we continue this conversation over lunch? If I remember correctly, the last time we had lunch together I made a rather abrupt exit."

"Yes, yes you did. Okay. Lunch sounds good."

"Great. You know, it just occurred to me. We could use a music teacher around here. Do you think you might be interested in teaching some classes?"

"I've already lost you twice in this life, Mukunda. The first time because I was blind, the second time because you were. I'll be damned if I'm going to lose you a third time. That's what I came here to tell you. So yes, I think you could say you've found your music teacher."

This time there was nothing confusing about Mukunda's smile. It was the one she had been waiting for all her life.

About The Author

Devashish holds an MFA in fiction from San Diego State University. He divides his time between Ananda Kirtana, a spiritual community in the Brazilian countryside, and his farm in Puerto Rico, where he has a yoga center and a tropical-fruit plantation.

www.ingramcontent.com/pod-product-compliance
Lightning Source LLC
LaVergne TN
LVHW091534060526
838200LV00036B/598